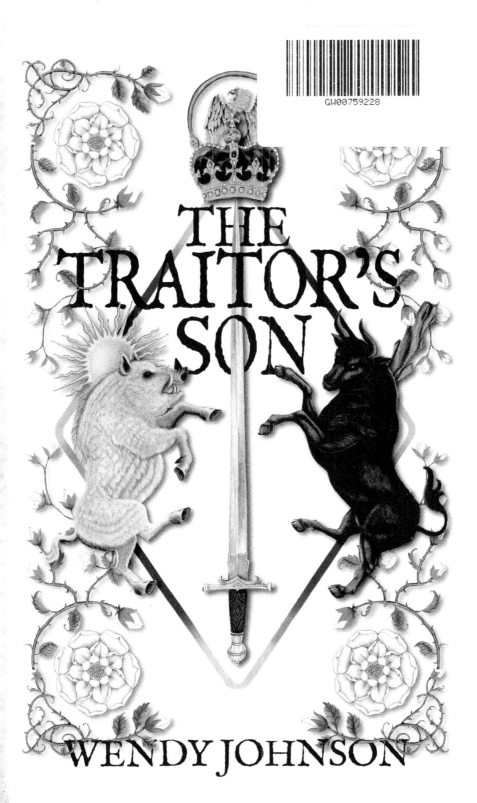

THE TRAITOR'S SON

WENDY JOHNSON

THE TRAITOR'S SON

Copyright © 2024 Wendy Johnson
ISBN-13: 978-84-125953-7-6

M

MadeGlobal Publishing

For more information on
MadeGlobal Publishing, visit our website
www.madeglobal.com

Cover Design: Tainah Lago

For Mam, with love and thanks always.

I should like to thank Tim Ridgway and all at Madeglobal Publishing for their support and belief in this book. Tainah Lago for her beautiful artwork and for re-imagining the heraldic devices of my characters in such an incredible way. I am deeply indebted to Toni Mount for her kind encouragement and for her time in reading earlier drafts of the manuscript. Gratitude is also due to fellow Ricardian Philippa Langley, for her abiding support and for helping me believe in myself, and to Carol Fellingham-Webb for her interest in, and enthusiasm for, my writing. I would like to thank historians Matthew Lewis and Dr. Joanna Laynesmith for kindly helping with queries, as well as historical researcher, Marie Barnfield, for allowing me to use her unpublished itinerary of Richard's early life as a guide to his whereabouts – it has been invaluable. My lifelong interest in the past began with visits to the children's section of my local library – weekly visits which I made with my Dad in the early 1970s – and my eternal thanks are due to him for introducing me to the fascinating subject of history. Finally, I would like to thank my dear husband, David, without whose love, support and unfailing encouragement this book would never have been completed. Thank you all.

Wendy

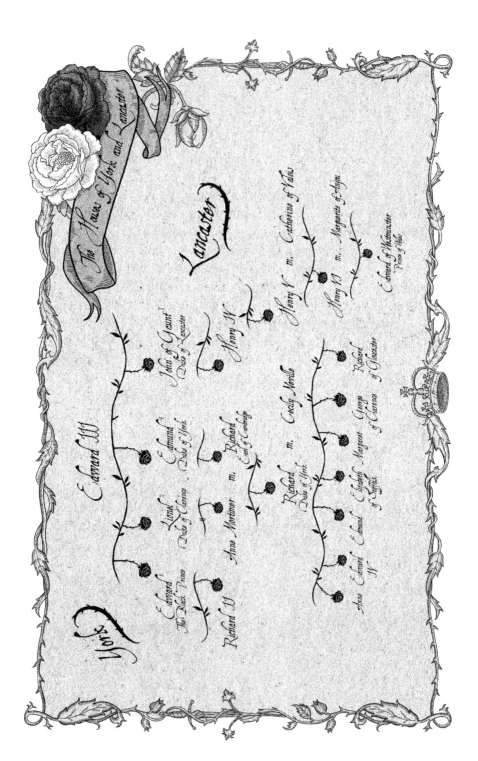

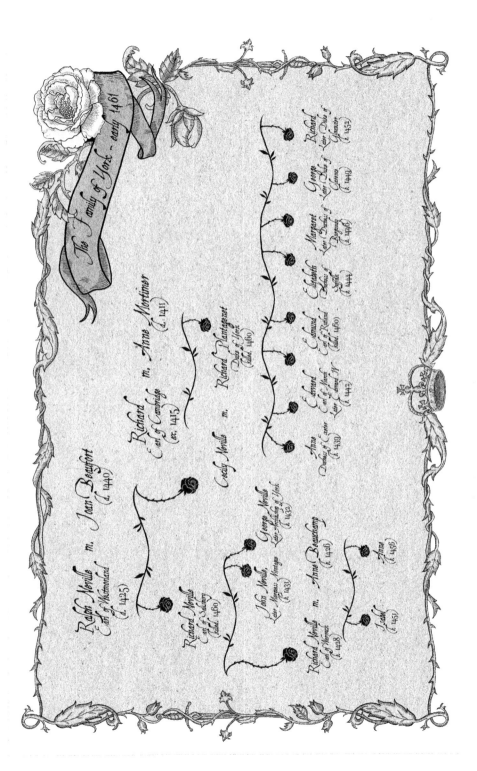

The Family of York – early 1461

Ralph Neville m. Joan Beaufort
Earl of Westmorland   (d. 1440)
(d. 1425)

Richard m. Anne Mortimer
Earl of Cambridge   (d. 1411)
(ex. 1415)

Cecily Neville m. Richard Plantagenet
Duke of York
(killed. 1460)

Richard Neville
Earl of Salisbury
(killed. 1460)

John Neville,
Later Marquis Montague
(b. 1431)

George Neville
Later Archbishop of York
(b. 1432)

Richard Neville m. Anne Beauchamp
Earl of Warwick   (b. 1426)
(b. 1428)

Isabel
(b. 1451)

Anna
(b. 1456)

Anne
Duchess of Exeter
(b. 1439)

Edmund
Earl of March,
Later Edward IV
(b. 1442)

Edmund
Earl of Rutland
(killed. 1460)

Elizabeth
Later Duchess of
Suffolk
(b. 1444)

Margaret
Later Duchess of
Burgundy
(b. 1446)

George
Later Duke of
Clarence
(b. 1449)

Richard
Later Duke of
Gloucester
(b. 1452)

Chapter One

HE WON'T cry out; still less will he weep. He must be strong. He promised.

The blood which had rushed to his head as he primed himself for punishment suffuses the boy's face with a crimson bloom, while his lower lip, compressed between neat square teeth, yields a warm metallic flow. The ordeal won't last long, he assures himself. A moment only. He can endure that.

His tutor inhales - a wheezing hiss through his bill-like nose. Brandishing the birch, he limbers up, emitting customary scents of ink and moth-repelling rosemary. The boy, inverted, considers the floor: the whirling knots in the oaken boards, the intricate weave of the rush mat. He senses the birch-rod slicing the air, hears it whistle in vengeful descent. As each stroke reverberates through his skinny frame, he knows he must be accepting, must adopt the manner of the meekly contrite. Outwardly, at least.

Inwardly, he knows he has done nothing wrong. When his father had ridden out, he'd vowed to return triumphant, and the boy had believed him. He still believes. Those who speak of York's death and defeat are mistaken. Not only that, they're liars: even his mother, and so he has told her to her face. If she believes he should be thrashed for it, he'll take the pain, but he'll not give up on his father.

'I take no pleasure in chastising you, Lord Richard.' His tutor's tone is detached, and it's impossible to tell whether the statement is true - or a post-birch apology delivered as an aid to conscience. 'But the duchess is weary of your continued defiance. It's beginning to distress her.'

He hasn't defied anybody. He's simply keeping faith, trusting his father's word. Why can his mother not see that?

'You do understand, my lord?'

Richard's mouth twists. 'Yes, Master Wadham.'

'Good.'

He commends himself on his resilience. To have wept would have been to admit that everyone else was right and that he was wrong, something he is not prepared to consider. Calming himself, he licks the blood from his bitten lip and waits to see what will happen next. From his upended position, he sees the fox-fur trim of his tutor's gown, the pointed toes of the man's leather shoes. If he had instructions to lash me further, Richard thinks, he would have done so by now.

His tutor expels a querulous sigh. 'You may stand.'

Richard straightens - fluid and giddy – and waits for the chamber to settle around him. Projecting his chin, he ensures his voice is as unwavering as he can make it.

'If it please you, Master Wadham, may I leave now?'

Wadham grunts, then waves him away with a stoical huff. 'Very well, my lord. You may go.'

Concealed within his pony's stall, he relishes the scents of the stable: horseflesh, clean straw, sour wizened apples. Earthy and honest, Richard knows he can trust them. Amber, his copper-coloured jennet, is pleased to see him. Responsive and genial, she nuzzles his shoulder, her breath warm and moist on his hand. Taking a pippin from the feed bucket, he offers it to her. She demolishes it in one bite, juice spraying his face as he presses close, seeking comfort. Amber demands nothing from him, only that which he is happy to give, and for as long as he remains here, he can assure himself that the past months have been an illusion and that all is fair and right with the world.

Sounds drift from the inner bailey: the clang-clang of the blacksmith's hammer, jests from the kitchen boys as they slop out their buckets. Sinking down, he settles amid the straw, stalks pricking bruised buttocks, and realises just how hungry he is.

He'd quit the schoolroom with as much dignity as a boy of eight can muster, abjuring breakfast and managing to evade his nurse. No small feat, and he'd felt proud of himself at the time. Now, however, his belly is growling. Resisting thoughts of manchet loaves, the refreshing tang of small beer, he sets his lips.

I'll be strong, Father. I will. I promise.

Closing his eyes, he sees once more the frozen courtyard, a sharp December dawn pierced by watery light. The clamour of his father's departure: the whip and slap of livery banners, the clinking of spearmen and hulking men-at-arms. His own hastily donned boots snapping the ice like brittle sugar. The precarious slither over slick and perilous ground to bid his father farewell.

'No need to fear, lad,' the blue-grey eyes, so like his own, had creased at the corners as the duke hunkered down to peer into his face. 'Those who threaten us will pay the price for their treachery. And when I return, I shall bring with me the assurance of safety. For all of us.'

'But I don't want you to go.' The admission had fetched a sob with it, but Richard had been swift to swallow it down.

A sweep of heavy wool had found him wrapped in his father's embrace, breathing scents of oily leather, of sandalwood and cinnamon. 'Have courage, my son. I ride to make an end of this - that I may finally assume my rightful place of honour. One day, when God in his mercy so determines, you shall be the son of a king. Do not forget that.'

Crushed to his father's brigandine, he'd sensed the steel plates stitched inside. It was Advent, and Richard feared for him. To make war in a holy season must surely be to incur God's wrath. 'Stay here,' he'd begged him. 'With us.'

Sleet began to slice the air, settling on his father's fringe, battering his lashes as he blinked. 'This has not been my decision, Richard, you know that - the malice of our enemies has forced it upon me. But, I give you my word; we'll return before Candlemas robs the hall of holly. Now, boy, remember, you are a son of York. Promise to be strong, for my sake.'

Yes, Father. I will. I'll be strong. I promise…

'Out you come, Dickon! I know you're skulking in here.'

A vicious jolt brings the world into focus. Startled, Richard hesitates, then creeps towards the stall partition. Finding a gap in the oaken boards, he peers through. His brother is blocking the stable door: a featureless shape against the dim afternoon. Richard grimaces. He should have known George would be the first to find him, that his artful, prying ways would lead him here.

'Out, you little worm.' No response forthcoming, George stumps in, brisk feet scattering straw. 'You can't stay here all day.'

It's true, he can't. And surrendering now, before the entire household is turned upside down, should enable him to salvage at least a little self-respect. Brushing his hose with a swift hand, Richard slips from the privacy of the stall.

'So, I was right.' George, triumphant, rakes a hand through his tawny curls. From his heaving breast, it's clear he's been tearing about the place, hunting down his prey. 'I tell you, Dickon, you're the most—'

'Richard. I'm Richard, like our father.'

George shrugs, dismissive. 'If I let Mother know I've found you, she'll have Master Wadham thrash you again until you learn some respect.'

'Where's our sister? Is she searching for me, too?'

'No. Why would she? Margaret is with Mother. Besides, I'm the one to look after you. Since Edmund is dead, and Edward is still on the Marches, I'm your guardian now.'

'Liar.'

'Well,' George rolls his eyes, 'everyone's a liar now, according to you, even Mother. Think yourself lucky she hasn't had you confined. A few licks of the birch, I'd say you've had it easy.'

Flicking straw into piles with the toe of his boot, Richard

ignores him. The stinging whacks, whether many or few, are hardly the point. The fact they were felt to be necessary at all is what bothers him. 'I won't recant, Brother. Father is coming home, he told me.'

George's mouth warps in a show of pity. Unbuckling his purse, he retrieves a soft white loaf indented with the marks of his sweaty fingers. 'Here, you haven't broken your fast this morning; you must be ravenous.'

Richard, thankful, breaks the bread and stuffs it into his mouth. Devoid of butter, it sticks in his throat. Choking, he wipes his eyes in swift circumspection lest his brother misread the tears.

But George is otherwise employed. Striding into Amber's stall, he snatches three pippins from the feed bucket. Tongue thrust out in concentration, he begins to juggle, cursing as one falls from his hand and lands with a thud close to Amber's hooves.

'That was your fault, Dickon, for staring.' Retrieving the apple, he presents it to the pony and proceeds to pet her.

'She won't take it from you,' Richard tells him. 'She doesn't know you.'

'She seems perfectly happy to me.' George smiles as Amber, bright head circling, devours the battered fruit. 'An apple is an apple, no matter who offers it.'

He has no right to touch her, Richard thinks; she's mine. Father said so. He watches with resentment as George feeds the creature another treat before wiping his wet hand the length of his thigh.

'Come on, Dickon. It hurts me as much as it hurts you. I know it's hard, but you must understand, Father and our brother, Edmund, are dead.'

'They're not, and you'll find out soon enough.'

George sighs and changes the subject. 'Cousin Warwick arrived while you've been moping in here. He's closeted with Mother. Something's afoot, but I can't tell what. I tried to listen but was caught with my ear to the door. I expect it concerns the queen - she's advancing south, I heard that much.'

'Queen Marguerite hates Father, doesn't she ?' The thought slips out unbidden.

'She hates all of us.' George's eyes dance with revulsion. 'We're a threat to her, and to her son – and you know how she dotes on that snivelling whelp. She's a vicious woman, Dickon. You don't know everything that happened last year at Ludlow when her army ransacked the town, but I do. Mother ensured we were safe and was careful to keep the worst from us. I only know because I asked questions.'

'You didn't ask questions, you pried, lurking behind wall hangings while Uncle Buckingham rebuked Mother for her loyalty to Father. Why didn't you show yourself? Why didn't you threaten him with what Father would do when he found out?'

'And bring more trouble upon us? I'm not as stupid as you are, Dickon. Besides, if the queen lays hands on us a second time, she won't place us in the care of Uncle Buckingham. I doubt she'll even let us live. As far as the queen is concerned, we're the sons of a traitor.'

Richard's head shoots up. 'Father is not a traitor.'

'Parliament decreed he should be king when Daft Harry dies. Marguerite's son was to be disinherited. That made him traitor enough in her eyes.'

'But Father is king by right. Mother says so.'

'He *was,* yes. And rights pass from father to son. So, now Edward is father's successor, we're all a threat to the queen. That's why she seeks to destroy us - all of us.'

Richard pops the last of the bread into his mouth while his belly howls for more. 'And if the queen reaches London, what will happen to us?'

'What'll happen?' As George's poise evaporates, Richard detects a subtle chink in his brother's blustering mien. 'I'll tell you what'll happen. She'll free the king from his confines and descend on us like a fury. And then, well…I wouldn't give a rotten turd for our chances.'

'*Sciant omnes.*' Glancing from his book of Latin orations,

Wadham narrows his eyes. 'Which mood, my lord?'

Richard shifts position, backless stool hard and unyielding. 'Imperative.'

'Imperative. Are you sure?'

'Yes, Master Wadham.'

'It is the subjunctive.' Wadham jabs the page with his pointer. 'You used to know this.'

Richard drops his gaze and considers his hands. He used to know a lot of things, but few seem to matter anymore. Life is not the same, nor will it be, until his father returns. His mother speaks of nothing but Edward. Your brother will bring victory, she tells him. With your cousin's aid, he will repel the enemy and take the crown in the name of York. We've nothing to fear. We need only trust in Edward, and in God's mercy.

'Lord Richard,' a sullen cough, as Wadham begins to pace, 'you are by habit an excellent pupil; your grasp of Latin exemplary for your age. Therefore, it is all the more vexing when you deliberately—'

Clattering hoofbeats in the yard below. Raised voices and the strangled whinnies of a horse. A messenger; it must be. Richard leaps to his feet. Lodging himself in the window embrasure, he presses his face to the yellowish glass.

'Return to your studies, if you please.'

Wiping the misted surface, he squints through the leaded pane. Unable to discern anything but the most distorted of shapes, he yanks at the latch, grunting in frustration as it refuses to yield.

'Lord Richard, I will not tolerate such behaviour. Resume your seat, and we shall continue.'

Undulating figures are bobbing into the yard: the darkest surely his mother's mourning gown. The news must be important. If it's word from his father, he must be the first to hear it.

Bolting from the chamber, he thunders into the stairwell: boots thwacking, echoing around the narrow space, as if there are two Richards, each desperate to outstrip the other. Emerging into the yard, he catches his breath, grins. He was right. A courier: the livery of York with the Lion of March. At last, a message from Edward.

Edward has found their father and is bringing him home.

'Dickon?' A sweat-drenched George, fresh from swordplay. 'News from our brother?'

And news of our father, Richard thinks with satisfaction, just as I told you there would be. Eluding George, he stations himself beside their mother's skirts, watching, rapt, as she accepts a missive from the courier's hand and hastily snaps the seal.

Their brother's square, untidy scrawl is easy to discern. Leaning in, Richard chases it the length of the parchment. This, at last, is the news he's been waiting for.

The courier bows. 'May it please you, Madam, your son informs you that his victory was ordained by God. On the eve of battle, three suns were visible in the sky, which he understood to be a sign of the Trinity.'

Richard smiles as a euphoric sigh escapes his mother. Touching the letter to her lips, she gazes about her as if seeing everything for the first time: including her youngest sons. 'Boys, Edward sends word. Upon Saint Blaise's Day, he took the field against the Earl of Pembroke and, in the name of York, gained a glorious victory.'

The parchment flutters in the rising breeze, her trembling hand struggling to secure it as she turns to the messenger. 'I shall, of course, compose a return. In the meantime, go inside and take refreshment; you have ridden far.'

But she has forgotten the most important thing. Risking a rebuke, Richard seizes her skirts. 'And what of Father?'

'Dickon.' George moves in. 'Don't.'

A dark shape is swooping across the yard: Roger Wadham, descending upon them like a wrathful crow. Richard's belly tenses. His mother must listen. She must answer him. Now - before he's bundled away.

'Mother, please, what of our father?'

The duchess extracts his fingers, squeezing them between her own. 'Richard, you know your father's claim is Edward's now. Henceforth, it is your brother we must look to.'

Desperation mounts. 'But surely Edward can find him. Surely, Edward—'

Wadham is looming, arms folded, face set. Frustrated, Richard watches as his mother returns to the missive and reads it over again.

'Brother,' George nudges him, 'is this not good news? Have we not been praying for Edward's success?'

Richard glowers into his beaming face. 'Leave me alone.'

'But, Dickon, can't you see what this means? The suns were a portent. Proof that we have God's favour. The family of York is blessed.'

Convinced his brother will never understand, Richard dodges Wadham's grasp and races from the yard.

'Stop being such a wantwit, Dickon, and let me in.'

'No.' Wedged against the chamber door, he strives to withstand the onslaught. Growling and huffing, George will tire first. Unable to gain entry, he'll lose patience and slump off like the petulant oaf he is.

But a frantic rattling of the latch proves his brother is not quite ready to surrender. 'For the hundredth time…open up, will you?'

Richard stiffens. 'Go. Away.'

Rising growls from beyond the door herald a determined shifting. Bit by bit, the oak begins to yield, and Richard is swept along by its inching movement, backside skimming polished boards. Gritting his teeth, he resists with renewed vigour, but enough progress has been made for George to poke a flushed and peevish face inside.

'You'll not hold me off, you little worm.'

'Begone!' Thrusting back with as much force as he can muster, Richard manages to gain some ground. He senses George moving off, but satisfaction dissolves as he dimly grasps his brother's plan. Having retreated, George intends to charge and throw himself at the door like a battering ram. Unwilling to be cornered, Richard scrambles to his feet as the pounding boots close in. Relieved of resistance, the door is cast asunder, and George, startled, catapults into the room.

Richard eyes him in triumph. 'Serves you right, fustilugs.'

'Come, Brother,' George's shoulders sag. 'Edward's victory is a cause for celebration, yet what do you do? Hole yourself up here like the whinging baby you are. Don't you know we two must stick together? What would Father think?'

'Father is coming home. I've told you.'

'He's not. Can't you see that? I wish to God you'd grow up.'

Enraged, Richard sets about him, pummelling his brother as if he were a bolster lacking in down. 'You know nothing of what happened. You're only listening to what Mother says. We've no proof—'

George pushes him to the floor. Sitting astride him, he clouts Richard's face; a swift, stinging buffet.

'Shut up, Dickon. What do you know about anything?'

Under his brother's weight, every breath is painful, but Richard refuses to capitulate. 'When he returns, I'm going to tell him what you've done. How you've all given up on him. How none of you believed. Only me.'

Resting on his haunches, George regards him with a mixture of frustration and pity. 'For Mercy's sake, stop this. We still have each other. Can't that be enough for you?'

Seizing the moment, Richard forces his brother onto his back and clambers on top of him. 'You've abandoned him. You traitor.'

'Get off me, Dickon.'

'Richard!' Unable to stop himself, he plunges his fist into George's belly. 'I'm Richard. Like him. Like our father. Dickon's a childish name. I hate it.'

'Get off me, you little shit.'

'No.' Control is slipping away – from his mouth, from his fists – and he's unable to rein it in. 'I won't believe your lies, George. I won't—'

'And what do you believe, eh? That a man whose head has been hewn from his shoulders can be brought back to life? Is that what you believe, you pathetic little wretch?'

'You lie!'

Richard attempts another assault, but George is quick to

react; snatching his brother's wrists, he grips them hard, his voice a quivering whisper. 'I promised, Dickon. I promised Mother I wouldn't tell you, but you've forced the truth from me with your damned disbelief.'

Richard's sobbing, when it comes – when it finally bursts its bonds – is loud and rasping. 'No… please…'

Unable to staunch the tears and incapable of wiping them away, he watches as they land, one by one, upon George's upturned face. Fixing his eye on a single drop, he follows its progress as if the whole world were enclosed in that single, tiny, clear mass.

His brother takes a juddering breath. 'Father was holed up at Sandal, awaiting reinforcements. When they finally appeared, he rode out to greet them. But they were false friends, Dickon, sent by our enemies to lure him out.'

'Please…I don't want to hear.' Wrenching his hands from his brother's grip, Richard clamps them over his ears, only to have George prise them away.

'When she heard of Father's defeat, the queen wanted to humiliate him further. His death wasn't enough for her; his dishonour was what she wanted. And so, she had his head hacked—'

'No—'

'—she had his head hacked from his body and paraded on a pike, like a fool's bauble. Edmund's, too. Sent them to York, where they were joined by our uncle of Salisbury's. You've forced the truth from me, Dickon, and there it is. Are you any happier for knowing it?'

Richard drags himself from his brother's belly. Crawling away, he curls up, knees towards his head, protective.

'I didn't want to tell you,' George's face crumples, 'but you wouldn't let it be. If Mother finds out, she'll have me punished. You won't tell her, will you?'

Richard feels numb. As though this is happening to someone else, and he's merely an observer, witnessing it all from another place.

'Promise me. Dickon?'

'I promise.' Shrinking into himself, he presses his cheek against the cool, polished floor while George's hoarse sobs batter the silence.

The following day, as dusk descends, he's called to his mother's presence. His nurse, Joan Malpas, says little on their way to the solar; her hand – plump, controlling – ushering him along like a herdsman driving calves to market. She deposits him outside the door, licks her fingers and smooths his hair, flattening the fringe to his brow. Assessing the result, she pats his back, then seats herself in the antechamber and takes up her stitching.

He doesn't think he can spare the room for any more ill tidings. The space within, set aside for sorrow and grief, is already full to the brim and spilling over. Further cares would herald a flood. Making a fist of his trembling hand, he knocks, waits, then crosses the threshold.

His mother sits amid a bevy of candles, their vivid flames capped with haloes, her women, with their sharp whispers and flashing needles, all strangely absent.

Pulling her lips into a fleeting crescent, she studies him, hazel eyes keen. She's afraid for him, he can see that, and the thought makes his bladder heave. He needs the garderobe but dare not excuse himself. Curling his toes inside his boots, he attempts to banish the urge.

A glance towards the window seat reveals the presence of his sister. Margaret's face, sallow in the candlelight, is fraught with equal concern, Paternoster beads slithering through her fingers like a glimmering snake.

'Come, Richard,' the duchess waves him towards the hearth, 'warm yourself. When your brother arrives, I have something to tell you.'

He does as he's bid, attempting to settle himself while his mind prickles with unease. His mother is lost in thought, garnets and pearls glinting with every rising breath as she caresses the book in her lap. He recognises the volume, its gilded clasps and decorative tooled leather: his father's *Life of Saint Catherine*. A week ago, he'd have asked when his father was coming home. Now he watches the flames dancing in the hearth, wondering if there are flames in Purgatory, as there are in Hell, and whether his father is burning.

The silence is tempered by the crack of kindling, the click and clack of Margaret's coral beads.

A scrambling at the door, and George arrives, breathless. Trussed in his padded jack, he must have raced all the way from the practice yard. Cheeks red from the cold, he nudges Richard aside to get closer to the hearth.

The bluster elicits a squawk, a tinkle of bells, from a perch in the corner. The popinjay, Criseyde, is ruffling her feathers, jet-like eyes bright with curiosity. But the bird is not alone in its observation. Having ceased her contemplations, the duchess is watching her sons, and Richard knows without doubt that whatever she has to tell them is of deadly import.

'Something to drink before I begin?'

He declines, terrified he may wet himself. George considers, then shakes his head.

'Very well.' Sliding a letter from the pages of her book, their mother deliberates, then clears her throat. 'I've come to a decision. Or rather, a decision has been forced upon me.'

Richard swallows. A decision had been forced upon his father, and look how that turned out.

Before she can resume, a commotion erupts in the antechamber and the door is thrown wide. A flash of white kerchief as Joan is thrust aside, and their cousin, Warwick, strides in, brisk, rotund, and exuding the chill of the Thames. Richard's eyes follow him as he makes straight for the duchess and plants a kiss on her upturned cheek.

'All is arranged, lady.'

Their mother grips Warwick's arm, relief visible and overflowing. 'Nephew, I shall be forever grateful.'

Warwick nods, and they lock heads, conspiring. George strains to catch what's being said while Richard shuffles from foot to foot, the dull ache returning, squeezing his bladder.

The earl straightens then looks the boys up and down. 'It will be tonight. Tell them.'

The duchess nods. 'George, Richard, London is no longer safe for either of you.

We've learnt from our spies that the queen is swiftly advancing, and your cousin is set to leave on the morrow to intercept her forces. Without his protection, I cannot allow you to remain here.'

Please, Richard thinks, *I must be excused. Please…*

In desperation, he focusses on his mother's fingers as they idly caress the letter, and for the first time, he detects the faintest tremor.

'Since your father's death, I have been in correspondence with Burgundy. The Duchess Isabella is a distant kinswoman and was supportive of his cause. As a mother herself, she understands my fears and has offered succour if the need arises. The time has come to take her at her word.'

Anticipating protest, Warwick is swift to reassure. 'Boys, this is for the best. Sending you away is the only solution. It's what your father would have done. He confided to me last year that he'd regretted not removing you from Ludlow when the danger looked set to increase.'

Richard ponders on his Uncle Salisbury: Warwick's father. Captured after Sandal and lynched by his own tenants, if George is to be believed. He imagines his uncle's head, set beside their father's above a city gate, and wonders if Warwick has nightmares. As he does.

'Have courage, boy.' A strong hand grips his shoulder, and his cousin grants a grim smile. How his eyes are like Mother's, Richard thinks, with green flecks amid the brown; the haughty thrust of his jaw, identical to hers. 'The queen is determined, but so are we. Determined and poised to crush her.'

His heavy signet ring is bruising Richard's flesh, but the pressure is reassuring.

'The Low Countries are a secure haven,' Warwick says. 'No danger will follow you there. Simply do as you're bid.'

George tilts his head in cocky fashion. 'Duke Philip is a great man. He'll protect us.'

A cursory glance from the earl and their mother continues. 'His… duchess, as I said, is sympathetic. You will be housed, if not in state, then decently and with respect for your rank. Few know of our communication, and for your own safety, you must sail immediately. Tonight. All has been settled. Your cousin has appointed a man to act as guardian. John Skelton has my full trust, and you must abide by what he tells you. I want no argument. We would not propose this if there were any other way.'

Richard stares at the floor tiles, the alternate squares of yellow and green. He finds himself counting them, rehearsing the tally in his head, as he tries to imagine the open seas and none for company but a man they've never met. He's never been aboard a ship. He doesn't suppose the journeys along the Thames in their mother's blue and gold barge count as sailing: not really.

A thought occurs, 'Mother, what of our ponies? Might I take Amber?'

'No, Richard. You'll take only those items which are essential: changes of clothing, your Psalters. I'll not have unnecessary baggage slow you down.'

He frowns. The pony isn't baggage; she's a gift from his father. 'But I want to take Amber.'

No response, and he sees the uselessness of pleading. A fluttering movement draws his eyes to the window. Large snowflakes, blown by the wind, stick to the glass for a brief moment before melting away.

'How long will the voyage take?' George is suddenly eager, as if they were bound upon some sort of quest.

'That,' their mother says, 'is in God's hands.'

'A day or two,' Warwick tells them, 'weather permitting. You shall not be sailing aboard the *Trinity*. Such a vessel would attract attention, but you will sail under my captain, Thomas Roger, an able man and loyal. Skelton, too, is my true liegeman, a fellow of good and sound judgement.'

And strangers both, Richard thinks. 'Cousin, what if the queen—?'

'That bitch shall learn a harsh lesson afore she ever reaches London. She'll be driven back to Hell if I must despatch her there myself.'

His cousin's threat is delivered with such brutish conviction that Richard can almost smell the coiling wisps of sulphur, the desolate whimpers of the condemned, as the pick of the Lancastrian crop is hurled into the pit.

He starts as a sharp knock announces a man in crimson livery, Warwick's device of the Ragged Staff stitched to the breast.

The duchess presents him. 'John Skelton, your cousin's man: intermediary between myself and the lady of Burgundy.'

Skelton bows, hair lank and greasy, large nose protruding from his face like the beak of a skinny bird.

George squares his shoulders, extending his hand like a man would. 'If you bear our mother's trust, Master Skelton, then we are content.'

Richard follows suit, but Skelton's clammy grip does little to subdue the fear that is gnawing at his innards. What if they never return? What if Queen Marguerite intercepts the ship? What if she cuts off their heads and sends them back to London?

A final word from their mother sees the boys dismissed. She clearly has much to discuss, firing orders at a tight-lipped Skelton while Warwick looks on, drumming his fingers on the back of her chair.

Richard pauses in the doorway, gauging the urgency between physical and mental relief. He needs the garderobe, but he also needs answers.

'Yes, lad?' Glancing up, the earl raises a bushy brow. 'Was there something else?'

Aye, Richard thinks - his mind a tumult of fevered questions - there's plenty.

'Well, out with it. Quickly.'

Necessity dictating actions, Richard shakes his head. 'Nothing, Cousin,' he says, certain that even if he were able to remain, he'd be hard-pressed to voice his fears. 'It's nothing.'

Chapter Two

February 1461
Baynard's Castle

*T*HE MOON, heavy and brimming with light, casts a blueish hue over the fresh layer of snow. Hurriedly dressed for the journey, Richard huddles into his cloak. He's unused to being outside at dusk, and this part of the castle, bordered by kitchens and wash houses, is unfamiliar. It's where the servants live, where food is delivered and where it is cooked. Glancing at the towering walls, the upper casements shuttered against the world, he feels like an exile already.

A door opens at the end of the range, spilling a shaft of buttery light. A small figure emerges: a boy carrying a bucket, picking his way in the direction of the well. Richard wishes he could remain here, like him. Perhaps he and George could disguise themselves as potboys; the queen would never seek the sons of a duke amongst a gang of sweating scullions.

From the kitchen, a clang of dishes, the delicious smell of roasted salmon. Supper is being prepared, but tonight their mother and sister will be dining alone.

Amber had known he was leaving; her eyes, large and glistening, had pleaded with him to stay. He'd made the stable boy an offer: some comfits from his mother's dish if he promised to care for the pony. But his mother wouldn't allow it. Bribery, she said, is a shameful thing which cannot honourably be practised. 'The stable boys are amply paid to tend the horses, Richard, and Amber is no different from the rest.'

But she is. Angry with the moisture that plays beneath his lids, he blinks, tilting his head towards the sky in the hope of a diversion. The task proves fruitless, however: no stars tonight, the moon itself halfway to being hidden behind a bank of rolling cloud.

'You'd better not disgrace me on this voyage, Dickon, do you hear?' George says. 'No snivelling.'

Richard squares his shoulders. 'Of course not.'

But he cannot guarantee it. The furthest he has ever travelled is to the family castle at Ludlow, to Fotheringhay where he was born, to Berkhampstead and Baynard's; each governed and regulated by their father. He knows little of the world beyond and nothing at all of the Low Countries. Glancing at George, he detects equal dread in his brother's trembling chin.

Catching his eye, George glowers. 'What?'

'I wish our cousin were coming with us.'

'Well, he's not. He's protecting London. Now, what did I just say?'

'That I'm not to disgrace you.'

'Yes. See you don't.'

Skelton bursts across the yard, rapping out instructions while his fellows unbar the gate that leads to the river stairs. Household pages emerge, slithering as they lug the boys' travelling chest over swiftly freezing ground. Small and battered, the chest contains everything the boys now own in the world: clean clothes, spare boots, their well-thumbed Psalters. It's as if their world has shrunk. As if it continues to shrink, moment upon moment.

'You understand why we must leave by the river stairs, my lords?' Skelton performs a swift bow. 'Better that few see us go.'

George concurs. Grabbing Richard's hand, he chafes it against the cold. 'Better we should escape, Dickon, than be captured by the queen.'

But it's not as simple as that. There are other concerns. 'What if the queen captures Mother and Margaret? You said yourself it would be worse than last time. And what if she slays our cousin and places his head on a spike as she did Father's?'

George huffs and releases his hand. 'You Jonah. If you can't think of anything encouraging to say, don't bother.'

Richard hangs his head. His brother doesn't seem to understand how much he hates concealment. Whatever may lie ahead, whatever they may be forced to suffer, he would rather know of it. Their father's fate had been kept from him for the right reasons, but the pain of discovery has been too much. He can't allow anyone to hide the truth from him again. Not now. Not ever.

'George?'

'Shut up.'

'But—'

'Silence, you little worm.'

Torchlight billows from the corner turret as their mother and sister arrive arm in arm, Margaret wiping her cheeks. Skelton swoops in before they arrive. Swift, pragmatic, and keen to depart, he stations himself between the boys and their womenfolk.

'All is ready, Madam. We must proceed.'

Framed by her widow's kerchief, their mother's face is tense, her manner unusually hesitant. If I beg her, Richard thinks, she may allow us to stay. If I say the right things, ask in the right way. But the words won't come, and he knows the moment is passing. Has passed.

We're going, he thinks, and there's not a thing on God's earth we can do about it.

'Richard?' The duchess sinks to her haunches, gown bunched and soaking up snow. Torchlight gilds her features, tracing contours, moulding hollows. 'We have little time, but my commands are these. Look to George and obey Master Skelton in all things. Your father would expect nothing less.'

Richard nods. He'll be watching; he knows he will. Perhaps from Purgatory, perhaps from the nearness of the shadows, his father will be observing them and must not find him wanting. His heart leaps as a figure emerges from the gloom, but it's only Skelton, eager than ever to be away.

'Madam, I beg you, we must make haste.'

'A moment, please. We must commend my sons to the

care of God.'

Richard clasps his hands as his mother recites a Paternoster. Margaret joins in, stumbling over the first two lines then falling silent, as if she has forgotten what comes next, while he and George make no response at all. The murmured words seem frightening and final, setting them on a road whose end is both uncertain and unknowable. At the final *Amen,* a wet drop lands on Richard's face, and he wonders whether it has begun to snow again.

Rising, the duchess flicks her cheek. 'Put your lives in His hands, and He will protect you. Have no doubt of that.'

Grasping Richard's hood, she pulls it over his head, tucking it beneath his chin with her icy fingers, while Margaret enfolds George in a tight embrace.

'Hurry, my lords. I must insist.' Ushering them towards the river gate, Skelton permits but one backward glance.

A rowing boat waits at the landing, dipping and bobbing as they climb aboard. Richard sinks onto the roughhewn plank that passes for a seat and longs for the silken cushions of their mother's barge.

Skelton, settling beside them, struggles to arrange his gangling legs in so cramped a space. 'All well, boy?'

'Well enough,' George says. 'I'm taking care of him.'

It's strange to be on the river after dark. And cold; waves slapping the gunwale, black and slick, like devils' tongues. At the prow, tallow flickers inside a battered lanthorn, a new cascade of tumbling snowflakes dancing in its glow.

Grim-visaged, the boatman wastes no time. Gripping the oars, he eases them from the jetty in a sickly, slopping rhythm.

'Be still, lads,' Skelton warns. 'No squirming about.'

George endorses the command with a sharp prod while their guardian engages the boatman in muted conversation. Determined to calm himself, Richard stares at the inky water, but the retreating presence of Baynard's burns the back of his skull like a brand.

To allow their home to disappear in such a way, unseen and unacknowledged, may be to lose it forever. He must take another look: to keep things right, to keep things safe.

Twisting his body, he peers towards the landing, where a pair of castle guards flex their legs and breathe white plumes into the frosty air. Torchbearers are emerging through the open gate, and in their wake, two black smudges blend and part before finally retreating inside. Mother and Margaret, he thinks, resolved upon a final glance. All at once he feels hollow, as if the very life has been sucked out of him. Too soon, the castle buildings are lost from view, and he settles with a sigh on the unforgiving plank.

'Sit still, Dickon. Has Master Skelton not instructed us?' George delivers another prod, then turns away, blinking hard.

Perhaps, Richard thinks, I should consider this an adventure, something I will be able to boast about in time. But he can't; he feels exposed on the water, unsafe, as if the whole world may know who they are and where they're headed. Retreating into his hood, he marvels at the vastness of the sky. The heavens look so infinite, and the boat a tiny, helpless thing nodding worriedly on the swell. He shivers as snowflakes brush his upturned cheeks. If it's this cold on the river, how shall it be upon the German Ocean?

Nearing Paul's Wharf, the bells of Saint Peter the Less are clanging for Vespers: a solemn sound, like a passing bell. Perhaps it tolls for them, sailing into a wilderness that is dark, cold, and forbidding, with no beginning and no end. Perhaps God has decided to rebuke them: taking away their father, depriving them of their mother, of Margaret. What sins have they committed that they should be so sorely punished? Richard ponders on the last twelve months. When he and George were sick abed, they ate meat instead of fish on fasting days. They'd possessed no Papal indulgence, merely the word of their mother's physician. Surely, in God's eyes, this had been a great sin: tearing the Lord's flesh in order to nourish their own. Then there was the day he'd argued with Joan, refusing to give up his hornbook when supper was due to be served, and refusing to eat when it was. Perhaps, if he's a perpetual sinner, God has turned his face from him. Perhaps that's why his father was slain.

Mea culpa. Mea culpa. Mea maxima culpa.

A gust of wind rips the water and the boat tilts. George makes a grab for his thigh, as if he fears his brother may be catapulted overboard.

Skelton eyes them both. 'Not too long now, my lords.'

He's told them they are bound for Queenhithe, where they will board their cousin's ship. From there, they'll sail down the Thames and cross the German Ocean to the Low Countries. *Queen*-hithe: Richard shudders at the word. What if she knows? What if her men are lying in wait?

'George?'

'What is it?'

He leans close. 'What if Marguerite knows we're leaving? What if she sends her men ahead to kill us aboard ship and drop our bodies into the sea?'

Snatching the hood from his brother's head, George hisses in his ear. 'And how could the queen's men board our cousin's carrack? They'd be cut down before they even set foot on deck.'

But Richard cannot banish the thought. They could be heading into a trap, just like their father. George doesn't seem to have considered that. 'What if there's a traitor amongst our cousin's men?'

'Quiet, will you?'

He eyes the boatman's meaty fists. For all they know, he could be the queen's man; could have fooled Skelton, and Cousin Warwick, too, could be luring them into the hands of the enemy. He inches closer to George: 'We can swim. We could jump overboard and swim for the shore.'

'Shut up, and don't be such an imbecile.'

Reluctant, Richard does as he's bid, blowing on his hands and marking the smack of the oars. At length, pricks of light pierce the darkness—boats with lanthorns: two, three, heading towards them. Richard stiffens. The queen's men, here already. He was right. He's been right all along, and George didn't believe him.

'Brother…'

Eying the craft, George appears undaunted, while Skelton pays them no heed whatever. As the vessels draw near, Richard sees they are but regular traffic; rowing boats like theirs and wherries sailing upriver to Westminster. His shoulders droop in silent relief.

'All well, Dickon?' George, suddenly attentive, replaces Richard's fallen hood, tucking it snugly under his chin, the way their mother had. 'We have a long voyage ahead of us. We'll be sailing with our cousin's men and mustn't let them think us afraid.'

Richard concurs, then asks: 'Are carracks great ships?'

'Of course. The earl was right not to set us aboard the *Trinity* or the *Grace Dieu*; we would have been a floating target. The *Anne* will serve us well enough.'

'But how shall a great ship sail under the Bridge?'

'Easy. The captain will have the drawbridge raised, and we shall simply sail through.' Instead of berating him for a fool, George grins. 'We're safe in our cousin's care, Brother.'

Cousin Warwick: Richard visualises the earl - solid, robust, fleet of mind. Mother's choice, Father's friend. Feeling his innards settle, he's certain George is right.

Skelton shifts. 'My lords, we are approaching Queenhithe.'

Ahead of them, a hulking shape looms in the moonlight: massive sail convulsing with every gust of wind, blobs of torchlight moving along the deck.

George fidgets, excited. 'The *Anne*.'

The vessel, while not as grand as expected, boasts raised structures at either end, like miniature castles with wooden crenels. Its standard, flapping madly from the topmost mast, is unremarkable, but that, Richard supposes, is precisely Warwick's intent.

The boatman eases them towards the jetty. Tying up at the quay, they rest in the shelter of the carrack, a tiny, cowering creature in the presence of a Titan. Skelton, budging up beside them, yells above the thwacking of its sails.

'Pay heed and do exactly as I say. No questions, no protests. I'm under orders from the earl, and you must obey my word.'

Richard's foot taps, reflexive, on the planks of the boat.

'Do you understand, my lord?'

'Yes, Master Skelton.'

'Good.'

Hauling him to his feet, Skelton helps him ashore while George follows, brushing his cloak with a nervous hand.

The crew of the *Anne* await them on the quay: roughhewn faces pitted and craggy, they could be agents of the queen, or of the devil, for all Richard knows. There's a stink of pitch and rotten fish, the tang of salt and seaborne sludge. Retching, he casts a wary eye at George.

'Save that until we're afloat, Dickon.'

A stocky man presents himself. Flat-faced but not unfriendly, eyes of a vivid blue, he greets them with surprising grace.

'My lords. I am Thomas Roger, the earl's liegeman and captain of the *Anne*, with instructions to convey you to safety. I ask merely that you obey my orders, look to Master Skelton, and trust in God.'

With a curt bow, he makes for the ship, barking orders and surveying the heavens before striding up the gangplank.

With a nudge from Skelton, the boys follow in his wake, the wooden ramp still quivering from the captain's heavy tread.

There's no way of knowing how long they've been at sea, the hours passing slowly in this heaving, stifling, water-borne coffin. Richard yearns for air, for the merest glimpse of day. Horn lanterns, suspended from the ceiling, squeal and sway with every lilt of the ship while their fitful splashes of light render him bilious. He imagines rolling into a black abyss, into the very jaws of Leviathan. If they die here, unshriven, they'll be cast into Hell. He wishes he could sleep, spend the whole voyage in oblivion, but the ship lurches continually, his belly likewise, and he wonders whether they are not in Hell already.

Skelton says they should be grateful. They're housed in the finest part of the ship, the Great Cabin, designed for the earl's own use, and it's true the space is comfortably furnished. There's even a bed: secured to the floor, a fur-lined coverlet offering some semblance of home despite its hardened patches of vomit. Skelton was very swift last night, but not swift enough to catch everything in the dented pewter basin. A fellow's first voyage, he'd told them, is always like this; the constant tossing and heaving is how it is at sea. But if either of them feels sick again, they must be sure to inform him so he can help them to the deck and they can spew over the side.

In all sense, Richard should alert him now. The base of his throat feels watery, and a bitter taste tells him that soon he shall be retching again. But he needs to hold out, especially now that George is composed, perched on the side of the bed and plying Skelton with questions. Richard wishes he could be like him. All his brother cares about is that in leaving London behind, they've eluded the queen. He seems to have left his fear behind, too, whilst Richard's remains, gnawing at his guts.

If he retches again, Skelton may be angry, but the incessant writhing of the ship will have its way, and soon, he shall have no choice. Already, he can feel it, taste it. It's coming. His hand flies to his mouth, but their guardian takes control, grasping him under the arms and propelling him onto the deck.

The freezing blast is cold and reviving. Richard gulps ice-laden air, but the thrashing of the sea is terrifying, and despite his need to retch, he yearns to return below.

George, insistent on accompanying them, huddles into his hood. 'If you need to spew, Dickon, get on with it. It's like the devil's cauldron down there.'

'I have you, lad.' Gripping Richard's cowl, Skelton hauls him towards the gunwale and angles his head towards the churning water.

Richard's body jerks. Vomit erupts, splashing the side of the ship and trickling towards the stirring depths.

'Watch that boy, now!' A tree trunk of a man bears down on them. 'Get them back inside. Can't you see there's a storm brewing? You must remain in the cabin, sir, until Captain Roger gives the word.'

Skelton complies, bundling them below. Once inside the cabin, he deposits Richard on the bed. 'Lie still, my lord. Any more retching, we'll have to use the close stool.'

Richard snuggles into the coverlet, shuddering at the thought of the close stool, of its wooden seat, its stinking, piss-stained pewter bowl.

You'd think that lying down would help. That remaining in one place, gripping the bedframe and steeling your guts, would make at least one ounce of difference. But it doesn't. Bile is rising again, and he tries to fight against it, diverting his gaze to the ceiling where a Calvary has been painted directly above the bed. Christ crucified, the Blessed Virgin and Saint John the Evangelist: a last comforting image for the eyes of a dying man. For they are all going to die, he's certain of it. Squeezing his lids together, he links his fingers: *Pater in manus Tuas…Father into Thy hands.*

'Haul the bowline!' All at once, there are cries from above. The same gruff voice they encountered on deck, bellowing commands, straining to make itself heard above the rising gale. The ship lists in one violent, sickening motion.

Richard opens his eyes. His brother is staggering across the boards, fighting to regain his balance.

'Lord George,' Skelton's yell battles the unholy sounds that seep through the timbers from the deck above. 'The storm will soon be upon us. I urge you, lie next to your brother, for safety's sake.'

George obeys as an almighty jolt sends the close stool careering across the cabin, and water slops under the door.

Steeling his nerve, Richard meets his brother's eye. 'We're going to sink, aren't we? If we are, you must tell me. Don't hide it. I won't be lied to, George.'

George squeezes him in a tight embrace. 'No. God won't allow it. We must set our minds on Edward. And on our cousin. Even now, the earl may be facing our enemies in open combat. We're fortunate in him, brother. He'll protect Mother and Margaret - make all safe for us to return.'

Richard recalls the day of their departure, the earl's hefty paw hard upon his shoulder, the certainty that in sending them away, he was doing what their father would have done. Bolstered by the thought, he raises his head. 'Before Father left, I made him a promise. I promised I'd be strong, for his sake – and I'm trying,

George. I swear to you, I'm trying.'

George grips him as they flinch from the impact of another wave. 'I know you are, and I'm proud of you, Richard. Very proud.'

For once, his true name, as if his father had spoken to him out of the tempest.

Chapter Three

'WELL, IT seems we must settle for second best.' George casts a critical eye around the musty chamber. Lifting the corner of a wall hanging, he beats it with the palm of his hand. Dust rising, he makes a show of coughing and drops the Arras in disgust, as if it had singed his fingers. 'This place has been empty for months.'

The huge courtyard, crenellated walls and steeple-topped towers of the Bishop's Palace looked grand enough from the outside, but it has proved a hollow shell of a place. Their host, Bishop David, is not in residence, and they're told not to expect him. The episcopal guards who escorted them here, their rasping French almost as impossible to understand as their grating Flemish, were clear upon that. It seems the bishop's dispute with the city of Utrecht has driven him elsewhere, to a place Richard and George could not even attempt to pronounce. He does, however, send them 'cordial greetings as brothers in Christ, and as sons of the late Duke of York, of most worshipful and exalted memory.'

When the guards have left, George barks with laughter. 'Cordial greetings? I wouldn't call this very cordial. There isn't even a privy.'

No privy, it's true, but as far as Richard can see, things are not all bad. A fire has been lit to welcome them, and the large tester bed, with its crimson curtains, is not unlike theirs at home. A mirror hangs beside the faded Arras. Beneath it, a small table holds a ewer and bowl for washing. Tall windows with square leads allow for plenty of light, and the shutters, brightly painted in green and gold, look stout enough to guard against the coldest of draughts.

'Look, Brother,' he points, cheerful, 'a window seat.'

George, unimpressed, wanders to the small oratory in the corner of the chamber. Richard follows, eager to compare it to their mother's chapel with its embroidered altar cloth and jewelled crucifix. By comparison, the alcove is tiny but brightly painted; Saint Michael crushing the serpent beneath his heel, the Virgin nursing the infant Lord. There's a small altar with a triptych, its painted panels closed for Lent; a prie-dieu with a cushioned hassock and a Book of Hours, pages open and inviting. Unable to resist, Richard runs his fingers over the vellum, smiling at the little creatures - mischievous rabbit, stealthy fox - which peer from the foliage bordering its pages. He wonders if the prayer book is the duchess' idea, whether she has gifted it to them for their evening devotions and will come to bless them before they sleep, as their mother does.

'We must remember to greet her properly,' he informs George, 'when she returns.'

'Who?'

'Duchess Isabella.'

'Why would the duchess set foot in Utrecht?' George is on his toes, reaching towards the triptych, tugging at its closed panels. Easing one open, he peeks inside.

'George, what are you doing? You know images must remain covered during Lent.'

Frowning, his brother moves to the bed and begins to prod, testing for comfort. Peering under the coverlet, he wrinkles his nose.

'He's one of the duke's bastards, did you know?' When Richard fails to respond, his head jerks up. 'The bishop. He's one of Duke Philip's many bastards. Skelton told me.'

'So?'

'Just that I would have expected the duke to receive us himself and to accommodate us in Bruges, not dump us here in this musty hole. We're miles from court, and the bishop can't even be bothered to greet us in person.'

Heaving an exaggerated sigh, George throws himself onto the mattress. Bed ropes creak in response, and he snarls at the sound. '*They'll* need tightening before we retire tonight. Do you think they've housed us in the wrong chamber?'

Wherever we stay, Richard thinks, at least we're on dry land.

'I wish the French looked more favourably upon us,' George says, adopting the worldly tone he uses to assert his seniority. 'If their old king were dead, we should fare well under the Dauphin Louis: that's what our cousin says.'

'But why should we want to go to France? Is King Charles not cousin to Queen Marguerite? He might sell us to her for a hundred marks, and then what would we do?'

George sets his mouth. 'I should hope we're worth more than that. Anyhow, Cousin Warwick says the Dauphin favours us and would support our cause. Our cousin favours the French as a people, says they're descended from the old blood, unlike the Burgundians, who have made their wealth through trade.' Snatching a pillow, he tosses it to the foot of the bed. 'Had we been housed by the Dauphin, we could have at least made ourselves understood. I just hope we're not in this dung heap long enough to have to learn their monstrous language.'

'But the earl told us this is what Father would have done.'

'Yes. Father might well have sent us away. But not necessarily here.'

Richard shrugs: George has an answer for everything. 'Mother said the duchess favours us. If she will keep us safe from Marguerite, then this is where we should remain.'

George's face puckers as if tacked round with loose stitches and the thread pulled taught. 'Can't you see, Dickon? Is this place not evidence enough for you? Mother mentioned the duchess, yes, but not the duke. If he really wanted us here, he'd have sent his steward for us, lodged us in his palace. They say his court in Bruges is the most lavish in Christendom. Look around you – no duke, no duchess, not even a bastard bishop. Duke Philip doesn't want us anywhere near him. He probably intends to forget all about us.'

When they were at sea, George had been eager to come here;

his confidence the only beacon in those few but agonising days when they were in little surety of their lives. Now, simply because the duke isn't here to greet them, he's acting like a churl.

Determined to win him over, Richard wanders to the casement and launches himself at the window seat. 'Want to see what's below?'

'No.'

'Well, I do.'

Unlatching the window, he casts it wide. Greeted by a rush of piercing air, he squints at the effect of sun on snow, then peers down at what looks to be a secluded bower, separated from the main courtyard by a high stone wall. Bumps and dents in the unspoiled layer of white reveal the position of flower beds and box hedges, and he's seized by the desire to hasten down; to leave a trail of frenzied footprints, scoop up handfuls of pristine snow and throw them at his brother. Were we at home, he thinks, George would be eager to throw one back.

Beyond the wall, to the town side, a bell tower points the way to Heaven. Its height cannot compare to the spire of Paul's, yet its open tracery, decorated in red and white, is much more beautiful. Richard gazes at it in sheer wonder.

'Brother! You must come and see.'

As usual, curiosity gets the better of George, and soon, both boys lean from the window, gaping at the huge painted structure. This must indeed be a great city, Richard says, to have so fine a church, and perhaps George is wrong, and the duke will visit them here after all. As they stare, a cascade of chimes tumbles from the belfry, a pretty, tinkling sound unlike the deep booming bells of London. Richard wonders whether they will be allowed to pray there, in that great building. Surely, so fine a tower would carry their prayers directly into the lap of God. He smiles, and George's eyes soften in response.

'Mes Seigneurs, méfiez-vous! Reculez!'

Startled, they turn from the casement, chamber dim and hazy green after the brightness outside. A man, lanky, all arms and legs, is lurching towards them in panic. Seizing the latch, he slams the window shut.

'Please, my lords, do not seek to escape. It is our honour to keep you safe here.'

The French trips awkwardly from his tongue, like jangling music. He's simply but finely dressed: short gown of crimson wool belted at the waist, green tippet and hood, and a strange square bonnet unlike anything Richard has seen in England. At the sight of their tense faces, the Fleming's lights up with an affable grin.

'Lord Joris, Lord Reichard, I bid you most welcome here. I am Jaagen Van Damme, your servant.' Snatching the bonnet, he crushes it in his fist. Thick hair, bluntly cut, flops over his brow: the muted colour of damp straw, it is the exact shade of their father's.

'You will want to wash, my lords, after your journey. I shall bring water and towels.'

George assumes authority. 'We were given to understand that the bishop does not reside here.'

'Alas no, Lord Joris. He lives at present in the castle of Duurstede. He is not on good terms with our townspeople, but those of us in his service who remain here are to act as your hosts.' Jaagen Van Damme smiles again, displaying a row of large square teeth. 'We have much here to entertain you: a library, many books.'

It's clear the young man is keen to please, and, in a bid to staunch his brother's complaints, Richard assures Jaagen that books will be most welcome: the *Roman de la Rose*, or a history of Troy, any romance where there are knights or soldiers.

'Do you have a chessboard and pieces?' George will not be outdone.

'Ja, the bishop owns a set made from the bones of a great creature, a gift from a wealthy Hansa merchant. His Grace also has many curiosities – a giant's toenail of ancient time, the horn of a unicorn dipped in gold—'

'A unicorn's horn? May we see it?'

'Alas, Lord Reichard, the bishop's greatest treasures travel with him.'

George huffs and strides towards the bed. Richard wonders whether he intends to raise the subject of the bed ropes, or whatever he found under the coverlet that he finds so disagreeable.

Jaagen looks undaunted. 'But we have many other things here that will interest you. His Grace has ordered mounts to be placed at your disposal. All boys like to ride, ja?'

Expect formality, Skelton had warned them whilst aboard the *Anne*. The Flemings are a formal people. Imagine being presented at court, the most elaborate ceremonials; your mother, your cousin, the king, the queen, the Patriarch of Jerusalem, the Holy Father himself, all in attendance. That is how formal it is there, even at breakfast.

From the brusqueness of the bishop's guards to the brooding silence of the palace, Richard might have believed such a statement, but when Jaagen grins, he can't help but do the same.

'I have a pony at home,' he tells him, 'her name is Amber. I wanted to bring her with me, but it was not allowed.'

Jaagen nods in sympathy. 'We shall find you a young mare, and a gelding for Lord Joris. We shall ride together. What else do you like? Running? Jumping?'

The Fleming places his bonnet on the floor and pretends to toss a ball into it. 'You play at petjeball, ja? Or kayles?' Lining up a set of invisible pins, he plays at knocking them down. George twitches, wracked by silent giggles.

Triumphant, Jaagen laughs. 'Tomorrow, we play. But now, hot water.' Spinning on his heel, he speeds from the chamber.

With a loud guffaw, George sinks to the bed, knees tucked in, body shaking. His mirth is contagious, and Richard flops down beside him. They laugh helplessly, ribs and cheeks aching, until all strength is spent, and they lie exhausted, overwhelmed by a sense of ease they have not felt in months.

Wiping his eyes, George points to the door. 'What need have we for the bishop's company when we have *him*?'

Beyond the palace walls, the tower bells sprinkle their melody. Breathing a prayer of thanks, Richard believes their pleas have already ascended and that Meester Jaagen Van Damme is himself a gift from God.

Utrecht may be second best, but Richard considers it a haven, and if George is correct and the duke considers them unimportant, then he is content. To be unimportant is to be safe. Provision has been made for their education, and the regularity of Master Geric's lessons in Latin and rhetoric is comforting. If Richard can be sure that each day, at the same time, the same things will happen, then life has assumed a pattern: a customary pattern with nothing to disrupt it. Disruptions are only ever bad, in his experience.

He's grateful, too, that his brother has ceased his grutching. It's impossible to be despondent in the company of Jaagen Van Damme, even for George. The most attentive of servants, Jaagen supplies their every need - bed turned down each night and made again each day; clothes folded, neatly brushed; food served; fire tended; water fetched; baths scented - he seems to fulfil the tasks of a hundred lesser men.

Three weeks after their arrival, ponies are delivered from the bishop's stables. It's good to be once more in the company of horses, solid, genial, their smell fetching up comforting thoughts of Amber. Saffier is a gentle grey, who snickers softly when Richard strokes her dappled hide, while George's gelding, Robijn, is a proud, golden beast, clearly aware of its charms. Horse and rider, therefore, have found an affinity, and Richard envies his brother's skill as George trots around the palace grounds, jumping with ease over the wooden hurdles that Jaagen has erected. Father, Richard thinks, would be very pleased with George.

Completing his circuit of the yard, his brother eases Robijn to a halt beside Jaagen's dun-coloured rouncey. Richard joins them, Saffier's hoofbeats muffled by the newly fallen snow.

George, pink-cheeked and gleaming, looks coaxingly at Jaagen. 'Could we ride as far as the Domplein square today? I should like to see the statue of Saint Martin you told us about.'

'*Nee*. My lord bishop is eager you should remain here, in the grounds of the palace. He is responsible for your welfare and writes that you must ride as far as the spinole but not beyond.' The spinole, an oddly shaped tower at the far end of the palace complex, is not so exciting a prospect as the Domplein. Both boys have already wandered to the tower on foot, disappointed to find it little more than a domestic building, as mundane as any at Ludlow or Baynard's Castle.

Faced with their dissenting scowls, Jaagen points to the great bell tower overlooking the palace. 'But see, my lords. Have you noticed the weathercock atop the Domtoren? You can see it well from here. Saint Martin, patron saint of our city, slicing his cloak to share with the beggar.'

They squint towards the lantern of the Dom Tower, the weathercock barely visible against lumpy grey cloud. Jaagen is undeterred: 'The cathedral houses relics – the very finger bones that performed such a charitable deed.'

George looks encouraged. 'Could we see them?'

If we could, Richard thinks, we could pray to the saint for Father's soul, for our cousin, for his victory over the queen. For Edward and for our journey home. For Mother, and Margaret, and Amber. 'Yes, Jaagen, can we see them?'

The Fleming tips a wink. 'My brother is attached to Canon Zoudenbalch's household. When next I see him, I shall beg a favour.'

The bed feels empty. Exploring the mattress with an outstretched foot, Richard finds nothing but chilled linen: his brother is not here. Grey light is seeping through a crack in the shutters, and a swift glance towards the cresset lamp shows it almost extinguished, yet no sounds drift up from the bailey. Nothing either, from the corner of the chamber: George is not at the pisspot. Turning over, he notes the smooth dent in the pillow where his brother's head should be, the sheet and coverlet tucked back into place to keep him warm. The garderobe, then. George shall return in his own time. Curling up, he sinks back to sleep.

Roused at length by the bells of the Domtoren, he finds he's still alone: no shared warmth cradling his back, George's half of the bed remains empty and cold.

Tension mounts. Where is he? How long has he been gone? Toes curling on the freezing tiles, Richard pads towards the oratory. Perhaps he's praying, mumbling Lauds over the Book of Hours. But the tiny space is dark and empty.

Wriggling into hose and shirt, he discovers a half-burned candle. Securing it atop a pricket, he guards the flame with a cupped hand. The clack of the latch is deafening as he slips from the chamber into the draughty space beyond.

He doesn't have to search far: by the casement near the stairwell, a dim shape quivers. George has hooked back the shutters. Breath misting up the glass, he peers into the early dawn, arms drawn across his chest. Richard creeps closer, palm shielding the pricket and smarting from the leaping flame.

George starts. 'What are you doing here, you little worm?'

'What is it? What's amiss?'

'Why no word?' Turning back to the window, George squints towards the gatehouse as if to conjure a messenger from the misty gloom. 'We've been here over a month and know nothing of what is happening at home.'

'Come back to bed.' Shivering, Richard grasps George's sleeve. Without his hand to guard it, a draught extinguishes the candle. In the blue-grey half-light, his brother could be made of marble.

'I had a nightmare.' George's voice is so low he can barely hear it. 'It woke me early, and I couldn't settle. Kept seeing them in my mind.'

'Who, George? Whom did you see?'

'I dreamt I stood on London Bridge. It was winter and cold. The place deserted; no people, no stray dogs, shops and houses shuttered and barred. It felt wrong. And the silence… an eerie, deafening silence. I wandered, looking for something, for somebody: anybody. Then a force took me, dragging me towards one of the parapets as if the devil himself was tugging at my collar. There, I saw a row of traitors' heads, each of them staring at me, accusing. As I moved closer, I could see the heads belonged to…to Father, Edmund, and

Uncle Salisbury. In the dream, it didn't seem strange that the heads were in London. I didn't question it, just stared back in fear, telling them I was sorry. Sorry I'd escaped; sorry that I live, and they had died. But they just glared back.'

George pauses, eyelids battering each other. 'Then, I realised that next to them, where before there had been only pikes, there were now other heads. One wore a bonnet and kerchief; that was Mother's. Her mouth was moving. She said, "We're all dead, George. Only you and Richard remain." Then I looked at the other three. One was Edward's, another Cousin Warwick's. But the final one, the one I dared not behold, but which called to me, was the most terrible.' Fear catches in George's throat. 'It was our sister. It was Margaret.'

Daylight shames George, and he's barely spoken a word. That it should have been Richard comforting him in the early hours, rather than the other way round, seems to have embarrassed him. And the fact they returned to bed wrapped in each other's arms has made him haughty, offhand. The nightmare appears to have deserted him, but the memory of it chills Richard to the bone.

'Your dream—'

'Here,' George stuffs a bonnet into his hand, 'don't dawdle. This is our chance to show the Dom Chapter just how important we are. The canons have agreed to receive us—no small honour, according to Master Geric—and have agreed to display Saint Martin's fingerbone. We must try to impress them, Dickon. That's the way we can best serve Father.'

Their garments are new. Made from sumptuous black velvet, they are a gift from Bishop David. George says His Grace must wish them well-attired, even if he's not prepared to saddle a horse and canter the few miles from Duurstede to visit them. Jaagen had them wear the gowns today to prove their worth to the Chapter. Unsurprisingly, George was in agreement.

'Black is the richest of colours its dye the most expensive. For that reason, it's worn only by the noblest of men.'

Richard tilts his chin, keen to appear at least a shade taller. When they meet the Dom Chapter, George will be sure to take control, but they each need to make an impression. They are both sons of York.

'How do we address them?' He dons his bonnet while George balances on his toes, assessing the effect of his own in the polished wall mirror. 'The clergy, I mean. Is it father or brother?'

'It would be easier if you did not address them at all, Dickon. Leave such things to me.'

'But we should both—'

'You'll not be required to say anything. Just follow what I do and keep your mouth shut.' Bounding over the threshold, George yells that Richard had better not let him down. 'Word of this visit may reach Duke Philip, and if we conduct ourselves well, he may invite us to Bruges.'

Richard grits his teeth and follows his brother through the maze of empty rooms, the narrow, twisting stairs. George remains ahead, striding with the distinctive confidence of the elder sibling, keen to uphold the customary order of things. They reach the outer staircase, slippery with compacted snow, and Richard sticks close, adopting his brother's swaggering gait. He must share the assurance and poise that George possesses. Must do as he does.

Jaagen is waiting below, swathed in crimson wool and blowing on his hands. Richard wonders why the bishop has not provided his servant with a better set of gloves. If God allows them to return home, they should provide a pair of lambswool and leather. It would be the right thing to do, an appropriate way to repay their friend and ease him through the Flemish winters.

Without warning, the steps slide from under him. Arms flailing, Richard gropes in vain for rope or rail, anything that will break his fall. With nothing to aid him, he slithers down the steps, backside striking each in turn, until he crumples, humiliated, at the stair foot.

George and Jaagen are on him in an instant; hunching, huddling, blocking out the light. Shock outweighs pain, but he swats them aside, assuring them that all is well despite the unwelcome certainty that it isn't. With an almighty effort, he forces himself to rise. An all-consuming pain shoots the length of his shin, and he flops down, snow seeping through the seat of his hose.

George seizes his ankle and rubs vigorously.

'Nee, Lord Joris.' A signal from Jaagen and guards hasten from the outer gate. 'Not until we know what ails him.'

Richard grunts. Nothing can ail him today; he won't allow it. 'George? Help me up.'

'Remain where you are, my lord.' Jaagen yells a command, and the guards disappear indoors, returning with a bedsheet, which they spread upon the frozen ground.

'I can manage.'

'No,' George says, 'you can't. Permit them to help you.'

Hoisted up, he's borne inside like a hunted quarry, Jaagen leading the way. George follows, brows drawn, mouth downturned. The relics, Richard thinks, anger and disappointment thrashing his core. I've let him down. I've let Father down. Deposited on the bed, he determines to bear the pain dry-eyed.

Jaagen leans across him. 'The bishop's physician is with him at Duurstede, but I shall send for one of the city surgeons. I command you, Mijnheer, do not move. And do not try to remove your boot.'

George watches him leave, then sinks onto the coverlet. 'We shall have to explain to the Chapter why we're not able to visit them. I hope they'll not consider it an insult.'

Surly with embarrassment, Richard tells his brother to leave: to go to the cathedral as planned, pray over the relics, and call down the saint's blessing. At least then, their father would have one son of whom to be proud.

'Certainly not. I shall remain here,' George assures him. 'Their surgeons may not be as well schooled as Mother's physician. You think she'd have me leave you to the ministrations of a stranger?' Rising, he removes Richard's bonnet and bolsters his pillows.

'You're angry, aren't you?'

'Yes, but what good will that serve? It's fortunate for you that I'm here; otherwise, who knows how you'd fare? Don't try to rise, you idiot; just rest and wait for the surgeon. But I warn you, if I feel this fellow to be lacking, I'll demand Jaagen fetch us another.'

Boot increasingly tight, Richard winces.

George's face rumples in concern. 'I tell you, Dickon, if I don't trust this fellow, then we shall have a better. We shall send to Bruges, to the duke. This city surgeon—' he waves a hand, dismissive, '— we don't know where he studied nor how successful he is. Truth to tell, I should ask for the opinion of the surgeon's guild before we agree to let him anywhere near you.'

'Why have you decided not to trust him? We've not even met the man yet.'

'Precisely. And until we do, I shall reserve my judgement.'

If only he would. With nothing to ease the pain, Richard gnaws his lip, convinces himself it's helping. 'I'm sure Jaagen will do his best.'

While the Domtoren strikes the hour, George speaks of anything and everything in an effort to distract, but his prattle makes for little ease. Letting his lids fall, Richard pretends to sleep until his brother nudges him. 'Dickon. Jaagen has returned. I've just seen him cross the yard. He has some fellow with him.'

Voices drift up from below: Jaagen's jangling chatter and the clipped undertones of a stranger. As the door opens, George stations himself beside the bed, eyeing the visitor with suspicion. The man is rotund, sombre-faced, wearing the long scarlet gown of his profession. His assistant scurries in his wake, an elaborate casket clasped to his chest, which he places on the table beside the ewer and jug. George watches, appraising, while Richard shudders. What should be contained in such a box but surgical instruments? Knives, razors - huge tweezers, like those used by the barber last year, to pull out George's rotten tooth. Surely nothing like that will be required today.

Folding back his sleeves, the surgeon grunts. 'The first thing we must do, my lord, is remove your boot.' His French is clear, crisp. 'This will hurt, but it must come off before your ankle can swell any further.' Cupping Richard's calf, he grasps the heel of the boot while George scrutinises every move.

Jaagen clasps the boy's shoulder, holding him down. 'No struggling, Mijnheer.'

A moment's pain and the boot is off. At a word from the surgeon, Jaagen loosens the leg of Richard's hose, rolling down the black silk and easing it over his ankle. Richard glances down; his joint a puffy swollen thing, ill-defined beneath a cushion of padded flesh. Grateful for the surgeon's cooling hands, he braces himself as his foot is prodded and examined.

'No break,' the man declares at length. 'My lord has merely suffered a sprain and must rest.' He turns to Jaagen, and they confer in Flemish, words clattering like dice.

Frustrated, George sets his lips. 'I'm his brother. Tell me what I must do to help him.'

Inscrutable, the surgeon blinks as though a draught has blown a dust mote into his eye. 'He must remain abed, my lord, as I said. No weight upon the ankle.'

'For how long?' George demands, hand hovering, protective, over Richard's foot.

'A fortnight.' An appeasing nod from Jaagen. 'But we will take care of him, ja?'

On the second day of his confinement, George appears with a chessboard and a box of richly carved pieces.

'Jaagen found this. It isn't the bishop's finest set, of course, but it'll do well enough. Here,' rummaging in the box, his brother thrusts a king into Richard's hand, 'start placing the pieces. I shall play white. And don't move once the board is set up, or you'll overturn everything.' He winks. 'Master Geric offered some texts for your studies whilst abed, but I convinced him to forsake lessons for a while. I can't imagine Wadham being so lenient.'

Chess is a great pleasure for George. Far beneath him in experience and skill, Richard is prepared for defeat but pleased with the distraction, a way of filling the long, inactive hours. Each day, George dines at his bedside, happily existing on bread, cheese, and smoked fish without any word of complaint. Richard is grateful. He knows how it must cost his brother to be cooped up in their chamber while, outside, the snow is finally beginning to thaw.

'You don't need to remain here, George. I'm not an infant.'

'What? Leave the chamber and let you move my pieces, Dickon? I'll allow no opportunity for cheating. For as long as we play, I shall remain.'

And he does. At night, with a game unfinished, he has Jaagen assist him in carrying the board to the table so they may resume upon the morrow. And they do: never tiring even when Jaagen insists that George, at least, would benefit from a dose of fresh air.

'I'll not leave my brother,' is the recurrent protest, 'he needs me.'

And Jaagen himself never arrives empty-handed. Pastries, sweetmeats, treats for the patient's good behaviour, are ferried on a tray direct from the kitchen. Books are fetched from the bishop's library: bestiaries, Bibles, the fables of Aesop. He's even discovered a *History of Troy* with gilt-edged pages. Eventually, George agrees to leave his brother unattended. On the days on which Richard chooses to read, he has Robijn saddled and trots around the palace grounds. Returning, he's full of stories: imaginings they build into adventures as a way of amusing themselves in the evenings.

Not all the tales they share are imaginary, however. Once dusk descends, with the fire banked down, candles lit, and shadows dancing, Richard begs George to relate his favourite tale: the story of their father and the King of France. It begins as it always does: Richard settling against the pillows and hanging on his brother's every word.

In a time before either of them were born, before even their brother Edward graced the earth, their father was a hero. King Harry's lieutenant in France, he led valiant military campaigns, gaining great renown, and all but captured Charles, their king. Storming the chateau where the Frenchman lay, their father was but a heartbeat away: one breath from glory.

George ends the tale with a flourish, eyes twinkling. 'And they say the king's bed was still warm.'

Richard's gaze flashes to the window, half expecting to see

Charles' skinny ankles disappearing over the sill. 'A moment more and Father would have taken him.'

'Imagine how all England would have applauded him,' George says, warming to his theme, 'how King Harry, and even the queen herself, would have been forced to recognise his greatness. He'd have put them all to shame, those knaves who pushed and buffeted him aside. Harry would have raised Father to his true place, the court would have demanded it, and the queen's favourites would've been ousted. Imagine, Suffolk and Somerset thrown out on their vicious backsides.'

Richard shifts as his ankle nips and throbs. 'Don't stop, George, tell me some more.'

Propping himself on one elbow, his brother all but salivates at the invitation. Richard doesn't doubt that whatever he's about to hear, he'll have heard a hundred times, but George is the best of storytellers, and to hear such tales brings their father close: as if he'd not died that December day but returned to Baynard's victorious. As if he's with them now, presenting his palms to the hearth and shuddering as the warmth thaws out his chilled limbs. *I'm home, Richard. No more journeys. No more wars. I'm home.*

'Father was the greatest magnate in the realm,' George says. 'In France, he strived to hold our domains as fiercely as did Harry the Fifth.'

The figure by the hearth is drifting closer; cloak enveloping Richard in a silent embrace, the snowflakes that pepper it sizzling, melting away in a hiss of vapour.

'There were none to match him, Dickon, but the queen denied his virtue, saw him as naught but an enemy. Though Father was only ever faithful, she dripped a trickle of poison into the king's ear.'

'Why did the king believe her? I'm sure I would not.'

'Because Harry hasn't the wit to see things for himself. He accepts all that Marguerite and her toadies tell him, as if they were the Blessed Virgin and Apostles.'

'But why did the queen lie about Father? Why did she convince Harry that Father was a traitor?' The question Richard is always compelled to ask, the one which always perplexes him.

'Because she hated him.'

This is the part of the story he can never understand. If their father's life had been recorded in a book, this is the point at which Richard should slam the volume closed, wrap it in its felt cloth and bury it under the bed. The romance, so finely wrought, so heroically told, has become a fabricated tale. Heroes do not die. Villains do not prosper. Not in the best stories, anyway.

It's inconceivable. 'Why?'

'Because he sought to rid the country of her favourites. Because he saw how Beaufort was leeching the exchequer, lining his pockets, while Harry drooled in his pottage and tried to remember what day it was. The saying was that the king was so poor he couldn't pay for his own meat. Imagine allowing others to slide their hands into the coffers under your very nose and be powerless to help it. What manner of king is that?' George is getting into his stride. 'For myself, I'd as lief suffer a crowned mute or a jacketed ape. Father would have made a fine king, and all knew it. His lineage provided him with a greater claim than Daft Harry's. The best Marguerite could do was to provide an heir and give the people a reason to support Lancaster. So, what did she do?'

Richard shrugs. All this talk confuses him; he'd rather talk about their father, not Harry and his evil queen.

'She rutted with Edmund Beaufort, then announced to the king that he had a son. They say that when the prince was born, Harry declared he must have been conceived of the Holy Ghost. I imagine Somerset was overjoyed, thinking that one day his bastard would be ruling the kingdom.'

Is rutting not something animals do? Why humans would want to act like animals, Richard can't imagine. And, as for the king, he must be a sinner, despite his holy reputation, since his speech was so blasphemous.

'George, if Edward dies, if our cousin dies, what'll happen to us?'

'We'll grow, and we'll fight. If Edward and Warwick are lost, then Father's cause must fall to us.' A conspiratorial grin. 'So, you had better make sure that ankle mends, hadn't you?'

Chapter Four

April 1461
Bishop's Palace, Utrecht

*E*ASTER DAY dawns full of rose-tinged promise. Following High Mass and a dinner of spiced capon to dispel the austerity of Lent, Jaagen guarantees a traditional celebration.

'My sister sends Flemish gingerbread, made in the form of animals.' He fashions shapes in the air. '"For the young lords," she says. You will enjoy. Then we shall join the festivities in the Domplein. My lord bishop has agreed, on my pledge that we venture no further.'

Richard grins. A stroll to the Domplein will provide a welcome test for his newly healed ankle. He's been making an effort to walk unaided; the crutches on which he'd come to depend now lying abandoned in the corner of their chamber. At his request, Jaagen has agreed to seek out a crippled child from amongst the poor of the city: a good and charitable act of which God will approve. 'Will there be music and dancing in the square?'

A comical grimace. 'You surrender your crutches, and already you look to dance? I think not, Lord Reichard.'

'No need to fear.' George, slipping his arm through his brother's, winks at their companion, 'I shall control him.'

'Ja,' Jaagen returns the gesture. 'But who, Mijnheer, will be controlling you?'

Laughter bubbles in Richard's belly, erupting in a great guffaw, and he tugs Jaagen's sleeve, eager for more. But the Fleming's attention is focused elsewhere: yells from the courtyard below, the tramping of boots on stone.

'Mes Seigneurs…' Tentative, Jaagen makes for the door. 'There are messengers.'

The visitors, resplendent in violet and black, present a letter from Duke Philip. Composed in ornate Burgundian hand, it is addressed to the boys themselves. George accepts it and breaks the seal.

Mark his face, Richard tells himself. You'll be able to judge its content if you just mark his face.

His brother's eyes flicker and dart, teeth nibbling his lower lip. When George finally glances up, his features gleam. 'His Grace has word of our brother. Edward is triumphant.'

'Truly?'

'Have I not said so?' George, euphoric, casts the letter in the air and throws his arms around Richard. 'Marguerite and Harry are fled. Our brother is king!'

Richard clasps him, and the news strikes home, thrumming like the shaft of a well-loosed arrow.

Jaagen, bemused, bombards the ducal messengers with a stream of questions. From the depth of George's embrace, Richard catches his eye. 'Home, Jaagen. We are going home!'

Their friend proffers a wavering smile.

Their final day in Utrecht is bright and warm: lingering scents from the bishop's fruit trees, the cooing of doves from his cote. The comparison to the day of their arrival could not be more pronounced; the yard swarming with ducal emissaries, with palace retainers eager to bid farewell to the brothers of the new English king.

'Show manners enough,' George gives instruction, 'but don't

be too generous with the gesture. These people make obeisance, yes, but remember, it is our due now and to be expected.'

Scanning the yard for their companion, Richard spies Jaagen astride his rouncey, preparing to join the cavalcade. He's to ride with them as far as Calais, but the boy would have him travel further. Regaling the Fleming with tales of London, he's spoken of its great river, its famous bridge and Tower menagerie. He's even offered to teach him the language, to show him Westminster and the vast spire of Paul's. Now Edward is king, he's told him, Jaagen need have no qualms about making England his home.

The Fleming always takes pleasure in the stories, but he never replies.

A commotion erupts as a group of chattering potboys are elbowed aside, and a painted carriage rolls into the yard.

George accosts one of the black-cloaked officials. 'What's this?'

'The duke would prefer you to enter Bruges together, monseigneur, and as your brother is but recently recovered, the duchess has sent her chariot to house you both. It is most luxurious.'

'And most unseemly.'

'These are our instructions, monseigneur.' Offered little choice, George clambers inside and throws himself down. 'Only women travel in chariots, Dickon. Women and infants.' He tugs at the leather curtain. Metal rings jingling, light spills into the carriage and illuminates his petulant face. 'I shan't be able to see anything properly from in here.'

And people won't be able to see us, Richard thinks. Perhaps that's what bothers him.

Lurching into motion, the carriage circles the yard. Soon, they're through the gate and trundling the lengths of the narrow streets: flashes of stone walls, passing carts, the shining flanks of horses. George snipes at him in irritation, as the city he has so desperately wanted to see speeds by obscured by the wooden framework.

'When we reach Bruges, we'll be received by the duke and his household. Can't you sit a horse - even for the last mile or so? At least then, we could enter the city with some degree of dignity.'

'The surgeon said I should not attempt to mount. It might delay my recovery.'

'You're such a milk sop.'

'I'm not.'

'Well, get out and ride then. Sitting there like a girl, you'll make fools of us.'

There's nothing guaranteed to anger George more than if one ignores him; Richard learned this fact long ago and has always found it useful. When he refuses to respond, George heaves the inevitable sigh and turns his back.

Richard shrugs. This may not be as exciting as sitting astride their ponies, but the carriage is comfortable, rocking back and forth over the bumps in the road with surprising ease. The interior is lavish, hung with green and black cloth, blue damask cushions bolstering their backsides and small silver bells tinkling for their amusement. Jerking his own curtain aside, Richard peers out.

'What's amiss now?' George: still peeved.

'Nothing.'

'Jaagen is following if that's what's bothering you. I saw him join the cavalcade as we passed through the gate. Do you know, Duke Philip has sent over twenty of his personal household to accompany us? I've been counting them.'

His view from the carriage is not so restricted then, when it suits.

'I suppose the chariot will be acceptable as far as Sluys,' George says. Seeking his brother's eye, he grins: the closest Richard will get to an apology.

Sluys' foremost inn, the *Teste D'Or*, is in the busiest part of town, and Monsieur du Moustier keeps a thriving and respectable house. Their chamber, above the courtyard arch, echoes with noise from the street below: clattering hooves, hawking street vendors, and the discordant chimes of at least four sets of church bells, interspersed with the mewling screech of gulls. After the quiet confines of the Bishop's Palace, Sluys oozes a heady mixture of excitement and unease.

'You're certain it's safe to return home?' News of Edward's victory still seems tenuous, as if it may be snatched away again at a moment's notice.

George, sitting by the open window, polishes the dagger the duke has sent him as a gift. 'The queen is in Scotland, and Edward holds London. She'll not head south again. She wouldn't dare.'

Richard frowns. No such gem-encrusted gifts have arrived for him. 'Why call her "queen"? If Edward is king, then Marguerite is queen no longer.'

'No, you're right.' George flashes a wicked grin. 'What should we call her? What about "the She-Wolf"? How does that suit?'

'What of the king? Harry, I mean. What of him?' Never, in the tales he's read, or had read to him for pleasure on winter evenings, has Richard heard of a kingdom with two kings.

George is dismissive. 'Who cares about that simpleton? I expect Marguerite dragged him all the way to Scotland by her apron strings, and if Edward ever manages to get his hands on him, he'll probably send him to the Bedlam.' He laughs. 'That's where lunatics are housed. Harry should feel at home.' Tilting the grip of the dagger, he allows light to play upon its garnets and pearls.

'What will happen to him, George?'

'Why?'

'I just wondered.'

'Well, don't. His fate is not our concern; it's Edward's.'

When their mother told them of Edward's victory in the west, of the miracle of the three suns, she said God had blessed him. She was right. God has indeed blessed Edward. Somewhere in the north, the country where their father died, Edward has now been rewarded with both life and crown. The fight is named Palmsunday Field, but with thousands of their enemies slain upon such a day, Richard fears for Edward's soul. George says it was the only way, and that they should be thankful. Richard is thankful, but fearful too. Fearful that retribution for their father's fate should blight the season of the Lord's passion. He worries that, for such a sin, holy bellows may stoke the fires of Purgatory and prolong their father's pains.

'Will they ever come back, d'you think – Harry and Marguerite? Will we have to return here if they do?'

'No. They're the exiles now, not us. Edward is king, and one day, he'll rid England of our enemies: every last one. And then, if Marguerite falls into his hands, he'll chain her up in a cellar full of rats and let them feast on her flesh.' Sliding the dagger into its sheath, George snaps it home. 'Revenge for our father, Dickon. Revenge on the She-Wolf.'

Philip, Duke of Burgundy, is an unattractive man: long, downturned nose, large unflattering lips, and jowls that wobble when he turns his head. Despite this, George says he has many concubines, and it's clear that any lack of beauty is countered by the elegance of his person. Arrayed in black, from chaperon to pike-toed shoes, the fineness of his clothes, the brilliance of his jewelled collar, reveal a man of immense wealth and fine taste. Beside him, his tiny duchess drowns in the depths of her voluminous gown. Eyes like amber beads glow with warmth as she assesses the boys with evident approval while her son, Charles, stands at her elbow, silent and subdued. Attired in black, a tall bonnet perched upon his ample curls, he is the perfect image of his father.

'My lords,' Duke Philip retains the formal distance regularly endorsed by the Flemish. 'I bid you welcome to Brugge.'

Richard watches his brother thank the duke for his hospitality; for the gift of the dagger in its tooled leather sheath, which has never left George's side since the day he received it. Heavily lidded eyes both appraise and approve, and under their scrutiny George expands.

'We shall speak privily,' Duke Philip confides. 'Later.'

'My lord Richard.' A drawstring purse, red embossed leather, dangles from the duchess' fingers. 'One hundred *Vierlander*, a gift from His Grace.' When Richard hesitates, she jingles the purse, making it dance. 'For you.'

Bowing low, Richard accepts the gift, his brother a pressing weight beside him. 'Dank je, Mevrouw.'

But George's peevish glare is as nothing to the lady's obvious pleasure, and Richard thanks Jaagen inwardly for the courtesy of his Flemish lessons. He wishes he could have addressed the duchess in her native Portuguese, that would have irked George even more.

'I am honoured,' the duke says, 'to be of service to the brothers of King Edward. Come.'

He shepherds them through the glittering hall, seating them at his right hand; a mark of deference hardly lost on George, who settles into his high-backed chair with a serene smile. While Richard would feel happier at the farthest end of the board, with the duchess and her brooding son, he settles himself beside George and agrees to keep his own counsel.

From the dais, it's possible to see everything: and everything Richard sees speaks of great wealth. The finest beeswax dripping light; jewels glinting on every hand, with every flash of silken sleeve. Walls adorned with vibrant cloths, vessels inlaid with gems: crystal, garnets, beryl. Not even Father, Richard thinks, owned plate as magnificent as this.

When the food is announced, he and George have pre-eminence: mawmenny, coloured with saffron and sprinkled with violets. Richard's spoon hovers over the richly flavoured soup. A memory, deeply submerged, of a Christmas feast, the garderobe shaft, his stomach rebelling and puking its contents into the dry ditch.

George shoots a glance. 'Make an effort, Dickon, else you'll look ill-mannered. Those of us at high table must taste everything that is presented.'

'In that case,' Richard leans in, whispering under the whine of hurdy-gurdy, 'I'll have done with this and wait for the next course.'

'You have to get used to it. When we return home, we'll dine like this all the time.'

Richard does his best, forcing down the rich delicacies donated from the duke's own plate. When the butler returns, it is with hippocras, and Richard grimaces behind his napkin.

'Now what?' George points to his brother's cup while the duke calls for wafers.

'I don't care for it.'

'Try. Remember what I told you.'

Richard suffers in silence until the subtlety is announced. It'll be like the Twelfth Night feasts when we were small, he thinks, fidgeting and eager. He and George revelling in the sugar creations, pitching a guess at what might appear. Their favourite had been two jousting knights astride their marchpane horses, hurtling towards each other, couching brittle sugar lances. They'd talked about it for days afterwards.

Keen to share the recollection, he vies for his brother's attention but finds the duke has the best of it. George and Philip have their heads together, hugger-mugger, for all the world like the best of friends. Very well, he'll take pleasure in the thing himself, if George chooses not to.

The creation, when it comes, is born aloft on the shoulders of liveried boys: a sparkling sugar unicorn endowed with a golden horn and harnessed with diamonds. Six flesh and blood maidens, bedecked with flowery chaplets and flimsy silks, cavort alongside.

The duke's attention immediately spiked, George tickles his brother's ear. 'Say nothing, Dickon, but Duke Philip has paid me the greatest honour. He wishes to negotiate with the king over the hand of his granddaughter, Mary.'

'He wishes to give her to Edward?'

'No, muddlehead. To me.' George jabs himself in triumph. 'A secret. Say nothing to anyone.'

'But—'

'But what?'

Richard budges closer. 'You can't marry.'

'Why not?'

'You can't marry and leave me alone. It wouldn't be fair.'

'Never fear. She's hardly likely to come between us, being an infant of four years. But you can see the wealth of this place with your own eyes, Brother.' George surveys the hall in one encompassing glance. 'Imagine what kind of dowry she would bring.'

'And where would you live? Here? What about me?'

'I'll remain apart from my bride until we're both old enough. But if I do have to live here, it shall present no difficulty.'

'So, you'd come here and leave me—'

'Keep your voice down. What kind of impression would you have us bestow upon His Grace? That we lack even the manners to remain sedate at mealtimes? Besides, you need have no fear of losing me for quite some time yet. You may have a wife of your own by then.'

Richard scowls, marvelling at the speed with which his brother's opinions are changing. When they arrived in the Low Countries, George considered it a land of upstart merchants, but now he's full of praise, continually asserting how fine a man Duke Philip is and how Edward is certain to make an ally of him. He watches, tight-lipped, as George converses once more with the duke and glances up from time to time to admire the fleshy maidens.

Is this how it'll be from now on? No more games, no more jests, no more racing around the practice yard? Is George to be considered a man from now on? Snatching a handful of currants, Richard sprinkles them on his plate.

'Where are your manners, Dickon?' George: sharp-eyed as a hawk.

'*My* manners? You're the one gawping at girls.'

The most comely of the maidens snaps the horn from the brow of the sugared beast, charges it with sweet wine, and presents it as a trophy.

Duke Philip nods, jowls bobbing like wattles. 'My guests shall be the first to drink.'

George accepts the vessel, takes a mouthful, then passes it on. His expression says, *Careful, you little worm. All eyes are on you.* Sticky with melting sugar, the thing is heavier than Richard supposed, and his heart sinks as cloying slops bleed into the pristine linen.

He's prepared for his brother's scorn, for a host of mocking, unspoken threats, but to his surprise, George's glance is warm, reassuring. *No matter, Dickon*, it says, *the duke failed to notice, and I, for one, am not about to tell him.*

The travelling chest they brought from home now brims with a surfeit of treasures. Newly tailored gowns, riding capes, shirts of exquisite lawn; each gift carefully packed, sprigs of lavender crushed between. There are offerings too - for Edward, for their mother – and George, gratified, has assured the duke that ample gifts will be proffered in return. Philip is flattered. Calling them his beloved and trusty friends, he rides for Saint Omer, while final preparations are made for their journey home.

Jaagen kneels, carefully packing the final few items, while Richard lolls against the door frame, trying to think of something to say. He's renewed his plea for their friend to accompany them to England, and while Jaagen keeps his counsel, Richard continues to hope.

George clatters up the stairs. Urging Richard aside, he strides into the chamber, paying little heed to their companion. 'I'm eager to see our brother again, aren't you, Dickon?'

Content that the trunk is locked and secure, Jaagen leaps to his feet. Striding past the boys, he disappears into the stairwell.

George continues to muse. 'Can you remember when Father was in Ireland, and Edward found us safe lodging at Fastolf's Place? He came to see us every day, without fail.'

The Southwark manor in Tooley Street. Their brother before them, boisterous and beaming. Whenever Edward left, George would adopt a swagger, as if he'd more in common with their eldest brother than he had with Richard. Yet both had looked forward to Edward's visits more than anything. Richard smiles despite himself.

Jaagen returns with household pages, and the trunk, a deal heavier than it had been on upon arrival, is lugged towards the door.

'George, when will we be able to see where Father and Edmund are buried?' This is what they should do first. Before they settle into whatever kind of world Edward has made for them, they should visit their father and ask for his blessing.

George adjusts his bonnet, a final glance in the polished mirror.

'I imagine Edward will arrange a visit to Pontefract to pay them due reverence.'

'Langzaam!' Jaagen guards the wall plaster as the pages struggle to navigate. Blowing out his cheeks, he removes his cap, raking his hair. 'Wees vorzichtig!'

'When, George?'

'When Edward thinks it appropriate.'

'And what about…you know?'

'What?'

'You know.'

'Their heads? Don't worry. Edward will have had them taken down by now.'

'And placed with their bodies?'

'I expect so, yes.'

The encumbered pages navigate the spiral; Jaagen, fretful, taking up the rear. Richard's gaze follows his misted image. 'Do you never wonder about it, George? About what will become of them? If their heads and their bodies remain in different places, what will happen on the Day of Judgement?'

'For Pity's sake, how can I know? I'm no priest. All I know is that we must look to Edward now, as Mother has told us. Our future lies with him.'

Richard forces a smile. 'As you say, Brother.'

There's a fair wind; ideal, the Flemings say, for the journey to England. Jaagen agrees, says they're lucky, that May is a good month for a sea voyage. Richard wonders how he can know, having spent all his life in Utrecht, never venturing beyond the shores of his homeland. But Jaagen seems certain, and Richard nods in agreement, shielding his eyes and gazing out over the expanse of water. He knows now that Jaagen is not coming with them. No provision has been made, and he carries no pack, no bedroll. His rouncey has been handed over to the keeping of a palace groom, and both horse and stableman await him above the quay.

Edward has sent a company of men. They do not wear the colours of York but a new livery of Edward's devising: deep murrey and vivid blue, like wine and water. Mingling with Warwick's red-jacketed soldiers, Edward's men seem young, cocky, and George watches them with approval. The vessel lying at anchor is not the *Anne,* but a huge carrack, flying Edward's new colours and a banner of the Virgin. Their trunk is heaved aboard, along with three tuns of Gascon wine - another gift from Duke Philip - and a popinjay for their mother, screeching in protest as its cage is shunted against the side of the ship. Richard wonders what she will do with another bird. She should gift it to Margaret, he thinks, that's what I would do.

George wanders up and down, itching to depart. Calling one of Edward's men, he plies him with questions. The man bows. George smiles, back straight, chest swelling. Choosing to remain with Jaagen, Richard wonders at the lack of stories this morning, the shortage of jests to ease them on their way. He steals a glance, but their guardian is shielded by wind-battered hair, bright locks catching the sun. Richard fidgets, knowing that soon there will be an ocean between him and this kindly man, who has cared for them so well, whose sharp blue eyes and wheat-coloured hair remind him so very sorely of his father's.

'Be of cheer, Lord Reichard.'

Finally, he has Jaagen's attention but finds he cannot look. Moist eyes are not to be expected of the brother of a king. Instead, he tracks the movements of a huge gull which struts about the quay, herring hanging from its bill like a silver jewel.

'The king, your brother, will take care of you now. But I hope you will never forget your friend, Jaagen.'

Richard offers his hand, and Jaagen takes the outstretched palm, squeezing tightly. Hunkering down, the Fleming busies himself in smoothing the boy's jerkin, removing stray threads, tightening his belt.

'May God keep you, Lord Prince.'

George arrives to lead him away, and Richard obeys, wiping his face when he thinks none can see, realising he can never look back.

Only when they're safely aboard ship, and the harbour is fading, dare he seek out a tiny figure in crimson wool and follow it intently until it vanishes from sight.

Chapter Five

June 1461
London

SUNLIGHT SPANGLES the rippling Thames as the barge draws up at Baynard's. Draped with the Leopards and Lilies, a canopy at its stern and trumpeters at its bow, it dwarfs all passing craft. The boys wait on the landing, dressed in the black velvets they acquired in Bruges. Their brother – their king – awaits them at Sheen, and they must display all due deference, not least in their own persons. He arrived only yesterday, and it's said he's never stopped travelling since his Palm Sunday triumph: moving slowly south, accepting surrenders, securing castles, and whatever else it is that new kings do; kings, at least, who have won their crown upon a battlefield. Their mother was summoned to his presence last night.

'He needs me,' she'd told the boys, face bright as they'd ever seen it. 'We have much to discuss. Important things. He'll send for you on the morrow.'

Richard knows he must acquit himself well. It isn't just his mother and George he needs to impress now.

Barge tethered, his brother insists on boarding first: his due, he says, as heir presumptive. Richard sinks beside him under blue cloth of gold, and they move off upriver; trumpet blasts, announcing their presence, ensure a path through the glimmering swell.

'See?' George is jubilant as a clutch of rowing boats changes course, oarsmen sculling in desperation. 'I told you. Life is different now. A king's brothers have precedence in everything.'

Leaving the city behind, they follow the flow of the river past widening fields: the green flash of dragonflies, a hazy, hovering mass of midges. As they pass the Abbey of Westminster, clanging bells summoning monks to prayer, George is at pains to point out the palace; a crouched mass of honey-coloured stone with a great hall at its heart. Regaling Richard with stories of their forebears, he speaks of the great round table the third Edward created for his castle at Windsor.

'Kings can do as they will,' he says. 'They can follow in the footsteps of Arthur.'

When the towers of Sheen appear on the horizon, George continues to enlighten. 'Richard of Bordeaux destroyed the former palace when his queen died of pestilence. Imagine that?'

If grief had caused him to do it, then yes, Richard says, he can imagine that. Squinting, he spots movement up ahead: tiny figures preparing their welcome. As the barge draws close, the figures become guards dressed in Edward's new livery. Shielding his eyes, Richard glances at the turrets where banners of the same murrey and blue flutter from every pinnacle and embroidered sunbursts wink in the light.

'The sign sent by God,' George observes, 'on the day of Edward's victory in the west. You see, even when we were in fear for our lives, God had a plan.' The barge slows and bumps against the landing. 'Ready, Dickon? Remember, we need to make a good impression.'

Ushered through the palace gates, they enter a swarming courtyard. Might and domesticity crushed cheek by jowl: sentinels in brigandines, scullions lugging buckets, larder men with shanks of beef, crimson-faced laundry women, black-robed chaplains, barking dogs, screeching fowl.

A man in a turkey bonnet bursts through the mass, his crisply pleated gown and gilded collar distinguishing him from all others. Bowing low, he makes a flourish. 'My lords—' A sudden clangour halts further comment. The man grimaces, sanguine countenance ripening in hue. As the chimes die away, he clears his throat. 'My lords, I am William Hastings, Chamberlain of the Household. On behalf of the king, I bid you welcome to Sheen.'

'And is your arrival usually occasioned by a peal of bells, Master Chamberlain?' George, the picture of innocence, tucks his smirk behind a charming smile. 'Or was that merely in honour of our visit?'

Hastings grunts and indicates a small turret in the corner of the yard. 'The palace is blessed – or one may say, cursed – with a clock, which strikes the hour. If it interests you, Lord George, I could arrange for you to view the mechanism.'

Serious again, George thanks the man in the eloquent, authoritative tone he has adopted since Bruges.

Aping his brother's gravitas, Richard nods. 'Thank you, my Lord Chamberlain.'

Once inside the palace, he follows Hastings' sweeping gown and George's shapely calves as they navigate the maze of chambers. The deeper into the bowels of the palace, the finer and grander the rooms. Light floods through soaring windows, basil and marjoram are crushed underfoot, and courtiers grow fewer in number. Finally, a set of iron-scrolled doors part to reveal a long, high-ceilinged chamber. Beneath a regal canopy, a figure is resplendent in blue damask. And beside him, their mother, proud, immutable, folding slim pale hands.

Hastings makes obeisance. 'Lord George and Lord Richard, Your Grace.'

The figure rises and hastens towards them, damask rippling over chequered tiles. Edward. Their brother. Their king. Gawping and ill-mannered, Richard cranes his neck. How tall he is, he thinks, I'd forgotten.

Despite the brightness of the day, beeswax candles scent the room, turning their brother's neatly coiffured hair to molten bronze. 'Come!' Edward throws his arms wide, vast sleeves billowing. 'Rise, boys. For the love of God, rise and greet your brother.'

George is first to his feet, glowing with pride as the king enfolds him and bestows a kiss of welcome.

'Your servant,' George says, 'in all things.'

Warm brown eyes alight on Richard, narrowing with pleasure, and a gush of laughter, warm and mellow, bounces from walls to ceiling. How comely he is: Richard had forgotten that, too. Prodded by a sudden memory, surprising in its clarity, he finds himself transported: the nursery at Ludlow, early morning. Dust motes spinning in a shaft of light. Hoisted onto his brother's back, his skinny legs dangling over Edward's brawny shoulders, small fists grasping his hair. A jiggling ride around the chamber: an Arab steed and its shrieking, squealing rider. The chamber aglow with the sparks of Edward's laughter, each circuit of the nursery taking them past the doorway, where their father lingers.

'Edward…' Richard's arms shoot up, all etiquette forgotten, but a furrow forms between his brother's brows. Edward clearly cannot remember. Worse yet, Richard knows he has disgraced himself. Mustering tattered dignity, he makes a formal bow. 'Thank you, Your Grace, for punishing Father's enemies.'

His brother's embrace comes swift and tight, slippery damask secreting a honeyed scent which teases Richard's nostrils. Staunching a sneeze, he is relieved when the king releases him with a fulsome kiss and a meaningful promise.

'I cannot bring our father back, boys, but I know my duty. The loyalty we owed him, we now owe to each other. I pray we may never fail in our task.'

George, spellbound, delivers a swift 'Amen.'

'I've arranged for you a fine suite of rooms where Lord Hastings awaits. Refer any requirements to his judicious attention, and aught I can provide will be gladly given.' With a glance towards their mother, Edward grins. 'I'm sure we have much to say to one another, and for myself, I would know my brothers better. The morrow, after Mass, what do you say? Until then, settle into your apartments. You should both enjoy what is your due.' He beckons, 'Clarice?'

A woman - white cheeks, rouged lips - detaches herself from a knot of onlookers and glides across the floor before sinking into her skirts. 'My lords, it is my honour to deliver you to the Lord

Chamberlain.'

They withdraw slowly, as they have been shown, never once turning their backs on their king. Edward watches, affection writ upon his upturned mouth, while their mother thrusts a sheaf of paper under his nose. Soon, the two are huddled together.

'Arrangements for the coronation,' George says as the boys retreat through the labyrinth. 'That's what they're poring over.'

Richard knits his brows. How exactly does George acquire his information? Already, he knows the names of Edward's gentlemen, who is blood to whom, where their estates are and into which family they're wedded. 'How can you be sure?'

'Stands to reason. If I were Edward, I'd want to be crowned as quickly as possible, wouldn't you? The sooner the commons forget Daft Harry, the better.'

'Will we be invited?'

'Naturally. As the king's brothers, we'll have roles to play in the ceremony. Or I shall, at least.' George shoots a reproachful look. 'Behind me, remember? It's the way of things.'

They reach a steep, curling stair, and the woman ascends first, ample hips swaying as she gathers her skirts. Richard's hand flies to his nose as a violent sneeze overtakes him.

'Her perfume,' he whispers before George can complain. 'It's overpowering. She smells like Edward.'

His brother pauses on the topmost step. With the woman out of earshot, he proffers a pointed smirk. 'No, Dickon. I think you'll find that it's our brother - it is Edward - who smells like *her*.'

True to his word, the king awaits them next morning after Low Mass and steers them to the palace gardens. Throwing back his head, he tilts his face towards the sun.

'Solitude, I've discovered, is a rare commodity for a king. And an arbour a more leisurely place to commune with my brothers than a chamber of state. Don't you agree?'

Glorying in his company, they try to match Edward's stride as he leads them to the heart of the garden, past a bubbling fountain and soil beds peppered with tiny flowers: reds and whites and purples. Pausing before a stone bench, the king invites them to sit. Richard flops down, enjoying the touch of sun-warmed stone, while George sinks gingerly, careful not to snag his new silk hose. Nudging them apart, Edward eases himself between. Crimson robe falling away to reveal a short yellow gown, he looks gilded, sun-kissed. They fall into a companionable silence, soothed by the arbour's many scents and the gentle plash of water.

Spontaneous, Edward extends his arms and crushes his brothers to him. 'I prayed for you both, you know. Braving the German Ocean in the depths of winter was no easy venture for two young boys, but I knew I could trust Mother's judgement. Sending you away was the right thing to do. I'm told you conducted yourselves prudently and well. I've commendations from our brother of Burgundy. He writes that you were – "well demeaned", "well composed", and a credit to me.'

'We were well cared for in Utrecht, too,' Richard tells him. 'Jaagen Van Damme—'

'Duke Philip was a most generous host,' George's chest rises as he puffs himself up. 'His receiving of us, most seemly.'

Finding a loose pebble, Richard rolls it under the sole of his boot. He wants to speak to Edward of their guardian, knows he would approve, couldn't fail to. The fur-lined gloves, he thinks, we must dispatch them. Perhaps later, if he can speak to Edward alone.

'The duke may prove an important ally,' their brother says. 'It's vital for our future that we recognise our friends. And in England itself, we must honour those who have supported us.'

'And punish those who have not,' George nods with certainty, as one man to another.

'Of course, but within reason. Often, it proves wise for a man to pardon his enemies. Rapprochement can be a way of acquiring skilful men, whose talents we may use for our own intent.'

'But we could never pardon Marguerite's supporters,' George says. 'What would Father have said? Those men deserve to die.'

In total agreement, Richard raises his head and sees the king squeeze George's thigh.

'Our father was not a man of war, Brother,' Edward says. 'Though it became his only option, conflict was forced upon him. Father tried for years to be a diplomat, seeking justice for himself through negotiation. Only when he saw no other way did he resort to the sword. A man, especially a king, should not wage war rashly or without consideration. There are other ways to gain the victory than to draw out a man's bowels.'

George considers. A moment later, he's smiling, apple-cheeked. 'Tell us about the miracle, Edward. The sign of the Trinity.'

Richard inches closer. He yearns to hear this story, too: of Edward's victory and his favour in the sight of God. A butterfly, shimmering into view, offers fleeting glimpses of speckled wings. Squinting against the sun, Edward follows its progress, then licks his lips with the point of his tongue.

'It was the Feast of the Purification. Piercingly cold and with a hoary frost. We were on the Welsh borders, at the castle of Wigmore. My scouts had not returned, and I was anxious for news of the enemy. About ten of the clock, word came from the ramparts: a change in the sky, an omen, they said, to herald the end of days. Eager to see for myself, I joined my captains at the top of the keep—a fearful sight, as they said. Not one sun rising, but three. That in the centre a huge glowing ball; those to either side, smaller, less defined, but glistening like flame.'

A sign from Heaven, surely: 'Were you afraid?'

'Yes, Richard, I was. This was my first command; I alone responsible for each of my men. If we were to engage the enemy, every order would be mine, every sword thrust, every volley of arrows. Those who were to die would do so because they had chosen to follow me. One glance at the sky, and I, too, wondered whether Our Lord was returning for the final judgement. But then I saw it for the sign it was: a token of the Father, Son, and Holy Ghost. Our victory was assured. I knew it. I felt it.'

Gazing steadily into his brother's face, Richard can see the amazement has not left him.

'What's it like to fight?' George is fidgeting, eager. 'The battle in the north country, on Palm Sunday – is it true that God sent a blizzard to blind our enemies and halt the flight of their arrows?'

Edward's smile dims. 'I didn't bring you here to speak of what has passed but of what I intend for the future.'

'But I want to hear,' George says. 'We both want to hear.'

'One day, I'll tell you, but not now. The future is what matters. So,' folding his arms, the king turns an enquiring eye upon them, 'tell me more of yourselves, how you've fared since last we met. In my youth, I had Edmund as playfellow. I know both of you have faced trials, but you had the comfort of each other's company, and of that, I'm glad.'

George grins at Richard. 'We did make good company together, and since our return, I've been encouraging Dickon with his riding. My tutor tells me I excel in the practice yard: running, jumping, hurling stones, all the pursuits necessary to build a man's strength.'

Edward's lips twitch. 'Indeed. Well, I must make time to witness this spectacle. And what of you, Richard?'

Retrieving the pebble, the boy rolls it back and forth, hating to be compared with George. But Edward is waiting; he must say something to please him.

'I'm fast. When George and I race each other, I always win.'

A snort from the far side of the bench. 'That may have been true - before you sprained your ankle.'

Edward shifts, a waft of musk. 'Well, you'll both have the opportunity to progress. And in your own establishment. I've decided upon Placentia. A journey by river will make it a simple matter for you to wait upon me at Westminster, or even here. Margaret shall be joining you; I think it fitting to keep the three of you together. And George, Placentia has a tilt yard where you can demonstrate your remarkable skills. What think you of that?'

George smiles, eyes bright, 'Perfect.'

The boys wear black doublets gathered at the waist by white leather girdles, crimson cloaks about their shoulders, and coifs tied beneath their chins. Exhausted from their nightly vigil but resplendent in ceremonial robes, they're finally deemed ready to assume the path of knighthood.

'All well, Dickon?' George eases on embroidered gloves, splaying his fingers to admire the leather.

'Can't you call me Richard? Even if it's just for today?'

'How can I be expected to remember? You're Dickon to me: always have been, always will be. How would you feel if I asked you to call me something else? Thomas, for example, or William—'

'But your name isn't Thomas or William, it's George, and that's what I call you. Father never called me Dickon; he always called me by my name. His name.'

George considers, lips compressed. 'It matters to you, doesn't it?'

'Yes.'

'Very well. I'll try to remember, at least for today.'

But he won't. Since their return, George has begun once more to ape Edward's gestures, his turns of phrase, adopting them as his own. He's moved on, and Richard will never be able to catch up, for George will always be three years older. Always one step ahead.

'What is it now, *Richard*?'

'Now that you're to have a dukedom, will things change? Between us, I mean.'

'Naturally, things will change. But for the better.'

'I don't mean that.'

'Then what do you mean?'

'Will you be our brother's friend now, more than you'll be mine?'

George smiles, gives Richard's arm an affectionate squeeze. 'Of course not, you little worm. How could I be? You're my responsibility, remember. We're bound together, and not even Edward can change that.'

On a bright windswept day towards the end of June, their brother is transformed. Richard understands now what it means to be a king. It means that God has decided, that He has chosen. He has chosen Edward, and all have seen how His power and benediction are received in the holy chrism of Saint Thomas: on head, and breast, and palms. Edward is transmuted; he is semi-divine, resplendent in white, and purple cloth of gold. Richard wonders whether God will send them a vision, like the suns over Wigmore, to prove His purpose for the family of York. He searches for seraphs amongst sunbeams, but there's no visible sign. Yet the Almighty is present, of that he's certain.

He hardly dares touch his brother afterwards. Edward feels the same as he did before, muscle and bone and sinew, but he's no longer simply a man: he's God's anointed and touching him is like placing your hands between the palms of an angel.

Yet, if God favours Edward, what then of King Harry? George tells him not to concern himself, says that Harry angered God by marrying the She-Wolf, and that when she took their father's life, God turned His back on them both. He's sure George must be right, for there can be only one king, and God will never turn His back on their brother. He will never abandon Edward.

The Keeper of the Great Wardrobe sends Robert Cousin upriver. On his first visit to Placentia, Cousin had provided arbitrary things: cushions, candlesticks, suits of green livery. This time, his men have fetched the boys' travelling trunk and two smaller chests from Baynard's Castle. Dragged aloft, the items are deposited in the solar while their owners gather to take receipt. George is particularly interested in the parcel of clothes sent with haste from the hands of the Keeper himself.

'Pass our good wishes to Sir George Darrel,' he says. 'And our thanks for his timely service.'

Richard observes his brother's excitement as garments are unwrapped and presented. Tonight, in the Bishop of London's Palace, there's to be a banquet in George's honour. Here, Edward shall confer upon him the dukedom of Clarence, and nothing could please his brother more. The gown of blue cloth of gold, bordered with vair and sewn with silver thread, has been made especially for the occasion, and his first sight of the garment leaves George dewy-eyed.

'Lionel of Antwerp was the first duke,' he is at pains to inform his siblings, as if they didn't know, 'our direct forebear. I must do well tonight.'

Margaret strokes the cloth with discerning fingers. 'How could you do anything else, you little popinjay?'

Cousin proffers the keys to the chests. While George makes a fuss of receiving them, Richard crouches fondly beside the battered trunk, scored by the clumsy ministrations of Bishop David's boys. Inhaling the scent of corroded metal and ancient oak, he recalls Jaagen, fretted and vexed, torn between the preservation of the shabby trunk and Duke Philip's pristine wall plaster.

The gloves: he still hasn't found the right moment.

He strokes the trunk with the flat of his hand. 'George, might I have the key?'

It's tossed in his direction. 'Ancient old thing. We'll keep firewood in there from now on.'

'Remember these?' Margaret, probing the contents of the smallest chest, flourishes a square of green felt before presenting it to George: his initial embroidered in gold thread and entwined with tawny vines. 'Here, Richard, yours too. They were practice pieces. I made one for each of us.'

Taking the cloth, Richard runs his finger over the monogram: gilded, glossy, finely wrought. Their sister took great pains with these, as he recalls. Their father had been in Ireland, and she'd said that when he returned, she'd make one for him, too. He doesn't know if she ever did. Smiling, Margaret closes the lid of her chest, and they place the cloths on top to admire her work.

George laughs. 'We played word games with them. Do you remember? We'd invent mottos.' Taking up the squares, he rearranges them: G for George, M for Margaret, R for Richard. 'Great and Mighty Ruler,' he says.

Margaret nods her approval. 'Yes. That is our brother. That

is Edward.'

December: the piercing scent of pine. Festive holly with its bloodied berries, a kissing bough suspended from the beams, entwined with mistletoe and ivy. The frugal days of Advent give way to celebration, and Christmas brings their brother, rising like Neptune from the foggy Thames. They greet him in the chill afternoon, proud and excited that of all the places he may have observed the season, he has chosen to spend it with them.

'Where else would I be?' Edward embraces them warmly, a great bear in his fur-lined cloak, sprinkling snow like holy water. 'We should be together to mark Father's obit, to observe his year mind. And that of Edmund, too. We shall remain together for the full twelve days, that our time of mourning may be cheered with moments of gladness.'

Confort et Liesse. Edward's new motto: Comfort and Joy. He has brought them both.

Chapter Six

September 1462 – April 1463
Palace of Placentia

*T*HE STAIRS are steep, but Richard - keen and happy - takes them two at a time. Reaching the top, he pauses before the door, grasps the ring handle and prepares himself for the pleasure within. A low moan and a clatter as the latch finally yields onto the vaulted library with its oriel window, squeaking floor, and colossal weight of stored knowledge.

George has accompanied him here once or twice, eager for military treatises and courtly poems, but it's Richard who visits most often, in the hour allotted betwixt lessons and meat, to marvel and to wonder. All the wisdom of Christendom must be housed here, he thinks, in the hefty book chests with their elaborate locks: enough reading for a hundred lifetimes.

He watches as his favourite treasure is unwrapped and placed on the lectern for his delight. He sits, thrilled, eager fingers loosening the clasps. Inhaling the scent of vellum and leather, he admires its crackling pages stiff with coloured inks, margins where proud swans paddle - the device of Good Duke Humphrey.

Humphrey of Gloucester, uncle to King Harry, was the one to amass the wealth of books, but George doubts he lived long enough to enjoy them. He says Humphrey was murdered, poisoned by his enemies with a cup of spiced wine. 'Humphrey's enemies were also Father's enemies,' George has told him, 'so it's only right that we pray for the surety of his soul.'

Yet Richard feels a greater obligation. As Edward intends to honour him with Humphrey's former title, he knows he must be tireless in his prayers, that the Good Duke's time in Purgatory may not prove overlong.

Aware of his moist palms, he wipes them on his hose. No sticky marks, no stains: if Humphrey remains heedful of his volumes, he would not wish to irk him. The latch clatters, and he starts, heart pumping, as the door swings wide. Edward ducks his head, squeezing his way through the narrow arch, and sweeps towards him across the screaming boards. His green gown, pleated, stylish, sways as he walks.

'Sit down, Richard, for Pity's sake. A man can tire of formality. Might I join you, or would I be intruding?' That the king should choose to visit him is honour enough, that he should ask permission is astounding. 'I thought it time we talked.' Hitching his gown, Edward perches beside him. 'George is settled here, what of you?'

Richard indicates the tall leaded windows, painted ceiling, and infinity of book chests. 'How could I be otherwise, Highness?'

'Our brother tells me you're enamoured of your romances. That you find as much joy here as in the stable yard.'

'Yes—' Richard hesitates, unsure of his meaning. 'I take great pleasure in them.'

'Ah.' An indolent sigh. 'May I see?'

Richard budges up. The king sits before the lectern, flicking pages with huge square hands until something catches his eye: a mounted knight entering a walled city, a crowned maiden observing him from its turreted walls. 'I suppose the knight is valiant and pious?'

'Of course. He lives by the chivalric code.'

'Even though he's painfully in love with the king's young wife, and she with him?' Edward's lips have begun to twitch. 'And I suppose the knight's loyalty has been tested by every means imaginable?'

'Lady Constancy has set him many tasks in order to test his worth, and he has remained true throughout. His love for Queen Bellamour is pure, and he's told the Lady he would rather surrender his very existence than befoul his beloved and betray his king.'

The king gives a wry snort. 'No Lancelot, then.'

'As chivalrous as Lancelot,' Richard says, 'but true of his body.'

Leaning in, he shows Edward his favourite part of the tale: the knight's greatest achievement, victory over the king's opponent in an act of single combat. He spies the jerk of Edward's belly as his brother strives to contain his laughter.

'I imagine that soon this fellow will travel into the heartlands of the king's enemies to offer his life in the lists on behalf of his lord?'

Richard lets the pages fall, dismayed his brother cannot see the value of the story.

'That is the usual conclusion to such tales.' Edward shrugs, 'The hero always wins, with honour and loyalty intact. Now, tell me if I'm wrong.' He judders with mirth, and Richard's mouth droops. The chivalric code is no idle fancy; it's real. How can Edward, of all people, believe anything less?

'I'm sorry, boy.' Edward's head dips, cajoling. 'It's natural to enjoy such stories; I enjoyed them too, at your age. I meant no ill. Forgive me. Come, what else takes your fancy?'

Richard presents a vivid illustration—a castle besieged by a great army: crossbows, scaling ladders, siege machines on wheels. 'I've not spent all my time dreaming, Your Grace. If you would give credence to my stories, you'd see that I've learnt something from them of the ways of war.'

'The ways of war? You think a book can tell you that? Even the Roman generals, in their military treatises, can't sufficiently prepare a man for battle. Romances are a pleasant diversion, but the ways of the soldier are a vastly different matter. If you would truly know the ways of war, you must understand they're not to be found in stories such as this.' Edward snaps the book shut. 'Now, are you sulking?'

Sincere, imploring, all mockery gone, it's clear that just like George, Edward is very easy to forgive.

'Your Grace, is it true you were but thirteen at your first field?'

'Ha! You've been listening to Mother. I accompanied Father to Saint Albans, yes, but he wouldn't let me fight. The idea was simply to observe and learn.'

'Was Father a good soldier?' Searching Edward's face, Richard tries to open a window onto the life he was too young, too much of an infant, to share with him.

'He was a good man. That's all you need to know.'

'But it's not enough. If I'm ever to be like him—'

'You can't live your life in the shadow of another, Richard. You must take what is good from the ones you love, cherish it, learn from it, then become your own man. We honour our father, as is right, but we must forge our own way. Is this not what George has been trying to tell you?'

'Yes. But Mother says we must look to Father as an example. Always.'

'An example, yes. But you must learn to live a life of your own. We pray for Father; we observe his obit. That's all we can do.' In the ensuing silence, Edward exhales. 'As I said, I thought it time we talked. I've been considering your future, Richard. You're happy here with your brother and sister, I know, but as heir presumptive, George will require a household of his own, and I must consider your education – your military education. I've decided upon our cousin of Warwick. I can think of none better. You will fare well with him.'

To join their cousin's household when he's so settled here? 'When? When am I to go?'

'Two, three, years, so there's time yet.' Edward deals him a soft blow. 'We must build these muscles. Our cousin shall appoint a tutor. Once he's finished with you, you'll have the strength to master the basic weapons.'

Richard sees him in his mind. Cousin Warwick: chestnut hair thick as thatch, hawk-like nose, all-seeing eyes. 'Are not our cousin's lands in the north country?'

'Some, not all of them. Besides, it may do you good to get away from George. He can prove too much of an influence.'

Richard studies the closed book. 'I believe our cousin has no sons. Are there other youths in his household?'

'He has wards. You'll not find yourself alone.'

Wards? Did their fathers fight for York? If not, he can't say he'd wish for their company. He would rather be with George.

'The earl has many traits you'll admire,' Edward says. 'He knows how to draw men to him. The Londoners love him - his house in Dowgate is forever assaulted by hungry mouths and empty stomachs. He doles out sides of beef and roasted capon like manna from Heaven. "Fill a man's belly," he once told me, "and he'll love you forever." And it appears they do.'

When Richard fails to respond, the king slides a brawny arm around him. 'The earl has been a great support to me, a mainstay. Without his support, I may still be a rebel, struggling to avenge our father's death—may well have met my own. Our cousin is loyal. He'll teach you well.'

Richard understands he has no say in the matter but weighs up the prospect just the same.

His brother's gaze is keen. 'And if anything should happen to me, I could trust you were in good hands.'

'Are we still in danger? Now that you are king—'

'Kings are as insecure as anyone when their enemies remain at liberty, and Marguerite will never give up whilst that cub of hers draws breath. She's desperate and will treat with anyone in order to win support. The Borderlands have proved a refuge, but our cousin has persuaded the Queen of Scots to withhold her aid, and Marguerite has been cast upon the seas to try her luck with the French. From what I hear, Louis is prepared to offer only slender help, but we must never forget the threat she still poses. We need men like the earl and his brother Montagu, strong supporters of our cause.'

'And if she returns? The Sh…I mean, Marguerite. Will she wage war on us a second time?'

'Not without considerable assistance.'

'George says no man would be fool enough to support Harry of Lancaster now. For it's clear he's a simpleton.'

'And George would know that, of course, being so worldly wise.'

Richard sinks into silence, out of his depths in this rugged political sea.

The king delivers a coaxing nudge. 'And so, what do you say?

Two to three years, and we'll have you in harness?'

Richard nods. His brother claps him on the back.

It's settled, then.

Edward rides in – unannounced – and George is hauled from his studies. Richard has received no summons to join them, but the temptation to seek them out is too much. If it's unwelcome news, he's not prepared to wait whilst it trickles its way down to him. Whatever is amiss, he would know it: and he would know it now.

He finds the solar door strangely unguarded. A private conversation then, but something, surely, of which he should be a part. Tentative and without shame, he flattens his ear against the cool oak only to hear his own name tossed between his brothers like a pig's bladder football.

'George, you're acting like an infant whose teething stick has been taken away.'

'*He's* the infant, yet you heap honours upon him as if he has earned them.'

'Cease your tantrum. You're far better provided for than Richard. What he has may sound impressive, but what it will ultimately fetch him is paltry.'

'Then you do not care for my opinion?'

'If your opinion is called for, be assured I shall ask for it.'

Shifting from one foot to the other, Richard hardly dares breathe.

'Why do you continue to treat me like a child?' George again, resentful.

'I've already told you. Because you act like one.'

'It's the only way to make you listen.'

'Oh, so you think I'm listening now?' Edward's mockery must be cranking George's pride like a windlass.

'The little worm informed me he's to become Admiral of England. He already has the lordship of Pembroke and a share of the Earl of Oxford's forfeited estates. Is that not enough for one so young?'

'And you, George, are Lieutenant of Ireland, as our father was when he was more than twice your age. One might wonder whether that is not enough for you.'

Silence. He pictures George's face, pouting, ruddy. 'I'll soon be old enough to administer my authority, he won't. He still pisses himself every time he has a nightmare.'

Liar. You damned liar. He's half minded to burst in, to confront George and pummel the untruths out of him. In his imagination, at least.

'If Richard remains distressed over our father's fate, then I see that as no shame. Rather, I see it as devotion to our cause. Don't you?'

'You think he is the only one who mourns?'

'George…'

'Well, you're wrong. Who do you think acted as comforter to him? You weren't there, and Mother was closeted with Margaret. Who was it who acted as father, brother, and mother to him? Ever thought of that? It was me. You think that was easy, when all the time I was grieving every bit as much as he was?'

'George, you played an admirable role in consoling our brother, and I thank you for it. But I urge you, don't think to use it as a means to get your own way.'

'But I'm your heir.'

'Honour enough, I would have thought.' Edward's sarcasm seeps through the door panels: slick and sour.

'Then I should have the greater number of awards. Father would have wanted me to have them. It makes sense; I'm the elder, and I must learn—'

'Yes, you have a lot to learn, boy, and you'd better start now.' Their brother is slowly simmering. If George possesses any wit, Richard thinks, he will cease before this goes too far.

'But—'

'Silence, boy. You already have more awards than Richard. You have four henxmen in your service – your brother has none. You have your own grooms, cooks, chaplains, your own wardrobe; you'll soon have your own herald. Your brother has none of those things. What more do you suggest I give you?'

'The lordship of Richmond.'

Richard springs back from the door, shocked and amazed by George's daring. Edward's cynical laughter entices him back.

'Richmond? Is that what all this nonsense is about? Why you have been whining like a woman with her monthly curse? Ah, I see. Then it's this latest grant to our little brother that riles you so much? Why so? Was it too generous in your view?'

The king's mockery is tangible, as is the silence which follows. Richard tenses. Suppose their brother should tire of bating George and quit the chamber? Suppose he should cast the door wide and find him, red-faced and cowering, like some prying scullion? A meddlesome boy asking to be flogged?

'Stop murmuring, George. Speak up if you expect me to listen.'

'I'm the senior brother, and you yourself have said how other rulers will be watching us, judging us. If Dickon and I are to be honoured in the same way, then we will be seen to be equal, which we're not.'

'No, you're not equal, George. That, believe me, is certainly true. You're not equal to your brother in attitude or in manners. If you expect anything more from me, you must prove yourself worthy.'

Sick with anger and embarrassment, Richard considers creeping away. But, like bursting a blister or prising a scab, the inducement is all-consuming.

George mutters, perhaps even weeps.

'What a display,' Edward snorts. 'The heir to the throne should show a little dignity, at least. Very well. If you want the lordship, you may have it. Richard can be compensated one way or another. But remember, it's my prerogative to give and to take away whatever I like from whomever I like. And don't imagine you can win me over every time you decide to stamp your feet. Now begone, you ungrateful whelp.'

The door is flung wide.

'And where are your manners, my lord of Clarence?'

Spying a niche by the stairwell, where an ancient archway

has been sealed up, Richard darts into the shadows. Soon, George emerges, shuffling backwards from the royal presence, in a belated show of deference, face blotched and crumpled.

In these brief moments, Richard loathes him; loathes him for taking away the royal gift, for calling him a child, a baby, a pisspot. He's tempted to leap out and render his brother's face more crimson than it already is. But then George will know; know that he's been listening, that he witnessed the derision meted out by their brother. Instead, he contents himself with the safety of the niche, watching as George strides away, wiping his face with the back of his hand.

'George hates me.'

Glancing up from her needlework, Margaret softens at the mention of their brother's name. 'Richard, you know that's untrue. He's hot-headed, is all.'

Having volunteered to sort his sister's threads, Richard has managed to untangle the emeralds, reds, and tawny golds, and wind them into tidy skeins. Now, it's the turn of the blues. A tedious, womanly task, but better than being with George. 'Then why does he behave like such a prick?'

'Language, Brother.'

'Sorry. But you must have seen him lately, mimicking Edward and strutting around like a farmyard cock. He wants to be part of everything. Last week, he insisted that for all the counties in which he is Justice of the Peace, he should receive reports of all trials and inquests. Can you really believe he'll read them? It's all an act to make him look clever – or to make him look cleverer than me. Yesterday, he took great pleasure in lecturing me on court leets and amercements, sniggering with his squires when I struggled to make sense of it. He's a boaster and a bully. Even you must admit that.'

Margaret is embroidering a shirt for the king, neat little borders of leaves and acorns to adorn each cuff. Sliding her needle into the linen, she sets it aside. 'We each have our foibles, Richard. George is Edward's heir, and whatever you say, I know he takes his position seriously. Besides, I think he's somewhat jealous – the king has been paying you a deal of attention of late.'

He laughs, incredulous. 'Why should George be jealous? He has much more from the king than I have.'

Margaret resumes her stitching. 'When I say that George is jealous, I don't mean he's jealous of you.'

The blue thread is so densely tangled that Richard cannot undo it. After a final, concerted effort, he tosses it to the floor in annoyance. 'What, then?'

'In George's mind, he has always been the one to guide you, to protect you. The king has usurped that place. Or at least, that's how it seems to George.'

Playing with the silks he's tidied, setting up skeins in a neat line, he'll do anything but look into his sister's face.

'Richard?'

He glances up, reluctant.

'Put yourself in George's position—'

'No. Why should I? He's an oaf. All he ever does is tell me how to behave. How I should listen to him, defer to him in everything, crawl along in his wake like a subservient slug.' This is not strictly true. Following in George's wake has been his own choice, and recently, it has proved no easy thing, the path being littered with other boys; the eldest sons of noble families only too happy to pander to the heir presumptive.

'He hopes you'll learn from him.'

'Learn what? How to be an arrogant churl?'

Shoulders drooping, Margaret sighs. 'The night you left for the Low Countries, I knew that as long as you had George, you'd fare well enough. You're the youngest; you don't know the responsibility one sibling feels for another. Had our sister Ursula lived, you'd have known, would've felt yourself responsible for her in the way George feels responsible for you. Oh, you'd have taken great joy in pulling her braids, hiding her favourite playthings, as do all elder brothers, but in your heart, you would have cared for her very deeply.' A fond smile. 'You know, when George was born, I spent the best part of each day crouched by his cradle, rocking him to sleep. The mistress of the nursery lost all patience, for I would refuse to go to bed if George was still awake. Would refuse to eat my pottage if he'd not been suckled and set to sleeping.'

Her grey eyes are heavy with feeling. 'Try to understand how it is for George. He may be arrogant at times, but believe me, Richard, he loves you. After all you've been through together, he simply finds it difficult to share you with our brother. Do you understand?'

Richard retrieves the tangled skein, makes another attempt to unravel it.

Margaret touches his arm. 'Don't think of repeating this; it would only embarrass him. And I beg you, don't judge our brother too harshly. Even if Edward does.'

The lordship of Richmond has been duly rescinded: taken from him and granted to George. By way of apology, George assures him that the lordship will be safe in his hands: he's older and more experienced, better able to administer its duties as their father would have expected. Except that he doesn't administer them, Richard thinks, not in person. They're merely titles to add to his growing list, along with the names of his henxmen, his officers, his servants of the body.

Remembering Margaret's words, he shrugs. *No matter, George. No trouble. I understand.*

George, delighted, embraces him and suggests a game of merrills. 'You'll receive your dues in time. Until then, let us be friends.'

Richard agrees and is rewarded with a mischievous wink.

'You always win at merrills anyway, Dickon. Here, open your hand.'

A dead frog, a fistful of maggots?

George fumbles for his hand. 'Come, what ails you?'

As Richard grits his teeth, preparing for the worst, a sweetmeat drops onto his palm: marchpane rolled in cinnamon sugar.

'I returned from Mass by way of the kitchens,' George grins, 'the confectioner was feeling generous.'

Producing another, he stuffs it into his mouth, and they laugh greedily.

Sometimes, Richard wonders whether he is the jealous one: jealous of those who surround George and help to give him airs. For without them, he would simply be George, his brother, and he would be able to love him again.

It's late August and the streets of Canterbury are overflowing. Narrow lanes, dry and dusty from the passage of countless feet, and ripe with the stench of horse dung. Richard is minded of London, the day of Saint Bartholomew's fair, except the crowds that gather here have not come to barter, nor for amusement. They've come to seek a blessing, and many, it's clear, have come for something more.

The mottled throng snakes its way along the well-trodden route to the cathedral close, inching towards the hallowed site with its shrine of Saint Thomas. Many walk, others crawl. The blind guided by friends, the palsied hefted on makeshift litters. All have but one desire: the cures to which the discarded crutches and begging bowls littering the tomb bear witness—the merciful intercession of the Blessed Martyr.

He and George have no need of a miracle but are as anxious as any to receive a blessing. Margaret has not accompanied them, a thing for which he is sorry. It would have pleased him to approach the shrine with her, stockinged feet skimming smooth stone. They can tell her of its glory, its gilded sarcophagus, the mass of jewels flashing in a sea of flame, but he doubts they can convey a true image of its beauty. The monks who guard the shrine are eager to exhibit its treasures. The greatest, a ruby, large as an egg and gifted by a French king. A perfect opalescent pearl, the rapturous offering of a grateful countess. And a string of golden beads from the hand of a convent plumber.

The following day, one of oppressive heat, they join the clergy for High Mass – Archbishop, canons, chantry priests – and process through the close into the cathedral proper. Richard's gown, stifling and stiff, pinches under the arms. His brother must be suffering more in his heavy velvets and cloth of gold. But how else should the heir presumptive present himself? George must offer the people a glimpse of majesty: a vision of their king in proxy form. City dignitaries, resplendent in purples and scarlets, bow their heads at the sight of him, at the unsheathed sword, carried before him point uppermost, in true regal fashion.

'Be sure to impress the populace,' Edward had told them, 'show all England that the family of York is strong, united. Show them the old regime is dead and that if aught should befall me, it is George the people should look to.'

Richard keeps expecting George to turn, to make sure he's following, that he's nodding at the right times, and to the right people. But his brother is too intently occupied. Rising above the crowds like a cloud of smoke, a waft of incense, George is playing his part to perfection.

Chapter Seven

September 1464
Baynard's Castle

An URGENT summons from their mother bids them forgo dinner and hasten upriver. The journey is tense; both boys poised in silence, lost in their own thoughts. There's word of plague in the city, and they would not have been bidden on a whim. It must be Marguerite – Harry and Marguerite – but neither dare voice the names, lest the words act as incantations and give substance to their fears. Edward is at Reading, heading the Royal Council, and is not here to protect them. Their cousin, Warwick, the same.

Tirewoman, Jane Lessy, greets them with nothing more than a dip of the head before ushering them up the privy stairs. The duchess is seated, jaw rigid, blue leather slipper poking from her skirts and tapping the floor in erratic rhythm. Their cousin, riding cloak soiled with dust from the road, has planted himself in the window recess.

Richard swallows at sight of him. If their suspicions are correct and Warwick has returned to defend the city, then where is the king? 'Edward…?'

'You may well speak his name, boy, but it finds no favour with me.' The earl turns from the casement, the spurs he has not bothered to remove jangling against the floorboards. 'Tell them, lady.'

Their mother's mouth twists. 'I cannot speak of him, Nephew.'

'Then you would have me tell them? I warn you, Madam, I shall not stint.'

A derisive snort. 'Then I shall utter no objection. The very thought of him disgusts me.'

Richard stares at his brother. George stares back, brows drawn. A late summer wasp, dazed, half-mad, darts in through the open window and circles the chamber with a vexing drone. Warwick tracks the creature with narrowed eyes.

'Your brother has debased himself, my lords, yet he sits, and he smiles, and he utters sweet words as if he were an angel sent by God, and all is right with the world. I fear that what I must tell you will not prove to your liking.'

The city bells chime the hours: the merry peals of Saint Benet's, the deep booming of Paul's. Their mother's chaplain should be here, observing the office of Sext, but as the peals die away, Richard hears no purposeful steps, no tapping at the door. Whatever is amiss has disrupted the order of things, and that very fact makes him nervous.

'The council at Reading,' their cousin chews the words, spitting them out like rancid meat. 'The matters for discussion: the coinage, the treaty with France, the marriage alliance.' Counting each item on stubby fingers, he eyes the boys as if expecting them to be versed in the business of all three. 'I bring him good news, how I have laboured these many months and how, by my efforts alone, I have Louis eating out of my hand. A treaty and a marriage in the offing, peace with our ancient enemies, and a settled realm: this is what I bring him. But what does he do? Panders to me as if I were a child, grinning like a lackwit and skirting the subject. I ask him, does he not wish for peace with France? A perfect opportunity now that Charles is dead. No, he has made his peace with Brittany and sent Duke Francis three thousand archers to use against the French.'

'But, Cousin, you expressly advised him against this.' George, keen to air his limited understanding of foreign policy, is ignored.

'I press the king on the subject of marriage. He admits he wishes for nothing more - so much so that the deed is done, and he's already espoused. Wedded, he tells me, in the month of May. Yet only now, as I stand before the council, rehearsing the success of my travails, does he openly admit it.'

The earl's raised, prickly brows demand comment. Unsure he

even understands, Richard gropes in the dark.

'The noblewoman of Savoy, Cousin? The match you have been negotiating?'

'No, boy, no. Not the match I've been seeking, no. Your brother, as he took such pleasure in regaling the council, has taken the matter of marriage into his own hands and chosen his own bride. A widow whose husband died fighting for Lancaster. An enemy of your father's and mine.'

This is wrong; it must be. Edward would never sully their father's memory. 'Perhaps someone has made a mistake—'

'A mistake? I assure you, there's no mistake. He confessed it with his own lips.'

George shrinks with loathing, body contorted as if struggling to void itself of poison. 'This woman...her family fought for Lancaster?'

Warwick nods. Motioning towards the buffet, he signals to the cowering page, who is pressed against the sideboard as if wishing for nothing more than to melt into the grain. Metal clanks against metal as wine is poured. An unsteady hand presents it, and Warwick takes a draught.

Richard tries again. 'But what of the Lady Bona, Cousin – the lady of Savoy? Of your peace negotiations?'

'It seems, boy, that your brother cares as much for my negotiations as he does for the filth on the sole of his shoe.'

Their mother rises, back straight, chin jutting, and signals to her women. 'I will to my chamber. My apologies, Nephew.'

Having failed to greet her sons, and showing no further inclination to acknowledge their presence, she leaves in a sweep of heavy damask. George's eyes, narrow and wary, swivel towards Warwick. 'Others knew of this, Cousin?'

'No. Your brother was very discreet. So discreet that not even his body servants knew. God alone knows how he managed it.' The earl begins to pace, and Richard is minded of the bears bated at Smithfield: how they pull at their leashes.

'Who is she?' he voices the obvious question while the earl steadies his breathing.

'No noble virgin, I can tell you that. No unsullied mare to breed upon.'

George exhales. 'If it please you, Cousin. Her name?'

'E-liz-a-beth.' Warwick stresses each syllable as if struggling with some outlandish tongue. 'The widow of Sir John Grey and daughter to Richard Wydeville, the jumped-up former squire. Your brother's marriage was a bounty I could have used wisely and well. It could have bought us a lasting peace with France; could have benefitted us all. Instead, it brings us nothing. How will Louis feel about it, d'you think? How will he look upon me, who has spent his time bartering, making promises? What am I to say? "I apologise, *Monseigneur le Roi,* but it appears the king has sought to conduct his own nuptials behind my back?" '

A frantic, angry buzzing. Richard's eyes flick to the casement, where the wasp is battering itself against the glass in a futile attempt at freedom.

'Is she carrying his bastard?' George ventures. 'Is that why he wed her?'

Warwick's laugh is like grating steel. 'Your brother can't even use that as an excuse for his folly. He boasts the woman was so chaste that, even had he held a knife to her throat, she'd have resisted him. Imagine that? A man as experienced as your brother having to resort to marriage simply to shaft a woman. There's no bastard in her belly, boy, simply ambition – both hers and her low-born father's.'

Wydeville. Richard recalls the name, but it means little to him. Grey means even less.

'However,' the earl shrugs, 'for all we know, the woman's belly could be waxing fat even now. As your brother prefers to keep his own counsel these days, the first we may know of it is when the brat finally draws breath. Besides, it's clear she's fertile: she bore John Grey two sons.'

George flinches. Edward's heir: but perhaps not for much longer. Richard scours his mind for something to say: something useful. He fails.

Warwick throws himself into the duchess' empty chair.

'Campaigning for your father in Calais, we heard that self-made shit, Wydeville, had been raising a fleet on Somerset's behalf. He was captured in Sandwich, thank God. He and his snivelling milksop of a son dragged from their beds. My father had them summoned, and we took our turns at rating them – your brother as much as anyone - calling Wydeville a knave's son and an upstart.' He pulls down the corners of his mouth. 'It appears your brother has forgotten all that. Or chooses to.'

Richard, retaining his silence, begins to feel trapped by it. He's thinking, again, of the day in the nursery. Ranged once more upon his brother's shoulders, giggling, squealing. He sees their father - or the vague shape that has become their father – smiling, happy. He wants to climb down from Edward's back, take his father's hand and tell him that if there's any disloyalty to be done, it shall not come from him. Never from him.

'Have you seen her, Cousin?' George: curious as ever. 'Grey's widow?'

Warwick rolls his eyes. 'Not yet. But I'm to meet her ere long. You too, George. After months of closet tupping, your brother has decided that his wife should live with him in earnest. She's to be presented to the council at Michaelmas. Reading Abbey. You and I are to have the honour of escorting her in.'

'Her lineage,' George is calculating, adding and subtracting names and titles. 'Her father, Wydeville, you say he is self-made. How so?'

The wasp, enticed by the sweetness of Warwick's cup, buzzes around the rim. Flicking it away, the earl takes another sip. 'My countess could readily advise you of the foul behaviour of that family, but for ease, let us say that Wydeville climbed the tree through marriage. Opportunism must run in the family.'

George ponders. 'So, the mother is noble? Who is she?'

'Jacquette of Saint-Pol. Bedford's widow. Married the brother of Harry the Fifth, and as soon as the duke was dead, married for lust.'

'Wydeville?'

'Wydeville the squire, keen to bed a lady of note and make a fine nest for himself. The nuptials, like those of your brother, were conducted in secret; evidence, if we needed any, that the family is well practised in the arts of matrimonial deception. In time, King Harry knighted Wydeville, created him Baron Rivers. Doubtless, he felt the need to give the churl something. Jacquette was, after all, Bedford's widow, and that she should choose to scrabble for a mate amongst the lower orders must have brought Harry no little sense of shame. However, the Wydeville coupling has been fruitful; our *queen* brings with her a brood of siblings. Watch out,' Warwick tips his cup, saluting both boys, 'she has a host of sisters. Edward will be searching for husbands.'

George scowls in disgust. The extent of the grimace would be comical, Richard thinks, were not the cause so dire. 'How can he have been so foolish?'

'I fear it is I who have been foolish,' Warwick says. 'Your brother's amorous ways had given rise to talk. I forced him to consider the inevitable – that he must marry, and marry well – but what did he say? That, whilst our enemies were still at large, making free with our Northumbrian castles, he could in no wise consider it. So, what did I do? Raced north, raised the siege at Norham, and forced Marguerite to take to the sea. And if it were not for John…' his mouth twists, '…your brother owes mine a fair reward. John's triumph at Hexham has brought Edward both victory and security, while all that time he was closeted away, wedding and bedding that low-born strumpet.'

Edward's paragon, Richard thinks, or Warwick's strumpet? Surely, a woman cannot be both.

'He may have deceived me,' their cousin says, 'but this business has taught me something. Edward does what he pleases and to hell with the rest of us.'

The wasp, ultimately dazed and exhausted, lands on the arm of Warwick's chair. The earl's fingers slide to the riding gloves tucked in his belt. A raised hand, a smack of leather: the creature is dead.

'Is this what we fought for? What our father died for, so Edward could spawn an heir on a Lancastrian sow?' George seems fit to weep. Silent and sulking on their way back to Placentia, he hangs on Richard's heels like a petulant lap dog. Throwing himself on the window seat, he stares down into the gardens. 'As heir presumptive, I shall have to stand aside once she breeds.'

'If she bears a son.'

'Yes. If she bears a son. But you heard our cousin; she's already proved her worth in that regard. And even if she hadn't, her mother's womb has popped a nursery full, so we can only presume the daughter's belly will be equally productive.' George's hands are making and unmaking fists; knuckles pale, upstanding. 'All we've done, all we've undertaken, has been to honour our father. He committed himself to war, Dickon, to rid the land of upstarts who were taking the rule upon themselves. Now Edward has allied himself to other such leeches, whose blood will taint our own. How could he do it?'

How could he? Good question. How could Edward, who has promised them so much, ally himself with their father's enemies? There must be a reason for it, Richard thinks. There must be something I'm failing to understand. He fingers the grip of his dagger: a present from their brother, embellished with a *rose-en-soleil*. He runs his thumb over the smooth petals, the rippling, jagged rays. Unlike George's gift from Duke Philip, it is not decorated with precious stones, but Edward had smiled as he bestowed it, and he'd accepted it with pride.

'Say something.' George is almost screaming.

'What is there to say? He's married her.' Richard draws the dagger, slides it back into place, draws it again.

'Didn't you hear what our cousin said? Her family fought against Father, and at the time, Edward himself rated Wydeville to his face.'

'I know.'

'Well, say something, then.'

Richard snaps the dagger home and meets George's eye. 'I don't know what to say.'

'You never do.'

'If the earl is unable to help the situation, then what can we do?' He needs time to think about what Warwick has told them, to try to comprehend it, but it's hard to think with George's frenzied tones hammering into his brain.

'I shouldn't become so taken with a woman that the thought of bedding her would chase all sense from my head. It's not beholden for a king to marry beneath him, Dickon. It's his duty to marry for the honour of the kingdom. Warwick says that he and Mother are not the only ones to object; many on the council were dismayed by our brother's choice. How can Edward have been so stupid?'

'Maybe you should ask him.'

'You're siding with him. You, of all people.'

'I'm not. I'm simply trying to make sense of it.'

'There's no sense to be made.' George is on his feet, pounding the floor. 'He married her because he wanted her, and she refused to submit to him any other way.'

'Do you think he loves her?'

'Now *you're* being stupid.'

Richard thinks, perhaps I am. The day in the library when Edward laughed at the chivalric code: should that not have alerted him to something? Maybe, after all, their cousin is right, and Edward seeks only to please himself.

'I shall demean myself,' George says, 'when I lead her into Reading Abbey. Imagine being forced to bow the knee to her, to speak softly to her kin, to consort with our enemies—'

Our enemies, Richard stiffens. What did this woman do in the depths of winter, he thinks, when their father's blood had spotted the snow, and their world had been destroyed? Doubtless, her family will have approved, raised pewter goblets in their manorial hall, calling down curses on the soul of York and a pox upon his kin.

'—I tell you,' George says, 'if it were not for the great duties incumbent upon me, I should disdain to grace this mockery with my presence.'

Richard glares at him, as much to goad him as anything else. He feels confused and angry, and George's ranting makes matters worse. 'Well, it's simple enough. Don't go. Feign sickness.'

'What, and let the honour be conferred elsewhere? I shall not. Escorting Edward's queen, no matter who she is, is another way for me to honour the family. After our brother's churlish behaviour, somebody has to.'

Stealing low over Baynard's Castle, the dying sun creeps with ease into his mother's apartments. Long fingers of light inch towards the far wall, licking painted fleur de lys, gilding roses. Richard pauses in the doorway. She'd told him once that the chamber had been specially chosen by his father, that she may enjoy the last of the daylight over her evening prayers. Tonight, she sits with closed lids, back to the window, ignoring the amber glow, whilst Margaret avails herself of its fading rays. Tilting her book towards the light, his sister reads aloud:

'*One night when she could not sleep for sadness, she heard the choirs of angels singing: "Cast thy burden upon the Lord and He shall sustain thee—"*'

'Richard?' His mother's lids spring open.

'How did you know it was me?'

'I should never mistake your footfall for George's. And if it were your cousin advancing upon me, he should already be engaging me in conversation before his boots crossed the threshold. No, it was obvious who had decided to pay me a visit.' There is no mention of Edward, of how she would have recognised him.

The duchess jerks her head towards the window seat, where Margaret is carefully placing her ribbon marker inside the book. 'The words of Mechtild of Hackeborn, a lesson for all humankind. If Our Lord, who was without fault, knew punishment and pain, then why not the rest of us? Have you come for my blessing, Richard? Or simply to evade George's whining?'

He shrugs, self-conscious. 'George has been listening to our cousin. He feels Father's plans have been set aside, that Edward's choice refutes all that Father would have wanted and that the blood of York will be tainted by Elizabeth and her kin.'

'And you, Richard? What do you feel?'

'Disappointed.' The first word that tumbles from his mouth is absurd: a disappointment in itself.

'Is that all?' It's clear nothing has transpired over the last few days to temper his mother's mood.

'But it's true. I am disappointed. I thought…'

'Yes?' The glare is expectant, unblinking, and Richard feels the weight of it.

'If Father thought Wydeville an upstart, then he must be. I think Edward's views should be our father's views. His beliefs, Father's beliefs.'

'But clearly, they're not. Is that all you have to say on the matter?'

Richard hesitates. His views are never called for; George only ever informs him of his own, and their cousin has never asked. The only person to have shown any interest in what he thinks about anything has been Edward himself.

'You have the right to an opinion, Richard. After all, you're shortly to enter your cousin's household and passivity is not a quality the earl appreciates – in anyone.'

Margaret rises with a swish of silk. 'I think we're all agreed, Mother, that the king has made a mistake and that it's against all our wishes that he should ally himself with former Lancastrians. But we can do little about it. Vows exchanged in the sight of God are binding. Edward is wed, and even if we abhor his choice, we must accept it.'

Margaret always knows what to say, what to think, how to act. She's been making regular visits here, praying with their mother, pacifying her, listening when needed, silent when not, smoothing the waters. Edward should have used Margaret as an example when he was looking for a wife. Surely, if he'd searched diligently, he could have found another like their sister amongst the lofty halls and palaces of Europe.

Neville eyes flash, indignant. 'That the issue is irreversible only makes it harder to bear. The marriage of a king is an opportunity for him to forge bonds with his fellow monarchs, to propose truces, make alliances. We had plans for your brother; they were never settled, but your father aimed high, as people of good estate are obliged to do. Marriage is not a matter of preference; it's a matter of duty. Choices are made after negotiation, once advice has been sought. Not upon the whim of a moment.'

Richard imagines his father, striving hard, meeting ambassadors, writing missives. How, as king, he would have chosen a fitting wife for Edward: a foreign match to honour the family. What must he think of them now, if he's marking events? How must he look upon Edward's choice, upon the daughter of Richard Wydeville, an erstwhile enemy who had been content to see them all dead and shrouded? Richard can't contradict his mother, can't disagree, yet Margaret speaks sense. There's nothing they can do. Nothing anyone can do. George says the only hope is that the new queen succumbs in childbed and that it won't be long before Edward can marry again, this time to a worthy bride.

Margaret's cool fingers creep into his, leading him to the settle where he sinks with her onto the scattered cushions.

'I'm sorry, Mother.'

'Sorry, Richard? What do you have to be sorry about? This mess is nobody's fault but your brother's.' She has yet to refer to Edward by name, and Richard wonders whether she ever will again. She's aged since yesterday, as if the anguish that afflicted her after Sandal has returned to salt the wound, to pummel the bruise. Something else has died for Mother, he thinks, and Edward is the cause of it.

'Cousin Warwick says the woman's family is extensive.'

A bitter laugh. 'Indeed. And yet, for all the births a woman suffers, half of her infants are laid in the earth. Henry, Thomas, John, your sister Ursula were all taken from me. Edmund…' The fading voice takes a moment to recover its force. 'Not so for Jacquette of Saint-Pol. The greater part of her brood is faring well, flourishing, creeping around your brother, seeking to suck him dry.'

Rising on impulse, Richard lays a hand atop his mother's, the knotty bulk of her signet ring jabbing his palm. 'Lady, your own family is strong. Our cousin's influence can still be brought to bear. Edward owes Warwick and his brother much; without them, Lancaster would have gained a foothold. The king needs our Neville kin.'

Margaret nods. 'Richard's right. The queen's family seems important now, but that's to be expected. Once they're established and settled to their manors, the king's true liegemen, his proven allies, will resume their places. Life will go on. The old blood must always triumph over the new.'

Their mother is barely listening. Folding her hands, she observes the perch in the corner, where a settled Criseyde preens and trills in her green feathery world.

Richard tries again. 'Mother, I trust our cousin, as I know you do. Edward will soon realise who is of value to him. As Margaret says, the queen's family can never uproot those of the old blood.'

Margaret, weary, catches his eye: *We're wasting our time, Richard.*

The duchess sighs, whether resignedly or from irritation, it's hard to say. 'Your father never strove for the crown. Never sought it. He claimed it merely to save his life – to save *our* lives – and died in the process. God has been kinder to your brother. He has granted him everything your father was denied, yet your brother seems content to defile it with his base impulses.'

Her voice is like a well-aimed missile. If Elizabeth Grey were here now, Richard thinks, she would be fastened to the wall, barbs through bonnet and kerchief, a final bolt aimed at her heart.

'The king has a sacred duty,' their mother says, 'not simply to his realm, not simply to his father, but to me. Yet I can only watch as that woman takes the place that could once have been mine. What did your father die for? Answer me that. So his enemies could wax and grow fat upon your brother's largesse?'

She glowers, fists balled. 'I swear before God, Edward is no son of York.'

The water is scented with rosemary and thyme, the bathtub draped with linen. Before George left for Reading, he granted Richard one of his boys to act as page. The youth is here now, topping up the water, face flushed and shining from the rising steam. Casting a nervous glance in Richard's direction, he snatches the napkin from his shoulder and crouches to wipe up the spills.

'Tell me,' Richard asks, 'how often did my brother beat you?'

The boy peers at him with the tell-tale squint of the short-sighted. 'Only when I made a mess.'

'And how often was that?'

The boy busies himself, laying footcloths around the base of the tub and fetching clean towels. 'Most days. He…he slipped on one occasion.'

Richard lifts the curtain of damp linen, laughter bubbling at the thought of George falling on his backside, fleshy cheeks slapping the floor.

'No, please.' The boy intervenes, dipping a hasty elbow. 'Allow me, Your Grace. It is my duty to test the water.'

George must have scalded himself, too, by the sounds of it. Satisfied, the boy nods, and Richard climbs into the wooden tub, taking his seat on the vast sponge while warm and soothing water laps his belly.

'What's your name?'

'Simon Kyngston, Your Grace. My father is in the service of the earl's brother, my Lord Montagu – oh, forgive me, the Earl of Northumberland.' Reddening at his faux pas, the boy is on the verge of tears. Warwick may bristle over such mistakes, Richard thinks, but the title has only recently been conferred on Cousin John, and pages cannot be expected to remember everything.

'Well, Simon, close the curtain if you can manage it. I should like to keep the heat in for a while longer, at least.'

Delivering a clumsy bow, Kyngston twitches the linen back in place. The boy would be in Reading now if he'd remained with

George. Inhaling the scented steam, Richard imagines his brother squirming and wincing beside Warwick as both kneel before the splendour of Edward's queen. He's pleased the privilege has fallen to them. He's not ready to witness it himself. Not yet.

'Fetch the soap, please, Simon.'

The curtain is swept aside, and a shock of cold air settles over the tub, dispelling the steam. Setting to work, the boy raises a lather over Richard's skin, rubs suds through his dripping hair. Richard wonders whether George has gifted his used soap as well as his disgraced servant. Task complete, Kyngston drenches him in a torrent of rosewater, badly aimed but sufficiently warm.

'I'm sorry, my lord. So sorry.' Cringing, the boy ducks from the projected punishment. When Richard makes no attempt to clout him, he stares, as if his new master is somehow lacking in his duty.

Richard smiles. 'Don't fret, Simon, I'm not my brother. Now, hurry, fetch me a towel before I freeze to death.'

'Well, I've seen her.'

George is fresh from the road, redolent with the scent of horseflesh, and surrounded, as so often these days, by a gaggle of henxmen. He flops on the bed, allowing them to divest him of his spurs and riding cloak. Raising each leg in turn, he grimaces as the boys struggle to remove his long, fashionable boots. If this had been one of Kyngston's duties, his successors don't appear to be faring much better.

Perching on the coffer at the end of the bed, Richard avoids the busying youths. One, with a jug of small beer, presents two brimming cups.

George nods his thanks, then wafts the boys away en masse. 'Are you not going to ask what she looks like?'

Richard was expecting eager tales of Elizabeth Grey but hadn't thought to hear them quite so soon; had assumed his brother would take at least one breath first. 'Is she fair?'

George slides his hand through his hair, raking curls. 'Not so fair that it makes all this debacle worthwhile.'

'Did you speak with her?'

'Yes, when she saw fit to grant me audience, but I can't say that what flowed from her lips altered my opinion at all.' His brother shrugs in worldly fashion. 'I'm sure the king must have had prettier bedfellows - there are more whores at Westminster than there are south of the river. If it were not for the fact that she's Edward's wife, I could see her as little more than she is: the widow of a knight from the shires.' A sip of small beer. 'I've seen her sons, too. They're almost of an age with us: gangly, arrogant-looking tykes trussed up in tawny silk. I imagine Edward will be scouring the Rolls to find titles and offices for them. If he's considered placing them in my household, he can think again.'

Richard, weary of twisting his neck, swaps the coffer for a stool by the bed. Leaning back on the mattress, George juts out his jaw. A year or two ago, his movements, his gestures, had been Edward's; now, the presence, the bearing, belong to Warwick. George could earn an admirable crust as a mimic, Richard thinks, if he ever lost his place at court.

His brother waggles his cup in the all-seeing, all-knowing fashion of the growing youth. 'There's more to this than we know. She must've coerced him somehow. You know what easy prey he is. She probably seduced him with her womanly skills.'

'Our cousin said she refused to succumb to Edward until he married her, so how is that the case?'

'As they say, there's more than one way to skin a cat. I expect she allowed him all kinds of freedom.' In a fit of laughter, George flops backwards. 'For Pity's sake, Dickon. You look like a nun who's taken the wrong turning and stumbled into the stews.'

Richard writhes under the mockery. 'Tell me about the presentation. Was it well attended?'

Still grinning helplessly, George heaves himself upright, ready and eager to make further report. 'Rather ask me whether it was well supported. Many attended, yes, but a sour taste lingered in most people's mouths, not least in that of the earl. He and I led the queen into Reading Abbey while her sisters followed, scrabbling for her train. It all seemed like a pretence to me: the lower orders raised, the higher cast down, like a Twelfth Night revel. I half expected the Lord of Misrule to pop up from behind the choir stalls and wave his bauble in my face.' The asinine grin subsides. 'How's Mother been?'

'Distraught, George. It's as if her life has ended.'

'Well, the life she expected for herself is ended, certainly. She planned a future at Edward's side, at least until he married. And even then, the bride would have been a woman of whom she approved. I suspect she saw her chance to fulfil the role Father would have granted her. What had she been calling herself? "Cecily, Queen by Right"? What Edward has done is shameful, no matter which way you look at it.'

Unable to disagree, Richard toys with his sleeve: soft velvet, jagged braid.

'Edward has made a mockery of everything,' George continues. 'To be forced to endure the woman herself is insult enough, but you should have seen her family: the proud father, the simpering mother.' His face takes on a series of contortions, but he doesn't intend to be amusing, and Richard isn't inclined to laugh. 'I hear Edward is already seeking husbands for the horde of younger sisters, so we would do well to stay out of their way. And as for the elder brother, our cousin was right to call him milksop. Although I believe I could think of other names.'

When his brother pauses for breath, Richard says, 'Do you think this is irreparable? With Mother, I mean. At present, she refuses to speak to the king, but how long can it continue? And what of us, in the meantime? We owe Edward our fealty and our lives, but our loyalty must also be to Father's memory. Mustn't it?'

The mask slips, George is in pain. 'I'm beginning to wonder whether family loyalty means anything to Edward. Aren't you?'

The court moves from Reading to Windsor, and it is there, in the first week of November, that they're summoned to pay their respects to the queen. The invitation, buoyed by informality, is extended with Edward's usual sense of ease, but there can be little doubt of the solemnity of the matter. His siblings will appear as a family to make due homage. They will acknowledge his choice of wife, in good faith – and in public. They will demonstrate to all that the house of York is united, and even George has found no acceptable excuse to refuse.

Autumn mists succumb to steely gloom as their cavalcade snakes along sodden roads, mounts stumbling in the slithering mire, Margaret's chariot churning mud. Richard's belly sinks as the squat keep appears, grey and bleary through mizzling rain, and he wishes the interview over and done.

Both lower and upper wards are awash with puddles, Edward's banners wet and limp. Hastings awaits, a familiar figure at least, eager to assist as Margaret descends from the swaying carriage. Refusing to be eclipsed, George swoops in, gloved hand raised and ready. Margaret, taking especial care in her wooden pattens, is a model of diplomacy. Granting them one hand each, she allows both George and the chamberlain to guide her over the sopping earth. Richard, eyes fixed on his poulaine boots, takes up the rear. *The customary order of things.* He hasn't forgotten: suspects the custom – and the order, in particular – will have yet more relevance for George today, under the scrutiny of the queen's kin.

The palace is aglow with sconces: gilded pools on ancient stone. Hastings, unusually silent, navigates them through a wealth of rooms towards a narrow stair. Clearly impatient, George strides ahead and vanishes into the spiral.

'The queen will see you in her apartments, my lord duke,' Hastings calls after him, begging Margaret to beware on the increasingly perilous stairs.

'And the king's grace?' George's disembodied voice echoes from above. 'Where is he?'

'The king would have you pay your respects to the queen, and once you have done so, bids me deliver you to him.'

Richard harbours a vague unease at the thought of greeting the woman who has caused their mother so much grief, raised their cousin to such levels of ire. Will she be as bland as George says? Or as sly and as scheming as Warwick would have her? Soon, he shall have formed his own opinion.

His brother has paused beside an ancient niche, where a rush light flickers in the gloom. As they ascend towards him, George glowers, his face a glowing mask. 'When the king is in residence, is it not customary that respects should be paid to him before any other?'

'It is the king's express wish,' Hastings says, 'that you, my lord of Clarence, His Grace of Gloucester and the Lady Margaret, pay due reverence to the queen upon your arrival. That is, I understand, the purpose of your visit.'

George takes the remaining steps at a run, and Richard loses sight of him.

When all emerge from the spiral, his brother snatches Margaret's hand from Hastings' dutiful grasp. 'Thank you, my lord, I shall conduct the Lady Margaret myself. I believe it fitting she should be led into the queen's presence by her brother.'

Raising his head, Richard is uncertain what to make of the face which has stolen his brother's reason. Slender and without blemish, it's as pale as expected, with fine, almost delicate cheekbones. The long, thin nose, the fashionably plucked brow exude an air of refinement, while the white and silver damask furred with vair, the gilded bonnet with shimmering kerchief surpass even the contents of his mother's Great Wardrobe.

'Arise, my lord of Gloucester, I bid you welcome.'

The ordinary voice surprises him; neither harsh nor beguiling, it could belong to any woman. Whether he is truly welcome or not – whether any of them are - he cannot tell. Rising, he delivers a swift bow and steps to where George, already acknowledged, waits, stiff and resentful.

Margaret, back erect, performs a formal curtsey. It's a show of deference bordering on defiance, which Richard can only admire. Mother, he thinks, has trained her well.

The dip of Elizabeth's head is slow and measured, and Richard detects a surprising hesitancy, a quivering unease. It reminds him of how it had felt when he and George had returned to England. As brothers of a king, their lives had changed beyond recognition. How much harder must it be for this woman, this widow of a knight, to learn how to become a queen? A surge of empathy takes him by surprise. He tries his best to batter it down, but it hovers: a moth around a pulsing flame.

He should feel offended by her, should be as angry and disgusted as George. Yet he can sense nothing in this woman's behaviour but a vague anxiety, a need to meld into the tableau the king has erected about her. She's lost without him, he tells himself. Without Edward to bolster her, she's nothing.

But Elizabeth is not allowed to suffer long. An elegant figure, peacock bright, swoops to her side to smother her trembling hands with his own. Richard wonders at his daring, but the slender nose and tawny languorous eyes give the man away.

'My lords, my lady Margaret,' Elizabeth beams, 'may I present my eldest brother, Anthony, Lord Scales.'

The peacock bows and Elizabeth is visibly imbued, his presence nourishing her like spiced posset.

So, Richard thinks, this is the 'milksop' of whom our cousin spoke. Casting a further eye over the modish gown and particoloured hose, he wonders whether Scales recalls the night he and his Wydeville father were captured in their beds and ferried to Warwick in Calais. He wonders whether his pride still smarts. He wonders if, when Scales kneels before Edward, he remembers the insults that were heaped upon him. If he does but chooses to forget them for the value of what he has gained, then it's certain he has no pride at all.

A fusion of silks and velvets forms about the queen. A woman, past middle age yet elegant and comely in her person, stands at the head of them. Elizabeth beckons her forward.

'May I also present the Duchess of Bedford – my mother.'

The woman sinks to the floor in one erect, sweeping movement. If Margaret had thought to convey defiance, then the gesture has been reciprocated. This woman may be Wydeville's wife, but it seems they must remember that she was once Bedford's widow.

Observing the queen, Richard sets himself a test. If the pity he felt at the sight of her nervous, twitching fingers had been genuine, he will allow it to return. He'll consider the scorn she has received at his mother's hands, the harsh mockery of Cousin Warwick. He shall try, despite all, to sympathise.

But the woman who had greeted them is no more, and her supplanter, buoyed and self-possessed, is of a wholly different sort. Flashing a complacent smile at Scales, Elizabeth shines, iridescent, while her family closes in around her.

Richard's pity fails to revive. Instead, he nods, bows, accepts the salutations in the mood in which they are given, and when he leaves the royal presence, he acknowledges the fact that his compassion had been totally misplaced.

The fluttering moth has singed its wings.

Chapter Eight

May 1465
Palace of Placentia

DULL, AND humid for the season, dense clouds grazing the rooftops and the sun a faded disk passing between. Gripping his practice bow, Richard inhales.

He'd imagined it would be easy, that archery skills would come as naturally to him as tying hose to points. After all, every youth, from the son of a king to the whelp of a gong-farmer, is taught to handle a bow, and the child's weapon he inherited from George had been easy to master. But he was wrong. His new bow is different, and he can barely draw the string as far as his nose.

Yesterday, he missed the mark by a hair's breadth. Muscles ill-primed for such heavy resistance, he'd felt weak, skinny, useless. Today, he will improve if it means remaining at the butts until Vespers.

His sixth attempt fails, but he cannot relent. Sweating, frustrated, one eye clamped so tightly the socket feels bruised, he forces himself to continue.

'Steady, Your Grace. Accuracy is vital.' His tutor, keen not to coerce, watches quietly from the corner of the yard. Richard knows the man has taught him well; he just wishes he could prove it.

Arrow nocked and ready, he draws, boot soles gripping the earth in an effort to hold his stance. Sapwood bends, but his left arm shakes. He tells himself he must summon the strength. From wherever it dwells, he must summon it. And he must succeed.

A scream rips the air as the arrow smacks home.

'Good shot, Your Grace.'

But good is not good enough. Another shot, then another. *Nock. Mark. Draw.*

Body taut, lungs compressed, he looses another arrow. It cuts the air with a whistle, thudding into the butt, shaft bouncing on impact. Stumbling forward, he sees the bodkin embedded in the marked circle. Now, and only now, can he honourably withdraw.

'Fine work, Brother.' The slap on his back comes from nowhere. Edward is towering over him, eyes warm as chestnuts.

A laugh – relieved, excited – twangs through Richard's body. Too late, he remembers to bend the knee.

'On your feet.' Edward grins. 'As I've told you a hundred times, a king can weary of formality.'

'How long have you been watching?' Richard runs a hand across his brow; it comes back damp and sticky.

'Long enough. You're determined, lad. I grant you that.' Edward takes his arm and leads him aside. Halting beside the low stone wall which separates the butts from the practice yard, the king squats on the moss-covered stone. He exudes the scents of clean linen: of rosemary, lavender, all the herbs of the clothes press. Perched beside him, flushed and beaded with sweat, Richard feels grubby: unfit company.

'Your tutor has spoken of your triumphs,' Edward says, 'of the fine progress you're making. And I can see for myself that when you bend your body to the bow, you're mastering the weapon. Perseverance brings great reward, and I've no doubt the earl will find you a resolute and skilful pupil. Oh, you don't believe me? You think your king a mere flatterer?'

'I've a long way to go before I can rival George.' Richard sounds surly, but there's no helping it: this is the truth as he sees it.

Edward laughs. 'I suspect that's what our brother has been telling you.'

'I've seen him draw a bow. He's stronger, and he's faster.'

'He's three years older than you; there would be something amiss if he were not.'

Richard shrugs. Had Edward sought him out like this a year ago, the conversation would have been different. He would have welcomed his brother's approval, gloried in it. But Elizabeth's presence has changed things. Even Edward must admit that.

'You've come a long way in recent months, Richard.' The king dips his head, coaxing. *Grinning like a lackwit,* Warwick had said of him - the day in council when he had broken the news. Grinning, whilst all around him gasped and snarled.

Richard wants to ask his brother how he feels. How he lives with himself. How he tips his cup with those who hated their father and willed him dead. How he beds a woman whose husband went to war to smite them, to spite them, to deprive them of their only hope. Had these efforts triumphed, Edward himself would be dead, Harry of Lancaster would still be king, and the family of York would be helpless. Does he ever think of that?

'You told me yourself you were quick on your feet.' Edward nudges him like a creeping George seeking pardon. 'Agility can mean the difference between life and death for a fighting man. Now, tell me how you fare with the rest of your training.'

Sulks are only effective for a certain length of time; Richard learnt that in the nursery. 'I'm trying to build my strength. I climb the knotted rope in the armoury. And there's the stone I must lift and carry about to strengthen my arms. My tutor tells me John le Boucicaut ordained just such a thing in his day.'

'And?'

Richard sags under the scrutiny. 'It's difficult.'

'I know. You forget, Edmund and I undertook the same training at your age. But I believe you are hard on yourself.'

A small group has accompanied the king: five liveried boys and four courtiers, who remain on the far side of the yard. One has a greyhound and is showing it off to his fellows as it circles their feet and sniffs the earth. Another is William Hastings, assured and stylish in a blue riding cloak. Walking towards the butts, the chamberlain stoops to retrieve Richard's discarded bow. Testing its weight with a grin, he offers some jest while his companions laugh.

Richard wraps his arms around his chest, petulant. 'I hate

being the youngest. The weakest. I hate it.'

'Time and patience, Brother.'

Richard huffs. Hastings' scorn and the king's scrutiny have him red-faced, wounded.

Edward snakes an arm around his shoulder. 'That day in the library, I was wrong to make light of your stories. Every man must have something, someone, to inspire him. The books and your memories of our father fulfil that purpose, and you're right to cherish them.'

Richard kicks at the earth. 'But I'm afraid I'll fail him. And to fail would be disloyal.'

The sun breaks from a mass of cloud, skims the yard, then disappears. A sudden gust blows Richard's hair across his eyes. With an angry gesture, he flicks it away.

Edward sighs. 'It is I who am disloyal, in Mother's opinion. Even though she has retracted much of what she said, I know I've gravely disappointed her.'

Richard sucks his lip. His brother's candour has surprised him, and he wonders whether Edward expects a response.

'And what of you,' the king says at length, 'what do you think?'

The last question Richard would have expected has him scrabbling for words. 'You took care of us when Father was in Ireland, and you take care of us now.'

It doesn't answer the question, but it's the best he can do.

Edward presses. 'But do you think I have betrayed his memory the way that Mother and George do? Because I haven't, Richard. I loved him as any son loves his father, but I don't live in his world; I live in the present. He left me a perilous legacy, and I couldn't wallow in grief; my family looked to me for survival. I was all you had, and I knew it. God has blessed me twice on the field, but I must be allowed to rule as I see fit and believe that wherever Father's soul resides, he trusts me with the crown that should have been his.'

The chestnut gaze is probing, hopeful. 'Can you bring yourself to trust me too?'

Supper at Baynard's is a tense, edgy affair. Margaret picking at her poached sturgeon, George silently crumbling his bread, while their mother recites the evening's Scripture from the Book of Proverbs.

"'A virtuous woman is a crown to her husband, but she who maketh ashamed is as rottenness in his bones.'"

Thoughtful, Richard reaches for the salt, seasoning what remains of his fish. The king's visit to Placentia had succeeded in settling his mind, and he'd placed his trust in Edward because he felt it's what their father would have wanted. But now, listening to his mother, witnessing George's growing discontent, he's once more unsure. The morrow will see Elizabeth Grey enthroned. That unalterable fact had planted itself among them as they took their places at table, and has remained throughout the meal, growing like a canker.

The duchess smooths the page. "'A wise son heareth his father's instruction: but a scorner heareth not rebuke.'"

A sage and knowing nod from George. Ill at ease, Richard takes comfort from the hunting scene engraved around his cup. When they were small, their father had commissioned a dozen from the workshop of a London goldsmith. One evening at Ludlow, as the boys were on their way to bed, their father lounged by the hearth. Along with his evening blessing, he'd presented his cup, tilting it towards the firelight.

'Can you find the stag? He's hiding from the huntsmen.'

Richard and George had peered intently, desperate to find the hidden creature. Eventually, their father had been forced to point it out. Richard picks it out now, cleverly disguised amongst the foliage, and caresses its pointed muzzle with the pad of his thumb.

Glancing up, he finds himself under scrutiny. It's time for evening prayer, and their mother and sister are keen to retire. The boys rise, then kneel as she recites the *Te Lucis* and offers up her hand to kiss.

'You promised me a game of chess, Dickon.' George is on his feet and halfway to the door before the women are over the threshold.

He's lodged in their father's apartments; spacious and overlooking the gardens. Fitting, Richard concedes, for the heir presumptive; a temporary honour to which George and their mother still cling like drowning men to flotsam. Pages in his brother's new livery of the Black Bull stoke the fire and thump the shutters in place, while a third pours small beer.

'How's the boy?' George tosses the remark as if he had been reading his brother's mind.

'Simon acquits himself very well.'

'Well, that was a swift transformation.' A soft smirk. 'While he was with me, he was worse than useless.'

'His…well—'

'What?'

'Only that his clumsiness may arise from his poor vision, is all.'

George considers. 'Well, how am I supposed to know these things? If his eyesight troubles him, he should have told me. Anyhow, I'm happy to hear he's settled. It's time you had your own page, and if Edward fails to arrange such things, then the duty must fall to me.'

A chessboard has already been set up. George, as usual, chooses to play white and waits for Richard to make the first move. As moments pass, it's clear the evening is not to be about chess; it's to be about George himself and his simmering anger.

'The scripture reading - you know who the "scorner" is, don't you?'

Richard contemplates the board. Their mother has declined to attend tomorrow's proceedings, and when he had dared ask why, she'd told him that unlike a king's anointing, where God invests the monarch with the wisdom and sanctity to rule, the crowning of his queen is mere ceremony, hardly worth the effort. Yet, he knows that were the coronation to have been the Lady Bona's, his mother's women would already be at work: brushing her velvets, scenting her furs, polishing her jewels. The duchess would have appeared resplendent.

'George? About tomorrow. Can you not convince Mother to attend?'

His brother blinks at the absurdity of the question. 'And why should I do that? Absenting herself is the only powerful measure Mother can take. It'll be remarked upon. The people will see that Elizabeth Grey would never have been our choice and that she'll never be truly accepted, by Mother, or by any of us.'

'But we two shall be present and be seen to pay homage to her.' Red rook captures white bishop.

'Yes, but only because we're compelled to. And because I have a role to fulfil.'

George is to be Steward for the day and is clearly pleased, no matter how much he tries to deny it. As for the invitation to attend the tourney the following day, he was hardly likely to turn that down. Richard watches as his brother pretends to study the chessmen. Dangling a pawn, George rotates it in small, distracted circles.

'Scales is to ride in the lists, did you know that? Apparently, he revels in this kind of thing. How would he have fared, do you think, had he lived out the rest of his days as a backwater squire? Not much opportunity for jousting at Grafton Wydeville, I wouldn't have thought.'

Richard sighs. 'Do you intend to make your move, Brother, or shall we still be here at dawn?'

George has lost interest in the game, if he'd possessed any in the first place. 'Don't pretend you approve of that godforsaken family, Dickon. You saw them with your own eyes, swarming about Edward like flies around shit.'

Richard shoots him a glance. 'That's unworthy of you.'

'No, Elizabeth is unworthy of *him*, and well you know it. Stop playing the plaster saint and tell the truth.'

If his brother is out to bait him, Richard refuses to bite. 'Edward doesn't see it that way.'

'No, I don't suppose he does, for as long as he can bed her. But once she's with child, he'll take up with his whores again.'

'George, please.'

'*George, please!* What does please me is that you're to be housed with our cousin; he'll beat the primness out of you. Henry, more candles.'

A boy shuffles from the shadows and lights a pricket at George's elbow. His master shoots out a hand, grasping the boy's wrist. 'What think you of the queen's kin, eh Henry?'

Kyngston's successor lowers his eyes, makes a fuss of extinguishing his taper. It's always the same with George, Richard thinks, not content with making his point, he must continue to push until he gets a reaction. The boy keeps his counsel and George sniffs.

'You know, Dickon. Sheen is more like a swine market these days. All manner of fellows dressing in chamlet and sarcenet, professing kinship to the queen in order to gain our brother's favour. I shouldn't be surprised if a gong-farmer presented himself and claimed to be her great-uncle. Edward wouldn't be clear of the stink for days.'

'Stop acting like a churl. Do you think Father would approve?'

George snatches his abandoned pawn and hurls it across the chamber. 'Do you think he would approve of *her*? It seems to me that Edward's victories have done little but replace one she-wolf with another.'

'Edward is our king, as well as our brother. We must respect his choices.'

'Come on, Dickon. If you or I had been Father's heir, d'you think we would have acted as Edward has? Wedding the daughter of an enemy and fawning over her kin? Edward's not like us. He does things we wouldn't do. Take Henry Beaufort. The son of our father's greatest enemy, yet Edward forgave him, treated him like a brother until Beaufort betrayed him and scampered back to Lancaster.' George peers down the length of his nose. 'Those are the actions of a fool.'

'Edward told us, when we returned from exile, that sometimes it behoves a king to pardon his enemies in order to sustain peace.'

'But don't you think he has taken that philosophy too far? Or do you enjoy prostrating yourself before the Wydeville whore?'

'We must be charitable. She's Edward's choice—'

Leaping to his feet, George strikes the board with his fist, scattering the pieces. 'He's won you over again, hasn't he? A few soft words and you accept anything he chooses to throw at us. What about Father, eh? What about your loyalty?'

Richard's stool crashes to the floor as he launches himself at his brother. 'Don't you dare question my loyalty to my father. I'm warning you—'

A swift movement and he's on his back with George's livid face pressed close to his. 'He was our father. Ours. You think you had him all to yourself, don't you? As if you were his favourite. Well, he was my father as much as he was yours, Dickon, and if you ever loved him at all, you'd see that what our brother has done is wrong.'

Richard raises a knee and strikes George in the gut, winding him.

A snide protest, belated and depleted, seeps through his brother's compressed lips. 'I'll say one thing for Edward. He's right to send you away. Despite your training, you're still as feeble as a girl.'

Richard yells as frustration rips through him. 'I hate you!'

A rap at the door, and both fall silent, united in surprise and confusion. The rapping comes again, harder, and the boy, Henry, races to the door in relief. George leaps to his feet as Margaret sweeps in, face crumpled in concern.

'May I ask what you're doing?'

'We had a disagreement.' George offers his hand. Richard takes it, hauls himself up, but refuses to look at him.

Margaret narrows her eyes. 'Have we not trouble enough?'

'Sorry—'

'Forgive—'

Apologies ring out, and they shuffle their feet like berated scholars. Flushed and embarrassed, George clears his throat as his boy scuttles to retrieve the scattered chessmen.

'What was it about?' Margaret gathers her skirts and climbs onto the bed that had once been their father's. Spine rod-straight, hands folded in her lap, she is a queen holding court. 'I thought my brothers had outgrown their childish tussles.'

Richard stoops to recover the toppled footstool while George sinks onto the chair by the hearth.

'Well?' Margaret's voice is firm.

He started it, Richard thinks, let the explanation be his. Their sister appears to be of the same mind. 'George? I asked what it was about?'

George tucks his hands into his armpits like a surly infant. 'The day Elizabeth Grey is crowned will not be a good one for our family.'

'No,' Margaret says, 'it will not. Therefore, the best thing we can do is stick together, not brawl like louts in a tavern yard.'

An accusatory finger is thrust in Richard's direction. 'He defends Edward, defends *them*.'

Margaret is unimpressed. 'Leave him be. This is not the time for petty squabbling, George. If you esteem family honour, you will make peace with Richard. Now.'

George squirms, the lash of Margaret's anger flushing his cheeks. 'Sorry.'

A raised eyebrow, a smoothing of the skirts. 'Not a particularly convincing apology. Try again.'

'I'm sorry, Dickon.'

It's not enough. Richard needs more from him. 'Don't ever question my loyalty to Father, George. I mean it.'

'Both of you. Come.' Margaret extends a hand, and they place theirs on top: a woven mass of fingers. 'I demand a promise from both of you. We three have suffered much, and yet always, with God's help, we have triumphed. We've a duty to uphold what He has given us, and if Edward's wife is part of God's plan, then we must accept her.'

'But—'

'George, we must accept her. Now, I want your word - and yours, too, Richard – for the sake of Father's memory. No quarrels, no brawling.'

Richard nods.

A silent, fleeting moment sees George acquiesce. 'Agreed.'

Dismissing her women, his mother beckons him towards the settle by way of a platter of sweetmeats.

'Marchpane, Richard. I know how much you like it.'

Slipping three delicate confections into a napkin, he flops amongst the vast array of cushions.

'Well,' she says, 'how was it really? I've heard George's description of yesterday's ceremony. Now I should like to know the truth.'

Detaching a candied leaf, Richard pops it in his mouth, allowing its sweetness to tingle his tongue. As a child, such confections were always his favourite. Tinted with saffron and spiced with cinnamon, he'd eat them slowly, fragment by fragment, prolonging the pleasure. He does so now.

'Richard. When you're ready.'

He passes his tongue over sticky lips. 'Where would you have me begin?'

'The people. How was she received? My spies tell me the climate is mixed.'

'George says the Londoners will applaud anyone as long as the Cheapside conduit runs with wine.'

'I didn't invite you here to reiterate your brother's opinion, as well as his flippancy. I want to know how it appeared to you.'

Wiping his mouth, Richard folds the napkin into a neat square.

His mother is snappish. 'I pay the boys of the napery for their skills with the linen, Richard. Leave the napkin alone and give me an honest answer.'

He reports on the pageant of Saint Paul at Southwark, the choir boys sprinkling song from the houses at the Bridge Foot, the peacock wings of the cherubim and the gilded wigs of the angels. He recalls the events at Westminster. Elizabeth's entry into the abbey church, bedecked in queenly wise, like the Virgin herself. He describes how Margaret, their sister of Suffolk and their aunt of

Buckingham carried the queen's train. He speaks of the banquet that followed; George, as Steward, preceding each course, clattering into the hall, mount caparisoned with spangles of gold. He makes no mention of his brother's ill-humour, of the petulance and pride that battled for dominance in his haughty face, how despite his promise of the night before, George had made no attempts to disguise his own disgruntled feelings. But he does commend Margaret and her admirable demeanour: quiet, dignified, an illuminated saint from a Book of Hours. It's difficult to determine whether any of it meets with his mother's approval. All he knows for certain is that he has her undivided attention.

'The woman's family, what of them?'

'The queen was waited upon by her mother and sisters.' He notes a slight withering in his mother's expression. 'Each dressed in crimson velvet. The youngest, lately wedded to Henry Stafford, was carried in so she might witness the ceremony above the heads of the crowd.'

'Lately wedded.' His mother's disgust is palpable. 'Imagine, my sister of Buckingham induced to squander her grandson's estates on the infant daughter of a former squire. Stafford's wardship was intended to be used wisely, but once again, your brother has eschewed good counsel and done solely as he pleases. Tell me, how were you and George received by… the queen?'

'Graciously. Why should it be otherwise?'

'Why indeed?' His mother's response, he supposes, is a lesson in rhetoric. 'Richard, you shall soon leave us for the earl's household. When you journey north, I would ask one thing of you. Observe the Neville patrimony, the lands wherein I was born, established by the royal hands of Cnut, long before the Conqueror set foot on English soil. The family name is strong there; it is honoured and respected. To be a Neville is to be proud, proud of one's lineage, proud of what the family has achieved. Behold your cousin's estates, witness the power of the Neville name, and try to understand how hard it has been, how hard it still is, for your cousin – and for me – to accept the consequences of your brother's folly.'

In the silky languor of Edward's presence, it's easy to see why they must forgive him and try to accept his choices. Under their mother's critical eye, the task is not so simple.

'Edward wants a peaceful realm. If his queen proves a loyal and a worthy wife, perhaps we should try to forget that her family once fought for Lancaster and enjoy the peace that Edward has brought us.'

'Forgiveness and forbearance are not unknown to me.' His mother swivels her rings with distracted fingers. 'For your brother's sake, I've accepted into my household numerous women whose families once opposed us. But the queen's former loyalties are not my only grievance, as well you know. The king himself acted rashly, without thought for me, without consultation.'

'But Edward risked his life for us. Without him, we could have been disgraced, exiled – or worse.'

'Disgraced, Richard?' The flesh around his mother's mouth creases and contracts. 'You think for us to have suffered in your father's cause would have meant *disgrace*?'

His face stings as readily as if she'd branded it with her palm. 'No. Of course not. I chose the wrong word – that is all. I would die for Father's cause; you know that Mother. If he still lived, I would follow him to the very jaws of Hell.'

'Not so flippant, my son. The jaws of Hell should stand as inducement to no man.'

He wishes they could begin the conversation again. His mother is twisting it. 'Please, my lady—'

'I trust you will never forget, Richard, how the blood of Neville, and of York, has been corrupted. For Edward has defiled it as surely as if he had married a Southwark whore.'

'Please, Mother. Edward has tried to encourage me. I owe him – we owe him – everything.'

'Everything?' On her lips, the word sounds meaningless, cheap. It is a talent of his mother's to demolish an argument with a single word. 'You've been fighting with George.'

Another talent is for a sudden change of course, designed to throw you off guard. 'How can you know that?'

'Servants talk. And it was not so difficult a matter to bribe that boy of George's.'

'Then you must know why we fought.'

Refusing to make it easy for him, his mother raises a brow. 'Come, Richard, tell me what you think. Don't hide behind your brother, either of them.'

'George exaggerates; you know he does. He looks for faults in everyone and if he fails to find any, he invents them. I believe we must accept Edward's actions. There's much good in him if George would care to look for it as readily as he hunts for flaws.'

An unrelenting frown has Richard struggling to defend himself.

'All I ever wanted was to please my father. I still want that, to be noble, honourable, everything that he was. He told me to be strong. If I can serve the king well – if I can serve Edward – perhaps I can become a true son of my father.'

His mother's eyes are moist. 'Richard, all I ask, all I beg, is that you remain faithful to his memory.'

Rising from the settle, he takes her hand and presses it to his lips. 'Until death,' he tells her.

Fallen leaves, crisp and curling, litter the courtyard at Placentia. It's cold for September, and George tugs his brother's cloak, drawing it together. When the heavy velvet fails to hold, he snatches the garnet brooch from his own bonnet and pins the folds in place. Standing back in appraisal, he admires his work. 'Well, Dickon. Time to say farewell.'

'It won't be forever,' Richard says. 'Edward will recall me in time.'

His brother's mouth twists in resignation. 'Well, when he does, you'll not find me here. There's little point in staying without you – and Margaret is always with Mother. Besides, I've heard Edward is scouring his holdings to find a place for the queen. Now she is *enceinte,* she's to have her own establishment. If it's a boy—'

'Brother, we need to face the inevitable. Elizabeth has already proved herself capable of producing sons. In any case, what makes you think the king will consider granting her this place?'

'My spies, and the fact that he's spending money on improvements.' George laughs wickedly. 'Who knows? He may wish to make way for a concubine at court. After all, he'll have little of Elizabeth until the child is born and will need to slake his appetite somewhere.'

Richard smiles. There was a time when he would have objected to George's lack of respect, but not today. He would not have them fight; they have been together too long, and the thought of separation is not easy for either of them.

'Besides,' George says, 'I'm to have Tutbury once I reach my majority, so shall be fending for myself next year.' He reminds Richard of an injured lapdog, gazing at its mistress, inciting pity.

'Are you saying you won't enjoy it? You'll fare well enough in your own household, George. Unlike me, you'll not have to face our cousin every day of the week. If I fail to meet his standards, what then?'

George grins in wry salute. 'But you won't fail. You're my brother.'

'You will write?'

'Of course, and you'd better respond. Come, Edward has sent his barge for you. He's keen to wish you Godspeed.' Taking Richard by the elbow, George ushers him from the courtyard and onto the landing. 'Westminster calls.'

Bidding farewell to his mother, to Margaret, had been far from easy, but taking his leave of George is the hardest task of all. The royal barge is moored up, lapped by the choppy Thames; with its canopy and its cushions, it's far too large for a solitary passenger.

'I wish you were coming with me.'

George sneers. 'I don't. Too many slobbering Wydevilles make it slippery underfoot. Make sure you watch your step, Dickon.'

A blast of wind threatens to steal Richard's bonnet. He makes a grab for it. 'Come with me.'

'No need. You're not an infant.'

Richard guffaws. 'And shall I remind you of that next time we quarrel?'

'Please do. But be assured, Dickon, I shall completely deny it.'

They laugh; heartier, merrier perhaps than the remark demands, and if their eyes are moist, it is because they are amused, or because of the wind on the water.

George takes him in a deep embrace. 'I'll miss you, you little worm.'

'And I you.'

Making no attempt to withdraw, they cling to each other as if the strengthening gusts will blow them apart.

George plants a kiss on his mouth, then nods to the bargeman. 'You need to embark. They're waiting for you.'

'May God keep you, Brother.'

The stench of the river rises as Richard picks his way down the steps. Boarding the barge, he makes more fuss than is necessary, keeping eyes and hands busy, distracted. A jolt as the barge moves off, and the giddy feeling of being afloat. Twisting his neck, he peers around the swathing canopy and finds George is still there, watching. Snatching his bonnet, Richard waves it in the air. Crushing his own in his eager fist, George waves back.

Flopping against the regal cushions, Richard blows out his cheeks. He steels himself, wondering how it will feel to make his own way in the world. Every day of his life, George has been there, with his grutching and his boasting and his irreverent jests. Without him, Richard knows he shall feel as he had in Utrecht when his ankle improved and he had cast away his crutches. Many were the times he'd found himself reaching for them.

The barge navigates the wider river, passing through its reedy banks and on towards the city. Placentia behind him, the spire of Paul's a needle on the far horizon, he settles into a watery limbo, soothed by the slapping of the oars. He's grateful for this time, this opportunity to clear his head, to seek the courage he'll need, the surety of purpose.

He acknowledges that life may be hard without George, but like the day he relinquished his crutches, leaving his brother behind will force him to move forward: by his own efforts and upon his own two feet.

'This way, Your Grace.' Hastings, another turkey bonnet - green this time, with peacock feather bobbing - ushers him through the throng of courtiers towards the presence chamber.

Westminster is crawling with people: courtly insects, fluttering, swarming, and a queue of supplicants in varying degrees of raggedness. One, a slovenly woman in a grubby kerchief, holds a tattered boy by the hand. As they pass, he stares at Richard with a hollow, vacant expression.

'Petitioners,' Hastings explains. 'Many will wait for hours to see the king. The keenest will huddle on the tiles overnight to be sure of a hearing the next morning.'

A backward glance confirms the boy still stares, mouth agape like a great landed fish. 'And does my brother help them?'

'His affability is well known. Whether he can always help such creatures is another matter.'

Richard finds the king seated at table before a pile of leather folios and parchment rolls. Two sombrely dressed clerks hover at his elbow. Another, shuffling documents, slides one under Edward's nose and passes him a newly inked quill.

Hastings bows. 'My lord of Gloucester, Your Grace.'

Edward glances up. Pushing back his chair, he throws down the pen and signals to his clerks. 'A moment with my brother.'

They slither away silently, as clerks seem bound to do, Hastings taking up the rear.

'So,' Edward says, 'you leave tomorrow.'

Richard finds himself straightening, standing tall: Edward has that effect upon a person. 'Yes.'

'Nervous?'

'No…yes.'

The king barks with laughter. Richard joins him, belly a mishmash of fear and excitement. 'Our cousin—'

'Is to be well provided for. Trusting him with you for the next few years is a sign of my favour. We're striving to patch up our differences, and whilst he still does not approve of the queen, he's had to grow used to her. Don't vex yourself over it, Richard. A Neville knows when to stay close to his king.'

'I shall write.'

A wry grin. 'I fear I'm not the most faithful of correspondents, but George, I suspect, will be happy to keep you informed of his doings. Small beer?'

As if he serves at table every day of the week, Edward busies himself at the buffet, returning with two gilt cups, their lowly contents more suited to his brother's age and status than to his own. Richard accepts one, grateful for the kindness, while Edward drinks to his health.

'God speed you on your journey, lad, and may you find pleasure north of the Trent.'

Richard tilts his cup and tries to count the rivers he will cross, the counties he will pass through before he reaches their cousin's northern lands. Not that the earl remains in any place for long; his countess's dower lands in Warwickshire, the French port of Calais of which he is captain, are all home to him. But it is the Neville fortresses north of York to which he's retreated since the news of Edward's marriage. Perhaps, Richard thinks, he sees them as bastions of defiance, relics of a world before Wydevilles.

Edward fingers a ring, caressing the garnets and pearls. 'Give my regards to our cousin. I know he's delighted you are to represent me at the enthronement of his brother as Archbishop of York. From what I've heard, the earl intends it to be a grand affair.'

A cacophony of voices filters from the palace beyond, the buzz and drone of industrious bees flittering in and out of Westminster's busy hive. As ever with kings, time is pressing.

'Come. Let us say farewell.' Edward holds out his arms, plants hefty kisses on his brother's cheeks.

Richard returns the gesture. 'May God keep you, lord king.'

Edward resumes his seat, picks up his pen, and gestures with a wry smile towards the towering heap of folios. 'Pity me. Whilst you're happily cantering along the Great North Road, I shall be slowly sinking under a hundredweight of paper.'

As Richard withdraws, he glances up from his labours:
'Do well, my lad– and come back to me a soldier.'

Chapter Nine

September 1465
Warwick

'MAGNIFICENT, IS it not?' William Hastings reins in, petting his mount.

Drawing level, Richard gazes with wonder at the moated fortress that glimmers through the trees. 'It's beautiful.' Hesitating, he juts out his chin as George would. 'Rather, that is to say, yes, it's magnificent.'

Hastings grins. 'Or, one might say, a fortress fit for the knight Tristan?'

Richard bristles at the chamberlain's ill-concealed mockery. 'That it is fit for my cousin, the earl, is surely the point, my lord.'

'Of course, Your Grace. I'm merely minded of your liking for the old tales.'

He hadn't expected the company of Hastings; the arrangement had been a belated idea of the king's. 'As you are both to attend the enthronement in York,' Edward had said cheerfully, 'what could be more natural than you travel north together?'

Richard, keen to please, had agreed with good grace. Company would be welcome, or so he'd assured himself, despite Hastings' seemingly habitual need to render him uncomfortable.

They process towards the ancient bridge, which spans the River Avon. The earl and his party await them, brightly attired, silks flapping. As they dismount, Warwick performs a sweeping bow. 'My lord duke, I bid you welcome.'

An unexpected warmth floods Richard's belly as he sinks into the ursine embrace. Locked against the barrel chest, he wonders how much favour Warwick has regained in the king's sight. That Edward is prepared to surrender his brother into their cousin's care must surely be a mark of his trust.

Releasing him, Warwick gestures. 'Your Grace, may I present my wife, the Countess Anne.'

The lady is tall, with a long, slim face; plain and unremarkable like the white loaves served up during Lent. And while the elegant bonnet, with its delicate wires and diaphanous kerchief, would make a gilded butterfly of a prettier woman, it does little to enhance the countess.

'Welcome, my lord of Gloucester. I trust you shall be happy in our care.'

Warwick, keen to move on, introduces his companion; a solid-looking man, dark curling hair, hook-like nose. 'My brother-in-law, Henry Fitzhugh, wife to my sister, Alice. When we move north, Your Grace may see much of him.'

Fitzhugh. Richard recalls the name; one who fought against his father at Sandal Castle, and against Edward at Palmsunday Field. Aware the man has made his peace with York, Richard emulates the king's magnanimity. 'A pleasure, my lord Fitzhugh.'

The reciprocal smile is both spontaneous and genuine. 'Your Grace. A visit to my castle at Ravensworth, perhaps, once you're settled in the north?'

Warwick, making for his horse, accepts the invitation on his cousin's behalf. 'And now the duke is with us, let us offer our thanks for his safe arrival.'

A Mass of thanksgiving is held in the parish church of Saint Mary and Richard stands beside the earl in the light and lofty interior, breathing silent prayers of gratitude. His cousin is proud and happy to have received him. That is good. He must do all he can to ensure things remain that way.

Prayers concluded, the earl leads him across the south transept and down a short flight of steps. 'Work continues on the decoration of the chantry chapel,' he says, as they navigate a forest of wooden scaffolding, 'when complete, it will be one of the wonders of Christendom.'

The chapel smells of plaster, of paint and linseed oil. Artists and labourers have been temporarily dismissed; buckets, tools and hogs-hair brushes cleared away in honour of the ducal visit. The Master of Works is presented and speaks to Richard of his craft; of pouncing and pin wheels, of red lead, azurite and vermilion. Conscious of Warwick's presence, Richard nods; keen to learn, to understand his cousin's interests, and to share them. When the earl takes his arm, he walks with him to a side wall where the newly painted faces of disembodied saints peer into the brilliance of Eternity. Entranced, he tries to imagine their future beauty: features complete, haloes gilded, and the space consecrated for worship.

'A wonder of Christendom,' Warwick repeats for the benefit of Hastings, who slinks through the scaffolding with the countess on his arm. 'A worthy mausoleum for my noble predecessor.'

The tomb, for which the chapel has been made, is like nothing Richard has seen before. Even the abbey church at Westminster, with its royal sepulchres, offers little to rival the vast sarcophagus; the effigy itself, gilded and in full harness, as splendid as that of any monarch.

Excusing himself, Warwick reaches for his wife's hand and guides her towards the twin prie-dieus set before the altar. Left alone with Hastings, Richard lowers his head. If the chamberlain seeks to engage in idle chatter, he would rather not. Fingers interlaced, he ponders instead on the chantries recited here, whether they will succeed in speeding the occupant of the tomb through the trials of Purgatory. How does it work, he wonders? Not even his mother has ever really explained. Does each mass reduce the torments of the cleansing flames by one day, one hour? Or can a whole year's worth of prayers offer but a moment's relief? He wishes he knew. He ought to know, for his father's sake.

'Richard Beauchamp was a man of legend,' Hastings says, voice pitched low in the hushed interior. 'The countess will let none forget how great was her father's reputation, both as soldier and diplomat.'

Richard's response is little more than a murmur, 'I'm aware of the late earl's fame; may God assoil him. He was acquainted with my own father.'

'Indeed.'

When the Warwicks leave, Richard and Hastings follow them to the nave, where the earl engages with the dean and treasurer. Hastings, ahead of the game, reaches into his money pouch. Fetching out four shimmering ryals, he flips them over on his fleshy palm. Plumbing the depths of his own hollow purse, Richard produces a solitary half-noble and squirms, embarrassed by his abiding penury.

One of the ryals slips into his hand. Hastings winks. 'Consider it a gift from His Grace.'

Grateful, Richard drops the coin into the treasurer's bag, where it vanishes into the glimmering ocean of Warwick's own personal donation.

Dean Berkswell raises a hand in blessing. 'My lords, your gracious sums offered for the salvation of Earl Richard's soul are most gratefully received.'

Glowing, Warwick informs his guests of the wealth of the establishment. Most of it, he admits, is the work of the Beauchamps: a promising collegiate foundation that he, in his turn, means to endow. Voice booming with pride, he points out the ceiling tracery, the painted bosses, and gilded angels. It's difficult to gauge whether Hastings is impressed, but Fitzhugh is clearly awestruck, substantial palms pressed together in silent adoration. All eyes raised, Richard dares to slip away.

In the throbbing silence of the chapel, a shaft of sunlight, alive with spiralling dust, illuminates the tomb chest. Richard knows he can't remain here long, that soon, at least one of his companions will come to seek him out, but the opportunity of gazing once more upon the magnificent structure has proved too strong to resist. He steals close: close enough to touch the prone and gilded figure.

Unlike most effigies, Beauchamp is not depicted as dead or sleeping, but as a real and living man. Head tilted, hands open in wonder, he seems to embrace a sacred vision invisible to lesser mortals.

Entranced, Richard circles the tomb, admiring the Italian harness, the tilting helm, the image of a perfect knight armoured for the lists. Stepping onto the stone plinth, he traces the armoured plates with his finger, flicks away a peppering of dust.

'You do know it's empty?'

Teetering backwards, he looks up into the ruddy features of William Hastings, the chamberlain's upper lip moist from the heat of the church's many candles.

'Yes, my lord. Of course I do.' He hadn't, but he's not prepared to admit it.

'Only, I thought you might believe he was already in there. The late earl is, in fact, still buried in the south transept; will be reinterred only when the work is complete and the chapel re-consecrated.' Presenting himself as well-informed, Hastings points to the chapel's west end and the huge, vacant space rising above it. 'I expect a Doom painting will be the final thing. The countess comes here every day when she and the earl are in residence, just to ensure her father's wishes are carried out to the letter. Have you noticed the weepers?'

He indicates the figures, cast in gilt relief, which adorn each side. 'The countess and her sisters on the left. On the right, their husbands. Here, this is your cousin, Warwick.'

Richard observes a figure draped in mourning robes and carrying a book of Scripture in a leather bag. He is reminded of the treasurer, the shame of his paltry coin buoyed by the chamberlain's dutiful gift. 'It does not resemble him.'

'When I first saw Beauchamp's effigy,' Hastings says, returning his attention to the recumbent earl, 'I wondered why his hands were open like that, why he did not appear to be praying in the usual fashion. You?'

Richard wants him to go away. He's like George: pestering, intruding when he would rather be alone. He came here to ponder, to offer some prayers of his own that one day Edward would erect just such a structure in honour of their father. 'I suppose I did wonder,' he says, summoning a smile for civility's sake.

Pausing at the head of the tomb, Hastings hunkers down. 'Here, Your Grace. Join me.'

'Why?'

'Kneel down and you'll see.'

Richard squats, as bidden, on the glazed tiles, hoping this is not some idiotic game, some foul jest the like of which George might play to embarrass him. From his brother, such japes might be acceptable, but not from this man.

'Now,' Hastings points to the ceiling, 'close one eye and trace a line between the earl's hands and that figure in the vaulting. See what he's doing? He's gazing upon Our Lady.'

Following his lead, Richard peers through the gap between the gilded hands to a brilliantly decorated roof boss; the Blessed Virgin, in her purity, invested as Queen of Heaven.

He crosses himself, abashed. 'Thank you, my lord. I should not have known.'

Before he'd left London, his mother had taken great delight in explaining to him the Beauchamp entailments, how both the son and the daughter of old Earl Richard's second marriage had wedded a Neville.

'My brother Salisbury was shrewd: he managed to wed two of his children to both of Beauchamp's offspring. Whichever survived and duly inherited, it was certain a Neville would benefit.'

One day, Richard promises himself, he will fully appreciate the complexities of the families into which he was born. For now, it's enough to wander in his cousin's shadow, to enjoy the beauty of his midland fortress, which is as wonderous at close hand as it had looked from afar. Hastings spoke true: Tristan should live here, or Arthur, or King Mark of Cornwall, but each night in hall, after supper has been cleared away, it's the exploits of the earl himself that rise to the hammerbeams, and Richard sees the king was right about their cousin's talents. Warwick's daring at Saint Albans, smashing through enemy palisades via back lanes and gardens, taking the city in the name of York. His command of the seas, crushing a Spanish fleet in the greatest naval battle for forty winters. Already, Richard can appreciate his cousin's worth, and the splendour of it daunts him.

Wiping his mouth, he sweeps the table at a glance: Hastings, moist-eyed and merry—yet still sober despite the endless supplies heaved up from Warwick's cellars. Fitzhugh, dark curls and heavy countenance, whose northern tongue sounds less outlandish the more Richard hears it. Countess Anne, a living replica of her father's gilded image, nibbling her honey-filled wafers. Finally, Warwick's sisters: Katherine Hastings, a decorous antidote to her effusive husband, and Alice Fitzhugh, placid, wide-eyed, and modest for a Neville.

This is, at present, the extent of his new family, and he tries his best to be courteous: answering their questions, offering polite comments. Any response that is well received, he counts a victory, a lever to slide him artlessly into their world. For their world must be his world now.

Chapter Ten

September 1465
York

'NOT LONG now, boy.'

Emerging from the fusty wayside chapel, with its peeling plaster and chipped image of Saint Christopher, Richard sees it has begun to rain. Again.

The earl mounts his muscular bay. 'A safe journey behind us, and the prospect of a warm and comfortable bed. You'll like my York townhouse, Richard. Monastery hospitality is charitable enough, yet I cannot help but crave my comforts.'

It's late afternoon, a forest of steeples pricking the near horizon. Richard's belly churns as he spies the city walls and fears he might void his guts. At Placentia, his tutor said that confronting your enemy is half the battle. Half, he thinks, but not all. Palms moist, he accepts there is no other way. Edward has beheld the gatehouse more than once. Beheld it when it still housed its sacred bounty, black with crusted blood and food for crows. He'd told him of it once—eventually, when Richard had wheedled it out of him.

'Why do you need to know?' Edward had asked. 'What good will it do you to dwell on Father's severed head?'

He'd tried to explain. 'I have to know. That I may remember as I pass. It would be disrespectful not to. I have to know,' he'd said, 'exactly where they placed it.'

Now the gate is looming - a grim, grey beast - and, already failing in his duty, Richard cannot bring himself to look. The cavalcade slows, inconsequential banter rippling through the ranks. A liveried man rides ahead and halts before the barbican.

'Richard Neville, Earl of Warwick, Captain of Calais, begs entry.'

A single voice resounds from the crenels. 'Enter, in peace.'

Richard gazes ahead through the cavernous arch. In the street beyond, crimson-clad aldermen wait to greet the second man in the kingdom and his skinny young charge. He counts them, these men with their bright gowns and their black bonnets, counts them over and over. Anything but raise his eyes to the parapets.

The line inches forward. Warwick clears his throat. 'All right, boy?'

Duty forcing him to raise his head, he's gripped by a surprising, urgent need for George.

'Richard?' Warwick's eyes are levelled at him—Neville eyes, like his mother's, like Edward's.

'I pray you, Cousin. The city gate, does it have a name?'

A moment's hesitation. 'Micklegate. Or the Micklelith as the locals call it.'

'Thank you.' Glancing his heels against his mare's dappled flanks, he urges her through the arch.

They could have entered through the eastern gate, he knows that now, for his cousin's family mansion lies on the eastern side, on Walmgate, amongst townhouses backed by gardens and orchards.

'Fulling sheds,' Warwick explains when Richard dares pose the question, 'brewhouses. All at the far end, close upon the gate. More pleasant to pass through the city and enter the street as we have, from the southwest.'

Richard is still bemused. Was this truly the easiest, the pleasantest, the most politic route to take? Or had his cousin thought to test his mettle? To see if he would weep, whether he would fail and flounder without George's brotherly arm to support him? Suspicion creeps over him and clings like damp homespun.

Can Warwick know how much of a trial it has been for him to enter this city, the city whose name conjures not merely a location but a face? He supposes he should think himself lucky that the turrets were free of heads, that no quartered flesh had been nailed to the iron-studied doors.

But there again, Edward would never do that, never think to place a traitor's head where their father's had once stood, for surely a felon's cop would defile the space.

'Here,' Warwick says as they process along the lengthy thoroughfare, 'is the church of Saint Denys, and here, Percy's Inn.' He gestures dismissively towards a solid timber-framed residence opposite the church, as if the house of Henry Percy, former Earl of Northumberland, must be discounted before they proceed towards his own.

From the depths of the city, the thundering bells of the minster church serve as a clarion call, and soon, the air vibrates with clangs no less frenzied than the heady peals of London.

The earl draws rein at the gates of a magnificent townhouse, equal to anything Richard has seen in the capital. His mother has primed him for grandeur, and Warwick's stone and timber mansion, built in three ranges around a neat courtyard, comes as no disappointment.

Duly impressed, the boy slips from the saddle while Warwick dominates the space, hurling instructions and scattering grooms like ninepins. Satisfied, the earl makes a grab for Richard's hand and, with great display, leads him up the outer stairs.

'It gives me pleasure, Your Grace, to welcome you to my home.'

The hall is a fusion of shades and scents: tapestries of hunting scenes and verdant woodland groves, floorboards strewn with marjoram and a host of sweet, crushed flowers. A swift fist tugs Richard's sleeve.

'You must meet my daughters,' Warwick beams, 'they are eager to greet you.'

Hastings, divesting himself of his gloves, catches Richard's eye and smirks at some jest known only to himself while Warwick manoeuvres the boy across the floor. Two girls sit on a low bench beneath a glimmering Arras. One, Richard's age, raises her head while the younger – a child – fondles a pet squirrel. Standing at his approach, they sink into their skirts.

'My elder daughter,' Warwick announces, 'Isabel.'

The girl is exceeding fair, all brown curls and dimples. Abashed, Richard seeks to address her; Margaret has told him the way: never to stare or be too bold, never to be clumsy or brash, compliment when necessary but keep a respectful distance. There's a lot to remember, and he is sure that, given the courage to open his mouth, he'll have forgotten half of it.

'Welcome, Cousin. We hope your journey north has been a pleasant one.' Against all forms of etiquette, the girl speaks first and delivers a fulsome smile.

'Thank you.' Does he take her hand? Does he kiss it? He should very much like to.

'And Anne,' Warwick says, 'the younger.'

This one looks him challengingly in the eye, the way her father does. 'Good day to you, Cousin.'

'And to you.' His bow, however elegant, leaves the girl's resolute mien unchanged. No sycophancy here, he thinks, but why should there be? To sit high in Warwick's favour is to require little acceptance elsewhere.

The earl's satisfied glance takes in all of his guests. 'Refreshment, I think, then a rest before supper.'

Hastings and Fitzhugh guide their wives from the hall while the countess ushers her girls. Anne, still petting the favoured squirrel, Isabel's movements polished and precise, long hands smoothing her glossy skirts. Richard's eyes follow.

With his sister's advice in mind, he is trying not to stare.

He ought to write to George. His brother will be eager to hear from him, if only for the opportunity of responding and regaling him with news of the Wydeville variety. Yet Richard delays. He cannot write to George of their cousin, beyond the usual recommendations of Warwick's good health, as he can't be certain his letters will leave the household unread. Neither can he write of their cousin's daughters, at least not in any detail. He wouldn't know how to describe them; to call them plain would be untrue, to call them pretty would serve only to embarrass him, and invite mischievous jibes from his brother's pen. He'll wait until he has something to report, and the investiture of the new archbishop should provide sufficient excitement.

George Neville, though brother to Warwick and Chancellor of England, is little more than a stranger to Richard. It would be fair, however, to say that his reputation precedes him. Chancellor of Oxford at twenty-one, Bishop of Exeter at twenty-six, and a renowned scholar of Latin and Greek, the man's intellectual skills sit comfortably alongside his gift for politics and diplomacy. As for vices, it's whispered he has a bastard daughter by a Beauchamp girl, but Richard can't vouch for the truth of it. Whatever the state of affairs, Neville's advancement to the See of York is another conciliatory gift from Edward to Warwick, and it is with great pride that the household moves from Walmgate to the white stone edifice of the Archbishop's Palace.

According to Hastings, the celebratory banquet has taken some time to organise. 'As steward, the earl is not merely presiding over affairs; he has arranged them, and from what I've gleaned, it's set to be the finest sight north of Westminster.'

And the chamberlain, as usual, is accurately informed. Warwick's hand is in everything, from ceremonial to culinary: from heads of cattle penned for slaughter to fresh fish and carcasses of game which roll in by the cartload. From his window at the palace, Richard watches them arrive from the game parks at Sheriff Hutton, the fishgarths of the Ouse, and the depths of the earl's great wine cellars. This could indeed be Westminster, or Windsor, or any of the king's establishments: the forthcoming enthronement as good as a crowning.

Leaning over the casement, Richard observes the laboured snorts of carthorses, the flushed faces of kitchen boys. 'Here, Simon, come and see.'

The boy, beating gowns and doublets in preparation for the morrow, sets the garments aside and joins him at the window. 'I spoke to one of the chamber grooms earlier, Your Grace. There are to be so many guests, pavilions are being set up in the palace grounds.'

Richard nudges him. 'Then you must ensure you get a fair serving yourself. You've earned it.'

A flurry at the casement opposite, a squeal as the window is unlatched, and a mass of chestnut curls spills out, buoyed by the wind.

'Richard!' Isabel waves, then points to the courtyard below. 'Is this not splendid?'

Returning the wave, he cups his hands to his mouth. 'Indeed, Cousin.'

Straining to hear, she inches over the sill, blue silk snagging. 'So splendid that people will imagine the king is here.'

Another head appears. Anne acknowledges him with a curt nod before scanning the scene below.

'Look!' Isabel giggles as a larderer's boy struggles under the weight of a great yoke, herons, capons, and plovers wobbling as he hurries towards the kitchens.

Unsure how he is supposed to conduct a conversation across a heaving space, Richard retreats into shadow.

'We three are to be seated together on the morrow, Richard,' Isabel yells over the din. 'Did you know?'

Richard's position at table has been well considered; the unrivalled view through the ancient arch and into the hall proper providing a magnificent demonstration of Neville grandeur. George Neville, Chancellor of England, now Archbishop of York, is seated on the dais, stiff in embroidered cope and shimmering mitre. He's like a papal father of ancient time, an idol hung with votive gifts. He could even be Saint Peter, gazing down benignly upon the whole company of Heaven.

Beneath him, narrow tables are draped with laundered linen,

adorned by golden plate, enamelled bowls and jewelled salts. Airless from the heat of innumerable candles, the hall pulses to the sound of tabor and pipe. Warwick, steward for the day, is a flash of sanguine silk, ordering, directing, baton in hand, navigating the hall like a burst of flame. His brother John, Northumberland's new-made earl, acts as treasurer; collecting alms and dealing coin into piles to distribute to the poor. Hastings is comptroller, overseeing the carver, the cup bearer, the keepers of the cupboard. Each server is a person of rank, and notwithstanding Edward's contribution of sixty royal esquires, the feast can rival anything the king himself could provide. Our cousin, Richard thinks, is making a point: under the canopy of estate, at the head of the most elaborate feast this side of Bruges, sits not an emperor nor a king but a Neville. His own tenure in Warwick's household, he's coming to understand, will be more than a training in the arts of war. As well as an acquisition of knightly skills, it will prove a novitiate in the art of ancestral pride.

Seated beside his sister, the Duchess of Suffolk, he swelters in his Burgundian velvets. Wedded whilst he was still in the nursery, Elizabeth is unfamiliar but keen to renew their acquaintance. Foremost of the ladies at table, she wears crimson silk and gold brocade, perspiration running the length of her neck and down her blue-veined breast. Imploring him to remember her, she produces stories of a youthful Edward, of a toddling, squealing, infant George. He searches his sister's face and finds vague traces of their mother in the upturned nose and rosebud mouth, but however hard he tries, he can't remember her. Any memories are the false ones she seeks to create; her familial anecdotes, snatches of a world he is too young to recall. But although she remains a stranger, Elizabeth can at least remember their father, and for that, he values her company.

The company which faces him across the crisp white linen, however, is of a rather different kind. As predicted, Isabel Neville, with her charm and dimples, and her youthful, sharp-eyed sister are too close for comfort, and under their constant gaze, his every move proves maladroit. Reaching for the salt, he spills innumerable grains upon the pristine cloth.

'Try not to worry, Cousin.' Isabel, reaching across the table, rests her hand on his long enough for his cheeks to grow shamefully warm. 'Though spilling salt is said to call down evil luck, I can't say I believe it. After all, if Judas really did spill salt at the Lord's table, you must agree that this was far from being his greatest sin.'

'Of course,' Richard agrees, 'but neither is clumsiness to be applauded.'

The earl's elder daughter unnerves him, not simply because she's flirtatious, but because she fetches up feelings that are new and disconcerting. Today, she shines in rose silk brocade, cuffs tightly fashioned and buttoned with seed pearls. Afraid to look her in the face, he fails in good manners, but books of etiquette don't allow for the wiles of such as Isabel Neville, nor instruct the reader on the act of blushing and the best ways to avoid it. His accident with the salt elicits no comment from her sister, who merely dips her bread and eyes him with disdain.

Isabel leans in, wafting musk. 'You know what Father said whilst he was planning this? That if the queen's relatives choose to demonstrate their power to the world, then they must prepare to witness that of the Nevilles.' Plunging her spoon into a hot custard tart, she tuts as its sweet centre bursts over her fingers. 'I hope the king doesn't regret giving the See of York to Uncle George.'

'Why would he? I'm sure His Grace seeks to reward your father and his brothers for their loyalty, and defence of the Borders.'

Isabel seems pleased with his response. 'And they've indeed served him well. Tell me, Richard, how do you find the queen and her ladies? They say she's a beauty and has a hoard of sisters.'

What kind of a question is that? Squirming, he wishes himself away from the table, with Warwick, or with Hastings, performing their duties around the hall, far from this silken trap of ineptness and embarrassment.

'The queen has many siblings,' he concedes, 'this is true.'

'But is she fair, in her person?'

'She is said to be.'

'But what do you think, Cousin?' Isabel tilts her head: the perfect coquette. 'Do you bow to her beauty?'

'Please, Isabel, cease teasing His Grace.' Northumberland's

countess rescues him with a charming smile and sugared dates. 'I imagine you will be presented to the queen soon enough, my girl; then you may decide for yourself.'

Anne takes a date and nibbles it, like the squirrel she seems so fond of petting. Having wiped her fingers, her head shoots up. 'I, too, have a question for our cousin.'

Richard meets the child's forthright gaze. This girl may resemble her mother, but the determined set of her mouth, the penetrating stare, come straight from her father.

When he invites her to continue, she says, 'Which, Cousin, do you consider the finest: the queen's coronation feast or this, given in honour of my uncle?'

An impossible question to answer. To speak of the richness and elegance of the queen's feast would be to cast a pall over today's celebration, yet to extol the Neville banquet would be to insult Edward. Truly, both are of a kind, and he tells her so. She nods with no attempt at artifice. Pealing a slice of coney meat from the point of her knife, she pops it in her mouth.

Richard stares at his plate. If a spy has been installed at table, it will not be Elizabeth, the sister he barely knows. It will not be Northumberland's countess, whose main concern is that they sample every dish that is served to them. No, if Warwick has inducted a spy, it will be one of his daughters, and for all her teasing smiles and secret whispers, Richard knows it will not be Isabel.

The one who will scurry to her father's side, who will assure him that his efforts today rival even those of the king, will be his favourite. It will be Anne.

Chapter Eleven

October – November 1465
Middleham

*I*N LONDON and York, he is the brother of a king. Here, he's merely a henxman, one of many. The rules which apply to his fellows apply equally to him. Seated together at mealtimes, they share a chamber at night. They train together, ride together, acquire the arts of singing, dancing, of serving at table. He's learning to hunt, he's learning to harp, early to rise and early to bed. Once a week, Warwick consults with his tutors, but although his cousin has the power to beat him, Richard has yet to feel the sting of the birch. It is administered to others, he knows that; he's witnessed the shrieks, the tears, the bruises of the unfortunates. If Warwick is sparing him, he wishes he wouldn't. Favouritism breeds contempt.

That said, friends are not so hard to find, and one evening after supper, Robert Percy, fellow henxman—a mass of auburn hair and freckles—seeks him out for a game of merrills. He wonders whether Percy acts at Warwick's behest. At the age of almost two score years, friendship with a boy seven years his junior may not be something Percy would have considered of his own accord. Whatever the case, Richard agrees to the game and helps Percy in arranging the pieces.

Conversation slips in, between the movement of wooden men and the strategy behind it. They speak of weapons, books, and Roman military tactics and soon settle on matters of blood.

'My family are cousins of the northern Percies,' Robert says. 'But whilst they fought for Lancaster, my father remained true to

York. He was captured at Sandal, with your sire the duke, but his life spared.' His voice trails away as if he fears Richard should think ill of his father for remaining alive whilst his own had perished.

'You're fortunate,' Richard tells him. 'God smiled on you.'

Perhaps, he thinks, Robert Percy is not truly fortunate. The other pages say he is a widower, despite his youth, that he had a wife who died in childbed and left him with a son. Percy has not seen fit to mention either dead wife or living child, and for his sake, Richard stays clear of the subject.

Drawing the conversation back to the board, he says, 'My brother, the king, excels at board games, particularly fox and geese.'

Percy eyes his black counters, set in a neat line at his opponent's elbow. 'And you, yourself, show like aptitude.'

Richard snorts. He supposes the others think Percy a sycophant, currying favour with the Duke of Gloucester in order to impress the earl. He doesn't want to make life difficult for his friend and tells him so.

'The earl takes men as he finds them, Your Grace,' Percy assures him. 'To find favour with him, I should have to do so upon my own merit.'

It sounds like something Edward would say. 'Call me Richard. It's easier that way.'

His smile is returned. 'Are you settling in?'

'I think so.' A swift glance shows their companions busy with dice, knucklebones, and the petting of hounds. 'It's difficult to know what is expected,' Richard says. 'King's brother, or earl's page. If I seek their friendship too eagerly, they may consider me false. Too reticent, they'll think me proud.'

'I find that to be oneself is always the best policy.' Percy captures one of his pieces and beams in triumph. 'Your move, Richard.'

Headings. The very word fills him with repugnance, but his cousin's order, received after supper, is explicit. Dawn. The practice yard. Preferably on an empty stomach.

Awake and restless, Richard watches the night light cast pulsing shadows onto striped hangings. In childhood, he and George would transform such shadows into fearsome creatures. The hump of the bedcurtains: Leviathan, the sea monster. A standing candlestick: the fork of Satan. But where the horrors of their imagination would dissipate by morning, tonight's morbid fears will be realised at first light.

His presence at tomorrow's event must be intended as a further test: a means to assess his courage as he stands in a yard full of bloodied straw and spews his guts on the filthy earth.

When he does sleep, he dreams about his father. About his father, and about Warwick, faces shimmering, bobbing as if emerging from water: drowning men rising from the sea at dead of night. He tells them, as if they didn't know, that all three of them are named Richard, and isn't that a strange thing? *One, two, three*: a voice, he cannot tell whose, counts aloud. The faces of his father and cousin slowly merge. It's difficult to tell them apart until Warwick's visage moves close, eyes bloodshot and staring. '*Four,*' he says, '*for my own father, Salisbury, was so named.*' '*Mine also,*' his father says, '*Cambridge. He lost his head.*' The faces fade, but his father's voice remains, reverberating like a bell in the depth of his ear: *Remember, my son, you are simply one of many.*

The practice yard has been cleared; no quintains today, no butts, no boys, no weapons, just a wooden block and plenty of straw. Castle guards mill about, flexing their shoulders, avoiding each other's eyes. One hawks, spits, glances towards the inner bailey, but there's nothing to see. Not yet. Even before he arrived at Middleham, Richard knew this day would come. Warwick had told him on the road north. Stray Lancastrians, remnants of those taken at Hexham, rounded up by his brother John and sent here for despatch, their fellows having already met their fates in this place a year since. Why could these hapless souls not have died with them? If they had, he wouldn't be here now, curling his toes, clenching his teeth, each moment akin to a year's duration.

His cousin keeps him close, on a raised dais opposite the block. Warwick's presence is immutable, and there's little chance of Richard escaping. The boy has fetched his beads but is unsure when to tell them. Are they obliged to pray for the souls of the condemned? Or are such sacred duties left to their kin?

'It won't take long, boy,' Warwick says. 'It never does.'

The yard throbs with an eerie silence. No sound, even from the henxmen, huddled en masse by the far wall. None have witnessed a spectacle like this, not even Robert Percy, who stands tall and grim-visaged in the midst of them. Richard catches his eye. With a curt nod, Percy turns his attention to a puddle in the centre of the yard, a product of the recent rains. One gangling youth, new to the household and more reserved than most, draws patterns in the mud with the toe of his boot. Warwick's head jerks as he spies the movement. Percy, entrusted with keeping order, nudges the youth with the side of his foot.

We're fortunate, Richard thinks, that these are to be headings only and not the full horror of a traitor's death. Were that the case, ladders would be fixed to the walls, the prisoners fastened to the rungs, facing their tormentors. There would be knives for disembowelment and a brazier close by for the burning of entrails. Considered that way, his cousin is right; this morning's events should be simple and swift.

A menacing rhythm erupts. A man with a tabor is the first out, leading a grim procession. Tasting sour bile, Richard swallows it down. He thinks, why do we need drums? To increase the prisoners' fear? To hide their quaking squeals? Or to give the rest of us something to do in counting the beats?

Four men lurch, blinking, into the early sunlight. Dressed in shirt and hose, they wear their bruises like brands; where an elbow has accidentally scuffed a cheek, a fist grazed an eye. A sergeant forces them into line, jostling one man against another. One of them turns, spits into the sergeant's face, and a swift kick is delivered in retaliation. The prisoner crumples, is hauled up again.

Already, Richard knows he shall not be able to face this. If the men were to be run through or felled by arrows, he's sure he could watch, could hold himself together. But the separation of head from shoulders will be impossible to bear. At least there is a block, and the heads will fall directly to the earth. George once spoke of executions, said prisoners could be forced to kneel upright, heads struck off with such force that they would shoot like missiles into the crowd. Richard hopes that today, the heads will be collected and disposed of. Hopes they will be buried with the bodies.

'Richard?' A hand squeezes his shoulder, 'All well, boy?'

'Yes, Cousin.'

At least a chaplain has been provided. The black-robed figure moves along the line, shriving, blessing, committing souls to God. Warwick's hand remains in place as the first man is hauled to the block. Richard's leg jerks as the axe is raised, and watery light strikes the blade. The whistle—sharp and swift—takes him by surprise. He baulks at the crushing, squelching sound, at the blood which pumps and flows like a hideous fountain.

A palpable tremor flickers through the crowd, and Richard lowers his head for the passing of the man's soul. Across the yard, henxmen shuffle their feet, cross themselves, and whisper behind their hands. The youth who dragged his toes swipes his cheek with a tremulous finger. When it comes away blood-splashed, he hunches forward and vomits.

Richard's relief is tangible but short-lived. The guards are busy, gathering up the remains of what, but moments ago, had been a life. It's nothing now, just a mess. A violent shudder overtakes him.

'Steady, boy.'

'I can't—'

'This is justice. For your father and for mine. Each time the axe falls, you must tell yourself that.'

Another whistle of steel, another crumpled mess. Richard tries to see it numerically, an act of subtraction: two dead, two to go. If this is indeed a test, then his cousin can be under no illusion, must be able to sense the boy's fear, the bones knocking together beneath his skin. More sawdust is heaped around the block, and a third body hauled onto the waiting cart. Now, only one remains.

When all is done, the rebels are taken for Christian burial on the edge of the churchyard: each body, as Richard hoped, united with its head. Silence descends, the air thick with the stench of blood and entrails. Stable grooms appear carrying buckets, the same vessels they use to muck out the horses. All eyes turn to the earl, waiting for his signal. When leave is granted, the crowd fragments without a word. Percy, pale and pensive, gives Richard a solemn nod, then nudges the snivelling henxmen back to the west range.

Richard isn't ready to follow. Instead, he hovers at Warwick's side, the earl's solid, stoical presence a thing of comfort. 'This was justice, was it not, Cousin?'

'Yes, Richard.' Warwick casts a brooding eye towards the heavens. 'Justice.'

With little desire for merrills, he suspects Percy feels the same. But there's an hour to kill after supper, and they both need something to do. Many of the henxmen gloat over the morning's events, boasting of how they barely flinched, how they anticipated every blow of the axe with eager fascination, cheering as heads rolled and bodies exsanguinated on matted straw. None of it's true. Every boy had recoiled as the blade cut the air, dropping their eyes or raising an arm in order to shield their faces. And as for cheering, the only sounds had been the intonation of the chaplain, the feverish confessions of the condemned.

When Warwick's man appears at Richard's elbow, the game, half-heartedly pursued, is almost concluded. 'A message from the earl, my lord of Gloucester. You are invited to attend him in his privy chamber.'

Percy counts his captured pieces and lines them up in a neat row. 'I can leave the board set up if you wish.'

Richard shakes his head. 'I shouldn't bother. I've but three men left and look set to lose even those. I can't set my mind to it tonight, Rob. Consider yourself the victor.' Making every effort to smile, he adds. 'I trust this shan't take long.'

He picks his way across the floor through groups of sprawling boys and their habitual games of knucklebones. It's all very well for them, he thinks; they don't have a cousin with rigid expectations. Belly lurching, he follows the earl's man down the tight spiral and out into the bailey. Kitchen boys are throwing out slops, bandying jests, sniggering. As he approaches, they fall silent, snatching caps and bobbing knees. The air is cool, pungent with the scent of verdure and horse dung, birds chirruping in the violet dusk. A solitary crow swoops from the keep, hops across the earth in the clumsy, jerking manner of his breed, then takes off again in the direction of the practice yard. If he goes in search of carrion, Richard thinks, then he's too late.

He should have fetched a cloak. It's so much colder here in the land of the Nevilles, plagued as it is with a perpetual wind sweeping from the moors and striking like a whiplash. He shivers, wondering why Warwick has hauled him from what little comfort there is to be had on such a dismal evening. To draw conclusions on the day's events? To tell him he has failed?

Torchlight bobs on towering stone as they mount the steps to the keep. Challenged twice in the ascent, he could be at Westminster, and Warwick a king at the heart of the labyrinth. Surely, he thinks, it's the dread of the moment that gives this impression, the creeping suffocation of growing darkness, the brilliance of the wind-torn flames. Warwick is my cousin and my tutor; he is not my sovereign.

The hall door creaks as they slip inside, the space within sombre and quiet in the semi-darkness. Trestles have been stacked away; the central hearth banked down. A single candelabrum guides them towards the privy chamber, where a shaft of light oozes beneath the door like a pool of melting butter. Voices can be heard as Warwick bids his family goodnight. Richard has no time for Isabel, for her teasing, glimmering looks, still less for her sister's probing eye. Not tonight, with his belly still pitching and the echoes of the axe still pulsing in his brain.

'His Grace of Gloucester.'

He steps into the inner sanctum. Rich with the tang of oranges, the glowing interior reveals the remains of an intimate supper:

empty cups, discarded nutshells, fruit peel, pastry crumbs. Two boys, poised in the corner with pipe and lute, continue to play despite his arrival. The countess and her daughters sink to the floor in a sea of velvet.

Warwick dismisses them with a hasty blessing, the relief of their departure moulded on his face in an air of quiet contentment. 'Women,' he waves in the direction of the door, 'speak of nothing but trifles.'

Richard, thinking of his mother and sister, is unable to agree. Taking the stool that is offered, he finds it still warm.

With a quiet belch, the earl reclines, legs outstretched and crossed at the ankles. 'I wondered how you'd take it. Watching a man die in cold blood is far harder than taking his life on the field. When a soldier slays an adversary, the blood lust is on him, and he's blind to the act. Occasions like today are not easy to observe for any of us.'

What is he saying, Richard wonders, that I'm as brave as any other youth or as craven as most?

'I know,' Warwick says, 'that today's events were particularly difficult for you. However, you did well, you proved yourself.'

Richard shifts on his stool. Compliments sit awkwardly; they always have. Word he has done well invites him to do better. Doing better proves he's yet to do his best. And he must do his best, he promised. Searching for something to say, he glances about him.

The chamber, like the York townhouse, is hung with cloths of green and gold, further depictions of sumptuous gardens and leafy forest glades. Where one would have expected a battle scene, the martyrdom of a saint, Warwick wallows in the shades of the outdoors, sprinkles his rush mats with hyssop and thyme. Richard feels they are encamped for the night in the open, that beyond the glowing pools of light lie miles of deepest woodland, sprawling heathland or rolling meadows. It makes for a strange yet welcome intimacy.

Deep in the hearth, a faggot falls, cracks, sparks flare.

With a gentle cough, Warwick tugs at his earlobe. 'After your father lost his life, my own was dragged from the field a prisoner, taken to Pontefract, and executed the following day. I was at your brother's side as we rode to York in the wake of Palmsunday Field, stood with him at the Micklelith as he ordered the heads to be taken down. Nothing I'd seen on the field prepared me for that moment: the heads of father, uncle, brother and cousin impaled and displayed as trophies of war. The fact that they're no longer there does little to halt the memory. It returns each time I ride through that gate, impressed on my brain like Saint Michael on a struck coin. What I'm trying to tell you is that I know how it feels. I understand.'

Taken off guard, words bubble up. 'Edward says I shouldn't dwell on the past,' Richard tells him, 'that I should offer it due reverence, but pass on, think ahead, to the future. He says that's the way to best serve our father.'

'But that's not your way, is it, boy? You're a thinker, a ponderer. And there's naught amiss in reverencing your father, as long as the memories serve to drive you on and not to hold you back.' Warwick raises the cup he's been nursing and drains it to the dregs. 'Duty was what guided your father. Duty to his family and to the realm. And he always held true to himself, to the principles he upheld. Never shied away from speaking the truth, even when he knew it may be dangerous to do so. As in the end, it proved.'

A lithe body slips from the shadows; one of the earl's hounds padding towards the hearth, sleek flanks catching the light. It sinks down, jaws snapping in a yawn, content with the caress of its master's palm.

'I'm a fellow of little patience,' Warwick says. 'In my opinion, life's too short. But your father's forbearance was a trait that bound men to him. Loyalty and fairness were the marks of the man.'

'Thank you, sir. I—'

A tight smile and the subject is closed. 'I'm pleased with you, Richard. You're learning. And to prove my pleasure, I'm giving you a youth to act as squire: the youngest son of Thomas Parr. The father was a good man, loyal, fought with both of our own fathers at Sandal. Edward thought much of him, as did I. The son, I believe, though a little older than you, is cut from the same cloth.'

Richard pictures the new addition to the household: the shuffling figure who'd swiped blood from his cheek and puked in the practice yard.

The earl smiles as the hound makes another play for his hand and licks his fingers with its lolling tongue. 'Tom needs a friend, as well as a master, someone to reassure him. I'd say you were well suited to the task.'

Margaret is to marry. News arrives with George's letter, and if anyone is to know, it's him, lingering in the shadows, sneaking up stairwells, ears cocked.

Don Pedro is Constable of Portugal and nephew of their former hostess, Duchess Isabella of Burgundy. But this, George adds, is not all, 'The prospective bridegroom is a contender for the throne of Aragon, so it may be that, in time, our sister will become *Reina Margarita*. The Duchess Isabella urges the match, and our brother is in agreement.' George hopes, however, that the marriage may be preceded by a long betrothal. 'If Margaret is to leave, then I would fain have you return in the mean season. I know that our cousin favours a French match for our sister, but I am uncertain as to whom.' It's typical of George to have more knowledge of the earl's business than those who share his household.

Richard refolds the letter. Margaret, a bride? The thought is disconcerting: the breaking of a circle that has existed since he was born. Uncomfortable in letting her go, he pictures the three of them slipping the anchor which has held them together and sailing slowly away, each in their own direction.

Unlike George, Edward rarely writes, but the messages he does send are treasured for that very reason. When the sporadic notes arrive, Richard slips them inside his Psalter. Were they placed in his clothes chest alongside George's, the inks may shift and blur, words may creep across the paper, mixing and mingling in a confusion of sentiments. And so, he keeps his brothers' missives apart, like his feelings, like the love he bears for both.

Filthy and aching from weaponry practice, the bath forms a welcome prelude to supper in Warwick's chamber. Thomas Parr, quiet and purposeful, helps Richard from his grubby shirt while Kyngston sets to, hanging sheets around the tub and scenting the water.

His cousin has been right about Tom. Six months older than Richard, he is a conscientious youth, and Simon has shown no manner of resentment at sharing his duties with him. That is only right. George's boys compete for his favour, but Richard cannot hold with that. If squires fail to help each other, they're unlikely, in turn, to give good service to their master.

'Hurry, Tom, or the water will cool. I hate a tepid bath.'

With no response forthcoming, he glances over his shoulder, finds Parr shuffling from foot to foot, Kyngston quietly folding linens.

'Tom? If you can't untie my points, just say. I'm not too proud to fend for myself.'

Parr looks up, cherubic. 'Your Grace, forgive me, but I wondered whether you knew of your injury.'

'My injury?'

A curse as Kyngston drops a towel, apologises. Parr looks to him for support, but the younger boy keeps his head down.

Richard considers the events of the practice yard, tries to recall each blow, each thrust of blunt weaponry. Surely, there can be nothing but bruises. 'You say there's a wound?'

'No wound, Your Grace.' Parr's voice wavers. 'What I mean is, your shoulder blade. Perhaps it's time to consult a surgeon.'

'A surgeon?' Flexing his shoulders, Richard makes exploratory circling motions. 'What are you talking about?'

Kyngston casts the towels aside and joins Parr in a show of fellowship. 'Your Grace, this is not new, but I agree with Tom. It appears to be getting worse.'

Bewildered, Richard lashes out, 'So, whatever it is, you've

noticed it before, but only now, when Tom points it out, do you choose to mention it?'

'Please, Lord Richard, I thought it impolite. As you never make reference to it yourself, I imagined you knew but put no store by it.'

None of this makes sense, but Kyngston's face, scarlet against the flat yellow of his hair, reveals that neither he nor his fellow are lying.

A knot forms in Richard's gut. 'And you, Tom?'

'May it please Your Grace, I thought the same at first. I thought…'

'What? You thought what? Don't seek to keep anything from me, either of you.'

Kyngston kneels, as well he might, given his experience of George's swift palm. 'My lord, I pray you, don't blame Tom. It was my duty to tell you, but it didn't seem right to speak of so personal a thing when you yourself made no mention. It seemed I would transgress. But Tom speaks true: your shoulder blade has sustained an injury in recent months. It looks…well, it looks wrong.'

Both can't be lying. 'Which side? Right or left?'

'The right, Your Grace.' Kyngston kneads his bonnet between clumsy fists while Parr fixes his master with a clear blue gaze, innocent as a chorister at Mass.

'Does it pain you, Your Grace?'

Impatient, Richard lets out a sigh. 'No, Tom. That's why I cannot understand what you're telling me.'

They do their best, fetch a looking glass and a smaller mirror of beaten metal in the hope that between them, he may catch sight of what they are compelled to reveal. But it's no good; a man cannot see the reflection of his own back, and if his shoulder is cast awry as they say, then the proof of it escapes him. Whatever the severity, it can only be conveyed to him second-hand. Exactly what he's always hated: reliance upon others to tell him the truth. Because, as he knows, sometimes they don't.

'The earl's physician is a good man,' Kyngston says. 'When my lord of Clarence suffered stomach cramps, the earl sent the man across London to attend him; a plaster of anise and wormwood made up for the duke's belly. The pain was gone by morning.'

Well-intentioned as he is, the boy is not helping. 'Tom, you say the shoulder blade looks out of place?'

'Yes, Your Grace. When you stoop.'

Richard gropes blindly, feels nothing but smooth skin pulled taught over bone: a shoulder blade like any other. But in bending forward, those same tentative fingers encounter a blade that rises up to greet them. So, it's true: something is amiss.

'Can we do aught to help you, sir?' Parr clasps his hands together as if initiating a prayer. Richard feels a sudden pity for him, for both of them, for their embarrassment and awkwardness. Should they be revealing such a fact to George, they would be wearing the brand of his boot on their backsides.

Straightening, he thanks them. 'No, but until I decide what to do, you must not speak of it to anyone. Swear it. Now.'

Chapter Twelve

December 1465
Middleham

A YORKSHIRE winter. On the ride north, his cousin and Fitzhugh had exchanged cheerful jests of how Richard's southern childhood, the damp landscape of the Marches would have done little to prepare him for the turn of the season. They bade him think of a frozen Thames, of a snow-covered Ludlow, of Fotheringhay when the ice melts and the rising Nene floods the fields, and to add all three together. That, they said, spells the essence of winter in the northern dales. He knows now what they meant.

At Middleham, a piercing wind presages snow. On the Feast of Saint Lucy, candles burn throughout the day, skies darken, and solitary flakes herald a fierce blizzard. The castle feels suddenly small, confining. Unable to ride or hunt, they're captives of a capricious foe from whom it is impossible to extract any reasonable terms.

Warwick assures him this is a regular occurrence, that a thaw will set in only when God sees fit. He speaks of Palmsunday Field, how he and their kinsmen had fought beside the king, ankle-deep in snow. In the north, he tells Richard, even Holy Week can be a continuation of winter.

'And now we have a peaceful border,' the earl says, turning to matters he can control, as opposed to those he can't, 'your brother has cause to be grateful.'

A leonine smile reflects his pleasure at his recent negotiations in Newcastle. Not only did he return home before the weather turned, he and his brothers have brokered a truce with the Scots for the duration of fifty years. The king is delighted, and Warwick's reward is the tutelage of a rich but pimply youth.

The wardship of Francis Lord Lovell is a great and generous prize, and when Warwick speaks of it, he chooses to call Edward 'the king' and not simply 'your brother.' It pleases Richard to see his cousin happy: to hear him offer praise and thanks to Edward. This is how it should be.

When the boy is presented, Warwick marks Richard's reception of him. 'As Lord Lovell is to train in the household, much like yourself, Your Grace. I thought you might take him under your wing.'

'Of course,' Richard tries to sound reassuring. 'And there's no better tutor than my cousin, the earl. I've already learnt a deal from him.' It will be gratifying to have the boy look up to him. For once, he thinks, I shan't be the youngest.

Lovell makes a formal bow, his features plain and unassuming: square face, brown eyes, a wide yet gentle grin. His gown is of the finest cut, but his bonnet is over-sized, threatening to blind him at any moment.

Richard warms to the boy immediately. 'Tell me, Francis, are you skilled at chess?'

Another bow, gracious and well-rehearsed, yet the lop-sided smile is distinctly honest. 'No, Your Grace. That is, not yet, but I'm learning.'

'Then it would be a pleasure to help you hone your skills. It takes a decent partner to make the game interesting.'

Warwick's mouth twitches, yielding to an expression of genuine delight. Sucked in by the warmth of it, Richard nudges the boy. 'When your game improves, we can make a wager on it, if you will.'

'Agree at your peril, Lord Lovell,' Warwick says. 'His Grace of Gloucester plays a deft game. You'll require a deal of practice before you embark upon such a wager with him. I lost a noble before I left for the Borders, and there's little likelihood of my winning it back.'

Not strictly true, Richard thinks, and Warwick knows it. What is lacking on his cousin's part is not skill but patience. An evening at the board, without the chance to stretch his legs, the opportunity for deep conversation, is not a thing Warwick relishes. When last they played, the earl had made a deliberate mistake in order to force things to a conclusion. Chess, merrills, fox and geese: all are trivialities to him. If he were moving people around a board instead of wooden pieces, well, it has to be said, that would be a vastly different matter.

Lovell, he learns, is without a father. The event recent, the obit still to be observed, yet the boy himself seems resigned to his fate. There again, Lovell's father died in his bed. Perhaps, Richard thinks, that makes a difference.

He feels compelled to probe. 'What ailed him?'

'A fever.' Lovell's eyes remain dry, cheeks smooth and pink as a babe's. 'His physician said he was choleric, but no amount of damp cloths seemed to help. My mother tried, of course, sitting by his bed each night and ministering to him.' He shrugs. 'He received only the best of treatments. His surgeon never bled him if the planets were awry or anything of that kind.'

'I understand you have no brothers.'

'None. Merely sisters, Joan—and Frideswide. The saint upheld my mother in her travail,' Lovell says, by way of explanation, 'she would have perished otherwise.'

'It is good to have sisters.'

Lovell shows little opinion either way. 'If you say so.'

The countess' women are handing round sugared dragées. Thrusting one in his mouth, Richard offers the dish to the boy. Lovell selects one with care, turning it over in his fingers.

'Don't worry,' Richard jests, 'they're not the medicinal kind. The earl would not have us belch in front of the ladies.'

George would have guffawed at this, elaborating on the jest until they both sniggered crudely, but Lovell remains quiet, sucking in silence.

Warwick has told him that John Lovell supported King Harry,

that when Richard's father returned from Ireland with an army to fight for his life, Lovell had defended London against him. Yet Richard holds no malice; the boy has lost his father and known but eight summers. Merciful saints, he knows how that feels.

Glancing the length of the chamber, he observes the seated earl, swathed in firelight, hands locked across his belly. His younger daughter sits at his feet, reading aloud. That is what Margaret will be doing, Richard thinks. While the Thames freezes beyond the confines of Baynard's, his sister will be perched at their mother's side, relating the Scriptures.

A sudden pang, sharp and swift, squeezes his heart then is gone.

Armies do not march in winter or, despite his family's bitter experience, would not choose to. War is made in spring, when the months stretch out, when the call of birds can sing a man to sleep on a battlefield and wind-blown blossoms shower his corpse. Yet, regardless of the season, they must continue weaponry practice.

'None can know the hour.' Their tutor is keen on quoting Scripture, making ill-matched comparisons, and twisting texts to suit his needs. 'The weather cannot be controlled nor conquered. When we face our enemies, we must be able to fight, whether God sends us sun, hail or blizzards. If you would fight for your king, you must learn to do so in fair weather and in foul.'

Richard's pitched, for the first time, against Robert Percy. An unfair match: Percy's developing muscles against Richard's slight but sinewy limbs. Stripping them down to their shirts, few would be foolish enough to wager upon his own scrawny carcass. Strip them to the skin, even fewer would take the risk.

'Our brother, Edmund, was skinny like you,' Edward had told him in Placentia days. 'Yet by fifteen, he was a worthy opponent.'

Fifteen. Two years seems far too long to wait, and if wagers have indeed been placed today, those who speculated on Percy must be revelling in the weight of their purses.

Harness squealing, they return to the armoury, Richard taking care that none but Parr and Kyngston should divest him. The injury is still apparent, or so they tell him, but he can still recall no accident, fall, strain, or wrench of the body that should have left its mark. He encounters pain like every other henxman, in buttocks, shoulders, thighs, in the muscles that run from armpit to breast, that span the ribcage and bolster the spine. They come, and they go, yet the anomaly remains, and he is no closer to understanding the reason why.

His instructor compliments him with a firm grasp of the hand. 'Well done, Your Grace, you are improving,'

Weaponry tutors are paid to encourage, and this man, it has to be acknowledged, is trying his best.

'Cousin Richard?' Isabel's fingers coil around his, their grip strong as twine.

Watery light filtering through leaded diamonds splashes on the polished floor of the countess' private solar. The chamber has been cleared, the henxmen in their scented livery, paired with her women in logical fashion. Percy, taller than most, is placed with the eldest and stoutest of the ladies; Lovell, the shortest, with the youngest female present, the Lady Anne. Musicians, purloined from Warwick's troupe, gather with flute and shawm while Raulin Gifford, dancing master, strikes the boards with his wand to still the chatter.

'The basse dance, my lords and ladies. You know the steps. Let us begin.'

Isabel flashes an impish smile. 'Remember to point your toes, Cousin.'

'Naturally. As Master Gifford says, we all know the steps.' Accustomed to her teasing, Richard has learnt to reciprocate. 'But it's Lovell I'm concerned for; your sister tolerates little error. Look at him, poor boy.'

It could be Warwick himself leading Lovell around the floor. For every mistimed bobbing of the knee, each misdirected bow, the boy receives a testy glance more meaningful than any rebuke.

'Father would have us shine at court,' Isabel says, 'and she wishes to please him. Our father's opinion matters greatly to Anne.'

At the tap-tapping of Gifford's wand, the music dies away. 'My lords, your partners have the better of you; they show you to be clumsy and ill-fashioned.'

Anne nods to Lovell, brows drawn together in her narrow little face.

'Whereas you, Cousin, are improving,' Isabel says, playful. He waits for the sting, but it is not forthcoming.

After three repetitions, they're allowed to rest, Gifford demonstrating an obeisance so low that Richard fears the man may tumble. Conscious of stooping, his own bow is less measured as he follows Isabel to where the countess perches on a heap of cushions, surrounded by her ladies. Anne is there already, feet tucked neatly beneath her, Lovell picking threads from his hose and flicking them to the floor.

'How is the dancing at court, Richard?' Isabel sinks at her mother's feet.

Hand still warm from her grip, Richard knows that if he held it to his face, it would smell of rosewater. 'I wouldn't know.'

'Why not?' Anne: head cocked, direct as ever.

'I'm surprised, Cousin,' Isabel says, 'for you're a natural dancer, the most graceful youth in the room.'

Both girls erupt into fits of laughter; Isabel's like tinkling water. Covering her face, she peers through her fingers while her sister stares at him pointedly with wide brown eyes. 'Does the king dance?'

'Of course. He enjoys it.'

'When the queen is delivered, there shall be great celebration at court,' Isabel says. 'The king has requested our father stand as godsib to the child.'

'If the child is male,' Anne says, visibly proud, 'I expect he shall be named Richard, in honour of him. Did our father stand as godsib to you, Cousin?'

'I believe so.' It's difficult to imagine himself a squalling babe in Warwick's arms, slavering and hiccupping over the earl's rich damasks. 'But it is my belief that I was named for my father.'

'May God assoil him.' The countess lays a gentle hand on Richard's shoulder. She knows how it is, he tells himself. In her worship of the Beauchamp earl, she understands. The respectful silence that follows renders her daughters immature, green, and untouched by reality. Beside him, Lovell coughs.

One of the musicians has brought a tabor with him; laying aside his shawm, he tests the drum skin and practises a skittering rhythm.

'Which instrument do you play, Richard?' Isabel leans close, a curling tendril tickling his face, a feeling not unpleasant.

'I can play the flute.'

'Good. I shall teach you the lute, too. You should fare well, having such long fingers.'

Another chorus of giggles has the countess calling for silence. He wishes Margaret were here. Margaret never speaks unwisely, laughs when she shouldn't, or makes him feel foolish. How, he wonders, can Warwick have sired such frivolous girls? Perhaps the countess was frivolous when she was young and unwed. Her sagging cheeks and thickening waist make her previous self impossible to imagine.

Gifford's wand thumps the floor. Percy has been assigned a new partner. Dark hair, pale cheeks flattered by a hint of pink. A great improvement on the previous choice.

Young and markedly slender, the girl is unfamiliar; she cannot have attended Warwick's women long, else Richard would have noticed her. Her bearing reminds him of Margaret's; understated, elegant. He feels happy to watch her, to admire her movements and skill, but there are other feelings, too, feelings that a sister never incites. Heat creeps into his face as Percy lowers his head to the girl and whispers into her hair. Why such a graceful partner? Unlike him, Percy is awkward on his feet. Even now, as the couple rehearse, Percy's lurching movements mar the effect of the dance, spoiling what might have been a beautiful display. The pair are ill-matched, Richard thinks; surely Gifford should have realised that.

Isabel rises, grin both perceptive and mischievous as he leads her into the dance. 'Perhaps next time, Cousin.'

The earl excels himself over the Christmas season: plays and pageants, dancing and disguisings, wine from Bordeaux, oranges from Seville, and surreptitious gifts from the lap of French King Louis. Richard wonders about the festivities at home and whether, during the York family gatherings and court masques, anyone is wondering about him.

His cousin's generosity, his warm invitations to ride out over the snow-covered hills, have prompted a decision, and on the Feast of Saint Sylvester, after supper, Richard dares to seek him out. Twitchy and tense, he ventures to the earl's inner chamber with its habitual scent of strewn herbs.

'Ah. What is it, Richard?'

Warwick is alone, merry and in good spirits, a gilt-edged volume open on his lap. He twists in his chair, his face genial, open and peachy red in the glow from the fire.

Richard hesitates, sad and unwilling to blight his cousin's contentment. Guilt tugs at him, an unexpected sense of sorrow for the disappointment he is about to engender. What he intends to say may change Warwick's opinion of him forever. And the disenchantment, he thinks, will all be of my own making. He need in fact disclose nothing. He could stop now before he begins, plead illness, tiredness, claim that whatever he intended to say, he no longer needs to.

'Come, lad,' his cousin indicates the stool so often occupied by the countess, 'sit you down. I trust the king's letter has pleased you. The Garter is a prestigious order, and I agree with him that as your brother George is now a member, so should you be.' The smile is affectionate, genuine and elicits a rejoinder.

'The honour brings me much joy, cousin.'

The earl's laughter draws a wet snort from one of his dogs. 'Well, I should not have guessed it by your demeanour, Richard. What ails you?'

Tell him. Just tell him and get it over. 'I need to ask you, Cousin… I've sustained an injury. At least, I believe I have—'

'What manner of injury? I've heard nothing from your tutor.' The unruly brows have drawn together, deep creases scored between. 'Are you in pain?'

'No, that's the point. This doesn't pain me, but it should, surely.' Words spill from Richard's lips before he can present them in any coherent order. 'I can make no sense of it. I can't recall anything which could have caused it. I'm afraid the other boys may see, that anyone may see—'

Warwick holds up a hand, fingers splayed. 'Slow down. What injury? Where?'

Richard hesitates but realises there is very little point. 'My back. Well, my shoulder blade. I know it isn't dislocated, but it is…damaged.'

'And how does your tutor believe this came about?'

'I haven't told him.'

'You make no sense, boy. If you have sustained any hurt, then your tutor should have knowledge of it.'

Richard is almost desperate now, wants for nothing more than to turn and run. 'I haven't told him, for I can't be sure the problem was sustained in the practice yard.'

'Where, then?'

'I cannot tell.'

Warwick's gaze is both intent and earnest. 'Might I see?'

Is this not why he came here? To have his cousin look and say, with his usual aplomb, that this is nothing, a minor inconvenience, something all boys suffer when they pick up a poleaxe and learn how to swing it.

'Richard?'

When he nods his agreement, Warwick leaps to his feet. Yanking the door wide, his cousin confronts the guards. 'No interruptions. You understand?'

A heavy thud, the click of the latch, the slap-slap of leather soles, and he's back: enquiring and expectant. Richard rises and unlaces his doublet.

'Stop dithering, lad.'

Dragging the shirt over his head, Richard turns his back. Gooseflesh rising, he stares at the painted wall before him: at the bears, the griffins, the golden letter Ms for the Mother of God. He jumps at the touch of his cousin's hand, the pressure of his fingers, the skimming of rough palm over smooth skin.

Silence ensues for what seems like an age, during which Warwick coughs, but fails to utter a word. He realises now how much he had wanted his cousin to deny it, craved reassurance that all was well, that whatever he thought ailed him didn't anymore. Well then, that being the case, his cousin must see the extent of it. Richard bends forward slowly.

The earl's considered breaths tell him all he needs to know. 'My physician in London. I think you should see him.'

Richard straightens. 'Then you agree, Cousin, it is an injury?'

'No. I believe it is a condition. One I've seen before,'

'Where?' Dressing, Richard emerges from billowing linen: a swimmer breaking the surface of water. 'Who?'

'A soldier I knew, fell at Saint Albans, one of my father's retainers. In his case, the spine had become crooked, one shoulder cast higher than the other.'

'And he fought? He could still fight?'

'Yes.' Warwick nods. 'The man was certainly not lacking in strength.'

Richard fastens his shirt with trembling hands. It seems unfair that his own body is playing him false, concealing its flaws, forcing him to rely upon the opinion of others. 'This man, he was a good soldier? He served my uncle of Salisbury well?'

'Indeed. And he was a man of good spirits, accepted his lot. May I have your consent to speak to my London physician? The king wishes to see me with regard to my forthcoming embassy, so I'll leave for the capital in a week or two. As will you, for your formal investiture.' Sucking his underlip, the earl calculates. 'What say we travel together? I could arrange for a physician to visit us. The man I've in mind is excellent, skilled in many things.'

Richard needs time to think. 'Cousin, I do not wish for the

king to know.'

'You have your squires to attend you. Your brother will be none the wiser.'

'And George. I wouldn't care for George to know.'

The earl shrugs. 'The choice is yours to make. If you prefer to keep your own counsel, then I respect that. It shows tenacity.' Smiling, he lays an encouraging hand on Richard's shoulder. 'As for the physician, what do you say?'

'Thank you, Cousin. I shall see him.'

Chapter Thirteen

February 1466
London

*U*NLIKE THE York townhouse, Warwick's London home on Dowgate is entirely built of stone. Its expanse of garden and the beautifully arranged herber, after which it is named, provide a pleasant outlook from the window seat of the earl's private chamber. Had they visited in spring, Richard thinks, he should be gazing upon rows of colourful borders, a host of blossoming fruit trees. As it is, the only hint of green can be glimpsed among the box hedges: tough, spiky fronds piercing the layer of snow. He wonders how it is at Middleham, whether Warwick's daughters have braved the weather, slithering over the frozen earth in their clumsy patterns with their slender, dark-haired companion. He wonders if Percy is on hand to assist: an outstretched arm and a charming smile.

'Hurry, Roger. We need a good blaze.' Presenting his palms to the fire, Warwick nudges the bellows with a well-aimed kick.

The tousled-haired boy sets to work, bursts of ash and flakes of charred wood shooting upwards amid yellow flames. The physician is still downstairs, enjoying the earl's hospitality: warm bread and spiced wine for his trouble. Edward was right about Warwick's munificence. Their cousin's servants are the most envied in London; indeed, Roger Fogge, still pumping the bellows, is well known to Richard. He used to light pricket candles at Shene, but L'Erber, he's told Richard, offers better pay - and its Calais-born pastrycook makes better pies.

Pointing his rump towards the growing flames, Warwick dismisses the boy. 'Doctor Brocas shall be with us anon, Richard. I'm to remain here during the examination. I trust you've no objection.'

'No,' Richard says. 'None.'

'You'll need to strip to the skin.' The earl shivers at the thought. 'I trust Roger has made good with the fire.'

A rap at the door, and their visitor sweeps in: black hair, sallow skin, crimson gown bunched around his scrawny middle. The man has a smell about him, herbal compounds: sage and borage, the bright, cleansing scent of lavender. Tucked under his arm is an ancient, scuffed volume, which he places with obtrusive reverence on a side table.

'My lord of Gloucester,' the earl seems eager to proceed, 'this is Ralph Brocas. I have familiarised him with your problem. Doctor Brocas, I trust my cousin to your care.'

Warwick retreats to the hearth while Brocas scrutinises his patient with dark, glassy eyes.

'The earl has indeed spoken with me, Your Grace, so I am aware to some extent of what is troubling you. However, I must consider the bodily humours in the first instance. So, how is your appetite?'

Richard is taken off guard. 'Reasonable, I suppose.'

Brocas blinks. 'Reasonable?'

Richard feels scrutinised already. 'I don't overeat.'

The glassy eyes narrow. 'I can see that. Do you sleep well?'

'Yes.'

'What of your dreams? Are they pleasant or unpleasant? Do they trouble you?'

Something prevents Richard from expressing the full truth. Blurred visions of his father still haunt him. Sometimes, the duke is alive and happy; sometimes, he is neither. Either way, it doesn't turn the dreams into nightmares. 'I do have dreams,' he says, 'but can barely recall them by morning.'

'Good. Would you care to disrobe?'

Richard shrugs out of his doublet and shirt, folds them, lays

163

them aside, playing for time. He shivers despite the raging fire, and Brocas circles him as you would a colt at Smithfield. Lifting Richard's arms, he peers at the clefts beneath, asks him to open his mouth, to show him his teeth. Yanking his hair, he peers at his scalp, looks into his eyes and pulls down their lower lids.

'A melancholic humour, I should say, the *Articella* is clear upon this. There may be an excess of black bile, although such humours are unusual in the young.' Striding to the table, the physician consults his tome. 'My lord earl, have your apothecary make up a tincture. Valerian root is good, and yarrow. Make sure the duke eats plenty of meat when the days allow, stewed or boiled in a soup. He may wish to avoid the more pungent of the spices, but basil, cumin and sage will do him good. Fennel, too, again, in hot sauces or soups. Now, Your Grace, let me see your back.'

Richard does as he's bid; holds out his arms, raises them above his head. Finally, Brocas bids him lean forward.

'Lower. Then return to the standing position. Slowly, if you please, I must observe.'

Blood rushes to Richard's skull. Brocas bids him hold the position while he examines his body from every conceivable angle. 'You may dress now.'

Straightening, Richard wriggles into his clothes, layers of linen and velvet serving as a refuge, a way of absorbing his shame.

'The condition is not entirely uncommon,' Brocas says, 'but its cause is unknown. The problem lies with the spine.'

'But does a person recover?' Richard speaks unbidden for the first time. 'Do things return to normal?'

Brocas sniffs. 'I'm afraid not, Your Grace. As a general rule, the condition grows worse with time. At present, your shoulders are aligned, but this will not always be the case. Eventually, as the spine becomes more affected, a discrepancy will occur.' He shrugs knowingly. 'But you're young, and measures can be taken, certain treatments. The body can be stretched with ropes to help straighten the spine, or exercises can be undertaken whereby the muscles may be strengthened. Sturdy muscle, so I've heard, can help the condition. Massage with certain oils can also assist.'

The earl strokes his chin. 'And what do you personally suggest?'

'As my lord is young and the condition not far advanced, I would suggest he consider all of these possibilities. A strong body can resist the change, even if it cannot entirely prevent it.'

Warwick thanks the physician. They discuss his fee, arrange further consultations where urine will be considered and diet fully discussed in an attempt to balance the patient's cold, dry humours. Brocas leaves, and Richard retires to the window seat. He knew how it would feel once the condition was known, once it was out in the open to be studied and stared at. At first, the problem had been his own, to consider or not, as it pleased him. Now, it belongs to other people to do with as they will.

Hitching up his gown, Warwick sits beside him. 'Well, what are your views? Are you prepared to submit yourself to the treatments he suggests?'

'I should need to learn more of them before I decide.' Richard makes a grab for his cousin's sleeve. 'If Edward knew about my injury, he would give up on me.'

'I think we've established that this is not an injury but a condition.'

Do well, Richard, and come back to me a soldier. Were Edward here now, would he still seek to encourage? Or would he divert his eyes, shamed at the sight of his skinny, malformed brother?

Exhaling, Warwick rises to his feet. 'Well, I shall leave you to think about it.'

Richard's heart sinks as he struggles to judge whose disappointment would hurt him most: the king's or that of the earl. He thinks he knows. 'Cousin, I hope you don't consider…'

'Don't consider what?'

He daren't even ask. 'The man you spoke of, sir - who fought at Saint Albans—'

The earl shifts the belt around his ample middle and adjusts his purse. 'What of him?'

'Did his fellows think him weak? Did they mock him?'

A sharp, pugnacious snort. 'I should've liked to see them try. He was a gristly bastard. Could have pitted himself against the best of them. In fact—'

There is a knock at the door and a letter delivered before the bearer shuffles out with apologetic speed. Heaving a sigh, Warwick breaks the seal and scans its contents. 'I'm wanted at Westminster. If your brother asks of you, I shall tell him you send your greetings.'

'Thank you.'

The earl taps the parchment on his open palm. 'I suggest you consider Brocas' advice. We'll speak further when you feel ready.' Taking his leave, he lingers momentarily on the threshold. 'Don't think this renders you in any way unworthy, boy.'

His cousin's pity, Richard decides, is harder to bear than any degree of disappointment. When the latch clatters into place, he returns to the window seat. Beyond the panes, the world darkens as pale flakes dip and flutter.

His injury—his condition—is not transitory, he knows that now, but at least his father was spared the disgrace. Gazing from the casement into a colourless infinity, it's as if he can see himself from a distance: a cowering insect, visible only to its Maker. Is this how he appears to the Almighty, when God casts down His eyes and seeks him out? A snivelling, shrinking, craven thing, fearful of his own shadow and content to fail?

His cousin had tested him. At York, as they rode through the defences that once held their fathers' heads, and again, at Middleham, as traitors fell foul of the headsman's axe. He'd not failed those tests. Warwick had said so.

Clangs from Saint Mary Bothaw jolt him back to the present, and he decides that, just like Warwick, the Almighty has chosen to test him. Rising, he smooths his velvet, tightens his girdle, then squares his shoulders as his cousin does.

I am a son of York, he thinks, a scion of the house of Neville. If God trusts me to succeed, then I will.

George awaits him at Placentia, eyes alight with genuine glee. Hauled into an overly tight embrace, Richard stiffens.

George recoils. 'What is it? What ails you?'

'Nothing, Brother. I strained a muscle in my back, is all.'

Suspicious, George's eyes narrow as they travel the length of him. 'That hardly surprises me; you're still as skinny as ever. Does Cousin Warwick not feed you?'

Richard smiles, pleased to have caused no offence. He's missed George but has no intention of admitting it. To do so would be to reduce himself to the quaking boy who left here almost six months since, and he'll not have that. They link arms, George leading him to his bedchamber in a wave of companionable chatter. The room has been repainted and hung with new Arras cloths, the bed draped with crimson curtains on which embroidered bulls frolic, flaunting their golden horns. Clearly, Edward has been generous.

'Look, Henry,' George calls to his boy, who hovers by the hearth warming a pan of wine. 'Duke Richard has returned to us. Hurry along with that, then get yourself away. My brother and I have much to discuss.'

The boy, nervous as ever, pours the contents of the pan into two waiting cups. George, divesting him of the vessels, waves him out. Richard finds himself predicting the way their speech will turn. It's simply a matter of how soon George will leap on the subject of their sister-in-law.

Keen to forestall the inevitable, Richard wanders to the far wall and admires the new hangings; their earthy scent of wool, the sharp odour of dyes, pungent yet not unpleasant. The fall of Troy is colourfully depicted: scaling ladders assault crumbling walls, soldiers hurling stones on the heads of besieging Greeks. The Greeks, of course, flaunt the banners of York, and Lions of March can be seen gambolling amongst the fray. Helen herself is leaning from a tower, encouraging the assailants with an enticing look. The high domed brow and slender nose seem somewhat familiar, and Richard wonders how generous the king has really been. When George moves on and Elizabeth moves in, she can recline on embroidered pillows and admire herself as the Queen of Sparta.

'This should serve to warm you.' George, bounding up, thrusts a cup into his brother's hand, then runs an admiring palm over the heavy wool. 'Beautiful, no?'

'Incredibly.'

'I'm fortunate to have them,' George cocks a wink. 'Edward may be playing the Burgundians at their own game and suspending trade, but he still managed to have these shipped in. I suspect that, as he commissioned them over a year ago, and because they were intended for me, the weavers of Artois were eager to oblige.'

There is no mention of Helen. If he's noticed her distinguishing looks, Richard thinks, he's unlikely to say so.

'My thanks for your letters,' George says. 'I wish you'd write more often. I'm certain the earl would allow you to tuck the odd letter or two into any correspondence he sends my way. You know,' he laughs, 'I had an idea. What say you to a game of chess in letter form? We could each set up a board, and every time we write, conclude our letters with a tactical move: I shall take white, as usual. Our boards will remain untouched until a new letter arrives as we must trust each other not to cheat. But of course, I know you wouldn't.'

Richard agrees they could try. 'Although I can't imagine how long it would take to conclude a match.'

'Well, it will encourage you to write. The more letters we exchange, the more exciting the game.'

Sympathy gushes as Richard realises just how pleased his brother is to see him. George must be lonely here, with no male companions of equal status. 'I thought to greet you at Westminster. Cousin Warwick tells me he's eager to see you.'

George nods. 'It will be a pleasure to see him too, but I'll visit him at Baynard's. I know he intends to spend some time with Mother.'

How does he know that? Warwick must have written to him. What else have they discussed in their frequent letters, Richard wonders. Not my condition, I hope.

George sips his wine. 'How did you find her when you first arrived? Mother, I mean. Edward spares her little time of late, and she spends much of her own at Clare. She likes it there.'

In fact, their mother's welcome had surprised Richard: an

embrace to rival George's and a flood of questions about the Warwick household. How were they faring together? Had the earl introduced him to the Neville affinity? Was Richard's health good? Was the countess making a gentleman of him? Responding to each in the affirmative, he'd relished the delight in her eyes as she took his measure.

'You're taller, I think, and your hair is darkening,' were the only comments she offered upon his person, but this, he had concluded, was good. His mother is nothing if not perceptive, and any change in his bearing would have been obvious to her.

He says, 'She has invited me to reside with her for a spell whilst I'm in London. Will you come, too, George? It'll be like the old days.'

A joyous beam. 'You know I will.'

'And will you come with me to court?'

'If it would please you, but I can make no promises. I try to keep away from them as much as possible.'

'You mean the queen's family?'

'Who else? They trail behind Edward like dogs sniffing out turds.' He shrugs as if the matter is of no account and they have better things to discuss. Except Richard knows this is not the case, that George would prefer, above all things, to speak as freely as he speaks before their mother and to feel secure in doing so.

'Dickon,' his brother indicates a chair by the bed, 'you must think me an unworthy host not to offer you a seat.'

While Richard sits, George perches on the mattress, his fur-trimmed gown riding up to reveal well-shaped legs, the kind that put a man in good favour with a woman. Richard tucks his own legs away, out of sight. In his tawny riding gown, he is a garden sparrow, plain and indistinguishable from its fellows. If the dark-haired girl were here and could take her pick of the king's brothers, whom would she opt for? He doubts it would be a difficult choice.

'Why not stay with me for a few days?' George is eager. 'I've had your old chamber prepared, and I'm sure Margaret will need no persuading to join us. What do you say? Our cousin won't object; he has business with the king, which should take them some days to discuss. You do know Edward would have him head an embassy to Burgundy to discuss Margaret's marriage?'

Richard knows their sister is not short of marriage proposals. They say Don Pedro has commissioned a large diamond. Duke Philip's son, Charles of Charolais, has sent a proposal of his own. And their cousin is eager for a French match. As for Margaret, he knows she will do whatever she's bid, but he would hope, at least, for her to be happy.

'Not all matters under discussion concern Margaret.' George, pleating the skirt of his gown with distracted fingers, clearly has a secret.

'No?'

'The king wishes for Margaret to wed Charolais, but he also has a proposal of his own,' George's eyes flick upwards. 'Charolais' daughter, to be married to me.'

'Mary?' An attempt at nonchalance. 'Yes, I heard that proposal has been resurrected.'

George's face contracts. 'You've heard nothing of the sort, you little worm.'

'Well, I know there's to be some kind of discussion.'

'You know it now, yes, but only because I've chosen to tell you.'

Richard glares, angry to have been caught out in a lie. 'My one hope, Brother, is that the girl has not inherited her father's swarthy looks.'

Like an arrow to the underbelly, the remark was a cruel one, and George looks genuinely hurt. Ashamed and embarrassed, Richard hangs his head. He should be pleased for George, but he's not, and it has nothing to do with the count's daughter, Mary. Beholding his brother in jewels and velvets, with his tawny curls and finely shaped calves, makes him wonder what George would say if he knew his spindly-legged brother had a secret of his own. At L'Erber, his resolutions had sounded very noble, spoken inwardly, with none but himself to hear. Yet the world beyond the townhouse shows him for what he is: a disappointment to his father, to his cousin, and to himself. He sees George's face as it was when he arrived: benevolent, smiling, and happy to see him. His own spiteful remark has cut the ground between them, and every moment that passes is widening the ditch. If he fails to span the crevice now, it may widen into a chasm.

'Forgive me, Brother. That was uncalled for. You know I didn't mean it.'

George is quiet, brooding, his pointed gaze slicing through to Richard's core and asking, *But do I?*

'George, please. What I said was unworthy of me. I don't even know why I said it.' Rising, he extends a conciliatory hand. His brother takes it grudgingly.

'What ails you, Dickon? Are you unhappy in our cousin's household?'

'No, not in the least. I'm more than contented.'

'What, then?'

Should he tell him? Should he trust George with his news and hope he will respect it? 'I can't tell you.'

His brother bursts with laughter, all antipathy gone. 'Is it a girl?'

An opportunity to digress finds Richard profoundly grateful. 'Well, there is a girl, but—'

'What's she like?'

'Just a girl.'

'She must be more than that to have spiked your interest. Come on, Dickon.'

Blushing, he has no choice but to acquaint his brother with the dark-haired girl: her green eyes with their sweeping lashes, her slim white hands.

'It seems you have observed her well. Surely you know her name?'

It doesn't pay to give George too much information; one can never be sure what he will do with it. 'Alice,' he tells him, 'that's all I know.'

'And does she like you in return?'

Richard shrugs, irritated to have divulged something he never would have admitted had the circumstances been different. 'I barely know.'

'There's no reason why she shouldn't,' George says.

'Isn't there?'

'None. But you've never been one to accept a compliment, Dickon, so I shan't bother trying. Just remember, if you ever manage to declare yourself, be sure to keep it from our cousin. I've heard stables are good for tumbling, but if I were you, I should find a sheltered piece of woodland somewhere—'

'No!'

George utters a loud guffaw, both hysterical and happy to have retained the power to shock. 'Oh, Dickon, I've missed you. Coyness is a rare commodity here. And you still haven't told me whether you intend to stay. The two pages you have with you, why not send them back to L'Erber for your travelling chest?'

'Not yet,' Richard says. 'I've business in the city.'

'Oh, yes? What kind of business? Or am I not allowed to know?'

'It wouldn't interest you.'

'And once you've attended to this *business,* you'll settle yourself here for a space?' The lop-sided grin is as persuasive as ever. 'You did promise, remember.'

Richard can't recall promising George anything but agrees, nonetheless. 'But I must beg our cousin's leave. I could do nothing without his permission.'

'Of course, Dickon. But, as I said, I doubt he will object.'

Dusk is closing in, and at L'Erber, servants touch tapers to wicks to chase away the gloom. The earl hunches over his writing desk. The candle at his elbow is dripping wax, glistening pools setting in opaque ovals upon ancient wood. He never ceases to work, sometimes far into the night; for the wealthiest man in London, the cost of beeswax can stand as no excuse. Richard knows he's working hard to narrow the gulf between England and France. For now, Warwick tells him, is the perfect time. Duke Philip is sick, and Charolais is running affairs: restricting our merchandise and crippling our trade—Charolais, who has never been a true friend to Edward.

Sensing Richard's eyes on him, Warwick raises his head. 'Worried about the morrow?'

'I suppose I am.'

Throwing down his quill, his cousin straightens up. 'I take it you've come to a decision. What will you say to Brocas?'

'I don't know.'

Closing his eyes, Warwick presses thumb and forefinger into weary sockets. 'I fear you'll need to know by morning.'

'There's a lot to consider. The stretching—'

'Are you afraid?'

'No. Well, yes, I am.'

Warwick snorts. 'Good. I'd worry if you weren't.'

Richard acknowledges the jest, if indeed it was one, but finds he cannot laugh. His mind is fixed on his condition, or rather, on what to do next. He needs his cousin's opinion but can't bring himself to ask. If Warwick were in my position, he thinks, he would know what to do, would have made up his mind before Brocas had even left the room. Edward likewise.

'Do you think this treatment—this stretching—would go on indefinitely, Cousin? Would I be required to submit to it for the rest of my days?'

Warwick leans back, his chair creaking in protest. 'Only Brocas would have the answer to that. But if you wish to consider it, I can employ the best of physicians. I hear there are fine doctors at Montpellier, and I'm sure Monseigneur Le Roi would be happy to supply one. Louis is keen to incur my favour of late, and I would swear his man to absolute secrecy. If you prefer, I'm sure Brocas could recommend someone here, in London.'

If you wish to consider it: torture on a yearly, monthly, weekly basis?

The earl places a hand on his arm. 'Richard, you may— not now, I grant you—but in time, you may wish to confide in your brother.'

'No. Not Edward. And certainly not George.'

'You don't trust them?' A mixture of sadness and curiosity, and again, that undeniable lick of pity.

'Not in this regard.' Richard surprises himself with the firmness of his conviction.

'Why?'

Surely, it would seem obvious. George would see it as confirmation of all his suspicions, that he is weak and could never be his equal. Edward would be disappointed for a while, but then he would find other roles for Richard to fulfil. A Garter knight who cannot wield a sword yet excels in matters of administration.

Richard compresses his lips. 'I need to prove myself first. When I've done so, they can make their own decisions about me, but not until.'

Warwick's face glows. 'Well said, boy.'

It's an honour to be invited to an intimate supper, more so when the invitation is extended by a king. But an intimate supper at Westminster would be a grand fête elsewhere, and any hopes Richard and George may have had of quiet discourse with their brother are dashed against the craggy outcrop of courtiers, servants, and musicians.

The air is thick with the scent of meat and spices, Rhenish, Malmsey, and the sweet allure of jasmine. Cushions are scattered around the floor, guests lolling cross-legged, women sprawled in pools of brocade. He and George pick their way to where Edward sits, Hastings at his feet. The chamberlain rises, unsteady in his pike-toed boots, while Edward beckons, bestowing kisses of welcome from syrupy lips.

'My brothers. Come, sit.'

He indicates two stools set at his elbows, and Hastings, yelling for a server, requests two brimming cups.

'Richard,' Edward laughs and grips his hand, 'it cheers my heart to see you. You're clearly thriving under our cousin's care.'

'Thank you, Your Grace.'

'Good lad.' Edward winks and looks content, if slothful and blurred around the edges. When he calls for music, minstrels pick their way through the sprawling guests and commence a Burgundian love song, sweet yet morose. George fidgets, plays with his cup, runs the pad of his thumb over the gilded decoration. Were it not for me, Richard thinks, he would have stayed away.

Servers draped with napkins fetch a delicacy for the king's brothers. 'Bream cooked in malmsey and flavoured with ginger,' Edward says. 'The queen has a penchant for it. Ginger is a particular favourite of yours, too, George, as I recall.'

'Most certainly, Your Grace,' a charming inclination of the head, 'and thank you. How fares the queen?'

Edward tips his cup in salute. 'Exceeding well, Brother, but I regret, confined—'

'If only.'

Richard gasps inwardly as the king turns to face their brother. 'Would my lord of Clarence care to repeat his comment so all may hear?'

George is undaunted. 'If only her grace were with us, she would most certainly enjoy the dish. Perhaps you might send her some, Highness, with our compliments.'

Edward smiles thinly. 'And if only custom allowed the presence of the male, I should entrust a platter to you and despatch you to the birthing chamber in order to serve it. A light but nourishing meal presented in person by her brother Clarence would be certain to cheer the queen's spirits.'

The king is too quick, too clever: George should have learnt that by now. A sidelong glance reveals him shamed, flushed and deep in thought.

Exhaling slowly, Edward raises his cup. 'Tell me, Richard, is Cousin Warwick proving an admirable tutor?'

'Very admirable. We fare well together.'

'Good. I knew I could rely on you.' The emphasis is cutting. 'And your training, how goes it?'

'I'm said to be improving. We practise in harness now.'

'Excellent.' Edward smiles, satisfied, as a napkin is placed over his shoulder and the bream is served. The fish has been cut into small pieces, easier for a casual meal, and served with a slice of the finest paindemain.

Richard crumbles the white bread, sprinkling it over the sauce. Why is it that friendship with one brother feels like a betrayal of the other?

'Eat up, lad.' Edward nudges him. 'We still need to make a soldier of you.' He moves closer, his breath a blast of spice, 'I'm sorry Mother is not here, but her absence is of her own choosing.'

Movements to the king's right; George scraping his spoon, head bowed.

Had Edward truly intended a family supper: Mother, Margaret, their cousin of Warwick? If so, Richard can only assume the invitations were declined, and the presence of Hastings, the minstrels, the lolling courtiers, are an afterthought.

As plates are removed, replaced with nuts, cheese and sweetmeats, a figure sweeps the length of the chamber: stylish chapeau with a tall, curling feather, iridescent sleeves of the best shot silk.

George produces a leather pouch and jiggles it under the king's nose. 'Dice, Your Grace? I owe you a noble from last time. Dickon can keep tally.'

Edward, ignoring him, salutes the approaching figure. 'My lord Scales. Your company is welcome to us.'

The chapeau is removed, the obeisance well-rehearsed; long, low, and lissom. Anthony Wydeville could grace any court in Christendom, Richard thinks, if he chose to do so. 'My Lord King, may I propose a game of fox and geese?'

Edward laughs. 'But I thought chess was your game.'

Another elegant bow. 'Indeed. But I understand fox and geese to be Your Grace's favourite, and I would consider it impolite to accept the most noble order with which you intend to endow me in the knowledge that I remain indebted to you. Please, accept this opportunity to win back the wager we laid two days ago, that I may feel settled in my mind.'

Richard squirms. George casts his eyes heavenward.

'If this heinous sin lies so heavily, Anthony,' the king laughs, 'then, of course, it would be most rewarding to grant you absolution.

Have a board set up, and I'll join you.'

He pats Richard's leg with brotherly affection. 'Do you mind? You're more than welcome to watch the game. There'll be wagers laid, should you wish to risk it.'

'Edward?' Richard leans in as the king gathers his gown. 'When I receive the Garter, is it true Lord Scales is to be awarded likewise?'

'As you well know, Richard, I shall be investing a number of knights. Don't become as resentful as our brother; it wouldn't suit you.'

Rising with a playful grin, the king crosses the chamber. Pages hurry ahead of him, making up a table, fetching stools, and setting up a gaming board with an army of wooden pieces.

George returns the dice to his purse. 'Come Dickon, let us retire. I detect the odour of dog turds around here.'

Accepting that the comparison between dog turds and the queen's family is commonplace for George, Richard retrieves his wine cup and follows him towards the gaming table. Edward and Scales are already considering their first moves, long backs hunched over the board.

A neat bow from George. 'Might we have your leave to retire, Your Grace?'

Edward eyes him, unblinking. 'No, you may not, my lord of Clarence. Richard is our guest, and it is our wish that you both remain. If you're eager for a game of dice, then I'm sure you have a willing opponent.'

George thrusts his arm through Richard's and draws him away from the crowd. Retreating to the oriel, they find it occupied by an embracing couple. At their approach, the man rises, and the woman dabs her lips as both make clumsy obeisance and shuffle into the shadows.

Richard sinks onto the warm cushions. George scowls and nods towards the gaming table. 'See what I mean? It's sickening. This was supposed to be a family supper, but they can't even allow us that. Edward could dismiss them all, but he chooses instead to dismiss us – his own brothers.'

'He did say he wanted us to remain.'

'I can't see why, if he prefers the company of that milksop.'

Richard knew it would be like this. He's equally disappointed that the meal is such an impersonal affair, but can George not at least try to enjoy himself? 'We have each other—'

'Ho! Did you see that?' Howling, George indicates a tall, slim young man in parti-coloured hose. 'John Wydeville, court fool – for certes, he dresses like one.'

'What of him?'

'Don't you notice anything? The idiot approached my lord Hastings in the vain hope of striking up conversation, but Hastings turned his back. Wydeville's face is as ruddy as a slapped arse.'

John Wydeville: their cousin has spoken much of him, or rather, of his infamous marriage. Their mother, for reasons of her own, has never allowed the bridegroom's name to pass her lips. Wydeville is little more than a youth, as his tightly laced hose and slender thighs confirm: his newlywedded bride, their mother's elder sister, Catherine Neville. 'She could be his grandmother,' Warwick told him once, lips curling in disgust. 'What kind of world has that godforsaken family created that even an aged dame is not allowed respect in her dotage.'

Richard notices the Wydeville stripling wander to a niche where a woman leans languidly in the stone aperture. She smiles at his approach, painted lips as crimson as the youth's livid cheeks.

'She's a whore.' George follows Richard's gaze. 'If Wydeville chooses to marry the Dowager Duchess of Norfolk for her estates, he ought to live the life of a celibate in recompense. However, I suppose such a command would be difficult for our brother to enforce, given the diversions he's found for himself these last few months. The queen being with child,' he adds by way of explanation.

'How do you know what he does?' Richard is beginning to feel uncomfortable: a yellow-beak with no experience to call upon.

George taps his nose. 'There's no such thing as privacy at court. Besides, I've a man in his service who's happy to keep me informed.'

'Someone in your household spies on Edward?' Surely this is outrageous, even for George.

'Why not? He spies on me. It's the way at court; you'll learn that in time.'

As Wydeville and the woman disappear through a doorway, another in a violet gown, attaching herself to a lutenist, runs her hand over the stringed instrument and giggles in his ear. The minstrel slips his hand from the lute, snaking it around her. Nothing of the sort would happen at Middleham, Richard thinks, at least not under the countess' eye. Suddenly, it's not the woman in the violet gown and a nameless musician: it's him, and it's Alice. Her sweet breath tickling his ear, his hand travelling the length of her bodice, over smooth, slim hips.

His eyes flick back to his brother. 'Whatever your opinions of court, George, I'm no longer a child. I can see and hear things for myself.'

'Clearly,' George smirks. 'I'm sure the woman would be happy to teach you anything you wish to learn, Dickon, although I wouldn't recommend it. She's one of Edward's and would be certain to tell him.'

There are celebrations at court, and in the city the conduits of Cheapside are flowing with wine. The queen has brought forth a living child: a girl named Elizabeth after her mother. Richard's own mother, standing as godsib, was awarded the honour of bearing her granddaughter to the font, where the Archbishop of York – and his brother of Warwick – awaited them.

'The infant may have Wydeville blood,' the duchess told Richard afterwards, in smug satisfaction, 'but she was baptised in the company of Nevilles, and a Neville it was who applied the Holy Chrism.'

George had smiled when he found out. 'A girl. That means I'm still heir presumptive. A woman can give birth to a nursery of girls before a boy comes forth. If he ever does.'

When it comes to diplomacy, one sees Warwick at his best. In spring, the earl is set for the Low Countries, in the company of Lords Hastings and Wenlock, to discover what exactly Count Charles is prepared to offer. Trade, he says, shall be high on the agenda, the rescinding of Charles' edict on the importation of English cloth. Matrimony, too; Charles' proposal to Margaret and the prospect of George's marriage to the count's daughter, Mary. He would rather set sail for France, of course, and barter with Louis, but to refuse the commission would be unwise. Were another to lead the embassy, it may appear to the world that his influence was waning. And that, for the earl, would be even harder to stomach.

Like George, Richard is learning to watch and to deduce.

One day, towards the middle of March, his cousin proposes a hawking trip. Richard is keen to agree; his new hawk, Angel, a gift from the earl, is keener still. He rides beside Warwick, beaters up ahead, the sky white and wide, heavy with stirring cloud.

'She's beautiful,' Richard tracks the bird's ascent, the powerful beating of her wings. He feels his soul is soaring with her, leaving the minutiae, the incidentals of life, far below amongst the sparse grass and sodden ditches.

The earl's smile is tender and as the creature returns to the glove, they each admire its poise, its undeniable grace. 'I'm pleased,' Warwick says, 'that you and she have found such affinity.'

Richard beams. Like Amber, the bird is more than a gift, and he knows he will treasure her well.

The shower takes them by surprise. Not that it should rain, but that in moments, the shower should become a deluge. Galloping through the torrent, they shelter in a neighbouring copse amid the tangy scent of wild garlic. The earl's entourage dismounts. A wineskin is passed round, men laugh, drink, and use the cover of trees to relieve themselves.

Cadgers wait at Richard's stirrup as he dismounts. Unwilling to surrender his bird, he carries her instead to the far side of the thicket, where Warwick leans against a gnarled trunk, deep in contemplation. Stationing himself alongside, Richard caresses the hawk's dappled plumage. 'I hope you shall not be too long away, Cousin.'

Warwick inclines his head. 'You mean you shall miss me?'

'Yes,' he says, knowing that he will.

'I understand your mother has invited you to Baynard's.'

'She has.'

'Well, you should go. We can travel together as far as London. You'd like that?'

A warmth spreads across Richard's belly. 'Very much.'

The earl grins. 'I can't say how long my sojourn will take, but no matter how Charolais receives us, our future lies with France. The French are our natural allies, from whom we are descended. They are a noble people, unlike the Flemings—a race of merchants grown fat on trade.'

'But should Charles' terms be acceptable to the king, then Edward may well agree to them,' Richard observes, keen to demonstrate his understanding.

'But consider, boy. Both Charles and Louis want our friendship, for whatever decision we make will secure England as ally against the other.'

Richard congratulates himself: he has worked this out, too. Curling his fingers, he runs them lovingly over Angel's glistening plumage.

'Your brother must reflect on what both have to offer,' Warwick tells him. 'Particularly when it comes to sealing such matters in wedlock. Louis has proposed his brother-in-law as a match for Margaret and the opportunity for a permanent peace, were Edward to join with him against the Burgundians.' The earl lowers his voice. 'In addition, Monseigneur le Roi has proposed a match for you.'

Richard's fingers pause mid-stroke.

'You're a valuable asset to us, boy. Louis intends to offer Jeanne, his second daughter, as well as the lordship of Holland, Zeeland and Brabant. But I pray you, keep your counsel on this. Your brother would have me treat with Burgundy, and so I must, although he will see in time that his policies are wrong and that France is the preferable choice.'

Marriage? There's been no talk of it, yet Richard trusts his cousin. If Edward had simply followed Warwick's advice two years ago, he would have avoided the problems he is facing now.

'How long will the proceedings last?'

A curt shrug of the shoulders. 'Impossible to guess, but in my experience, these things never run smoothly. Duke Philip is not a forthcoming man, as I'm sure you recall, and since he's on his sickbed, we must, unfortunately, confer with his son, who by all accounts is a sullen individual and even less accommodating.'

'Duke Philip was gracious to George and me,' Richard reminds him, 'but only once Edward's position was secure.'

'My case *en point*. I believe this alliance is driven by the queen's kin or, more likely, by her mother, Jacquette. Due to family ties, that woman has influence in the Low Countries.' Warwick huffs then forces a smile. 'The shower appears to be easing; should we depart?'

In time, news arrives at Baynard's directly from the Low Countries. Richard watches as his mother breaks the earl's seal and devours his news in silence. George flashes him a look. They both know from experience that she'll only tell them what she wants them to know.

At length, she raises her head. 'I regret, George, your cousin's dealings with the Count of Charolais have not been easy. There is, he says, a lack of rapport.'

'So,' George glowers, 'they want Margaret, but they don't want me. I'm right, aren't I?'

Margaret, perched beside him, takes his hand. 'Can they not reconsider? George and I had hopes of remaining together.'

'No. Your cousin is clear upon that, although he does tell me he has another proposition.'

'What proposition?' George is up, eager to grasp the letter and read the news for himself. Their mother is faster, folding the vellum and tucking it into her skirts.

'Your cousin says he must speak to me first. He has not hinted at anything further in his letter, so we must wait upon his return.'

George spreads his hands. 'But Margaret and I have planned so much.'

'Silence. You would be well advised to take a leaf from Richard's book. Discretion is a virtue.'

Richard proffers a look of sympathy, but George has no appetite for it.

'In fact,' their mother smooths the backs of her hands, ironing out the creases, 'your cousin feels we should not ally ourselves with Burgundy at all. He has, as you know, always favoured France and seeks to find a suitable husband for Margaret amongst King Louis' kin. And, of course, there's still Don Pedro.'

Richard finds Margaret watching him: calm, dignified, pragmatic as ever. She sends him a brief smile. *You know George as well as I,* it says, *he will recover.*

Chapter Fourteen

June 1467
Baynard's Castle

RICHARD WAKES to the shriek of gulls and the yelling of boatmen, sunlight searing through gaps in the shutters. He struggles to understand his surroundings until familiar shapes form in the half-light, and his mother sinks into the mattress, relief tugging the corners of her mouth.

'Ah, you're awake. Would you care for something to drink?'

Flashes of recent days: the seemingly endless journey south, sun pounding dry earth and bouncing up to blind him. The gatehouse at Baynard's, hands slipping from the reins as he slithered to the ground, lurched to the garderobe and spewed into the long drop. Yet, he can't recall how he got here, to his old chamber, nor by whose hands he was divested and put to bed.

He jerks upright. The chamber spins, and he flops back against the pillows.

'Easy, Richard. The physician attributes it to something you ate on the road or a reaction to the hot weather – or both.'

'But who brought me to bed? Who undressed me?'

A shape materialises from the murky haze: Simon Kyngston, cup in hand.

'Small beer,' the duchess says. 'Drink.'

The rim knocks against his teeth as he gulps the contents in one mouthful.

'You're dribbling like a baby, Richard. I've half a mind to send

Joan Malpas for a slavering clout.'

His weak laughter leads to a coughing fit. 'The journey. It was so hot.'

'*Too* hot.' His mother raises her eyes heavenward. 'God send us some rain.'

'George?'

'Has visited twice, fussing like a Dorking cock in a farmyard. I said I'd summon him once your fever broke, which I will. He bade me tell you he shall miss your company at Smithfield. The joust. The Burgundian visit. You do remember, Richard?'

'Of course. But surely, I shall meet him there.' The tournament, organised by the king to impress his Burgundian visitors, is the sole reason he's here, why he travelled down in this ungodly heat.

'No. Doctor Brocas advises against it. You're too weak.'

Brocas has been here? Richard's belly lurches. 'But—'

'The decision has been made. You're to remain here and rest.'

'Mother. About Doctor Brocas—'

'Rest now, Richard. Sleep is the best remedy.' With a quiet word to Kyngston, the duchess leaves by the stairwell, the door-latch clacking behind her.

She returns before supper, the realised threat of his old nurse quivering by her side.

'I've made provision with the kitchen, Lord Richard, something light.' Joan, pink-cheeked and perspiring, hasn't changed a bit. 'They're preparing a caudle for you, adding honey and saffron: the way you used to like it. If there's anything else you need?'

'Nothing, thank you.'

When she blusters out, the duchess takes a seat by the bed. 'Don't concern yourself, Richard. None shall hear of it from me.'

Silent, he presses his back into the yielding pillows. His mother seems content to wait, but the longer the silence, the less certain he is of how to fill it.

He takes a deep breath. 'Mother, you said Brocas has been here while I was sick. Why him? How did you know?'

'Your cousin has been occupied with this new embassy to France, but not so busy that he failed to make arrangements for you. He told me that, should you have need of a physician, I must summon Doctor Brocas and no other. He said you'd sustained an injury last year, for which Brocas had treated you, that you know and trust the man.'

First Burgundy, then France. But it seems the earl's new embassy has not precluded his concern for his young cousin. Richard is moved.

'So,' he says, 'you know all about it now.'

His mother blinks. 'No. Not all about it, for I have yet to hear anything from you.'

Panic creeps in. 'Edward is unaware? And George?'

A click of the tongue. 'As I have just told you, none shall hear of it from me.'

'That's what Cousin Warwick said.'

'And he kept his word. Your cousin revealed nothing, and those boys of yours are so discreet, I had to prise it out of them. Don't distress yourself; my purpose was only to learn how I might help you.' A wry smile. 'But from what I've gathered, you're managing well enough on your own.'

He curls up under the bedsheet. 'Brocas says it's not unheard of. And the earl knew a man in a worse condition who fought at Saint Albans.'

His mother teases his hand from the coverlet and cools it between her own. 'I consulted Brocas at length. He tells me you receive certain treatments from him but have chosen not to submit yourself to others.'

'There's a reason for that.'

'And I believe you're right. My prayers and contemplations lead me to the same conclusion. God will give you the courage to overcome, so that His mercy may be made known to you.'

Richard passes a tongue over parched lips. 'Another drink. Please.' Sated, he says, 'Can you tell me how it looks? I can't see it for myself. Kyngston and Parr are dutiful, but that may prevent them from telling me the truth.'

'But you are inclined to believe your mother?'

'Of course.'

'Then know that what the boys say is true. The condition was only noticeable to me when they stripped you bare. And then, only when I helped them get you abed.'

'*You* helped them?'

She laughs. 'Don't look so surprised. Young Parr is the most loyal of servants. Would let none but himself and Kyngston attend you. A thing he was insistent upon, even in the presence of the king's mother. But I demanded they allow me to assist.'

'Then I do not appear... crooked?'

'Not in the least. You're as strong as your brothers. And, I believe, more fiercely determined.' A glimmer wafts between them, dust motes dancing in a shaft of light. 'You are your father's son, Richard. How could you be anything else?'

'If the doctor prescribes mushed food and bedrest, then that's what you must have.' George, resplendent in green silk, looks flushed and uncomfortable. 'We don't want you to sicken any further, do we? This heat is not doing any of us any good.'

Sliding a finger under his collar, he moves it back and forth, glancing down at Richard as if he envies his imposed confinement. 'At least you don't have to witness Scales showing off. You know, I'd love to see him bested. They say Antoine, Duke Philip's bastard, is a skilled jouster.' His lip curls in derision. 'I've been given the honour of carrying Scales' helm. Did you know that?'

'We have the better part of a week before the joust,' Richard assures him. 'I believe we shall both be present.'

'What?' George is sceptical. 'And have you spewing again? You're better here, out of the way. Margaret says she's been helping Mother to tend you. Do you want their ministrations to have been in vain? Besides, I'm sure Edward is too preoccupied in pleasing his Burgundian visitors to care whether either of us attend.'

Things would have been different, Richard imagines, had the proposed match between George and Mary met with Charolais' favour. Rather than perching on the bed, helping himself to the supply of small beer, his brother would be acquainting himself with *Le Grand Bâtard*; demonstrating his riding skills, his swordsmanship, besting the man at chess. Still, George has chosen to ride here in the relentless heat when any number of excuses would have sufficed, and for that, Richard is grateful.

Yet, he'd have preferred to have been up and dressed. Lounging here, naked, he feels vulnerable, as if he wears his condition like a brand. Pulling the sheet to chest height, he tucks it around himself.

'You can't be chill, surely?' George frowns. 'Not in this heat.'

'No.' He's still a child in his brother's eyes. His reasons for doing anything open to question.

George thrusts out his lip. 'Think of me,' he says, 'acting as little more than a squire while Scales is shining in the lists. I should rather be here with you.'

'No, you wouldn't.'

'No, you're right. I wouldn't.' Stirring himself, George drops a kiss on his brother's brow. 'Never fear, Dickon. I shall tell you all about it.'

And he will, every last detail. How he'd sweltered in his embroidered tabard; how glib Scales had been as he'd trotted round the tiltyard; how attentive Edward was in his appreciation of all things Wydeville. Oh, George will tell him everything, Richard's certain of that.

Brocas returns towards the end of the week and, following a host of questions about giddiness, vomiting and bodily fluids, declares him much improved.

'Massage would be advisable after keeping to your bed. You still have a supply of oils?'

He tells him yes, and that Parr and Kyngston are proving themselves capable in their application of them.

'And you will continue to perform the exercises I showed you?'

'Certainly.'

When Brocas leaves, Richard wonders about his fee. Of how many marks each visit adds to Warwick's running tally. The physician, he knows, is expressly paid from the earl's personal coffers. *No need to trouble the king, lad.* Sighing, he reminds himself how much he owes to his cousin's continued discretion.

He wonders how the earl is faring in France. Warwick told him little of last year's sojourn to the Low Countries other than that he and Charolais had fallen foul of each other. France, however, is a different matter, and Richard knows Warwick is determined to negotiate with Louis: 'And return with such an offer that will send the Flemings scurrying back to their warehouses and their looms, in the knowledge that they've been bested.'

But it's clear, even to Richard, that it's the Burgundians who sit high in Edward's favour, and no expense has been spared in the arrangements for the coming visit. London, he's heard, is a riot of colour, the Cheapside conduit again running with wine - and Westminster, according to George, the embodiment of Camelot. The Bastard Antoine will see much to impress him.

Frustrated, Richard throws off the coverlet and calls for Parr and Kyngston. He recalls what his mother had said of them, how careful they'd been of him. They must have their reward. At length, he says, 'Would you care to watch the lodges being erected at Smithfield?'

'Us, Duke Richard?' Kyngston, selecting a shirt from the pile of fresh laundry, unfurls it in a wave of lavender.

'Why yes,' he casts about him in mock pretence, 'unless there's anyone else, loitering behind the bed hangings.'

Parr, kneeling at his feet with an unlaced boot, whips up his head. 'May we?'

'With my express permission. I've a mind to know how the tourney will be arranged, and, as I'm forbidden to attend, I thought you might be my eyes and ears.'

The youths grin like schoolboys.

'But remember, I want a detailed report of how the settlements are laid out. It will help to make sense of what His Grace of Clarence has to tell me. I can spare you after dinner if you like.'

'But you are newly risen from your sickbed,' Kyngston holds out his lightest silk gown, something suited for the weather. 'You may need us.'

'I'll be content with a book and some small beer.'

A commotion from the river draws Parr to the casement. 'The king's barge, Your Grace.'

Richard joins him by the open window. The royal barge with its Leopards and Lilies, its Garter pennant limp in the heat, is moored beside the river stairs. The sun strikes the water as the king disembarks and vanishes into the depths of the gatehouse. Edward must have some business with their mother, and that he should come in his own person is promising.

'Still feeling well, Your Grace?'

Richard glances into the mirror held up before him, smooths hair still lank and greasy from confinement. 'Perfectly, Simon. Don't concern yourself.'

A sharp knock draws Parr to the door. The king bursts across the threshold, a giant in crimson silk. Parr and Kyngston, overawed, make hurried bows while Edward, insouciant, waves them away.

'Get you gone, lads. My brother and I are capable of looking after ourselves.' The youths shuffle backwards like scuttling beetles while the king peers at Richard with ill-disguised concern. 'By the mercy of God, boy, you look like a corpse.'

The royal embrace is overwhelming, and Richard feels as if his bones will snap. 'The physician advised a sparing diet. But I'm well enough to take pottage now, and Mother is plying me with treacle mixture. I believe I'm much improved.'

'And who are you trying to convince? Me, or yourself? No, no, you take the chair, I'm happy here.' Squashing his long body into the window embrasure, Edward settles on the cushioned seat. 'I pray you'll forgive me for not attending you earlier.'

'Of course.' Whatever delayed his brother, Richard is thankful for it. Thankful he's dressed, that he doesn't have to face Edward naked and abed. 'It's kind of you to come. I know you have the embassy to entertain.'

'I wished to see your progress for myself. One can never trust the word of others where sickness is concerned.'

'You've been talking to George.'

'Ha!' Edward smacks his knees and lets out a bark of laughter. 'With our brother, one can never tell where truth ends and exaggeration begins. But I believe that, in this case, he spoke true. I'd a thought of coming here and rescinding, of allowing you to attend the tourney after all. But I can see I was right to deny you. Besides, your physician has confirmed you're not well enough, especially if the hot weather continues.'

Richard's heart sinks to the pit of his belly. 'Doctor Brocas? You've seen him? Spoken to him?'

A dismissive wave of the hand. 'Of course. You think I wouldn't make every effort to acquaint myself with your condition?'

No, please. 'My condition? What did he tell you? What did he say of me?'

'This ungodly heat, he thinks, or something you've picked up on the way. He said you were lucky to have reached London when you did. That had you spent another day in the saddle, you may have fallen sick by the wayside. And I know you, Richard, you'd feign recovery simply to take up your place at Smithfield.'

His sickness, then, is all they have discussed. *Deo Gratia.* 'But there are a full four days before the joust, Your Grace. I shall be myself by then.'

'So, you're a physician now?'

Richard scowls, like George in a fit of pique. 'No, but—'

'I appreciate your disappointment, Brother, but we can't risk it. The heat remains unbearable, and you're better served by remaining here.'

'But I feel well enough, even now.'

The king will not be gainsaid. 'Then let us keep it that way, shall we?'

The duchess crumbles her bread in silence: a snowfall of soft flakes settling over saltfish and eggs. Her head is lowered, kerchief obscuring her face. At length, she exhales. 'I can't believe it, George.'

Richard casts a worried glance at his brother. George, newly arrived from Westminster, is wild-eyed and excited, happy to have found his mother and siblings together: a captive audience.

'It's true, I can assure you. Edward bade me – rather, demanded - that I join him and march to the Archbishop's Palace at Charing Cross, where he disturbed our cousin of York at his prayers.'

Raising her eyes, the duchess gazes steadily at George. 'And?'

'The archbishop emerged from his closet most surprised.' George's cloak, drenched from the summer storm, drips onto the polished boards. 'His clerks scattered, but some huddled around him as if he were holy Saint Thomas and we, the four knights of Henry Curtmantle.'

'Please,' their mother heaves an irritated sigh, 'just tell me what happened.'

George, incredulous, throws a glance towards his siblings, then back again. 'I thought I was.'

'Then continue, if you please.'

George licks his lips, chest juddering. 'Edward informed Cousin George that he no longer held the office of chancellor and that he must surrender the Great Seal. "Indeed," he said, "I shall not leave without it." My lord archbishop explained that such a thing was inaccessible to any other in the house and that the king must allow him time to retrieve it. Edward escorted the archbishop to his chamber, and to my shame, I was charged to accompany them. Cousin George produced the seal in its white leather bag and placed it in Edward's hands.'

Richard and Margaret are silent while their mother continues to stare at her uneaten supper. 'And how did my nephew appear?'

George spreads his hands. 'How you would expect. It was a shock to most of us to have to witness such a shameful display. If

192

the earl were here, Edward should not have dared.'

Richard pushes his plate aside. 'Do you think our brother may reconsider?'

George regards him as he would a lackwit. 'Hardly likely, is it? He's shamed my lord archbishop in public and made an example of him. I tell you, if our cousin of Warwick had been here—'

'But he's not,' their mother seethes, 'so there is little point in speculation. Did the king offer a reason for his actions?'

'No. Too eager to return to his Burgundian guests. But he's been put out since the archbishop failed to make the opening address to parliament.'

Suddenly conscious of his drenched cloak, George shrugs it from his shoulders. With no page to hand, it falls in a heap at his feet. 'Cousin George has been unwell,' he sniffs, sinking down beside Margaret, 'a perfectly good reason to absent himself, one would suppose. With the Bastard Antoine and his retinue in attendance, the session could have dragged on for hours.'

Margaret touches his arm. 'We must remember the archbishop in our prayers. What ails him?'

A brief pause, during which George rinses his fingers in the bowl of rosewater and avails himself of the remaining loaf. 'Summer ague, not uncommon. But Edward appeared to care little. Mother,' he continues between bites, 'did you know that our cousin of York has written to His Holiness the Pope with a view to a cardinal's hat?'

'No, George,' their mother says. 'I…no. Well, that is to say, not in relation to a cardinal's hat.'

A look passes between them, a brief moment of mutual enquiry, with which ultimately both seem satisfied.

Richard sucks his lip. The chancellorship wrested from Neville hands in the discernible absence of the earl. And now, he thinks, some covert scheme closely nurtured between Mother and George.

If battlelines are being drawn, he wants no part of it.

A final visit from Brocas and Richard's recovery is confirmed.

His mother's care, the physician assures him, has played no small part. Enforced confinement has aided him, too, but it has also shielded him, excluding him from developments. When he bids farewell and sets off for L'Erber, it is with the knowledge that Warwick's household may be a different place in light of recent events. And his cousin, a different man.

Yet, he hopes he's wrong. He has missed his cousin, and only now, as he clatters through the gates of the townhouse, does he realise how much. Slipping his reins to a groom, he passes the time of day with the steward, seeking to divine the earl's current mood. The man, giving nothing away, leads him to the solar.

The room is like the office of a government clerk: huge table strewn with papers and inkhorns, with the perceptible scent of melted wax—evidence of a half-eaten supper: manchet loaves with hardening crusts, two discarded cups. And George, pouring over a newly penned letter while Warwick looks on. Richard's smile fades.

'Cousin!' The earl propels himself towards him like a cannonball. 'How good it is to see you.'

George, discarding the letter, springs from the settle and locks him in an effusive embrace. Warwick, sniffing, clears his throat.

'As you see, Cousin,' Richard says, discomforted, 'I'm much improved.'

Yes. Good. Excellent. Praise God. So ebullient are the greetings, he knows he must have timed it very badly indeed. Perhaps he should return on the morrow when Warwick is alone and more ready to receive him.

George resumes his seat. 'Have you come from Edward?'

'No. From Mother.'

Warwick takes his measure. 'You were always skinny, boy, but this sickness has taken its toll. Have you supped?'

Leyched beef, he assures him, before he left Baynard's, and hot custard tart. With a grunt, Warwick calls for his servers. 'A platter of mutton for my lord of Gloucester and a jug of Gascon.'

Two suppers in one day: Richard wonders whether he can manage it. The earl has a space cleared at table, a chair fetched, a cushion plumped. Silence settles as boys arrive with cutlery and napkins, fetch up slices of roasted mutton swimming in spiced wine gravy. Encouraged by the delicious aroma, he sets to.

George flashes a wink. 'You remember my telling you of Scales' behaviour at Smithfield, Dickon?'

Wincing as hot gravy burns his mouth, Richard sets down his spoon. 'You mean his charging before his opponent was ready? Yes, you told me.'

George snorts in derision. 'I was just relaying the story to our cousin. Not only did Scales charge before the Bastard Antoine was ready to receive him, but some would attest the Bastard's horse was slain by a spike Scales had attached to his saddle. Not the kind of behaviour you'd find in one of your romances, eh, Dickon?'

This last, Richard feels sure, was said to bait him. But if true, it is indeed an act of dishonour. 'I wish I'd been there, that I could have seen the business for myself.'

George's mouth gapes in outrage, but the earl interjects, 'George speaks true. It appears he was not the only person present to have noted this offence. The fact that Scales went unpunished is yet further proof of the influence exuded by his tribe.'

They seem to be waiting, expecting Richard to respond. He returns to the steaming mutton, but Warwick hasn't finished.

'I'm sure you know, boy, that in addition to this, the king, encouraged by those who would lead him astray, has treated my brother of York grievously. It is an insult, a direct assault upon me, and upon the name of Neville.'

'Mother—'

'Shut up, Dickon.' His brother leans forward, clasping his knees. 'Mother is in agreement with us. In his promotion and adherence to his wife's family, Edward has besmirched his own.'

George seems set to continue, but their cousin throws him a warning glance. Laying a hand on Richard's shoulder, he says, 'It's my belief that, separated from those who seek to lead him astray, Edward holds great promise. But whilst he's in the sway of Richard Wydeville's kin, he'll bring us all to ruin.'

George's silk-clad leg twitches in irritation, bouncing movements from the ball of his foot. 'Listen, Brother. Edward has snubbed the French, sent our cousin here chasing wild geese, while all the time he's treating with Burgundy. I presume you heard about the death of Duke Philip and the Bastard's hasty return? Edward is keener than ever now to unite with Burgundy and to use Margaret to seal the agreement. I admit, I once thought it a good idea myself, but not now. An alliance with the Low Countries means Wydeville influence. We need to stop the king—'

Warwick glares at him, then turns to Richard. 'Cousin, it was not my intention to concern you with this. Not yet, but as usual, George is too ready with his tongue.'

Chastened, George curls back onto the settle and examines his cuffs. Richard sets aside his spoon. What do they expect him to say? Perhaps he should just excuse himself? Feign tiredness, a full belly?

Warwick sits beside him. 'Edward must be rescued from bad counsel. Much as your father strove to separate King Harry from those who sought to influence him in their own favour.'

Richard wipes his mouth, smearing the napkin with gravy. 'I know.'

'Then you would not think ill of us for trying?'

He folds the napkin and lays it down. 'I would see Edward as the king our father would have been, if that's what you mean, Cousin.'

Warwick smiles, 'Spoken as a true son of York.'

Chapter Fifteen

July 1467
London/Warwick

*P*LAGUE, RIFE in the suburbs and creeping closer, has thrown London into a frenzy. At L'Erber, servants work through the night, stuffing clothes chests, mobilising cooks, servers, pages, and by morning a miniature army has gathered in the courtyard. The earl is moving northward to his Neville lands. He intends to break his journey at Warwick and has included George in his plans. Richard waits with his brother in the courtyard, mounts jostling flank to flank, cloths pressed to their faces to ward off the pestilence. Soaked in vinegar overnight, the linen stinks like the devil.

Eying George, he's reminded of their journey to Utrecht: the sudden departure, the fear for life, their desperate need to cleave to one another. Part of him wants to renew that intimacy, to feel close to his brother again. But relations are not so simple these days. They are no longer frightened boys adrift on the German Ocean. When George opens his heart to him now, it is with caution. It's as if, while Richard lay sick abed, the world swivelled on its axis. Things have altered course, moved on without him, and he has nothing with which to determine his position.

Free of the capital and its contagion, tensions are beginning to ease. In Warwick Castle's towering hall, the earl makes a fuss of his daughters, presenting them to his cousins as if for the first time.

George makes equal ado, complimenting and kissing hands like the courtiers he so despises.

Isabel, all concern, grasps Richard's arm. 'We hear you fell sick, Cousin.'

'But am much recovered. As I keep reminding everyone.'

'I'll insist on marchpane and comfits after supper,' she smiles, 'to fatten you up.'

Before he can respond, George steps in, once more taking Isabel's fingers and pressing them to his lips. 'Time spent in your company, my lady, will act as restorative to us both.'

The coquette vanishes in an instant, and Isabel becomes a demure maiden, blushful colour rising. It's embarrassing enough to suffer Warwick's teasing daughters, but the image of a flirting, flattering George is beyond endurance. Over his brother's bowing head, Richard catches sight of Alice, bobbing the knee then rising from her mass of skirts, budding mounds visible above her stomacher.

'Cousin Richard,' Anne: eyes sharp as a sparrowhawk's. 'We thought a game of fox and geese this evening. After your marchpane and comfits – of course.'

Her adoring eyes seeking out her father, the girl evokes a sudden, inexplicable wave of pity, and Richard finds himself dropping his guard. 'Tell me, are you still in possession of your pet squirrel?'

Anne grins. 'Yes, but Mother would have him remain in his cage. He scurried up the bed hangings last night and made her angry. I told her that climbing is a natural pastime for a squirrel, but she fears he'll make an assault on Father's best Arras cloths, and we'll not be able to tempt him down.'

It's the longest conversation they've ever shared. Richard laughs. Anne joins him: a bubbling, childish giggle.

'London has never been a safe place in the summer months,' Warwick announces unnecessarily as pages gather, removing his gloves, his riding whip, 'best out of it.'

'I've no objections,' George says. 'It's a filthy place at the best of times.'

'How does your mother fare, my lord of Gloucester?' The countess' smile is more charming than Richard recalls. 'And my lady, your sister?'

'Very well, I imagine,' George butts in, 'now they're out of London. And much as our cousin says, it hasn't been the safest place over the summer months. Best out of it.'

The countess claps her hands, and pages appear in droves. 'My lord of Clarence, my lord of Gloucester, I shall have hot water sent up to your chambers. You must wish to bathe after so many days on the road.'

Richard squirms. 'My squires, Parr and Kyngston?'

Warwick inclines his head. 'Are in your chambers already, Cousin.'

Richard shoots him a grateful smile.

He forfeits the luxury of scented steam to ensure his ablutions are swift. An opportunity for banter is never wasted on George, and the thought of his brother sauntering through the door, ripe for chatter, while Richard still bathes, is a thing not to be borne. If he does arrive, Richard decides, I will face him fully clothed.

When he's scrubbed and dry, Kyngston fastens him into his gown while Parr, entranced, is drawn to the view beyond the casement.

'Impressed with the earl's fortress, Tom?'

'It's magnificent, Your Grace. King Arthur can have lived in no more splendid a place.'

A knock as expected, and when the door is not immediately opened, another.

'Oh, let him in, Tom, will you?'

Kyngston sniggers as he buckles his master's girdle. 'Anything else, Your Grace?'

'No. Thank you.' Richard leans in. 'It might be an idea to leave my brother and me alone. You know how he is.'

He dismisses the boys as George strides over the threshold,

noticeably genial, nodding to the squires and grinning as they scurry out.

'It's good to spend time together, Dickon. We don't see enough of each other these days.'

Richard rakes his damp hair before donning his bonnet. 'I'm sure we can make up for it over the next few weeks. How long do you intend to stay with us?' He and the earl intend to continue north; he cannot tell what George will do.

'Is that your girl?' George, sprawling, avails himself of the bed.

'Who?'

'Who do you think? Dark hair, green eyes…long, tapering hands.' His brother's own fingers take a stroll around the coverlet, creeping over the heavy damask. 'She's very pretty, Dickon. Fits your description exactly. Did you ever—?'

'Certainly not.'

When George snorts with laughter, Richard is tempted to ask whether he has, and with whom, but he wouldn't know how to begin. And besides, his brother is almost eighteen now, he must have.

'Well,' George says, reining in his mirth, 'perhaps it's just as well.'

'What do you mean?'

'You'll find out soon enough.'

'About what?'

George is temptingly evasive. 'Our cousin will tell you. But in his own time.'

George is right, it is good to be together again, and they intend to make the most of it. Warwick has granted his cousins the use of his hunting parks, his lymerers, his vast array of hunting dogs, and, on hawking trips, the company of his elder daughter. Stroking her merlin's speckled breast, Isabel grieves over its moulting feathers and that soon it must repair to the mews for the season. George, eager to console, never leaves her side and smiles at everything she says. Richard notes how the girl responds. How she tilts her head, amused at George's jests, how her tinkling laughter eddies and spills over with the gushing flow of his brother's shimmering wit.

Today, however, Isabel has fetched a companion, one with slender hips and sleek dark hair: mischief, Richard feels, which can only have been set in train at his brother's behest. Conspiratorial, George and Isabel trot ahead, spirals of laughter wafting like a kerchief, and leave him alone with Alice.

Embarrassed and unsure, Richard aligns his mount with hers. 'I understand your father is retained by the earl.' Unable to look at her, he focuses on George's back as his brother sways languorously in the saddle.

'Yes, indeed.' This is the first time he has heard her voice, and the deep, sensual timbre does not disappoint. Like everything else about her, it is faultless.

'And you are happy in the household?'

When she answers in the affirmative, he sees the stupidity of the question. If Isabel's temerity or Anne's bluntness troubles the girl, is she likely to say so?

Ahead of them, George and Isabel continue their merriment. If their laughter is aimed at him, then it belittles Alice, too, and that is unkind. Grinning awkwardly at the girl, he's rewarded with a sweet smile.

'I heard you were unwell, Your Grace, and for that reason, had to forgo the great tourney.'

He laughs, incredulous. 'It seems the whole of Christendom has been appraised of my sickness. Soon, I shall find myself in receipt of a papal indulgence to allow for meat on fast days.'

'Forgive me. I ask merely to ensure that you are recovered.'

'Recovered and hearty as ever.'

The green eyes glint with mirth. 'Then I'm glad.'

Few of the squires at Middleham talk about girls. No, that's untrue: they do discuss them; they just don't choose to include him in their conversations. Perhaps they think it unfitting to discuss the charms of the fairer sex in the company of the king's brother. He wishes they would, for he can't speak to George of such things; he fears his ridicule too much. He could never broach the subject with Edward - and their cousin is entirely out of the question. Laughter bubbles in his gut at the thought of such an uncomfortable conversation, and he struggles to staunch it.

'It's good to be out of London, Alice.' Another stupid remark. Who would not be glad to be out of a plague-infested city?

Alice nods, the breeze whipping her hair into glossy spirals. How, he wonders, can a girl be so perfect? So modest, yet so alluring. Enchanting, yet pragmatic. He stares unashamedly, and she lifts an enquiring brow.

In an absurd gesture, he casts his eyes heavenward, at the grey churning clouds encroaching on the white. 'I fear it may rain.'

She glances up in appraisal. 'Perhaps you're right.'

Is she the kind of girl who tells her mistress everything? Will they giggle after supper as she takes down Isabel's hair and tucks it into her night coif? Is this all some monstrous jest they have planned between them? Perhaps this isn't George's doing after all. Perhaps it's Isabel's.

He looks to where his companions are perched above a sprawling prospect of meadow and shrubland. George has sent the beaters out, and Isabel is slipping the hood from her merlin. 'Come,' he says, 'let us join your mistress.'

The girl's lips curve in a dutiful smile while her eyes flicker with disappointment. 'Yes, of course. Let us join them.'

Supper à la Warwick—and, unlike Edward's populous affair, the earl offers a private meal in the company of his wife and daughters. All are merry tonight, even Anne. Smiling, she offers Richard a peach from the dish at her elbow.

'Our orchards have been bountiful this summer, Cousin.'

She is trying hard to please. Taking one, Richard thanks her and runs his palms over its curving flesh. His mother still holds with the dangers of eating raw fruit, but the countess believes there are benefits to be had. And she may may well be right. For him, the peach induces thoughts of Alice's soft skin: daring thoughts that both please and shame him. Sensing Anne's scrutiny, he looks up to find her staring boldly. Girls are supposed to keep their eyes lowered in mixed company. Has her mother never told her that?

The sisters exchange glances. Richard knows them well enough now to guess that if they have the slightest knowledge of his feelings for Alice, their teasing will be unbearable. That is to say, Isabel will tease. Anne will simply sit back and enjoy the show.

When supper concludes, the women retire. Kisses are proffered, bows performed, and when the servers have cleared away, a jug of wine and bowls of dragées are fetched for their enjoyment. Richard pops one into his mouth: the sweet taste of violets and the spicy smack of cinnamon and ginger. While Warwick reclines, patting his belly in a show of contentment, George snatches the jug, eager to serve the earl with his own hand. In his haste, he misjudges, Gascon slopping and seeping into the tablecloth.

'Damnation!'

Fighting the urge to laugh, Richard grabs his napkin and holds it to his mouth. What an exquisite image to present to Simon as he readies him for bed tonight.

Satisfied with his efforts to clean up the mess, George is keen to distract. 'A pleasant evening. A truly intimate supper, unlike that occasion with Edward. You must remember, Dickon.'

Refusing to be enticed, Richard lowers his eyes. A pleasant evening should remain pleasant, in his view.

Unwilling to be ignored, George turns to the earl. 'Dickon and I were invited to Westminster for supper. One like this, or so we supposed. But it turned out otherwise, didn't it, Brother?'

Warwick's eyes swivel in Richard's direction. Richard is reminded of Isabel's merlin: observing all, missing nothing.

'As it transpired, we were not the only guests,' he says. 'But intimacy is rare for a king.'

His brother barks with laughter. 'Well, it certainly is now. Edward probably has a Wydeville wiping his arse every time he uses the stool. Oh, stop looking so offended, Richard.'

Richard? His given name for once? His brother could at least have chosen a better context wherein to use it.

Warwick lays a bejewelled paw on George's silk brocade.

'Forgive me,' George says. 'I thought Dickon might find the remark amusing.'

So, I'm Dickon again, Richard thinks. Make up your mind, Brother.

The earl recharges their cups then settles back, livery collar glistening; pendant bear, muzzled and jewelled, winking its garnet eye. 'Richard, you must see that your brother is in danger of losing his honour. My spies tell me there are mutterings in the city, Edward's policies are unpopular, and many of those who supported his claim feel disappointed. I'm afraid I must agree with them. What Edward achieved for his father, for George, for you, has become secondary for him.'

'No, Cousin,' the words are out before Richard can stop them. 'Edward is true to the cause.'

Warwick spreads his hands. 'You think so? Even now? Those who've served him well are being cast aside. He chooses to make a mockery of us.'

Richard feels hemmed in, cousin and brother inclining towards him, faces yellow and heavy in the candlelight. Under the table, he links his hands, clasping, unclasping.

Warwick sighs. 'Your brother has great abilities, I admit, but they are being eroded. He allows himself to be led in only one direction: that of his in-laws. Edward proved himself a worthy successor to your father; at Mortimer's Cross, where God showed his favour, and at Palmsunday Field. But the king's cause is no longer that of York. It is his own, and that of the family he has made for himself.'

George inches closer, avoiding the sticky remnants of his earlier spillage. 'When we were children, Father struggled to establish his place at court. He, the most noble, the most royal man in the kingdom, had to fight to find a foothold under Marguerite's rule. But now, a man requires no such virtues in order to be exalted. He needs only Wydeville blood in his veins. Provided he has that, he can become anything he chooses. Don't you see this as an insult to our father and the struggles he had to undergo simply to survive?'

Oh yes, George, Richard thinks, you know what to do. You know how to slide a dagger under my ribs and twist it.

George persists. 'The earl and I wish to draw Edward away from the queen's family and their poisonous influence. Surely you must understand?'

'Yes,' Richard nods, 'yes, I can see that.'

'We want Edward to be himself again. Don't you want our brother back, Dickon? The brother who avenged Father's death, who fought for us against the odds?'

It's true. They can't allow Edward to destroy what their father strove to build. If Warwick and George simply wish to separate Edward from ill counsel, then that is good; their father would approve. Had he not striven to do the same when the old king lay under the influence of Suffolk, of Somerset?

'We must set Edward back on course,' George says. 'At present, he's like a ship caught in a storm; he needs our cousin to steer him home. You do agree with us? You do agree that this is our only choice?'

'Perhaps.'

'Perhaps? Come on, Dickon.'

Warwick eases himself against his cushions. 'Then you must also agree, Richard, that the best way to proceed would be for us to unite.'

Richard glances from cousin to brother, brother to cousin: confused, unsure. Imagining the treatments Brocas spoke of, he conjures an image of the tortuous rack. Yet it is not Brocas himself who turns the handles: it is Edward, stationed at his feet, and Warwick at his head, who draw his extremities slowly towards them until he fears he will snap in the middle.

'You do want to preserve the cause of York, don't you?' George, almost weeping, reaches for his hand. 'Dickon?'

'You know I will serve our father's cause until I die, George. I'm surprised you feel the need to ask.'

Warwick allows Richard's words to reverberate around the table, then gently, and with precision, takes a breath. 'A solid alliance, boy, is what is required. York and Neville: a union your father forged for himself and which, I can assure you, your mother is keen to see upheld.' The pause is brief, but meaningful. 'George to wed Isabel. You to wed Anne. What do you say?'

Anne? Richard squints at him over the candle flame. 'You once spoke of marriage into France, Cousin. Is this not to be the case now?'

'Ha!' George throws his wine-stained napkin onto the table. 'Think yourself fortunate, Dickon. Louis' daughter is but a child – and malformed. Hump-backed, is that not so, Cousin?'

Anger flares. Richard is on his feet. 'And that in itself, you feel, is reason enough to refuse the girl?'

'Richard, please.' Warwick reaches up and grasps his arm. 'On consideration, marriage into France is no longer politically desirable. Much better to strengthen ties at home, don't you agree?'

They've been discussing this behind my back, Richard thinks. Meeting in the balmy evenings at L'Erber whilst I was laid low at Baynard's, rehearsing what they would say, anticipating my response. Warwick and George, like conspirators, like comrades: like father and son. He throws himself down, the bench jarring the base of his spine, as George slides close to their cousin, usurping the place that should be his.

'Think upon it, Richard,' Warwick says. 'That is all I ask.'

Richard's night light burns low, a floating wick amidst glimmering oil. It's the watching hour, and the castle has woken from its first sleep. He rubs his face, throws off the coverlet and slips out of bed. Forgoing his shoes, he pads to the livery cupboard. Parr has left a cup of wine and a small manchet loaf. He slams the creaking door with the heel of his foot and returns to bed. Slumping against the pillows, he breaks his bread and tries to imagine what others will be doing. George, complacent, munching on cold meat and green cheese. Warwick, regaling his wife with hearty assurances that the king's brothers are eager to ally themselves with the family.

The daughters themselves, sharing foolish fancies within the confines of their bed.

His own thoughts tread an exhaustive path and make no manner of progress. It would be easy to agree with their cousin. In many respects, his offer makes sense, and you might say Warwick has no choice: there are no worthy husbands left for his daughters, after all, since the queen's sisters have had their pick of them. He recalls the earl's letter from the Low Countries. George had been rejected, but Charolais' daughter was not the only option. Warwick had another proposition. Presumably, this is it: York's sons joined with Warwick's daughters, a firm alliance to stand against Edward's chosen regime. And what is more, Richard thinks, Mother agrees.

Yet this business of marriage is not the real matter at stake. The vital choice is between cousin and brother. Between Warwick and Edward. Between tutor and king.

To refuse his cousin's offer seems unthinkable, would be to deny the trust and filiality that has grown and blossomed, and which hangs heavily on the bough. It would form a cleft between them, a cleft which George would seek to fill, and Richard knows he couldn't bear to see that: Warwick means too much to him. Yet, to question Edward's rule would be to betray God's anointed, to deny the brother who had risked everything for them.

To betray Edward would be treason.

'How in God's name did you expect to get away with it?' Edward towers over them like a Titan, eyes bulging, lips flecked with spittle.

The summons had caught the brothers by surprise. The accompanying letter, hastily penned, and delivered by the clammy hand of a royal messenger, allowed for no excuse: summer waning, plague receding, they were to proceed to London without delay to answer for their conduct. And they must appear alone. Their cousin was to remain in Warwick. Edward was adamant about that.

'Well?'

George is both unimpressed and unafraid. 'We would have told you. Eventually.'

'Oh, you would, would you? You faithless little shit.' The king casts an appraising eye over them both, and it's as if what he sees revolts him. Richard shrinks, imagining how they must appear to him—two rain-drenched rats, sodden and unkempt.

Edward has learnt of Warwick's marriage plans, and Richard understands that in their brother's eyes, he is as guilty as George. That he has made no promises, harboured no plans of his own, will make little difference. He's guilty by association.

The freak summer hail continues. Lashing the windows like fistfuls of pebbles, it casts the privy chamber into a haze of thickening gloom. A scuttling in the shadows: Hastings creeping forward, stooping to recover the papers Edward has scattered in his wrath. Richard lowers his head, avoiding Hastings' eye, while George throws the chamberlain a filthy look.

'What's he doing here? This is a family matter.'

Edward curls his lip in disgust. 'It's more than that, boy; it is a matter of treachery.'

George shrugs as if caught out in nothing more than stealing an apple from the orchard, a slice of mutton from the larder. 'We have committed no crime, Brother.'

'You have deliberately disobeyed me.' The king's breast rises and falls, velvet bellows kindling flame. 'Marriage to the earl's daughter was mooted some time ago. I refused. You know that, and yet I am aware that the Archbishop of York continues to do all he can to procure it.'

'Why should I not marry her?' George demands. 'Who else am I to wed? Duke Charles is only interested in our sister. I could have been his son-in-law, I could've married Mary, but he didn't want me. Was it you who talked him out of it, or your new Constable of England?'

Edward's snarls. 'The queen's father, at least, is a man in whom I can place my trust.'

George tilts his jaw in a show of defiance, but Edward is on him, prodding him with a vicious finger. 'You can't deny that I've been patient with you, Brother, more so than you deserve.'

'But I have reasons,' George shrivels under Edward's pummelling, 'good reasons.'

'And what makes you suppose, for one moment, that I'm interested in your reasons, eh?'

George stumbles backwards, foot slithering on the one piece of parchment Hastings has overlooked. 'You ought to care what I think, what our cousin thinks.'

Edward's breath comes swift and hard. 'I might listen to your opinions, George, if it were possible for you to show yourself as anything other than the insufferable, ungrateful churl you are. If you could pull your head out of your arse long enough to see that our cousin is merely using you as a tool with which to strike at me.'

Seeking the chamberlain's eye, Richard utters a silent plea. If anyone can soothe Edward, it's Hastings. The response is little more than a brief acknowledgement: studying his boots, Master Chamberlain is unwilling to engage.

'Dickon,' increasingly desperate, George sees fit to drag him in. 'Dickon and I are assured of our cousin's loyalty. The earl is true to the cause.'

'Whose cause?' Edward's laughter is pained, bitter. 'His own?'

'Father's cause. The cause of York.'

The name serves as a charm, and Richard throws himself at Edward's feet, 'Your Grace, I beg you.' When the gesture does little to placate, his head snaps towards George. 'Please, Brother. Do you think Father would approve of this? If we have disobeyed our king, we must seek his clemency. Only then—'

George's boot, crusted with mud, strikes him in the ribs. 'You coward, Dickon. I might have known you wouldn't have the courage to speak up for our cousin.'

Richard curls upon himself, defence against further attack, but the kick is not the only thing to have injured him. George's accusation has pained him more.

'The boy is your brother,' Edward yells, 'leave him alone.'

But George is thundering onwards, like a wild horse, like a battering ram. 'I have the courage to tell you, even if he doesn't.

Our cousin is faithful to you, to the cause, but his place has been usurped—'

The king grasps the cords of George's riding cloak. 'You speak to me of the cause? It was I who understood Father, I who wreaked vengeance on his enemies.' Tugging the cords, he twists them. 'Father's cause became mine. So, I would suggest that if you desire to follow the cause of York, you look to me, and none other, for your survival. Do you understand?'

Edward loosens his grip. George, crimson and quivering, shrinks into a heap of rain-soaked wool. Still clutching his ribs, Richard feels a gentle nudge. Hastings has drawn up a stool and is offering his arm. Nodding his gratitude, Richard sinks down, while George continues to diminish in size—David before Goliath— but a cowering one, whose sling is short of stones. Edward stoops to retrieve George's bonnet and places it on their brother's dampened curls.

'Do you understand, George?'

A curt nod, a sniff, 'Yes.'

The king lifts George's chin. 'Know this. The earl will always have a place at court. If he chooses to serve me well, I will reward him. I owe him much. But if he chooses to work against me, then I must consider him my enemy—'

George licks his lips with a quivering tongue.

'—and the same goes for you. You're my brother, and I love you, but if you work against me, I have only one choice, and that is to consider you an enemy also.'

Richard feels oddly ashamed. Perhaps he had deserved George's boot. After all, he's done nothing to defend their cousin. Does that make him a craven? All he wants is for those he loves to be reconciled. Is that too much to ask?

George's nose is running. He wipes it with the back of his hand as Edward grasps him around the shoulders. 'Well, let us see how much we can trust you. Richard will return to Warwick, and you shall remain here until the earl's household returns north. And then we shall release you.'

Richard hangs his head. There's nothing he can say—to

either of them.

Chapter Sixteen

April 1468
Middleham

COUSIN WARWICK is playing the host. Resplendent and cheerful, he welcomes his guests to the dais and has them sit beside him. He feeds them delicacies from his own plate: snipe in galingale, parmesan pies, fresh brown trout from the waters of the Cover. He captivates, he entertains, he tells a pleasing tale. Yet Richard, stationed before an Arras cloth and melding into the weave, knows this is more than a companionable dinner, a neighbourly invitation. Acting the page, he is nothing more to this gathering than a henxman serving at table, but matters are afoot here from which he is excluded, and he feels once more the trifling child, tinkering, playing at life, as it falls apart around him.

Henry Fitzhugh, he knows. Scrope of Bolton is familiar. Conyers, Sheriff of Yorkshire, he's met, but knows little about. Rapt and attentive, each man is crouching at Warwick's elbow, ears cocked to every word that falls from their master's lips. Such meetings occur with regularity, sometimes over dinner, sometimes over supper, sometimes by the late-night glow of the Paris candle in his cousin's privy chamber.

The fact unsettles Richard, as much as the memory of Edward's anger still shakes him to the core. Even now, months later, his brother's furious visage still creeps up on him, blasting into his mind unannounced, and he dares to wonder whether it haunts George, too. After the confrontation, Richard had been dismissed, and packed off under the auspices of Hastings, while the king chose to keep George close. Richard had spent a sleepless night before returning to Warwick. It had been an agonising ride through the late summer storms, teeth clenched against the pain in his ribs, his mind fearful of the questions that would invariably greet him upon his arrival.

'Your brother's doing?' Warwick, waiting with his dogs in the inner bailey, had spotted his disquiet immediately.

'Cousin?'

'Well, your face is deathly, and no rider dismounts with such lack of grace unless he's suffering some level of discomfort. I take it Edward had you beaten?'

'No.' He'd clamped a hand to his ribs, defensive both of his pain and of what had befallen. 'I had a slight accident on the road; my mount shied, threw me, and I fell awry. That is all.'

Kyngston, taking his riding cloak, had passed him a knowing glance. *My lord of Clarence's boot*, it said, *I know it well.*

Warwick had made no further attempt to discover what had transpired at court, and Richard supposed he must already be in receipt of the facts. A lengthy transcription in George's hand must have found its way, by covert messenger, into their cousin's eager palm. The boot, the maltreatment, the lash of words would all have been Edward's. No culpability would have found its way to the doorstep of Saint George.

That said, George has apologised—as far as he ever allows himself to apologise—and now takes the trouble to enfold a brotherly missive into every communication he sends to the earl. Admittedly, the letters are brief. They speak of generalities, providing news of their mother, their sister, and offering an occasional flash of humour. But Richard is troubled by their frequency, especially so by their counterparts intended for their cousin's hands. Warwick never discusses these; merely refolds them, locks them away, then sends for his elder daughter. Nothing further has been mentioned upon the subject of the younger.

As for Isabel, she seems to have renounced her flirtatious ways, exhibiting a modest countenance more closely akin to that of a duchess, and Richard is under no illusion that this is what she is set to become. At sixteen summers, she's ripe for marriage, and the earl shows little sign of seeking any other husband for her.

The last time George put pen to paper, he'd been at Coventry, observing the Christmas season with Edward—not from choice, but because he had been summoned. The missive had been short and regular in form: no chess moves, no jests, no grutching about the queen's kin. This, more than anything, had told Richard all he needed to know: the letter would be read before it was sealed, contents scanned, its tenor determined. He knows also that George had not been the only one summoned to Edward's presence.

Warwick, however, has told him nothing of what had taken place when he had finally swallowed his pride and obeyed the king's command. He rarely speaks, these days, of what he calls his 'business,' and Richard is more often delegated to the company of the women or the henxmen. But he is aware of the visitors, who are well received and feasted: the earl's secretary, Robert Neville, and a Scotsman fresh from the French court. News from Calais, Warwick says, whenever he dares to ask: his captaincy, keeping him busy.

'A penny for your thoughts.'

Richard starts. 'Hmm?'

Robert Percy, fellow server, edges in, that he may hear him above the whistle of pipe, the drone of hurdy-gurdy. 'Is it a girl?'

'Why is it that whenever I'm lost in my own musings, everyone assumes they're centred around a girl?'

Percy stifles a grin, eyes wandering the length of the hall to the lower table where Alice sits, head dutifully bowed. 'Girls are generally the cause of my musings.'

'And you newly betrothed?'

'And unable to wed until my lady Joyce reaches her majority. Is it any wonder I muse? Richard, you've been in an odd humour for weeks. What's amiss?'

'Nothing,' he shrugs, irritated. 'Nothing's amiss.'

On the dais, talk is gushing, thick and deep as forest mud. Richard's innards turn to water.

A light touch on his sleeve, Percy's face close, concerned.

'Richard. Do you realise you're trembling?'

Early morning in the practice yard; air cool and punctured by the bubbling call of pigeons. Richard inhales the delicious chill, a gulp of refreshment before consigning himself to full harness. His arming doublet stinks of sweat, but he sees it as a private accolade, the satisfying reek of spent force. Proof that he has pushed himself to the limits, and an inducement to push further.

Each morning, when he wakes, there are pains, every muscle, every sinew stiffened by sleep. He convinces himself that others feel the same, that it's merely the result of the training sessions, of consistent, aggressive combat, and that he's nothing if not the same as the other youths in every conceivable regard.

The only concession he makes to his condition is to emerge early, like this. To allow his squires to arm him while none are present to watch, to preserve privacy of a kind. None have challenged his routine, his prompt departure from the breakfast table, not even Percy, and the countess knows better than to interfere with her husband's household arrangements.

Parr and Kyngston, discreet as ever, are more than proving their worth. He suspects they're grateful for his skinny shape, for the advantage it gives them over those who struggle to fix breastplate and backplate to the husky frames of some of his fellows. The act of arming is a great responsibility for any squire; one error and his master could pay with his life. To this end, Warwick has given him Thomas Huddleston, whose duty is to oversee Parr and Kyngston, to ensure each strap, each stud, is well secured and snapped in place.

'He'll find naught amiss today,' Parr grins, blue eyes dancing astride his wide-bridged nose. 'And we were faster this morning, don't you think, Your Grace?'

Richard smiles. Parr is becoming more sure of himself, confidence grown of battling it out with the other squires, of wrestling with Percy's boys, of learning dagger thrusts. 'For sure, Tom. You must've been buckling plate in your sleep.'

Kyngston pulls Richard's arming cap over his skull, tucks in wayward hair, as a gaggle of boys files into the yard. Francis Lovell trails behind, smaller than the rest, and Richard recalls himself at that age: dispirited, forced to trudge in George's wake, to watch his brother clashing about, and knowing he could never contend with him. He raises a hand in greeting and Lovell beams. Clamping his arms to his side, the boy makes an elegant bow before skittering off to join the others.

'Early as ever, I see.' Percy has crept up on him, hair flaming in the early light.

'Well, as the earl has pitted us against each other, I don't wish to be found wanting. After all, I cannot fail to recall the last time you bested me.'

'True,' Percy flexes his shoulders, 'but you've improved since then.'

'I'd rather you didn't flatter me, Rob. I'd much prefer to hear the truth.'

Percy laughs while his squire, crawling around in the dust, slides his master's feet into their sabatons. 'Then if you would hear the truth, Your Grace, it's that I'm almost six years your elder, and six years more experienced.'

'That, I cannot deny.'

Kyngston lowers Richard's sallet, springing the visor open, as Parr nods in the direction of the armoury. Huddleston has emerged: rubbing his palms against the spring chill and striding across the yard, he's a shaft hurtling towards a butt.

Richard greets him and remains stock still as the youth sets to, circling him slowly, tweaking plates, tugging straps. In this daily ritual, nothing is overlooked, yet Richard trusts his cousin enough to know that this is as far as Huddleston will ever come, that the youth will never divest him of his arming doublet, never strip him to the skin. To his new squire, as to everyone else, Richard is as well-formed as the rest of them.

At length, Huddleston nods, satisfied. 'Excellent work.'

'At least those boys of yours are learning something,' Percy says, extending his arms to receive rerebrace and couter.

'Meaning?' This is where the contest begins, not with the first blow, the initial clash of steel on steel, but as combatants, standing alongside each other, trading insults.

'That they can make a pretty job of arming you.'

'But?'

'But you'll need more than a good set of harness if you are to claim victory today.'

'Arsehole.'

'Arsehole?' Percy bares his teeth, 'Is that the best you can do?'

'Whoreson, then.'

'You can do better than that, surely.'

Richard glowers, trying with all his heart to hate his friend, and failing miserably. His cousin says that hatred is essential, that it's easier to face the carnage of battle if you truly abhor your opponents. Allow any charity of mind into the crucial moments of an encounter, he says, and you're a dead man. With this in mind, they are encouraged to engender loathing of a kind in their challengers. For how can friends engage in combat, Warwick says, if they consider only the polite conversations, the games of dice, which follow once supper has ended and the household takes its ease? Those who come to blows as friends make for poor opponents indeed. And so they must find, even for a short time, a reason to hate.

For Richard, and for Percy, false enmity has been easy to concede. While they assume their positions, a mutual vision hovers between them: Alice and her slim hips. Richard's trick is to recall their dancing class, Percy's hand on hers. To imagine his friend's hand, bold and libidinous, creeping unreservedly over soft rose damask. Whatever Percy chooses to imagine, he cannot tell; trusts only in his own provoking thoughts and allows them to enflame him.

A delicious scraping as they draw their weapons. Alerted, fellow henxmen leave their business and gather round to observe. Any wagers laid on Percy today, Richard thinks, may stand on shakier ground.

Percy strikes first. Richard dodges, hooks his blade under the hilt of Percy's weapon, and tries to hurl it free, but his friend thrusts him away with an immense show of strength, and he staggers to regain his balance. Sword flailing, he steadies himself, parrying Percy's repeated blows. Arm muscles weakening, the strain is beginning to tell, but he cannot yield.

Hate your opponent, boy. It's the only way. Imagine him taking all that you hold dear and trampling upon it, crushing it into the dust.

Screaming, Richard launches himself at Percy. If we were met upon the field of battle, he thinks, this would be a last attempt at life. Those gathered around have begun to yell, baying as if the blood lust were on them.

Force vibrates from hand, to arm, to shoulder, juddering through Richard's entire frame. He has the advantage, but not for long. Percy bears down, and, like George before him, his strength is superior to anything Richard can summon. Buckling under the onslaught, Richard crashes to the ground, winded, with Parr and Kyngston peering into his face. He thrusts them away frustrated, spies Percy, sallet removed and gasping for air.

Fumbling to retrieve his weapon, he hauls himself upright. 'Come on. I'm not finished.'

Screeching and scraping his way towards him, Percy extends his hand. 'A fair contest. You fought well.'

Ignoring the gesture, Richard resumes his stance. 'I said, I'm not finished.'

'Perhaps not. But I am.'

Vulnerable and unsuspecting as Percy is, Richard knows it would now be a simple matter to wrench him off his feet. But this would not be chivalrous. It would not be what his father, nor his cousin, would have him do.

Accepting defeat, he forces a smile, conceding that Alice is undefiled and Percy once more a friend. 'You, too, fought well. Were this a true fight, I should now be your prisoner. Or worse.'

'And I must commend you, Your Grace, as a worthy opponent. For a moment, I could have sworn you really did hate me.'

Taking the letter from his cousin's hand, Richard examines the seal: the king's personal signet impressed into the blob of wax.

'An invitation to accompany your sister on her wedding journey,' Warwick informs him. 'I have received the same.'

Richard scans the missive, re-folds it and slides it into his purse. 'It appears the king has settled upon the feast of Saint Thomas the Apostle as the day for the ceremony.'

'Yes.' A faint snort from the earl as cynicism seeps in. 'Edward has finally managed to scrape together the first two dowry payments. The talk in the city is that crown plate has been pledged to the London goldsmiths.'

That's as may be, but the talk at Middleham is that the king has been forced to it, Warwick having refused to contribute a penny towards the fifty thousand crowns.

'My sister will be happy we are to accompany her to Dover, Cousin. I assume George will be joining us.'

Warwick nods. 'To be sure. But my daughters are sorry not to have been invited.'

Here he is, linking them together again. Edward's brothers, Warwick's daughters: like gold and silver, bit and bridle, hips and haws. Items which, by their very nature, make for natural bedfellows.

Reaching for his wine cup, Richard takes a sip. His cousin does the same. 'You did well today, lad.'

If the earl wishes to compliment him, he should invite him here more often, like he used to. A cold meat supper washed down with tales of their fathers - of York and Salisbury, of knightly brotherhood and friendship. If he would encourage me, Richard thinks, we should sit up late, as we once did, in the days when all was well, and there was complete trust between us.

'Today,' Warwick repeats, by way of explanation, 'in the practice yard. You fought well.'

'I could have done better. Perhaps my tutor has spoken more

favourably of me than I deserve.' He's being surly and he knows it. He just can't help himself.

'I had no need to consult your tutor, Richard. I witnessed your efforts myself. Oh, I made sure you didn't see me. I stayed out of view; I wouldn't have you distracted. You were pitted against Percy for a reason, and you did not let me down.'

'But I let myself down. Percy bested me.' Richard compresses his lips. Like Edward's flattery in days gone by, the tributes do little but frustrate him.

'Only after a struggle, and if he'd taken you up on your offer of another bout, well, who knows?' The smile, warm and genuine, takes Richard by surprise, but he's unable to return it. He refuses to accept praise, where none is due. Warwick shakes his head. 'By God, boy, you take a hard view of yourself.'

'But surely that's the only way to progress? Only a fool believes himself to be greater than he is. I thank you, Cousin, but I fell far short of what was required today.'

'You must know, Richard, that such misplaced modesty does you no credit.'

'No modesty, merely a matter of truth.'

'You must allow me to disagree.' Hauling himself up, Warwick fishes a key from his purse and moves to the chest by the window. He returns with a bundle of crimson velvet. If this is intended for the fashioning of gowns, Richard makes up his mind to refuse. He hasn't earned it. 'I know you better than you think,' Warwick says. 'You can't be satisfied because you seek the approval of one who is unable to grant it.'

'I seek only to improve.'

'I can't speak for your father, Richard. Can say only that if you were my own son, I couldn't be more proud of you.' As Warwick speaks, he's unfurling the velvet. No longer velvet for its own sake, for the making of doublet, sleeves, or riding cape - it is a covering for something more precious. Casting the cloth aside, the earl extends a beautifully crafted sword. 'Please, accept this as a gift.'

Closing his hand around the grip, Richard draws the weapon from its fine leather scabbard, says softly, 'Sir, this is of the finest quality.'

'A French estoc made to my specifications. Louis recommended the most skilled of his craftsmen.'

'You had this made … for me?'

'And no more than you deserve.'

Warwick's noticeable relief, even joy, that the gift has been well-received tears at Richard's heart. 'How can I thank you?'

'You approve,' the earl says, 'of the inscription?'

'Inscription?' He hadn't realised. Tilting the blade to the candlelight, Richard spies a series of letters. Below the hilt, exquisitely engraved, is a single word: *Optimo*. The best. He blinks as the flame swims, blinding him. 'Perhaps not the best—'

'Well then,' Warwick grips his shoulder, pudgy fingers pummelling flesh, 'you must become the best. If not for my sake, then for your father's.'

'Cousin…' Richard falters, the surge of conflicting emotion far beyond his ability to express.

'Enough, lad.' The earl awards him a tender smile. Fondly, Richard returns it.

Chapter Seventeen

June 1468
London

CHEAPSIDE: AWASH with splashes of colour. Citizens, in their best worsted, gathered en masse, their wives in rippling kerchiefs. Doors are festooned with floral garlands, and from every casement, blossoms fall in scented spirals in honour of the future Duchess of Burgundy.

They have been lucky. A wet spring, day upon day of relentless rain, and early summer no better, yet today a brilliant morning: the elements, once more, declaring God's support for the family of York. Richard processes beside his brother, pride in their sister and sorrow at her departure prompting a strange blend of emotions.

Sweat sits on George's upper lip, and his hair lies in damp curls. 'Charles is greedy. The fifty thousand gold crowns are only part of his demands. He wants, in total, two hundred thousand.'

Richard flicks petals from his brother's sleeve with a playful blow. 'Every bride comes with a dowry. Would you have our sister go to her husband empty-handed?'

George grunts. 'Margaret is an excellent prize in herself, with or without a dowry. What Charles desires most is Edward's support against the French.'

Jerking the reins, Richard steers his mount clear of the pressing crowd. 'Then he's a fool. Scripture says that a worthy wife is like a jewel to her husband.'

But George is in no mood to agree about anything. He's staring straight ahead, eyes fixed on Warwick's mount: a huge chestnut bay, Margaret riding pillion, crimson skirts rippling over its glimmering flanks. 'We should be going with her. Her own brothers, not Scales. Why should he be granted the honour?'

Richard cannot disagree, for the simple reason that he knows Margaret herself would wish to prolong their tripartite alliance, if only for a few more days. Despite their separation over recent years, no distance has prevented the three of them from spending the occasional Christmas together, celebrating Easter in one another's company, if and when they wished. This marriage will not simply separate us, Richard thinks; it will redefine us. Whilst he and George will remain their brother's subjects, Margaret's loyalty must now be to her husband, and to Burgundy.

'The Londoners make a veritable to-do,' George indicates the heaving crowds, 'but we all know they don't really approve. They've never favoured the Burgundians. It's our cousin they applaud here. The cheers, the flowers, they're for him and for our sister, not for Edward and this damnable alliance. We can only hope the union will incline Charles to lift his restraints on trade, perhaps then the Londoners might look more favourably on him.'

From Warwick's saddle, Margaret acknowledges the cheers; elegant bows, gracious waves confirming her as a suitable consort for any ruler in Christendom. Richard's admiration swells. 'Do you think she'll have a good life with him? With Charles?'

George snorts, nudging his mount. 'She'd better. If not, he shall answer to me.'

Dusk consumes the abbey of Stratford Langhorne. Compline concluded, candles extinguished, the monks have withdrawn; pale smudges shuffling towards the night stairs. Enveloped by the scent of dying smoke, the congregation splinters into factions as each seeks out familiars.

Richard rises from his knees, genuflects, his sister's hastily penned note crushed in his fist. Margaret wants to see him privately, says there's something she would have him do for her, and he's determined not to let her down. The claustral walk, she suggests, after Compline—and he's to come alone.

His keen eye picks her out amongst her growing entourage. Resplendent in grey silk, she is a young dove smothered by pecking, cooing mother birds. Elizabeth, Duchess of Norfolk, Joan Lady Scrope, fussing and flapping, straightening her skirts, smoothing them down. With a swift gesture, Margaret excuses herself and slips through the throng towards the south door. Richard makes to follow. They'll have to be quick. Her women won't leave her alone for long.

'Dickon,' George sidles up, the earl alongside, 'the abbot has favoured our cousin with a jug of Gascon. Will you join us?' The tone is welcoming, inclusive, and Richard shuns the petty jealousy that rises at the sight of brother and cousin, arms linked, united in their disapproval of the forthcoming event.

'I thank you, but I wish to walk before I retire.'

Warwick lowers his eyes. 'A great shame.'

Richard knows he's disappointed him. Excusing himself, he says that were it not for a slight bellyache, for a feeling of sleeplessness which might only be remedied by a lungful of evening air. If—

George is clearly bored. Clearing his throat, he nods to where Scales is kneeling in the ante-chapel, palms joined in an act of private devotion. 'It is argued that an ostentatious faith is no faith at all. You do know that Brother Anthony scourges his flesh?'

Richard shrugs. Margaret will be waiting. 'If the queen's brother chooses flagellation as a means of reaching God, then who are we to criticise?'

'I've heard it said that certain folk find pleasure in punishing themselves,' George raises a mocking brow, 'a pleasure which is little akin to faith.'

'Please. I must beg your leave.'

When George makes to protest, Warwick stops him. 'Your brother wishes for solitude. Let him be.'

George huffs in a show of exaggerated toleration. 'Of course, Dickon. I forgot. Your bellyache.'

Richard tries once more to apologise, but brother and cousin have already turned away, heading for the guesthouse, velvets merging.

Easing himself through the tarrying worshippers, he makes for the south door. Plunging into the dim cloister, he pauses in the half-light, ears cocked for George's creeping footfall. It would be just like his brother to retrace his steps, to pry, to satisfy himself as to Richard's true intent. But the passing moments yield nothing save the eager call of chirruping birds, the thud of a door in the bowels of the abbey. Unfolding Margaret's letter, he squints at the florid script. Whatever she seeks from him, he prays it will be within his power to accomplish.

'I knew you would come.' Shadows dissolve, relinquishing his sister.

'How could I not? You have a task for me?'

Margaret glances swiftly about her. 'We may not have long, so I'll speak plainly. George and Cousin Warwick. They must make their peace with the king before this business goes any further. And you are aptly placed to act as diplomat to both sides.'

A cynical laugh escapes him. 'If you believe that, Sister, then you overestimate me. My influence is not so great that either our cousin, or Edward, would pay me any heed. And as for George…'

He could go on but knows it's merely envy which prompts him; truculent and childish.

Margaret snatches his hand. 'Please, Richard. I'm afraid of what may happen if things continue in this way. I saw George and the earl enter the church, deep in conversation. Don't shake your head. You know as well as I that they're not passing time together to speak idly of the wedding celebrations. Things are occurring, there have been rumours—'

Footsteps. The slap and scrape of leather soles. Margaret tenses then sags with relief as one of the abbey's boy servants hobbles into view. They sink into silence, allowing him to pass, but as he moves into the failing light, they see the boy is lame, one foot hideously twisted, each movement slow and seemingly painful. At sight of them, he pauses, unsure.

Richard nods. 'May God give you good night.'

It's clear the boy is unused to being acknowledged, still less addressed. Stammering his gratitude, he makes a clumsy bow. 'And to you, my lord.'

Richard watches him lumber towards the abbey church, the south door groaning as the boy wrenches it open and limps inside.

Margaret senses his disgust. 'What is it, Richard?'

'The poor boy should be free to partake of God's grace with the rest of them, not forced to steal into church after prayer simply because he's malformed.'

Surprised by Richard's sudden fury, Margaret squeezes his hand. 'I'm sure we all pity such unfortunates, but please, my women will not allow me my freedom for long. You must listen. I'm afraid of what might happen to George if he and our cousin continue to oppose Edward.'

'Our brother is old enough to take care of himself.'

Pity for the boy-servant and anger over his plight ignite Richard's frustrations as he relives the evening's events: Warwick linking George's arm and whispering like an intimate, inviting him for wine and discourse, treating him in the way he should treat Richard; the way he used to treat him.

'Brother, I'm afraid.' Margaret, wrapped in her own private despair, closes in on herself, becomes a tight, defensive bundle.

Richard fumbles for her hand. 'Forgive me.'

'I need to rely on someone, need to know that our family will not be damaged beyond mending. I would not have us divided. Not because of a woman we all despise but whom we must endure for Edward's sake. If George is drawn into treason—'

'Treason?' He steers her into the shadows. 'I doubt he would really go that far. That either of them would. Our cousin isn't stupid. Howsoever Edward has chosen to wed, we each of us owe him our loyalty.'

'Then tell them. Tell George.' Margaret's whispers are growing in force, her fingers locking around his wrist. 'I've always been able to contain him, to control his rashness. But you must know that it's only a matter of time until his dissatisfaction spills over. I need to be able to rely on you to do as I would. To stop him – them – from making a fearful mistake.'

'Perhaps if I spoke to Mother.'

Margaret closes her eyes, damp lashes fusing. 'Mother is scrupulous, discreet, but her anger is still raw. Even now, if she thought that between them, George and our cousin could force Edward to cast the queen and her family aside, then she'd encourage it. You know she would.'

'Yes.'

'I have only you, Brother. Can you give me your word? Can you?'

Her solemn grey eyes, demanding, beseeching, pierce Richard's soul. 'Of course.'

'Speak to Edward, too, if you can. Speak well to him of George. For my sake.'

He nods as his sister swipes her face with her hand then composes her features.

'Do I have your promise, Richard? In the name of all that is holy?

'Yes, so I have said. You have my promise.'

'Thank God.'

'Come,' he links his arm through hers, 'let us walk.'

Waning light traverses the cloister, bleeds onto the smooth stone paving along which their shadows glide, black and elongated in the sanguine glow.

'Sister,' Richard says, voice hushed, 'you spoke of rumours. If you've heard aught which may harm the earl, you must tell me.'

A patter of feet, a swish of silk, announce the arrival of her women.

'You've given me your word,' Margaret says as they bear down upon them. 'Don't forget.'

Richard bows, watching with regret as his sister is gathered up, like a bundle of laundry, and spirited away.

Edward has surprised them, a sudden decision tearing him

from civic duty to take a personal farewell of his sister. Hair flapping in the salty breeze, he squints to survey the flotilla anchored off the Margate coast: the impressive *New Ellen*, which Margaret boarded yesterday, the *Saint John,* the *Mary,* and twelve smaller ships bobbing gaily in their wake. A spectacular fleet, good enough to bear the king of England's sister and grand enough to impress her new Burgundian husband.

George peers towards the flagship, shielding his eyes as he tries to pick her out. His shoulders settle as he spots her, close to the forecastle; hair, loose and virginal, whipping around her like a pennant.

Drawing rein beside him, Richard wonders how their diminutive figures must appear to her. Which of us, he thinks, will hold her gaze the longest? Edward, glimmering and throbbing with life? George, eyes fixed on the ship as if bidding his soul goodbye? Or me, the one upon whom she has placed her greatest burden?

All three wait in silence, watching the vessels decrease in size as they navigate the rolling waves. A gentle thud of hooves, the chink of bridle bells, as Warwick settles his mount beside them.

'A fair wind. Two days at most.'

Richard gives a tight smile. 'Let us, at least,' he says, 'be grateful for that.'

The king's mount whinnies, and Edward tugs at the reins. 'A man could wish for no better sister. She will make a fine duchess.'

Something upon which they are all agreed. Yet already, Richard feels he's failing her. What possible influence can he have over anything? Edward, Warwick, George: why should any of them listen to him? But he must try. The problem is when, and how.

The earl takes his leave, and Edward follows, trotting in good humour over the sand-strewn tussocks. George pets his mount in silence, gloved fingers combing its chestnut mane. Its colouring reminds Richard of Robijn and their pony rides around the bishop's palace. Odd, he thinks, how past troubles lessen with the passage of time. If any had told him that their sojourn in the Low Countries would one day seem nothing more than a curious interlude, he wouldn't have believed them.

'Never fear,' he says, a hand on George's arm. 'We'll see her again, Brother.'

George's head whips round, eyes moist. 'How do you know?'

'Because we will. We're her family, and she loves us. Duke Charles will surely allow her to visit, and I'm certain Edward will arrange for us to visit her. He does not forget how close we became after Father's death.'

George stares at the horizon, at the vanishing speck of the *New Ellen*. 'But you can't deny we should be making the voyage. With her. If Edward bore us any love at all, he would have granted us that.'

The court returns to Westminster, and Richard's opportunity to fulfil his promise to Margaret is swiftly receding. George will not dally here, and he himself will soon be returning north. There are but a few days. He can't let her down, yet shrinks from the task. Psalter open, he fingers its worn pages and runs his eyes over the text:

Thou sittest and speaketh against thy brother: thou slanderest thine own mother's son.

Slapping the book shut, he kneels, rush mat pricking his knees, snagging his hose. What would his father do? How can he know? How can he even pretend to guess? His father had no brothers, did not experience that particular manner of mixed blessing.

Breathing a swift Paternoster, he crosses himself, dusts his knees and goes in search of George.

Finding his brother alone but for his page, he delivers a prayer of thanks. There's no sign of their cousin nor any indication that he has even been here. George is intent on a game of chess, ivory queen tapping the board, satisfaction apparent as he swipes an opposing knight and adds it to his collection.

'You ought to have foreseen that move, Harry.'

Richard recognises the boy: bumbling, anxious, maladroit Henry. His brother seems to collect that kind of servant. Perhaps he uses them as a mirror, holding them up and comparing reflections to make himself feel better.

'Dickon!' Flapping his arms, George indicates a vacant chair. 'Please. Sit you down. Move that book, Harry, allow my lord of Gloucester to seat himself.'

Henry does as he's bid, then melts away, flopping onto a stool in the corner, obscured by the bed hangings. Richard recalls their mother's pert remark, her pragmatic shrug of the shoulders. *Servants talk. It was not a difficult matter to bribe that boy of George's.*

'Brother,' he says, 'might I speak with you alone?'

'We are alone, aren't we?' George looks incredulous, laughs. 'What? You're not worried about Harry?'

Richard peers awkwardly towards the bed curtains. How can George be so unaware of himself, of his own complete lack of discretion?

'Oh, very well,' George makes a face. 'Find yourself something to do, Harry. A game of hazard with the kitchen boys. Here,' fumbling in his purse, he tosses a coin, 'make a wager, if you will.'

Scrambling for the groat, the boy is out of the door in a moment. Scurrying downstairs—or skulking outside, ear against oak? Richard can't decide.

George links his fingers, cracking the knuckles. 'I've been thinking about Margaret. She must be on Burgundian soil by now. I wonder how they're receiving her?'

Richard's nerves settle, pleased George is heading in the direction he wishes to take him. 'Very well, I should think. If you recall, we both found the Duchess Isabella to be a most gracious lady.'

'And sympathetic to York. But it's Charles who worries me. He was disloyal to his own father, and he supported Lancaster. Edward is foolish to expect too much from him.'

'But the duke has his mother to guide him – and the talk is that they're very attached to one another.'

George offers a half smile. 'I dare say you're right. But this is

Margaret we speak of. Her welfare is of great concern to us both. I wouldn't wish her anxious or unhappy.'

Excellent, George. This couldn't be better had the words been placed in your mouth from above. Richard takes a breath. 'I'm pleased you mention her because before she left, Margaret entrusted me with an errand.'

'You?' George inclines himself, beetle-browed. 'What kind of errand?'

'She is concerned about the unrest that is felt in some quarters. The dissatisfaction with our brother's rule.'

A rolling of the eyes. 'Well. If Edward were to cast aside his wife's family, then all dissatisfaction would follow. Our brother has the power to solve everything, but he chooses not to. He's not particularly far-sighted.'

'But our sister is. Far-sighted enough to see what could happen to you, and to our cousin, should you persist in your aversion to the queen.'

George cackles. 'You speak as if the earl and I are the only souls who object to that family, but I assure you, Dickon, there're many who feel the same. Were we, even now, to approach the queen's grace with open arms, it would do little to appease others of the nobility.'

'But men take their lead from you, from our cousin.'

'Indeed they do, Brother.'

'George, this is exactly what Margaret fears. You and—' with an eye on the door, Richard pauses, then continues in hushed tones, '—you and the earl taking things into your own hands. To act against the queen's family is to act against the queen. To act against the queen is to bring Edward's judgement into question.'

George closes his eyes as if searching for the patience to deal with a frustrating infant. 'If men had thought to remove the She-Wolf or convince Daft Harry to control his wife for the good of the common weal, Marguerite wouldn't have grown in power, and our father would still be alive. Think on that, Dickon. Would you have a woman poison our brother's ear as Marguerite poisoned Harry's, until he cannot think for himself?'

'George, keep your voice down, for Mercy's sake.'

'You have no idea, have you, Dickon?' George's face is piqued and flushed. 'No idea what Elizabeth is capable of. At least we knew Marguerite for an enemy and could not be surprised by anything she did. Edward's wife acts behind his back. And he lets her.'

He glares, daring Richard to question him. When he doesn't, George springs to his feet. Crouching before Richard's chair, he grips its arms, making a prisoner of him, forcing him to listen. 'Thomas Fitzgerald, Earl of Desmond,' George's voice drops until it is barely more than a whisper, 'my deputy in Ireland, a onetime friend of Edward—'

'Has but of late lost his head.'

George swallows. 'At least you know that much. He did indeed lose his head, and on a charge of treason. Fitzgerald was a good fellow, popular, until incidents of petty unrest were laid at his door, and our brother, mindless of their former friendship, chose to consider the man incapable of his duties. The role of deputy was taken from Fitzgerald and given to the Earl of Worcester.'

'John Tiptoft.' Richard shudders. 'An evil name to conjure with.'

'My man at court says that despite removing Fitzgerald from his position, Edward had perceived no treason in the man's behaviour, merely considered him ineffectual.'

His brother's breath battering his lashes, Richard blinks. 'Then why was he arraigned? For treason, of all things?'

George licks his lips with a trembling tongue. 'I've heard Fitzgerald's execution came as a surprise even to Edward, for he himself had uttered no such order.'

'But such a commandment would be issued under the privy seal. Wouldn't it?' Under other circumstances, Richard would have revelled in proving how much he has learnt of the laws of the land, but this is not the time. He's too busy recalling the headings at Middleham, the whistle of steel, the founts of blood. He's too busy feeling sick.

George nods. 'Indeed.'

'I don't understand. If the order didn't come from Edward, then…?' Richard hardly dare pose the question.

'You forget Fitzgerald was also a friend of Warwick's and confided in him. Upon one occasion, he told our cousin a tale.' George shifts on his haunches but remains close. 'Fitzgerald said that once, whilst he was in Edward's favour and visiting our shores, our brother posed him a question. This, it must be remembered, was not long after Edward had married the queen.'

Richard's palms have begun to sweat, his supper stirring itself up in the pit of his belly. 'What manner of question?'

'Edward, proud of his mésalliance, sought Fitzgerald's opinion on his choice of wife. Fitzgerald spoke openly, told our brother that, in his opinion, Edward had abased his princely estate by marrying beneath him.'

'What are you saying, George?'

Staring pointedly, his brother rises from his haunches. 'I think you know.'

'Surely not. It cannot be.'

'The whisper is that letters were devised under the king's privy seal, but if the king did not append the signet, then someone did. Someone able to access it. Someone close.' With a suggestive shrug, George resumes his chair, where he remains silent, allowing his words to sink in.

Richard feels as though a steel band is encasing his ribs. 'More reason, surely, to have a care for yourself.'

No response, save a soft, almost inaudible snort.

'You wouldn't do anything rash, would you, George? Please, consider our sister, consider Mother. They've been through enough.'

George stares, unmoved. 'Whatever I do, Dickon, it will always be for the good of the cause.'

When Richard finally plucks up the courage to leave the room, the boy, Henry, is nowhere in sight. Sconces smoulder, conjuring shadows along the route to his own chamber. The dank, musty smell of the river has settled in every niche, while the draught-blown hangings respire decades of dust.

Not for the first time does he find himself craving the brisk air of Yorkshire.

All traces of Margaret, the panoply, the celebrations, have been swept up like debris. In the palace yard, Warwick's men are saddling horses, rolling up banners, securing chests onto sumpter wagons. George's men are doing the same.

In the royal apartments, Richard finds himself smothered in a shower of brotherly kisses. 'God knows,' the king says, 'I'm sorry to see you leave. All of you.'

Edward is lodged within the casement, watching the commotion below, his gown of cloth of gold, the final vestige of celebration. He's sorry to see us leave together, Richard thinks, perhaps that's more to the point.

'If you're concerned about our sister, Richard,' Edward murmurs, 'then don't be. She is in good hands with Anthony, and if she's anxious at the thought of leaving us, I've loaned her two of my fools to keep her entertained.'

'No,' Richard says, 'I don't fear for Margaret.' If his brother considers this to be the depth of his trouble, then he sorely misreads him. 'There's none more capable than she; any man would be fortunate in taking her to wife.'

Turning his back on the activity below, Edward changes the subject as surely as if he had slammed the shutters. 'You shall be sixteen in October, Richard, and have reached your majority.'

'Yes.' *You'll be sixteen in October, therefore...?* Where is this leading?'

'I believe your training is at an end and would recall you to court before Martinmas.'

Why keep it until now, until they are about to depart? It would have been good to have discussed this in detail. 'Our cousin—?'

'Tells me how much you have achieved during your time with him. Says that he's proud of you. And I agree, you are a great source of pride. For him, and for me.' Another spontaneous embrace and Richard starts at the slap of his brother's huge palms.

'He knows? The earl knows I'm to be recalled?'

'I've spoken to him. He understands you will soon have duties to fulfil. Your involvement in affairs, such as commissions, has thus far been nominal. But you need responsibilities, Richard; you are a boy no longer.'

Responsibilities. He would welcome them. But he'd also have welcomed his cousin's inclusion in any decision to extract him from the Warwick household.

'You do want responsibilities, Richard?'

'Of course.'

'And so, we're agreed you shall leave your cousin's establishments by Martinmas?'

He doesn't know why it has come as a surprise. It ought not to have done, but it has. It's the timing. As if Edward wants him under his control. As if he suspects him of going the same way as George.

'Yes. Martinmas.'

Edward's face softens. 'Concerning our cousin. You know I would have his friendship, and our brother's also. We're not natural enemies, nor should we be. And though I'm the first to admit his opinion can be swayed by no man, I trust that you might make good account of me to the earl in the time remaining. If the words came from you, perhaps he may listen.'

Margaret's burden, secured with tight cords, increases in weight as Edward lodges his own beside it. 'Rest assured, Your Grace.'

Middleham, gleaming under the snows of early winter, is stark, white and beautiful. In the brilliance of the morning, they crest the incline, bridle bells tinkling, and halt to squint across the dale. He's pleased to be alone with the earl. Warwick, the most direct man he knows, has been finding reasons to avoid him. Constant business, the stream of messengers, arrangements – always arrangements, for travelling to this, or that, place – have taken up, it seems, every moment of his cousin's time. The earl's unexpected suggestion of a gallop across Sunskew Park has been grasped tightly before it can be rescinded. Richard needs to speak to him, and as they draw rein, the stillness of the crisp air provides a tableau for his final, abject plea.

'Cousin—'

'If you've made up your mind to leave, Richard, then I cannot stop you.' Patting his horse's withers, Warwick turns to face him. It is a weary countenance, the cruel winter light picking out each line, each crevice. 'You reached your majority last month and are receiving ample honours from the king's hands. Your training is at an end, and I have no hold over you.'

The response sounds overly pragmatic, rehearsed. One may even call it banal. Richard would rather his cousin speak his mind. If he would prefer him to remain, let him say so. At least it would show he cared one way or the other.

'You think I want to go?'

Warwick turns his attention back to the sweeping blanket of white. 'I know you do not wish to stay. Go with my blessing back to your brother. That is, after all, where your heart lies.'

'It's where my loyalty lies. The two are not necessarily the same.'

Following the flight of a buzzard as it dips and rises, the earl remains silent.

Frustrated, Richard edges his mount closer. 'The king has recalled me. What would you have me do? Disobey?'

Warwick remains expressionless.

Richard sets his mouth. At least he can say he has fulfilled his promise to Edward. Since returning north, he has tried more than once. But their cousin is determined to disregard all he says, to deliberately misunderstand. Sometimes, he thinks the earl wants rid of him; at others, he wonders whether it's a ploy to keep him safe: the less he knows, the less he is involved, the safer he'll be.

'Sir,' he tries again, 'I beg you, consider what I've told you of late. Edward would have your friendship. Yours and George's. He would not have the family divided.'

'He divided us when he married Lady Grey. How then can he place the blame anywhere but at his own door?'

'The recent grants he's bestowed on you, upon your brother of Northumberland—does that not show the king open to reconciliation?'

A sharp laugh. 'So open that he sends an untried boy to negotiate with me?'

The insult, if that's what it was, cuts deep. 'If he thought you were prepared to do so, he would welcome you to court in person and with open arms. He said so.'

Warwick's smile is sardonic. 'And the viper in his bosom? If I were to accept the king's embrace, you know as well as I that she would sink her fangs into my flesh.'

'And the alternative?'

The earl tugs at the reins, wheeling his mount. 'Of that, Cousin, you need not concern yourself.'

'Richard?' Robert Percy loiters in the doorway, bonnet in hand, lanky in his black gown and hose. 'I came to wish you Godspeed.'

Richard beckons, although he hates farewells, they conjure too many memories. A diminutive figure follows; Lovell has taken to trailing Percy in anticipation of Richard's departure. That's good. Francis is on the verge of adolescence, and Richard can appreciate the experience, especially when one falls short, in height and in bearing. Rob will encourage him, he thinks.

Smoothing down his fiery locks, Percy replaces his bonnet. 'Please, Your Grace, know that if I might serve you in any way—'

'And I.' Lovell's bows, having been worked upon, are now quite spectacular.

How dutiful they are, Richard thinks, the pair of them. How different this conversation from the convivial banter once traded after supper, the relentless boasting, the irreverent jests shared in the armoury. 'Come, my friends. Surely, we are too comfortable in each other's company to employ formality now.'

Percy fidgets. Lovell wipes his face with his sleeve. Richard, blinking, sucks his underlip until the moment passes. Until now, he had not appreciated the depths of their companionship. At court, he has no friend but Edward.

He clears his throat. 'I've learnt of late that a king's brother need not lack for company, but company does not always equate to friendship. The two of you have offered me both in good measure. Thank you for…'

Percy, practical as ever, sees fit to rescue him. 'Keep us in mind, Your Grace.'

A final glance around the chamber succeeds in conjuring spectres: shadows of a boy in crimson livery, keen to learn, afraid to fail, delighted by any word of praise that falls from his cousin's lips. Fighting the urge to linger, Richard makes for the door.

The Countess and her daughters wait in hall: silent, detached. When he first arrived, they had welcomed him so warmly, encasing him in their colourful world; teasing, flirting and cultivating the awkward, restive boy, and burnishing the courtier to a glimmering sheen. Richard owes them much, has given nothing in return, and today, he will turn his back upon his lord and master, throwing every kindness Warwick has ever shown him back in his face. Or, at least, that's how it feels.

The door to the earl's privy chamber is closed. The countess says, 'My lord husband will be with us anon.'

He wonders if the earl is hunched over his desk, perusing some furtive French missive, or whether the delay is intentional, designed to extend Richard's agony, to demonstrate his diminishing place in his cousin's vigorous world.

'Please extend my goodwill to His Grace, your brother.' The countess coughs delicately, and he hears echoes of her husband. *His Grace, your brother.* Not His Grace, the king.

'I shall, Madam.'

'Godspeed, Cousin.' Isabel's eyes are glassy. If Edward is correct about her father's intentions, then where does she see herself in the course of a year? As the newlywed Duchess of Clarence, or something more? Richard thanks her, returns the blessing, and takes the liberty of placing a kiss upon her smooth, ivory cheek.

Anne throws swift glances towards her father's closet, like a supporting player keen to deliver his lines before the hero takes the stage. 'Farewell, Cousin. We wish you well.'

'And I, you.' The girl's loyalty to her father is absolute, and Richard cannot condemn her for it. Instead, he kisses her hand.

Alice, tawny-clad, hovers on the margins, bobbing the knee. He makes a cool bow, ignoring the empty space opening in his belly, the twisting in his breast at sight of her, deluding himself that those green eyes hold no lure for him, and that perhaps she is not the beauty he had first thought her.

The chamber door is yanked wide. Thrusting a parchment into the hands of a page, Warwick groans. 'I apologise, Cousin. Business.'

'Yes. Yes, of course.'

Awarding Richard a lingering glance, the earl throws an arm around him. The gesture says, *We were close once. I know your innermost secret and have kept it. If you remember nothing else of me, then remember that.*

Whisking him through the doors, Warwick ushers him down the outer stairway and into the bailey. There's still time, Richard thinks, still time to tell him I've changed my mind, that I'll stay and give him the support he was once so keen to win. But with each step, the words recede, unspoken. Both he and his cousin know he cannot remain, cannot espouse a cause contrary to the king's will. That he can never, while his breath remains, commit any act of which his father would not have approved.

The wind is bitter; rasping his cheeks, it lays them raw, open to whatever may come. His mount stamps with impatience, hooves squelching the filthy slush of the yard. Parr and Kyngston, having overseen the loading of his goods, sit alongside the sumpter horses on their fat rouncies.

'Farewell, lad.' Warwick's rough embrace takes him by surprise, and Richard cleaves to the solid bulk, breathes in sandalwood and sweat. It takes him back to Baynard's, to a grey December dawn infused with agony and fear. Gripping the back of his cousin's gown, he squeezes gilt brocade.

'I beg you, Cousin. Please. Edward has said—'

'No, Richard.' Warwick releases him and pins him with his eye. 'No. You know I can't.'

'I will be eternally grateful to you,' Richard fights to control the tremor in his voice. 'I would not be the man I am without your care, without your concern.'

'Well then,' a meaty fist grips his shoulder, 'time will tell what kind of a man I have made.'

It is as final as the raising of a drawbridge, the ultimate crank of a windlass, and Richard doesn't know how to answer him. Mounting his horse, he makes a fuss of settling into the saddle, hoping his cousin will call him back, offer a word, a promise, to convey to the king. Instead, Warwick joins his wife and daughters at the foot of the keep: a splattering of colour against grim, grey stone.

Chapter Eighteen

December 1468
Palace of Placentia

TREASON: RICHARD'S first Christmas at Edward's court is blighted by the stink of it. Even the king's gifts to him, of manors and estates, have come about through sequestration, the forfeited lordships of those who have lately conspired against Edward's rule. In the aftermath of Epiphany, Henry Courtney and Thomas Hungerford, condemned on the evidence of a captured Lancastrian, are to face the ultimate charge. And Richard, the king decides, is to personally head the commission. It's to be a baptism of fire. A test which makes those imposed by their cousin, three years since, seem almost prosaic.

He sups tonight in the king's chamber. Edward has ordered cold fowl and manchet loaves, butter that melts in the heat from the hearth, Rhenish that warms and soothes. Richard has partaken a little too keenly of each, and it is helping.

Edward, dissolving into a pool of liquid gold, raises his cup and peers at him over its glistening rim. 'And how are you finding the celebrations at court, Richard?'

'Different.'

'Different?'

'From what I've known before.'

A sliver of charred wood falls onto the hearthstone, red glow fading. Edward covers it with his soft leather boot and crushes it to dust. 'I'll say one thing for you, lad, you do not waste your words.

The influence of your cousin's blunt Yorkshiremen, doubtless.'

Your cousin, Richard thinks. And when did Warwick cease to be ours? Perhaps he should pursue it, but anxiety lies low tonight, the Rhenish has seen to that. Curled snugly at the base of his stomach with no inclination to rise, his fears are too seductively, too deliciously, constrained as he feels himself descending into a state of hazy indulgence.

'It's kind of you, Your Grace, to invite me to sup.'

'Nonsense, you're my brother, and it's high time I saw more of you. Tell me, how did you survive those hostile northern winters?' Edward scans his face as if it were a map upon which were impressed the villages, hills, and valleys of Yorkshire: every stream, every copse, every sheepfold.

'I agree the winters are ungodly, but the summers can be as sweet as those of the south. It is a fair land. I came to feel at home there.'

'Did you?' The king's gaze is exacting. After a pause, he says, ''Tis a pity our cousin didn't sire a son. I've heard that even his bastards are daughters.'

To picture Warwick and the countess abed is an embarrassing enough proposition without speculating how far he may have scattered his seed. Against his better nature, laughter tickles Richard's throat, but instinct is swift to conquer. The subject of Warwick's progeny is dangerous ground.

Edward wipes his mouth. 'Did you make any friends in the household?'

Robert Percy, he tells him, Francis Lovell. 'It was our cousin's idea that I should take Lovell under my wing. The boy was unhappy when he arrived, having just lost his father. Despite the difference in age, I believe we made good company.'

'Did you miss George?'

The Rhenish, the bluntness of the question, will not allow Richard to lie. 'Yes, I did. Very much.'

A crack bursts from the depths of the flames, and tiny sparks pursue each other into the vastness of the flue. Edward watches them and smiles. 'Edmund and I, you know, were much the same.'

If this is to be a tale from Edward's youth, then Richard would hear it. Availing himself of more Rhenish, he settles himself, invoking the past.

'The huge oak at Ludlow,' Edward says. 'Edmund and I could see it from our chamber and were forever challenging each other to climb it. One day, in the practice yard, when our tutor was called elsewhere, we made for the tree. I, being the tallest, let our brother climb upon my shoulders to reach the lowest limb. Lithe as a monkey, he was, with his skinny body, far nimbler than I. You know what I did then?'

Richard shakes his head, light-headed and eager.

'I left him there in jest. Went back to the yard. Picked up my sword. When Master Apsall returned and asked where Edmund had gone, I shrugged and told him I really had no idea.'

'What happened?'

'Our brother remained there for the rest of the morning, too abashed to call for help. I owned the deed, of course. Eventually.' The king snorts with laughter, eyes bright and moist. 'Master Apsall was furious, had a groom fetch a ladder from the orchard, to help bring him down. Edmund never forgave me. That he should be rescued like some hapless maiden was too shameful a thing to bear.'

Richard smiles. Had this been himself and George, there's little doubt who would have been the dupe. 'I wish I had been old enough to know Edmund better.'

'He was my greatest friend. You would have liked him.' Edward is quiet for a space. Taking the edge of his sleeve, he exhibits no shame in dabbing his eyes. 'The sweetest memories always hurt, Richard. That's a lesson we all learn, in time.'

If George were to die, Richard thinks, I would weep, too. He cannot raise the subject of their brother, nor that of the earl. Soft and comfortable, he would be too loose, too free, with his words. There is something, however, that he must ask the king. 'Edward?'

'Yes?'

'Tomorrow.'

'I have not forgotten the date, Richard.' His brother regards him over steepled fingers. 'I trust you will attend Mass with me in the morning. We can pray for our Father together. Would you like that?'

Embraced by warmth, wine, and comfort, Richard nods as his brother's face swims in the depths of his glimmering pool. 'I should be honoured, Your Grace.'

A sharp thump and a squeal as Kyngston opens the shutters and grey light creeps in like an accuser. The solemnity of their father and brother's obit has given way, over recent days, to further seasonal celebration. Unlike any Twelfth Night revels Richard has known, the festivities have been loud, boisterous, visceral; the hall a glittering casket awash with gems, a pungent bower of greenery and candleflame, an inverted world where the Lord of Misrule holds sway, encouraging mischief.

'Softly, Simon. Please.' He shifts with care, unwilling to raise his head, knowing any further movement would result in an undignified display on his part.

Parr, swift-minded as ever, thrusts a bowl under his chin. 'In here, Your Grace, if you can.'

Breathing deeply, Richard studies the coverlet, applying his concentration to the pomegranate pattern, its green and gold curling leaves, its bulbous fruit. The wave of nausea eventually passes, and he smiles at the boys' anxious faces. 'Fear not, I'm well enough.'

Kyngston retrieves Richard's shirt from the floor. Shaking off the strewing herbs, he makes some effort to fold it before setting it aside with the rest of the soiled laundry. Richard makes the effort to rise. Stomach rebelling, he flops back against the pillows, blushing as snatches of last night's merriment begin to surface.

As Parr reaches once more for the pewter basin, he waves it away. 'No need, Tom. As I said, I'm well enough. And I believe I owe you both an apology.'

The boys grant each other a knowing grin. 'You were sick but twice, Your Grace,' Kyngston informs him, 'and Tom soon cleaned it up.'

Richard winces, trying to remember how exactly the evening had panned out, once Edward's cellars had furnished well the cup of every reveller, and the line betwixt ribaldry and decorum had begun to smudge for most. The girl had fair hair, he remembers that much, and blue eyes, as unlike Alice as it is possible to be. He recalls little of their conversation, if indeed any had taken place, recollects only a darkened niche, the sensuous feel of silk beneath his eager palm, a warm, fervid mouth open to his. And a throbbing in his veins, even now, despite the shame. Along with it, a tender regret that the act itself could not have been as he'd so often envisaged: a clean and welcoming bed and Alice, arms held out in welcome.

He eases himself from the mattress, floor cold and hard beneath the foot sheet, and allows himself to be dressed. He'll feel better once he's eaten, but he can't break his fast before Mass: that would only be something else to confess. Fetching warm water, Parr combs his hair, smooths it with scented pomade, then peers into his face.

'Well,' Richard asks, 'how do I look?'

'Like death, Your Grace.'

'Ah. To the point.' A laugh explodes inside his head like canon fire, and Parr's face is the epitome of embarrassment. 'Fear not, Tom. I cannot hold to admiring a man's honesty if I shy away when it doesn't suit.'

What would Margaret say if she could see him like this? If she had observed him last night, willing and eager in the embraces of a court whore? His sister, ever the pragmatist, would doubtless shrug. *I care nothing for your Twelfth Night capers, Richard, as long as you hold with your promise.* And how has he gone about fulfilling that? A half-hearted conversation with George. An evening by Edward's fireside floating in his own intoxication, happier to see his cares bobbing away on a tide of Rhenish than to grasp them and look them in the face.

'Simon?' A sharp movement of his head sends the chamber spinning. 'Not that old green worsted. Brush the blue velvet, will you? I would beg an audience with the king after Mass and prefer to look presentable.'

He hears the laughter before he's even admitted. Edward's melodic, genial swell; Hastings' nasal snigger and mocking guffaw. It's me, he thinks. They're talking about me, about my conduct, about what they consider to be my initiation into their world.

Ushered inside, he hovers, almost gagging at the stench of stale wine still lingering from the night before. It's a chamber he knows well: a room where, during their habitation, he, George and Margaret had amused themselves with harmless pastimes: reading, singing, telling stories. It suddenly seems so long ago.

He makes a low obeisance, notes how the conversation has dried up, how both sets of eyes snap towards him.

'Come to join us, Brother?' Edward, lounging, smothered in furs, tips him a wink and delivers a knowing smile. 'How fine you look. I fear last night's entertainments have rendered me a little coisy.'

Self-conscious in his brushed velvet, black silk hose and pike-toed boots, Richard feels his colour rise. 'I would speak with you, Highness, on a privy matter. But would not wish to disturb your business with Lord Hastings.'

'Please, Richard,' Hastings smirks, 'call me Will. You know your brother abhors formality.'

He would rather not call him anything, would rather the chamberlain remove his mocking, blood-shot features elsewhere. A clatter of dice reveals a tight group, pressed into the oriel space, exploiting the glancing light of sun on snow. One, he notes, is John Wydeville. Another, Thomas Grey, the queen's son: one of George's *arrogant tykes in tawny silk.*

'That business we discussed, Will,' Edward says, 'could you see to it now?'

Hastings sweeps from the chamber intent upon his errand, be it real or imaginary, while Edward pats the stool by his chair.

'What is it, Richard? Does it concern our brother?'

The perceptiveness takes Richard off guard. 'How did

you know?'

'Well, I think I can hazard a guess. The forthcoming trial of Hungerford and Courtney. You're aware, of course, that George and the earl were invited to sit on the commission along with yourself.'

'Yes. George knows of the postponement and that you wish to attend the trial in your own person. He wrote to me saying he'll be in Salisbury for the commencement.'

'In that case, he told you more than he has told me. I've received no correspondence from him whatever. Or, need I say, from the earl. I don't expect them in Salisbury, Richard, and nor should you. Neither intend to obey the summons. And why do you think that is?'

However much Edward drank last night, it's done little to dull his wits. Toying with his purse buckle, Richard remains silent.

'The Lancastrian agents recently apprehended,' Edward says. 'You cannot fail to have heard that they implicated Lord Wenlock in their treason.'

Wenlock? An associate of Warwick. In fact, more than that: a friend. 'But that doesn't necessarily mean—'

'Doesn't it?'

'Of course not. Our cousin would never associate himself with our enemies.'

'There has been much unrest, particularly in London. Ask yourself, Richard, who has the hearts of the Londoners? Who holds them in the palm of his hand?'

'Many would say you, Edward.' But many wouldn't.

'It's Warwick, that Colossus straddling both England and France, who seeks the rule here. Our cousin has long sought to bend me to his will, and for a time, he succeeded, but he's losing his grip on me, and that does not please him. It's true that whatever Wenlock is engaged in need not implicate Warwick. But I know the earl's hatred of the queen is bitter enough to drive him away. And yet,' Edward throws up his hands, 'I prefer not to believe the worst of him, so I continually delude myself. I grant him and the archbishop estates to feed their pride. But I fear there may come a time, and soon, when I can delude myself no longer. When I must believe that his intentions, and those of our brother, are indeed contrary to my own.'

'Your Grace, surely this requires nothing more than a discussion with our cousin, and with George, that our courses may meet in the middle.'

'And I would be more than willing to agree. If I could trust them.'

Richard exhales: this is more than he could have hoped for. 'Send me. I can be your envoy. I can mediate.'

Edward studies him. 'If I thought you could.'

'I can.'

Their conversation has piqued the interest of the dice players. Edward glances over his shoulder and lowers his voice. 'No. Let the forthcoming trials act as a deterrent to all who seek to stand against their king: in whatever way.'

The subject is closed. Temporarily thrown off balance, Richard's tongue is tied, and he begs his brother's leave.

Salisbury. A January morning, bitter wind slicing flesh as they enter the Bishop's Guildhall. Solemnity shrouds the limewashed interior, freezing every coil of breath and settling into their spines like death's rigor.

For all his majesty, Edward is here merely to intimidate, to strike fear into those who would seek to harbour treason. Richard, it is, who must *hear and determine* and deliver the verdict upon which the court is so firmly resolved. He must show he's not afraid, that he's able to condemn a man to the rope, to the hurdle upon which he will be disembowelled, to the sword, dagger, tongs with which the penalty will be exacted. He must, in every regard, be his brother's right arm.

Taking his seat upon the constable's bench, he sees that below him sit Edward's staunchest supporters, those who stick to the king like kid leather to sweating palms: Hastings, Rivers, Scales. Belly churning, Richard wishes he had not broken his fast, that his wine had not been watered. Anything which would have softened the ordeal. Looking a man in the eye and condemning him to a traitor's death is not the most desirable way to start the day.

Hungerford and Courtney are accused of plotting the king's destruction, of communicating with Marguerite, one-time queen of England. The verdict is a foregone conclusion, an example of what can befall those whom Edward forgives but who choose to transgress a second time and revert to their old allegiance. It's to show the king cannot be trifled with, cannot be taken for granted. It's to be a lesson to all would-be rebels. But most of all, it is designed as an example for George, and for Warwick. A lesson Richard is expected to deliver without allowing it to stain his conscience.

He's shivering. A brazier has been lit, but the blaze is slow to take, and the warmth doesn't reach him. He laces his fingers, hides his hands in the folds of his gown. It wouldn't do for Edward to notice their trembling.

Four years ago, he was compelled to view an execution. Now, he's obliged to initiate one. Licking his lips, he steadies his breathing and calls for proceedings to begin.

Chapter Nineteen

May 1469
Windsor Castle

'TASTY?' EDWARD indicates his brother's plate, raising his voice above the hubbub. 'I ordered it especially, knowing your fondness for pies.'

Richard dusts his fingers free of crumbs. 'Thank you, Highness.'

There's been no lack of concern, no want of attention since he arrived at court; his appetites catered for, both in kitchen and buttery, collections of books finding their way to his chamber—as well as the occasional girl. But that doesn't mean he's settled; three months after leaving the Warwick household, he still finds himself longing for their cousin's company.

Edward smiles at Richard's empty plate. 'A custard should be on its way—'

Screeching and scraping cuts across music and chatter. Drowning the tones of gittern and shawm, it has all heads twisting in the direction of the door. Howls of mirth ensue as a man, wobbling atop a pair of stilts, totters through the throng. With the aid of a huge staff, he navigates the floor, avoiding lolling hounds and a collection of discarded wine cups. It is Wodehouse, Edward's capricious fool, clearly dressed for some imaginary journey, riding cape daubed with mud for effect, legs encased in elongated boots that all but reach his loins. Even his cheeks, ruddy and inflated with the enforced effort, are smeared with dirt as if spattered by the wheels of a passing cart.

'What in God's name?' Hastings, hunched on a stool at Edward's feet, wipes his eyes as the fool approaches, making what form of obeisance he can in his discomforted state.

The king explodes into peals of laughter. 'Wodehouse, you lackwit! Come, what have you to say to us?'

The fool retains his pained expression. Facing his audience, he pulls down the corners of his mouth in feigned dismay. Richard grins, recalling the revelry he and George had enjoyed as children when their father's fool would tie his limbs up in knots and crawl around the floor like a crab. Edward, sharing the memory, squeezes his hand.

Wodehouse is enjoying the attention; waggling his backside, he bemoans the weather. 'Fair Prince and mine own good sirs, please, I beg you, do not decry my poor state, for the wind blasts foul in the nether parts, and I am beset by misery.'

Mighty guffaws erupt. One of John Wydeville's companions, helpless with drink, presents his silken-hosed rear and a vulgar riposte; Edward's shoulders judder.

Delighted with the effect of his buffoonery, Wodehouse shuffles forward and essays a bow. 'Highness, my journeys have sore wearied me. I've travelled far and wide, throughout many parts of your realm, and the rivers be so high that I could bare scrape through them but was fain to search the depths with this long staff.'

The king is suddenly still. Sniggers from the depths of the chamber are swiftly stifled. The rivers to which Wodehouse refers are surely not the natural, flowing kind, with silt beds and a wealth of pebbles to score the toes of paddling boys. Earl Rivers, the queen's father, is surely the butt of the jest: a jest, Richard thinks, which would doubtless cast George into paroxysms of delight and cause their cousin to beat his breast with glee.

A cough, a clearing of throats, a shuffling of feet. In the unnatural silence, Edward's guests find something with which to engage themselves: raisins of Corinth grasped from the bowl, another mouthful of filberts.

The king fakes amusement. 'An incomparable wit, Wodehouse.

As ever.' Fishing a rose noble from his purse, he flicks it towards the fool. The coin lands, spinning in bright, quivering circles, before settling on the tiles. 'Jump down from your stilts, man, and take your fee.'

George smells of musk and ambergris, his hair of sweet pomade. Eyes bright with pleasure, he holds Richard at arms-length and looks him up and down. 'How do you, Brother?'

'Well. And you?'

George makes an elaborate flourish. Any meeting of the Garter chapter is, by nature, a splendid occasion, but this evening's ceremonial supper, held in honour of the absent Duke Charles, is set to be lavish, and George seems intent upon outshining even the king.

A furtive movement, and the threadbare patch in the crook of Richard's sleeve is hidden from view. 'I asked how you fare, George. I can see how you look.'

'Hearty enough. I'm pleased Edward has seen fit to honour Charles with the Garter. It will have pleased Margaret. Our cousin says his recent visit to Burgundy on Edward's behalf found the duke much amenable.'

Warwick stands at George's side, fixed, solid, every inch the Colossus to which Edward has compared him. Richard extends a hand. Snatching it in his fist, the earl pulls him into a tight embrace.

'Richard!'

'And how was Margaret?' The query for Margaret's welfare is instinctive. 'Is she faring well?'

Warwick loosens his hold. 'Indeed. The Burgundians respect her, and Madame le Grande, whom you remember, has become a valuable companion. After all, Margaret must miss your mother.'

Richard's heart sinks. His interest in Margaret's welfare has outrun concern for his cousin, and Warwick's disappointment is plain. Rueful, he grasps the earl's hand, encasing it in his own. 'And how do you fare, Cousin? Truly, I'm most happy to see you again.'

Warwick's gaze remains wary. 'And I you. Life at court still suit?'
Richard's shoulders fall. 'Not really. Truth to tell, I'm lonely.'
George deals him a clout. 'That's because you don't have me.
No pretty girls here to keep you company?'

'Your brother has ever been discreet in his personal concerns,
George,' Warwick says with meaning. 'Don't push him to reveal
his secrets.'

A gush of feeling rises, and Richard wishes they could begin the
conversation again. 'Edward was pleased you sought Margaret out
during your sojourn, Cousin. And that your dealings with the duke
were successful.' Petty talk, he thinks, can I do no better than this?

Warwick inclines his head. 'I fear the Garter I delivered may
be a little plain for Charles' taste. You yourself have observed the
splendour of the Burgundian court.'

'Well, I'm sure the duke's man will witness a grand ceremony
today. Tell me, how fares my lady the countess?'

'She sends her regards.'

'And your daughters?'

George twitches and flashes a brief glance at the earl.

'Again,' Warwick says, 'they are faring well.'

'Our cousin has ordered the *Trinity* refitted, along with the
Anne,' George says. 'You should come with us to Sandwich to
inspect them, Dickon.'

The implication is not wasted on Richard. Memories of the
Anne, of their younger selves clinging to each other in terror, are
guaranteed to resurrect feelings of amity that not even Edward
could destroy. However, Richard won't be accompanying them. He
can't, and George knows it.

He watches the progress of the raindrops. Splattering the
window, they race one another across the leads before slithering
into oblivion. The casement offers a clouded view of the castle
buildings. Somewhere, in their depths, Edward is with the queen,
petting their new daughter as George and Warwick ride away. The

infant is named Cecily, and on Richard's recent visit to Baynard's, his mother told him she is once again to act as godsib.

'Another daughter,' she had asserted. 'Perhaps Our Lord is making a point.'

The birth of his third daughter doesn't appear to have caused the king any degree of anguish, however. The event simply tells him that his queen is fecund and that by the very laws of nature, a male child must follow. During their visit, George and Warwick even deigned to visit the baby, and to offer Elizabeth their formal respects.

On the face of it, Richard should be pleased. He should feel settled at court, content with Edward's friendship and generous gifts of land, even if his monetary income barely covers his needs. But he doesn't. Feel settled, that is. The nagging desire to see his family permanently reunited cannot be quelled. It plagues his dreams and intrudes, with increasing ferocity, upon his waking hours.

There are messages: trouble in the north, uprisings, the emergence of petty rebels. It appears that eight years of Edward's rule have failed to exorcise the ghosts of Lancaster, which hover in the misty dales and lurk in the backwaters. The family of York should be united, Richard thinks, as it was under our father. Differences need to be forgotten before our enemies use them to their advantage. For they will. That is what people do.

The shower persists, and he has his eye on a single, bulbous drop: Warwick, he thinks, racing ahead of his fellows, bobbing over the milky glass, then disappearing from sight.

A firm hand on his shoulder has his head jerk up in hope. 'Cousin?'

'Is aught amiss, Your Grace?' Hastings tosses a cushion aside and sinks down beside him. That the chamberlain should have caught him out in so stupid a mistake makes Richard feel like a fool. Again.

'No.' He sounds ill-mannered, even to himself. 'Should there be?'

'Well, you make for a sorry figure, huddled in the casement with nothing more to entertain you than a dismal rain shower.' Hastings' hands are clasped over his knees; thick fingers, like venison sausages, sprinkled with golden hairs and a surprising array of keens; some healing, others gaping and sore.

'Forgive me, my lord,' Richard returns his gaze to the window. 'I was merely intent upon my own musings.'

'When will you learn to call me Will? Or did the earl tutor you to shun familiarity?'

Richard concedes. 'If my cousin's household taught me anything, it was how to be respectful, and so I apologise. You must think me very haughty…Will.'

'No, just young, inexperienced. But that's to be expected.'

Always the lad, eh Will?

'My brother the king was leading an army at my age,' Richard says, 'and so could I, if it came to it.'

Hastings holds up his hands. 'I'm sure you could, but let's hope it doesn't. Come to it, I mean.'

Richard glowers. 'Why should it come to it? My cousin of Northumberland has dealt commendably with the northern skirmishes. Just a handful of Percy retainers making trouble, that's what Edward says.'

'Aye, John Neville is to be relied upon. Since he was awarded the earldom, it's been in his own interest to put down any Percy nonsense.'

'John and his brothers have always been loyal,' Richard stresses the word to make a point. 'Loyal to York.'

Silence settles, and he feels himself observed. At length, Hastings sighs. 'Ned has told me of your fondness for your cousin.'

As always with Hastings, Richard finds himself waiting for the counterpunch. When it doesn't come, he provokes one: 'And what do you say, my lord? That this is…unwise?'

'On the contrary, I think it admirable.'

'But you think it misplaced?'

'No, Your Grace, you wrong me. Loyalty is always to be commended. I simply note that the youthful are often dazzled by the influence of great men.'

What's the inference? That Richard's feelings for Warwick are nothing more than the simpering fondness of a yellow-beaked boy?

'The youthful, perhaps. But, as you see, I'm a youth no longer.'

A good-natured laugh and Hastings pats his shoulder, as he would some pet hound. 'Forgive me, Richard. I'm a plain-speaking man, true to the black and the white of a matter. I see things for what they are, and though the earl is my kinsman, I can see what he's about. He labours under a vision of righting that which he feels is amiss with your brother's governance.'

Richard narrows his eyes. He can see what Hastings is up to. The chamberlain holds in his mind a set of scales and would seat him in the balancing pan opposite George. He's curious to see if one would dip below the other or whether their loyalties would weigh the same. 'The earl would never betray the family of York,' Richard says. 'It means too much to him.'

'Not the family of York,' Hastings says, 'I agree. But if it's his intent to insult the queen's family, then it's my personal belief he would not hesitate to act against the king in order to make his point.'

If the chamberlain has a spy in the earl's household, Richard thinks, it wouldn't surprise me. 'Why are you telling me this, Lord Hastings?'

'Because I feel the king has not been plain with you. But the truth is, you've made a choice and are bound to remain true to it. No matter what comes.'

Rumours of northern unrest still circulating, the king wishes to pray for harmony in the realm. Saint Edmundsbury, he tells Richard, then on to Walsingham, which houses the replica of the Holy House: a shrine revered by their father and frequented by women yearning to conceive. The significance for Edward is clear. Whilst there are those who would rebel, the lack of an heir renders him vulnerable. The dearth of male children has not bothered him before. It does now.

Called to the king's private chapel, Richard finds his brother on his knees: bulk quivering with intensity, fingers kneading

Paternoster beads, the very image of a troubled man. Sinking beside him, Richard adds his own exhortations. Peace is what's required. Peace and reconciliation.

With a whispered *Amen*, the king gathers his gown and rises to his feet. 'Thank you, Brother.'

The confined intimacy of the closet allows Richard the freedom he might well subdue elsewhere. 'We will be reconciled: with George, and with the earl. I'm certain of it. Neither would seek to destroy that which our father sought to build.'

Instinct urges him to offer his hand. The king takes it, squeezes, but quits the chapel in silence.

Chapter Twenty

June 1469
Dominican Friary, Norwich

LATE EVENING, and the sky is bloodshot. In the priory guesthouse, the king has ordered the shutters left agape until the brazen sunset fades. He had been about to retire, a basin of water beside the bed, servants hovering with kerchief and comb. The last thing any of them had expected, at this hour, was an importunate visitor.

'Let him be admitted.'

The abbey's guest master scuttles from the chamber. Hastings, face reddened by the heat of the day, watches him leave. 'A Percy retainer? Here?'

Edward waves away his body servants. 'If, whoever he purports to be, this man brings news from the north, then we must hear him out.'

Scales gropes on instinct for the sword he dutifully left at the priory door. 'But Henry Percy's been in custody since Palmsunday Field. We must be wary. It could be a trick.'

Richard's eyes are fixed on the open doorway. 'Well, if it is, the man is taking an enormous risk.'

Men-at-arms hustle a dishevelled figure across the threshold, the black-robed guest master bringing up the rear. 'If it please Your Grace, I am obliged to inform Prior John.'

Edward's attention is fixed on their visitor. 'By all means, brother, but I would ask that he not interfere. This does not concern him.'

A thrust propels Percy's man towards the bed, and he sprawls at Edward's feet. Richard moves close, takes in all that can be seen of him: shuddering frame, dust-stained jerkin, the bruises already forming on neck and wrists.

Edward is on his feet, casting a menacing shadow over the prone figure. 'Who are you?'

The man is young: sharp eyes, bulbous nose, a messy thatch of hair. 'I am Lord Percy's man, I come—'

'Your name?'

Whatever courage the man possesses, and it must be considerable, is beginning to ebb. Moistening his lips, he cranes his neck in an effort to look his inquisitor in the eye. 'Pygott, Highness. Adam Pygott.'

Edward has the man hauled to his knees. 'Well, Adam Pygott, if your allegiance is to Henry Percy, then my first question must be whether your lord and master is aware of your activities. After all, as our prisoner, he has no true reason to show himself a friend.'

'Those of us who serve the earl—'

'*Lord Percy*,' Edward sets the man aright. 'The earldom of Northumberland, as I'm sure you know, now resides with our cousin, John Neville.'

'Beg pardon, Highness. Those of us who serve the Lord Percy,' Pygott stresses the name through tense lips, 'are eager to disassociate him from the activities of any who seek to rebel against Your Grace's rule.'

The king appears unconvinced. 'If, as you say, there is further trouble in the north, then why must we rely upon the word of a Percy retainer? The current Earl of Northumberland can be entirely trusted to put down any insurrection, as he did but lately prove when he suppressed the antics of your master's associate, Robin of Holderness.'

A man-at-arms aims his boot at Pygott's rump and delivers a vicious kick.

Hastings throws the man a savage glare. 'Leave him.'

Pygott, saluting his saviour with a grateful nod, continues to plead, 'Highness, I was sent here to tell you—'

'Sent by whom?' Edward demands. 'Your master?'

'Indeed, sire.'

A space during which the king's thoughts are impossible to discern. 'Then, it appears Henry Percy is in receipt of news that even our own spies have failed to deliver. So, tell me what you know.'

Pygott swallows. 'The rebel force is adhering to a new leader. Like the last, this one takes the name of Robin.'

'Don't they all?' Scales' cynical laugh fades as Edward calls for silence.

However, Scales is correct. Any would-be champion would make himself a hero: Robin Mend-All, Robin of Holderness. For Robins are not ordinary rebels. They fight against injustice, never for themselves, but for the people, like the most famous Robin of all. Robins, as each man here knows, are dangerous.

Edward's eyes narrow. 'What else is known of him?'

'Little, Your Grace, but that he goes by the name Robin of Redesdale.'

'Robin of Redesdale was dealt with in the spring. Thanks to our cousin of Northumberland, he went the way of his Holderness counterpart. What do you say? That he's once again at liberty?'

'May it please Your Grace, but my master knows naught of this man, only wishes you to know that he himself plays no part.'

'Then who does?' The king's fist clenches. 'If you know more, man, then I would have it from you. One way or another.'

Richard chews his lip. A northern-based rebellion not instigated by a Percy can have support from only one other quarter. Please God, Warwick would not be so foolish.

Pygott's chin begins to wobble. 'My master is informed, by way of intelligence, that Redesdale and his following may be of Neville affinity.'

It's as if a mailed fist has engaged with Richard's belly, reverberations rippling to the very edge of his being. Slipping closer to the king, he eyes Pygott with distrust. 'This accusation should come as no surprise, Your Grace. It's in Henry Percy's interests to lay this at our cousin's door.'

Scales crosses his arms; scarlet sleeves bleed into white cuffs. 'We cannot dismiss this claim lightly. But I agree with my lord of Gloucester, we require greater proof.'

Edward sinks onto the bed, kicking away the slippers placed there when the evening had looked set to be a peaceful one. 'Pygott, your master has given you a perilous task, to come here and to coolly implicate the earl of Warwick in this sorry business.'

'My task, Highness, is to disassociate my lord Percy from this present trouble. He would have you know this recent unrest is none of his doing, nor does it involve any of his retainers. He prays you to remember the blood affinity that exists between you. That his grandmother and the duchess, your mother, are sisters.'

'And in so doing, ease his way into our favour?' Edward's cynicism is palpable. 'It seems to me that Percy has an interest in this matter other than fulfilling his duty to his king.'

'You ask for proof?' The messenger's hand flies to his hip. Richard lunges forward, placing himself between Pygott and the king. Hastings and Scales are of the same mind.

'Good God,' Edward bellows. 'He's only one man. Step away.'

Richard holds his ground. 'He could have a weapon concealed about his person.'

'What? In that paltry purse of his? Talk sense.'

Duly chastised, Richard and Scales both stand aside allowing Pygott to extend a trembling, outspread hand. 'My master, fearing his word may not be enough to convince Your Grace, asked me, as a last expedient, to offer you this.'

In the centre of his palm sits a ring with a heavily decorated bezel. A nobleman's ring certainly, but has it truly come from Henry Percy?

With the king's leave, Richard snatches the ring from Pygott's hand. Delicate gold enamel, a blue lion rampant, surrounded by exquisite lettering *Esperance en Dieu:* Hope in God. Percy's cognizance. Percy's motto.

'This proves nothing other than that this man comes from Henry Percy. It doesn't prove that what he says is true.' Richard passes the ring with reluctance, and Edward's fingers snap around it. Jiggling the token in his fist, the king looks to Hastings.

'Speak to the abbey hosteller. Ask him to arrange a pallet for this man.' His eyes flick back to Pygott. 'We'll speak at length in the morning.'

The chamber is a confusion of flickering shadows: Hastings and the men-at-arms making for the door, Pygott held firmly in the midst of them.

Kneeling before the bed, Richard speaks softly, 'Your Grace? The name Robin of Redesdale indicates nothing. Redesdale is as much Percy territory as it is Neville. More so, in fact. There's no reason to believe that our cousin has any hand in this.'

The king considers. 'No, I agree. But you can't deny that Pygott himself appears honest enough.' Opening his fist, he studies the ring. 'And why would Percy go this far?'

'A ruse to get his earldom back.'

Edward laughs. 'You're learning fast.'

'And if that isn't the case, then perhaps, as with Robin of Holderness, the rebels may be acting upon Percy's behalf but without his consent.' Richard feels his heart pumping. 'I beg you, please, consider this possibility.'

Edward tosses the ring in the air, catches it. 'I must consider all possibilities, Brother, whether I want to or not. Anthony? Do you wish to say something?'

Turning, Richard finds Scales twitching, eager to be away. 'Saving Your Grace, I would to my prayers.'

A sweep of Edward's hand. 'Of course. God give you goodnight.'

Scales departs, eyes downcast, hands clasped before him like a penitent. Off to convey the news to his father and brother, is what George would say. Off to wallow in the potential shame of the House of Neville.

Another wave. 'You may take your leave also, Richard.'

Before he can object, pages close in, surrounding the king like diligent ants. Hurt and frustrated, Richard makes obeisance.

'May God keep you, Highness.'

The night is long and fitful. When his mount is fetched next morning, the scent of newmade ale rising from the abbey brewhouse, Richard suspects Prior John will be happy to be rid of them: soldiers slumbering in his stables, envoys arriving as the sun goes down, his community hurled into a state of unrest. Lest Pygott speak true, Edward chooses to think ahead. Issuing orders for harness and livery, he commands artillery from the Tower. Calling for troops, he's written to William Herbert and the Earl of Devon, arranged to meet Norfolk and Suffolk at the priory of Walsingham.

'A precaution only,' he assures Richard. 'As I told you, we must consider all possibilities, whether or not we welcome them.'

Richard still feels uneasy. What if Percy's man was right? He thinks of all the missives that had taken up Warwick's time during his own final weeks in the household. The messengers crossing land and sea with letters strictly for the earl. Lavish suppers and closet meetings with his northern affinity. If only Edward would use me as an intermediary, he thinks. If only—

Hastings sidles up. 'Ned, I've sent despatches to Leicestershire. My men are to join us at Fotheringhay.'

Scales and his father are doing likewise, missives tucked in saddle bags intended for Northamptonshire. The letters Richard himself must write will be for ready money: a knight cannot raise a body of men if he lacks the wherewithal. Yet neither can he do so with an easy mind if those whom he raises are to ride against his own blood.

They arrive at Walsingham as regular pilgrims, surrendering their weapons as well as their shoes and completing the journey barefoot.

'This is no place for hauteur,' the king says as they pass beyond the gatehouse and into the monastery proper. 'A walk after supper,

Richard. Just we two. What do you say?'

It's as much a command as an invitation, but Richard welcomes it with open arms. It's time they spoke privily. It's time he fulfilled his promise to Margaret.

Later, they enter the prior's garden as the bell sounds for Vespers, a light meal of stewed pigeon settling in their bellies. The tranquil enclosure is gilded and fragrant. Suffused with the scent of rose and periwinkle, it offers a respite from the disquiet of recent days. They know of their father's devotion to the shrine here, his donations of land and property. Speaking fondly, they speculate, wondering whether York's funds were used to beautify this garden, whether the income from a tithe or a rent helped to build the enclosing walls, or fund the carvings of Saints Joachim and Anne, set either side of the arch.

At length, boots crushing wilted grass, they fall silent. Faint snatches of plainsong infiltrate the garden, and its mistle thrushes take it up.

'Richard?'

'Yes?'

'I have to be honest with you.'

So, now we get to the nub of it.

'Life is not like the romances you enjoy so much.' The king's laugh is forced, nervous even.

Richard tenses. 'Have we not had this conversation before? Placentia, if I recall. But I've grown since then.'

'Yes. And a man needs to face the truth.'

'Edward, I would rather face the truth than any number of forced excuses. But if you speak of our cousin, I still maintain we cannot accept the word of Henry Percy over that of our own flesh and blood.'

Edward shrugs, shoulders like hammerbeams. 'And for myself, I don't wish to believe the worst of the earl, though many would rebuke me for it. I propose to write to him, and to George, that they might prove themselves true. I may have sent Pygott back to his master, but I can't forget the conviction with which he spoke. And he's right. There are rumours of Neville involvement. My own spies have at last confirmed it.'

'Rumours. What fool believes rumours?'

Edward halts. 'Then you agree I should write to them?'

'And by so doing, you shall understand the falseness of this talk.'

'But I must ask you now, Richard, must assure myself that if the rumours do indeed prove true—'

'As they will not.'

'—if the rumours do prove to be true, then I must have your commitment.' The king turns towards him, blocking out the setting sun. 'Richard, when you left our cousin's household, I knew you'd made a decision. You'd reached your majority, yes, and I had recalled you, but you had a choice. You could have defied me, but you didn't. You could have stayed with the earl.'

And there we have it, Richard thinks, the problem which keeps me awake at night. 'I want what God wants. What Father would have wanted.'

Seizing Richard's shoulders, Edward shakes him as he would an obstinate child. 'This is not about our father. It's about us. It's about Warwick, about George, and whether or not I can trust them.'

Richard, defiant, holds his brother's gaze. 'Edward, you must give them a chance to deny any involvement. Please, you owe them that.'

The king loosens his grip. 'I agree. Besides, our enemies will consider any division within the family of York as a weakness they can exploit. We must, at least, be seen to be united. I shall compose a letter to the earl before I retire. Then we shall see what transpires.'

Chapter Twenty-One

July 1469
Nottingham Castle

'*Y*OU WANT me to leave? Why?'

Summoned to the king's presence, Richard finds him in the solar, hunched over a heap of newly penned letters. Nicholas Harpisfeld, signet clerk, stands alongside directing affairs.

Edward glances up from his labours long enough for Richard to see how his features have shrunk: eyes narrow, lips withered and downturned. 'I want no argument. It is a temporary measure. I have a task for you.'

'Your Grace, whatever the task, I can think of a better. You now claim to have proof that our cousin has decided to challenge you, yet you refuse to use me as intermediary.'

'Allow me to conclude business, Brother, and I shall explain all.'

The impervious scratching of quill on parchment has Richard grinding his teeth. 'If you let me, I could speak to him. I could convince him to desist.'

The king's chest heaves beneath gold brocade. 'Don't overestimate your influence in that wise, boy.'

'Send me, I pray you.'

'God's Blood!' The king's hand upsets the ink horn, and a glistening trail covers the desk, eradicating Harpisfeld's latest despatch. While the clerk rescues the remaining paperwork, his colleagues fret and fuss, swabbing black mess with black silk sleeves. Disengaging himself from the upheaval, Edward glowers. 'Richard,

I warn you, do not try my patience.'

'Send me to speak for you. That is all I ask.'

'Tell him, Ned,' Hastings says, rubbing his sore, red hands together. 'It's the only way he'll understand.'

'Sit down, my lord of Gloucester.' Indicating a vacant stool, the king drags another across the ink-stained tiles and throws himself upon it. 'Listen, and do not dare interrupt me.'

Subdued, Richard sees Rivers and his sons loitering; John Wydeville squinting, as if the distance does not allow him the intimate aspect he so desires.

'My communications with Coventry,' Edward says, 'in the wake of the northern revolts, served to furnish me with certain information which, at the time, I chose to keep to myself: namely, that our cousin had informed the city how his daughter was soon to be wedded to the brother of the king. I kept my counsel because I chose not to believe it; I wished to consider it an evil rumour, a thing of no substance. But today, I've learnt otherwise. The Earl of Warwick and our brother have at last revealed their intentions.'

Edward's anger assures Richard's silence—this, and the fact that, for as long as he fails to acknowledge what he's hearing, the situation doesn't exist. For this brief moment, Warwick is still their confederate, George still little more than the simmering firebrand he's always been.

The king takes a ragged breath. 'It seems that whilst we were on our knees at Saint Edmundsbury, praying for reconciliation, the pair of them were at Sandwich. Our cousin of York was censing the *Trinity* with holy water, and they were planning a sojourn in Calais. Any idea why?'

Richard stares him earnestly in the face. 'No. Other than that, as captain, our cousin's presence in Calais is perfectly justified.'

'If I told you that Warwick's wife and daughters accompanied him, in addition to brother George, would that help?'

Richard's pulse quickens. 'George and Isabel. They're wedded?'

'Wedded and bedded. Against my express wish. And there's more. My spies in Calais inform me that the day after the wedding, the earl – and our brother – issued a manifesto. So similar in tenor to the proclamations given out by Robin of Redesdale that it's difficult to imagine no collaboration between them.'

The king pauses, allowing the facts to be absorbed. 'My kingship,' he says, shoulders sagging, 'is likened to those of three deposed monarchs: the second Edward, Richard of Bordeaux, and the erstwhile King Harry, my predecessor. I'm a spendthrift; my "deceivable, covetous rule" sows discord amongst the nobility by honouring my favourites, and I do not care for justice. Three excellent reasons to suggest I meet the same fate.' A cynical laugh. 'Unless, of course, I renounce my ways and follow the advice of he who has always sought to rule through me. He, whose knowledge and ability is, of course, so much greater than my own.'

Richard meets his brother's challenging glare. Warwick's conditions are not unprecedented. They're simply those presented by their father in his attempt to separate Harry of Lancaster from his queen and her favourites. 'I say again, Your Grace. Offer to negotiate. It is what Fa…it is the right course to take.'

Harpisfeld's pen scrapes and scratches. Hastings picks his flaking skin. The king ruminates, while beneath Richard's feet, the earth shifts.

'I realise that,' Edward concedes, 'and am prepared to negotiate, but on my own terms, and in my own time. It's my belief the earl intends the manifesto as a threat. His intention, so he says, is to present a proposal for "remedy and reformation." However, it pays to be prepared; we still have the presence of Redesdale. You've done well in gathering forces, Richard, and that is why I would have you leave me: to win more. I shall remain here, wait for Herbert and Devon to join us, and the archers we have requested from Coventry.'

Gather an army, crush the rebels, then negotiate with Warwick—a good decision: the only decision. 'The estates you granted me in Lancashire, Your Grace. I could, perhaps, raise support there.'

'That would have been my suggestion. Make your presence felt. Ensure the region is loyal. And whilst there, you'll be able to keep an eye on Lord Stanley. Let me know if he makes any movement to join up with our cousin. As his brother-in-law, it's always possible Warwick may write to him.'

'But you said you did not envisage open revolt.'

'As the king says, Richard, a precaution only.' Hastings lays a hand on his shoulder. 'Any intelligence we receive is scanty, to say the least, and at present, we cannot be completely sure of what's afoot. Therefore, we must consider all possibilities: your cousin is slippery.'

An objection forms on Richard's lips, but Edward intervenes, 'If it makes you feel any better, you're not the only one to be departing from me. I'm sending Earl Rivers and his son, John, to Wales – my lord Scales to Norfolk.'

'Do you need anything for your sojourn, my lord of Gloucester? The king has set aside a little ready coin.'

Thanking Hastings, Richard declines. He's satisfied with his loan requests; accepting funds from the treasury would only tarnish his success, confirm his dependency. Edward is watching him, and for the briefest of moments, he detects a flash of brotherly pride.

Chapter Twenty-Two

August 1469
Clitheroe Castle, Lancashire

SCAFFOLDING, LIKE a timber skeleton, has been erected in Clitheroe's bailey, and work has begun on repairs; raising crenellations, replacing weathered stones. Strictly speaking, responsibility for the castle's upkeep lies with Richard, but it's unlikely to benefit from the contents of his mutable purse. At Nottingham, his gallant refusal of further coin had felt heroic, but like all actions pursued in haste, leisure finds time to regret them. Edward, at least, had had some foresight. Prior to the current troubles, the king had put aside two hundred pounds for repairs at Clitheroe, and Richard is grateful.

He'd be more grateful yet, had he been granted leave to approach the earl as a go-between, but he won't give up hope. He can't. He owes Edward and Warwick too much to allow them the opportunity of destroying each other.

Earlier in the day, he had clambered up the scaffolding at the invitation of the chief mason. From his vantage point, it had been possible to take in the vast expanse of rugged valleys, the austere beauty of Bowland Fell. He'd recalled Edward's instructions to inform him of any covert movements enacted by Thomas Stanley in support of the earl. But he has no concerns: despite the man's kinship to Warwick, Richard can recall little conviviality between the two.

For himself, Richard's never met the man and has heard

nothing from him since his own arrival in the north; no letter of welcome, no offer to indulge in the delights of Stanley's park at Lathom. And yet, even if such an invitation were extended, Richard can't guarantee he'd accept. His father's relations with Stanley had been far from warm, and that is enough to discourage him from proffering any friendship of his own.

The chamber darkens as dusk creeps in. Yawning, he finds a discarded taper and lights more candles. He wishes he knew where George was and what he was doing. Whether he and Warwick have taken supper, whether they've retired to their beds, dreaming of a world without Wydevilles. He'll labour for them tonight, pray neither of them will be foolish enough to challenge Edward further. Pray while there's still a chance of reclamation.

A light knock. Kyngston enters juggling basin, towel, and ivory comb. Pausing, he blushes at the inescapable scent of rose and musk lingering amid the beeswax. 'Ready to retire, Your Grace?'

Richard stretches. 'Yes, thank you, Simon. As I'm sure you're aware, my guest left some time ago.'

He's found company here of late: a discreet girl, quiet yet decidedly willing. He feels sure of her, and, unlike the girls at court, has trusted her with sight of his back. The anomaly makes little difference, she says, why should it? Sharing the long summer evenings with her has served as a curative to the equally long and tense days, when all he can do is pen letters for support and wait upon Edward's call.

Kyngston makes a fuss of setting out his wares. Something is troubling him more than the embarrassing hint of Katherine's perfume. He hangs the towel on a peg and places a clean night coif on the pillow. 'Your Grace? Forgive me, but I've been thinking about my lord of Clarence.'

'You, too? What of him?'

'There were, as Your Grace knows, times when the duke dealt with me sorely. But he could be generous also, and I wouldn't see him disgraced or…'

'Nor would I, Simon. But it won't come to that. I believe the king will come to terms with my lord Warwick, and it's my intention to act as intercessor with Duke George.'

Helping him from his shirt, Kyngston seems unconvinced.

The following day, in the hour after dinner, the sun's rays pound the wall walk. Keen to exhibit the building works, he ushers his visitor to the top of the keep. James Harrington shows considerable interest but appears to be suffering in his unseasonable attire. Although of excellent quality, the crimson gown with its sleek squirrel trim is tight under the arms, and across the barrel chest, of the unfashionably-bearded, middle-aged man. Something about Harrington, however—the candidness of his gaze, his genuine deference—makes Richard warm to him immediately. The man's stewardship of Amounderness renders them close associates, and Richard assures him they shall work well together.

'My cousin thinks highly of you. And, as I'm sure you know, Sir James, the earl is not a man easily impressed.'

Harrington, eager to please, accepts the compliment with grace, but Richard longs to know what has brought him here. A polite introduction, in all likelihood, but a promise of men, God willing. Pressing a hand to the merlon, Harrington leans over the parapet to survey the view.

Richard is drawn to the impressive sapphire that adorns the man's middle finger and to the death's head, a memento mori, which sits alongside. 'A father and a brother lost at Sandal Castle. We have common ground, I think, besides our regional duties.'

Harrington squints against the sun. 'My father served with your uncle and also with your own father; may God assoil him.'

'I know it well. And your grandfather carried Harry the Fifth's banner at Agincourt. An honour of great moment.'

Harrington's grin reveals a perceptible gap between his front teeth. 'My lord is most gracious.'

'Yet I feel you have further business to discuss other than that which jointly concerns us.'

'Indeed, yes.'

'Then please, elucidate.'

Harrington takes a breath. 'There is a matter which sits heavily with my brother and me.'

'Concerning?'

'Concerning Lord Thomas Stanley.'

Richard swallows. Any movement by Stanley must indicate a call to arms. And one instigated by the earl. 'What do you know?'

A ripple of cynicism mars Harrington's benevolent features. 'Enough to know that without your good lordship, our lands may be lost to us.'

Richard smiles as relief washes over him. 'Then I assume this to be a private matter and not pertaining to my lord Stanley's loyalty?'

'Quite so, Your Grace. It touches upon the hereditary rights of my family.'

Richard recalls some talk of a sojourn in the Fleet. Although the king himself had been involved, it had been a legal case, Chancery business. He knows little of what it entailed other than Warwick's attempts to mediate between the families of Harrington and Stanley.

'If there's aught I can do, be assured I shall do it to the best of my ability.' It is the customary response, by mouth or by letter. But if Warwick, the diplomat, failed to solve the issue, Richard doubts his own potential to heal the breach.

Harrington hesitates—a vague dip of the shoulders before he wets the lips lying virtually unseen between moustache and beard. 'The feud between our family and Stanley's is of long-standing and cannot be unknown to Your Grace. Through the proximity of our lands and nearness of blood, our own fortunes and Stanley's have intertwined, although my family has always prided itself in its allegiance to York.'

'You've shown more than allegiance, Sir James. Hard upon our cousin John's victory at Hexham, you were one of those who recovered King Harry and delivered him to my brother. What greater task could a man perform for his liege lord?'

Harrington sucks his teeth. 'Lord Stanley, in recent times, has proved himself valuable to the king's grace in raising men against the threat of a Welsh rebellion. The king was grateful, and the matter betwixt our families was found in Stanley's favour.'

Interest piqued, Richard urges him to explain.

'It concerns my nieces, the daughters of my brother John, who died with Your Grace's father. It pleased Stanley to appeal for their wardship, desiring their marriages for the sake of what he sees as their inheritance – my father's castle of Hornby.'

'And legally?'

Harrington blinks. 'My brother Robert and I believe that our nieces' wardship, and the castle of Hornby, are legally ours. Stanley holds that when our brother John died upon the field, our father had already perished in the fighting and that for a brief space, John was our father's heir.'

'And if your father were the first to perish, then Hornby fell to John and, with his death, to your nieces. And from there to the girls' prospective husbands. I can see, Sir James, where this trail is leading.'

'I assure Your Grace that we had word of John dying upon the field and our father of his wounds the following day. For a matter of hours, Hornby remained with him.'

'And yet, Lord Stanley's interest in the matter depends upon the reverse being the case.'

'Indeed.' Harrington fingers the glinting sapphire. 'But I assure you that however the matter might appear, Robert and I act upon the word of those present at both our brother's, and our father's, deaths.' Removing the ring, he places it in the centre of his palm. 'This was bequeathed to me, taken from my father's own hand.'

Richard is suddenly aware of the tautness of his jaw. 'You need make no further case, Sir James. All is clear.'

He offers Harrington a chamber, and a supper which lasts long into the night. By morning, they are firm friends, united in sorrow, and in understanding. A reciprocal agreement is made: a company of Harrington retainers in support of the king's cause for Richard's personal intervention in the ongoing feud.

Next morning, as Harrington saddles up, Richard grasps his hand. 'Continue to hold Hornby. I believe it is yours by right.'

'Contrary to the king's judgement?'

'Perhaps His Highness is not in full receipt of the facts. I promise you, James, that very soon, he will be.'

When news arrives, it comes early and is delivered by Simon Kyngston. Tumbling, red-faced and breathless from the direction of the keep, the boy slithers to a halt in the circular bailey as Richard and Parr return from weaponry practice.

The rebels: it must concern the rebels. 'What is it, Simon? Tell me.'

The boy gulps in air. 'Lord Hastings is here. We've placed him in the solar.'

Gripping his riding gloves, Hastings slaps them repeatedly against his opposite palm. As Richard enters, he makes a hasty bow. 'Your Grace.'

The chamberlain's appearance is startling. Tired and unkempt, square frame sagging, he's like a heap of bed curtains pulled down in spring and hauled to the river for scrubbing.

'My lord, please, be seated. Are my people attending to you? Wine? Something to eat?'

Hastings dips his head. 'Thank you, yes. I'm already well attended.'

A moment of silence, each waiting for the other to break it.

'You have tidings, Will?' Richard uses the epithet without thinking, familiarity easing him towards whatever it is which has caused the chamberlain to ride through the night.

A clack of the latch brings a jug of wine, a manchet loaf and a hunk of cheese. Hastings waits until the boy has retreated before breaking the bread and stuffing it into his mouth. 'You are in receipt of my letter?'

Richard shakes his head. 'I fear you may have outridden it. If the king requires my presence, then I'm ready. I beg you, if you have word from him—'

'The king is in ward.'

'If my brother has any word for me, I urge you to deliver it. I wait only upon his instruction.'

'Did you not hear what I said, Richard? Edward was taken into custody at Olney, where he was resting for the night.'

'Taken? By whom? Robin of Redesdale cannot dare to challenge the king's person.'

'Redesdale, whoever he is, may not dare, but there remains one who does.'

'Not the earl. I won't believe it.'

Hastings delivers that familiar look: the raising of the brow, the wry twisting of the lip. 'I pray Your Grace may believe it, for it will make the remainder of what I have to tell you so much easier to relate.'

Richard lowers his head in the surly manner he thought he had outgrown. 'How can you be sure?'

'Because I was with the king. We'd decided not to ride against the rebels – not until we had more support: Herbert, Devon, and any men Your Grace may have been able to raise. Even then, the king was minded to consider this only as a last resort. I believe, in his heart, he has always acknowledged Robin of Redesdale as your cousin's man.'

Richard's mouth feels parched, his tongue like a leather strap. 'Pray don't tarry over this, Will. Tell the tale, and tell it swiftly.'

'The king, as you know, decided to leave Nottingham. Word from his spies was meagre, and he felt the only way to gain clearer intelligence would be to move out. There had been word of an engagement near Banbury, that Herbert and his brother had been captured—executed, according to one report. Another said that rebel numbers were increasing and that the north was rising. His Grace had no option but to move on. We received other reports—'

'Of what? Out with it, Will.' Name of Mercy, he's dragging it out.

'Those at Banbury reported sight of the Ragged Staff. Although others swore the earl was not present in his own person.'

Aware that his hands are shaking, Richard anchors them together. 'And so, Olney. What happened at Olney?'

'We were visited by the Archbishop of York at night, around nine of the clock. The king was abed and sent a reply that if the archbishop had come to conduct evening prayers, then he'd left it too late. Poor jests from Ned are always a warning sign; they show he is afraid.'

So, there can be no doubt. Their cousin has made his move.

'Archbishop Neville demanded the Great Seal,' Hastings snorts, 'which must have given the supercilious pizzle a certain degree of pleasure. Warwick's idea of revenge, I suppose, for the loss of the chancellorship.'

'You're telling me, Will, that my lord of York took the king into custody? Was any attempt made to resist? Did you not try?'

Hastings holds up his hands. 'Ned sought the archbishop's permission to dismiss me. And thank God for his foresight. At the very least, you and I are now free to gather further support.'

Richard sinks down opposite him. 'Do you believe the earl's intention is merely to separate His Grace from the queen's family, from Earl Rivers? Or to imprison him?'

Hastings chafes his hands together, scattering dried skin and breadcrumbs, before starting on the cheese. 'At the moment, he appears to be intent on both.'

Richard closes his eyes. Please Jesu, let his cousin see sense, let him sue for peace before it's too late. 'What did he say? The king? What did he say to you?'

'That it would be best if I left him. That he was the one the earl wanted and that, given the situation, this was the only way. But I believe Ned has allowed himself to be led into a trap. If he's relying on his charm to outwit Warwick, then he's misjudged affairs, for few can be more charming than my lord of Warwick when he so chooses. The Londoners love him, and he has the Kentishmen eating out of his hand.'

The earl has shifted his chessmen expertly across the board, and his plan is clear. First, lure Edward up country with tales of unrest. Next, ensure the loyalty of the City. Rouse the north into open rebellion, force Edward back onto the road south, then trap him. *Checkmate.*

'What now, Will?'

'We wait. We can do nothing until we see how the land lies.'

'Our duty…' Richard hesitates, barely trusting his voice to remain steady, '…must be to the king.'

Covering his mouth, Hastings belches. 'And that is why we cannot afford to err.'

'And the queen's family? Earl Rivers, where is he?'

'You heard the king say at Nottingham that he thought it best Richard Wydeville made away, given the earl's antipathy towards him. But the archbishop informed us that both Rivers and his son, John, have been apprehended: captured and arrested by the earl's men, close to the Welsh border.'

'On what charge?'

Hastings looks weary. 'God alone knows. Warwick has been waiting for this opportunity since Edward married the queen. I don't hold out much hope for them if the earl's behaviour towards Herbert and his brother is anything to go by.'

Richard feels as if his innards are shuddering, as if his whole being is simply a vessel crammed with quivering, slithering guts. 'If the rumour is true, my cousin has acted hastily in executing William Herbert and his brother.'

'*Illegally*,' Hastings stresses the word. 'He has acted illegally.'

'Yes.'

Hastings is right. Warwick's waited almost five years for this. He has a grip on the reins, which he'll not loosen until this erratic and determined beast has carried him as far as it can. Richard feels thirsty, so damnably thirsty. 'What do we do?'

'The archbishop informed the king he'll be taken to the castle of Warwick, where the earl will join him.' Hastings huffs in a show of contempt. 'Your cousin would have the rule, and make of your brother a gilded poppet. In France, they already believe this to be the case, that *Monseigneur de Warwick* is England's ruler *de facto*, if not by right. Make no mistake, Richard, the earl's plans amount to treason and nothing less.'

Richard recalls his cousin's eyes glowing as he spoke of the French king, admiration oozing like honey. One evening, after a visit to the Valois court, he had praised Louis to the skies. 'Le Roi has earned himself a nickname, "the Universal Spider",' Warwick had grinned. 'A great talent he has for weaving webs.'

Richard thinks of Courtney and Hungerford, remembers their faces as they shrank upon the scaffold, their entrails removed and held aloft before their eyes. *Behold, good people, the innards of a traitor.*

Rising from his chair, he kicks the strewn rushes. 'I assume my lord of Clarence is with them?'

Hastings consigns his empty plate to the floor. 'D'you think your brother would forgo the opportunity of telling the king where he went wrong? I've no doubt he's polishing his speech already.'

Richard scowls. 'My lord of Clarence, I'm certain, will show all necessary respect.'

Hastings no more believes that than he does. Grimacing, the chamberlain rubs the back of his neck and jiggles his shoulders. 'A bath and a soft mattress wouldn't go amiss.'

Richard claps, makes arrangements. A feeling of helplessness has engulfed him, and he despises it. 'So, Will. What do you advise?'

Hastings stands and throws his napkin on his discarded plate. 'As I said earlier, we wait. I shall return to my estates in the morning, retain my numbers in reserve. You, Your Grace, must do the same. Edward is sure to get word to us, and when he does, we move out.'

A summons arrives, but it is not what Richard expected. Written under the privy seal, the directive is delivered with the thrust of the Ragged Staff.

Laying the parchment aside, he massages his temples. If Warwick would rule in the name of the king, then he's compelled to conduct a king's business. He must appoint a council, call a parliament, as if the coup had never taken place. In the eyes of

Christendom, England must be seen to be functioning; its courts holding sessions, its clerks scribbling, its castles garrisoned, its priests praying, its labourers labouring. The earl must ensure that all men feel secure and confident in his authority. They must believe that, in his hands, each city, each village, will prosper, that the corn will be harvested, the tithes paid, and the coasts guarded. He must assure every man of his livelihood, every woman of the wool for her spindle. He would say that he's guiding Edward, showing him the error of his ways, demonstrating how a king should rule if he's to retain the support of his people.

And their cousin, no doubt, believes he can do it.

Richard reads the summons again. It's dated the seventh day of September, a little less than a week ago, and calls him to a parliament in York, arranged for the twenty-second. He must either attend and, by implication, throw in his lot with the earl, or abstain and make an enemy of him.

A recent despatch from Hastings spoke of a rumour: the queen's mother charged with invoking the dark arts to bring about Warwick's death; a leaden image, broken in the middle and secured with a wire, has been made and practised upon. If Jacquette burns for it, then she'll simply follow her husband and son to the grave, for Hastings has been clear upon that point also: Richard Wydeville and his son, John, faced the axe on the Feast of Saint Hilaria.

For Warwick, and for George, there can be no going back.

Chapter Twenty-Three

October 1469
Westminster Palace

As A phoenix slipping its fetters and rising from the ashes, Edward shimmers in cloth of gold. The forest of candelabra is no mere antidote to the creeping gloom; it is deliberate, an aureole of light that separates the king from the host of mortals gathered at his feet. Casting his eyes around the Presence Chamber, the king notes every face, challenging them with the sparkling allure only he possesses.

At royal behest, a figure moves forward, resplendent in blue velvet: Henry Percy, fresh from the Tower, clearly celebrating his newfound freedom. Placing his palms between the king's, he lowers black-pebble eyes and repeats the oath of allegiance in a resoundingly clear voice. He's young, of an age with George, and as he has so keenly sought to remind the king, almost as close to him in affinity as Warwick. He swears, upon his faith, to be the king's man, to observe his homage in perpetuity. Satisfied, Edward rises and grasps Percy by the shoulders, kissing him on the mouth.

Richard cannot be the only man present who wonders how Henry Percy's newly pledged friendship will be ultimately rewarded. There's only one thing, surely, that he would truly desire: the return of his family's earldom—the earldom which currently resides in Neville hands.

Warwick, suitably cowed but bedecked in scarlet and Venys gold, is easy to spot amidst the throng. Events of recent months have aged him; jaw clenched and grim, eyes dull and disillusioned, he's like a man who hasn't slept in the course of a week. How long had he imagined he could keep Edward confined? A country must function, and more than that, the people must see their king. Especially if their king is someone like Edward.

George, hovering at their cousin's side, looks equally jaded. Richard catches his eye: his brother's weak smile, an unsurprising mixture of longing and self-pity. Surprisingly, Edward hasn't sought to keep George and Warwick apart; indeed, he has pronounced them to be his best friends. But then, Richard supposes, he can pronounce anything he likes: it's not every man who could inveigle his way out of Warwick's custody with naught but his charm as a weapon. Hastings was wrong to have doubted.

With all eyes fixed on the king, Richard crosses the floor unnoticed. George is the first to acknowledge him, bowing in formal greeting, then folding him in a tight embrace. 'My Lord Constable.'

'I trust you'll not commend me on my new office quite so emphatically in the queen's hearing,' Richard warns. 'The honour has, after all, been granted to me upon the death of her father.'

Which, he wonders, Warwick or George, had decided to pass sentence on Earl Rivers and his son? Which had dared to act the part of a king, while the king himself played merrills with his gaolers to while away the time?

George is silent. The earl, distracted, observes how Edward has thrown his arm around Percy in his habitual gesture, and is parading him like a newly fashioned jewel he's had made for his bonnet.

Richard coughs, uncertain how to begin. 'Cousin?'

Drawing his gaze away with reluctance, Warwick inclines his head. 'My lord of Gloucester, how fare you?'

'Well.'

'I'm happy to hear it.' The earl's smile is genuine. Offering his hand, he searches Richard's face in the way he would scan a text, anxious to locate the verse whereat he ceased to read.

Taking his cousin's hand, Richard pumps the meaty fist. 'And it pleases me yet more to see the two of you at court.' They can never know how many times he's lain awake, how he'd pictured them, manacled, condemned, and facing the butcher's knife. 'I was pleased to learn of the forthcoming betrothal,' he says, 'the Lady Elizabeth and the son of the Earl of Northumberland.'

Edward's idea of an alliance between his infant daughter and the only son of John Neville must be seen as encouraging. Mustn't it?

Warwick, tucking his gloves into his belt, adjusts his signet ring. 'I wonder, Cousin, what the king intends for Henry Percy, since the Earldom of Northumberland now sits, as you say, with my brother.'

'I'm afraid he's not confided in me.' If Warwick hopes for enlightenment, then Richard cannot help him: he's as much in ignorance as anyone. 'George, how does Isabel fare?'

George's grin is both proud and affectionate. 'The Duchess of Clarence fares well. She is with child.'

Richard slides an arm about him. 'Accept my felicitations and offer them fulsomely to your lady.'

'Thank you, Dickon.'

For once, it feels good to hear the name, and Richard gives his brother a gentle squeeze. Katherine, his leman, has written by way of a scribe; she too is *enceinte*. It would be pleasing to be able to tell someone.

'With your brother's leave, I shall be returning to Warwick,' the earl says. 'You're always welcome to visit, Richard.'

'You know that nothing could please me more.' And nothing could, apart from a full and genuine reconciliation, an end to all doubts and suspicions.

The earl nods, knowing as well as he that such an invitation could never be accepted without Edward's permission. Warwick's greatness has been diminished, Richard can see that. An earl who takes control of a kingdom, only to find that kingdoms need a king, must feel thwarted, aware of his own expendability. Yet, he must be aware of how fortunate he is. For a noble, even one as mighty as Warwick, to have rebelled against his monarch, executed two members of his queen's family, and still find himself at liberty is nothing short of a miracle. George is fortunate, too. Heads cannot be placed back upon the shoulders, nor life breathed anew into the lungs of a corpse, but Edward has decided to be magnanimous.

Richard prays each can find it in his heart to be grateful.

The king peels a costard with the blade of his dagger, divesting the apple of its skin as he might a woman of her chemise. The peel drops to the floor: a lifeless snake.

Richard recalls how Margaret once spoke of the girls in her household, that on the eve of All Hallows, they made a ritual of such a thing, gathering with a bag of pippins to divine the initial of their future husbands. Taking an apple in turn, they'd remove the skin in one continuous piece, this being essential for the love magic to work. As each skin slid to the ground, the girls would huddle together, trying to identify the letter it had formed.

'Then surely each must marry a Stephen or a Clement,' Richard had told her, 'for I can't imagine it forming any other letter than an S or a C. Or perhaps an O.'

His sister had laughed. 'Trust you, Richard.'

He wonders whether she'd ever been tempted to try it for herself. If she had, she'd have found his prediction to be close to the mark.

'If you're still inclined to heed Mother's warning on the dangers of uncooked fruit,' the king says, indicating the bowl at his elbow, 'there are filberts.'

'Thank you.' Richard snatches a handful, crunching the nuts between his teeth.

Watching Edward, he thinks, you'd never suspect that a little over a month ago, his kingship had hung in the balance. Only yesterday, he'd once more declared the earl his best friend. Considering his brother's nonchalance, Richard can almost believe him.

The king raises a brow. 'What did you want to see me about?'

'The Stewardship of Halton. I've learnt from Sir John Say that Lord Stanley is still collecting revenue when, by Your Grace's own grant, the estate is now mine. Surely, that is not right.'

'Don't concern yourself, Richard. The money you speak of is owed to you from Duchy of Lancaster funds, and he cannot withhold it. Rest assured, the matter will be resolved.'

'It should never have arisen in the first place.'

'No, it should not, but Stanley is Warwick's brother-in-law, and perhaps recent events had emboldened him. He may have been waiting until he was assured of my fate. We cannot be sure of what the earl may have promised him.'

Richard compresses his lips. 'I don't know why you tolerate him.'

'Of whom are we speaking, my lord of Gloucester?'

Accepting the hint that he may have forgotten himself, Richard performs a respectful bow of the head. 'Lord Stanley, Your Grace. The behaviour of his family towards our father was reprehensible.'

'For Pity's sake, Richard. You can't judge every noble in the land by their dealings with our father. I have said I will resolve the matter, and I shall. You'll receive what is your due.'

'It's not simply about the funds.'

The costard has been whittled bare. Edward tosses the core onto his plate, sets his knife ringing. 'What, then?'

'Through my duties in the north, I've become acquainted with Sir James Harrington.'

'And, doubtless, he has bemoaned his fate.'

'Edward, his father and brother died for our cause. Do we not owe him much? The possession of his rightful inheritance is surely the least we can allow him.'

'As ever, your devotion to Father's memory does you credit, Brother, but it's a luxury in which I am unable to indulge. Recent events have proved that to some, blood and sentiment matter less than the power to control. I'll be fair when I can afford to be. At this present time, it's important to keep Stanley close. His lands and estates, his family name, are important to him. In Lancashire, the name of Stanley holds as much dominion as the names of Neville and Percy do in the north. I took a risk in placing you within his sphere. The grants have aggrieved him, and I'm not prepared to push him any further.'

Duly chastised, Richard drops his eyes. At times, his brother's objectivity seems little short of callous.

'Is there's something else?' Edward says.

'A personal matter.'

'Spit it out, then.'

'I…there is a girl—'

The king's face lightens. 'With child?'

'Yes.'

'Well done.'

Richard's cheeks burn. 'I owe it to her to find her a husband, but you know my fiscal position.'

Laughing, Edward taps his nose. 'Allow me time to consider, and you'll find that there is always a solution for such predicaments.'

The shift and shuffle of silk, the yelping of lapdogs, as the queen's ladies crane their necks with interest. Planting a kiss on Elizabeth's hand, Richard wishes he could dig himself a hole and jump in it. Delivering a sweeping glance towards the rapt figures, Elizabeth fastens her fingers around his. In one swift, graceful movement, she's on her feet.

'Walk with me, my lord of Gloucester.'

Dismissing all but one of her women, she allows him to draw her away, a scent of jasmine rising with every movement, until they reach the furthest end of the chamber. He's grateful for her consideration. To reveal an intimate secret to the queen is unappealing enough without her flurry of gossips revelling in every detail. Head tilted, curiosity piqued in the heart-shaped face, Elizabeth offers a smile which is not unkind.

'I know, of course, a little of the matter in hand. Tell me,' she says, 'something of the girl.'

'I suspect you would find little in her life to interest you, Your Grace.'

'Her father?'

'Dead.'

'Her mother, then?'

'Equally so.'

A sigh, soft yet audible. 'The girl must have something to recommend her, my lord, after all, she did attract your attention. Shall we start with her name?'

'Katherine.'

'His Grace has assured me that, should my cousin James Haute take the girl to wife, he'll be generous until you have sufficient funds to support the child yourself. James is not his father's eldest son, but he has a small manor in Kent. Katherine will fare decently enough.'

The queen's chief tirewoman still follows in their wake but stations herself apart. Immobile, hands crossed over her belly, elbows at right angles, she assumes the sedate stance of a well-mannered and virtuous woman.

Elizabeth, following his gaze, lays a hand on his arm. 'Once the girl is related by marriage, then perhaps I could honour her with a similar place in my household. You may be able to see her.'

Richard inclines his head. The idea is delectable. 'Thank you, Your Grace.'

Elizabeth pinches his sleeve, and he wonders if it's intended as an act of endearment. 'Your loyalty to the king is valued, my lord of Gloucester,' she says, 'particularly of late. Valued by both of us.'

Chapter Twenty-Four

March 1470
Baynard's Castle

THE SOLAR is rich with the scent of griddled salmon, of roasted leeks and onions. When the plates have been collected, and marchpane served with honeyed wine, the duchess eyes her sons in turn.

'I'm trying to recall the last time we were together like this, informally.'

'I pray you do not trouble yourself, Mother,' George says, dipping his fingers in the comfit dish and passing it round the table. 'It's surely more important we are here now.'

His jovial, fraternal letter, sealed with the device of the Black Bull, has seemingly achieved the impossible, bringing the king by barge from Westminster to converse in genial fashion as if recent events had never occurred. But if the idea is that the family of York embrace in peace and love, then surely their cousin should be here, too.

Invited but busy, George says, when Richard voices the question. Recruiting a retaliatory force to ride into Lincolnshire, where a new host of insurgents have risen against the king.

'Ah, Lincolnshire,' Edward muses. 'I wonder why Lord Welles should feel safe in renewing his feud with Thomas Burgh.' He taps his teeth in the detached manner that shows he doesn't wonder at all – he knows. Or rather, he suspects. 'Given his Lancastrian tendencies, he surely can't suppose I would approve of such conduct against my Master of Horse. What, do you think, has emboldened him to act in such a manner?'

'Lincolnshire is a seedbed of revolt,' George says, munching another comfit. 'It's hard to credit how the people of those parts still adhere to Daft Harry. Enough that they'd like to see his bony backside once more warming the marble chair.' He shakes his head. 'This misplaced loyalty to Lancaster needs to be stamped out, once and for all.'

Edward's eyes fix on George with the intensity of a lymer ahead of the hunt. 'And how many men do you intend to offer me?'

'As many as I can make ready, Your Grace. This discontent needs to be eradicated.'

'And that, my lord of Clarence,' Edward graces formality with formality, 'is my intention. I march north upon the morrow.'

'Good.' Inspecting his finger ends, pink from melted marchpane, George pops each into his mouth and licks like a pernickety cat. 'I'll send what I can, of course, but as for myself, I must return westward. Isabel is close to her time and would have me and her mother close. Natural, under the circumstances, this being her first travail.'

He proffers the comfit dish. Their mother declines with the merest shake of her head. 'I've always understood the countess to be skilled in that regard,' she notes, 'despite her own sad dearth of infants. I'm sure Isabel will be in safe hands, George.'

Richard finds it all very stilted, like a civic pageant with shoddy actors, where the best man the butchers' guild can offer stumbles through his lines with the clumsy aid of the skinners. He wishes Margaret were here. Things are always easier when Margaret is here.

Edward's chair creaks. 'Does the earl intend to be at Warwick for the birth?'

'As you can imagine, the arrival of his first grandchild is a matter of great import for him.' In a swift change of course, George catches Richard's eye. 'How's life on the Welsh Marches, Dickon? His Grace has been generous of late, and you're swiftly becoming a man of prominence. Chief Justice of North Wales, quite a responsibility.'

Richard nods. 'Presence on the Marches is essential. Since his father's death, William Herbert needs to be assured of assistance in strengthening our hold on the Welsh borders.' At the mention of the elder Herbert's execution, George blinks. 'Since I joined him,' Richard says pointedly, 'William has become a good friend. His sire, you will know, was a valuable supporter of our own father.'

'I heard you worked a wonder, Dickon,' George performs another volte-face. 'The trouble at Carmarthen and Cardigan subdued without bloodshed.'

Complimentary or not, the meaning is lost on Richard. When he fails to reply, George leans in. 'And so, your return there is imminent, Brother? Or do you ride with His Grace?'

'I go where I am bid.'

Their mother signals for more wine. 'A welcome gesture, George, inviting your brothers here.'

Edward glances at Richard before launching his own swift attack on the marchpane. 'Perhaps my lord of Clarence simply wishes to be genial. After all, circumstances have not yet afforded us the opportunity of celebrating his marriage and impending fatherhood.'

'I thought it might be pleasant,' George says. 'We've seen little of each other since the council in November. I thought we should act upon our reconciliation.'

The king seems unimpressed. 'A little ill-timed, I would have thought, given we are each of us set to leave London tomorrow.'

'Surely,' George laughs, 'acts of friendship are never untimely. Perhaps, once we are concluded here, we could make an offering at Paul's?' He leans across the table, round face shiny as a babe's, and Richard finds himself concurring.

If their brother is proposing a silent surrender, then this may be his way of sealing it. Never keen on apologies, one has to read between the lines with George, and if he's chosen to hold out an olive branch, it's important Edward understands. If their brother is truly reconciled, it may be that their cousin will soon follow.

The nave of Paul's is crawling with jobbing scribes, with touting whores, and rogues collecting gossip they might peddle for a penny. Richard follows his brothers to the Lady Chapel. He finds it awash with light, and a growing host of pilgrims Edward's men are swift to disperse. This doesn't seem right, he thinks, disturbing the prayers of the poor. It might not sit well with God.

As his brothers spill coin into the offertory dish, he surveys his own purse. He's minded of his first visit to Warwick, and Hastings' timely rescue. Things have changed, but his pouch is none the heavier despite Edward's grants. All that comes to him departs from him by the same means. What the king gives with one hand, he takes with the other, and yet one might ask, what choice does he have? Defending a kingdom costs money.

Edward and George kneel together while Richard remains at a distance, respecting their privacy. He should be overjoyed, but the longer he stares at his brothers' backs, the distance between their stilted forms, the more unsettled he becomes. George's apologies have never been effusive, but this quiet, demure affability holds none of his customary élan. It's almost as if he's playing a part.

Something is amiss, Richard thinks. I can sense it.

The king's chamber is like Candlewick Street: shirts, gowns, strewn about as if it were a draper's shop. He's to leave on the morrow, early. Hastings and Arundel are to accompany him north and, so it appears, is his newmade friend, Henry Percy.

'You're to return to Lancashire,' he tells Richard. 'Your lands in the northwest were not granted on a whim. I've placed you there for a reason. You are required to observe, and to quell any actions which appear contrary to my interests. And before you bring up the question of Hornby again, I've already told you I am considering it.'

Servers arrive with the king's supper: manchet loaf and cold herring, meagre fare designed to satisfy hunger but little else.

'But my place is with you, Your Grace.'

A bedgown is placed around the king's shoulders. Edward shrugs into it. 'Your place is where I choose to send you.'

'When, if, you encounter the rebels—'

'I will have sufficient men to deal with them.' Flopping down, Edward launches into the herring. 'I don't intend to be taken captive again, if that is what's troubling you.'

Through the open door, Hastings can be seen pricking items off a list and rapping out instructions. Dipping his head, Richard decides on one last plea. 'You think our cousin is behind all this business in Lincolnshire, don't you?'

'Yes. That's why I need you to keep an eye on Stanley's movements. As I've said before, it's possible Warwick may look to him.'

'What about George? This afternoon saw him make his peace with you.'

'I don't believe a word he says. And neither should you.'

'But you prayed together.'

'So?'

Another cautionary glance towards the antechamber shows Hastings still busy: organising pages, counting coin, securing chests with a plethora of keys. 'George is our brother.'

Edward picks at his bread. 'Then you should know him as well as I. In fact, you should know him better; you grew up with him.'

'Despite his failings, he's loyal to York. Loyal to Father's memory.'

'Neither he nor the earl claims to be anything else. It's their loyalty to me that's in question.'

'They're not traitors, Your Grace.'

'Sir Robert Welles has other language. His father, so he says, has been approached by the earl in request for support.'

'Against the rebels?' Richard hardly dares anticipate the response. When Edward remains silent, he says again, 'They are not traitors.'

The king pushes his plate aside. 'Well, if you are correct, they'll soon have the chance to prove it. Both Warwick and George have been summoned to join me in my pursuit of the Lincolnshire rebels. You yourself heard our brother promise as many men as he can spare, and the earl is purportedly gathering a force as we speak. If they come to me, I shall welcome them. If they don't, I'll assume they have chosen to oppose me. And if they have, even you must admit to their treason.'

Hastings is winding up business. Richard is running out of time. 'There must be some way—'

'God's Teeth, Brother! How many more times must I hear this? Surely, you can see that no man could have been more forbearing.'

Richard inclines his head, heart pumping. 'Of course, Your Grace. No man could.'

Ferocity diminished, the king makes a grab for his arm. 'Loyalty, Richard, is what is required, not your continual pleas upon my clemency. Your brief, for the present, is to return to Lancashire and see which way the wind blows. Now, do you think you can manage that?'

Chapter Twenty-Five

March 1470
Ribble Valley, Lancashire

*T*HEY'VE BEEN on the road for what feels like a lifetime. The dappled palfrey, Liard Gris, a recent gift from Edward, is generally a comfortable mount, but continuous riding is taking its toll. Buttocks numb, back screaming, Richard grits his teeth and glances at the leaden sky.

His scouts are up ahead. The sight of a Stanley-led army moving southeast is to be noted and reported. He's managed to convince himself that even if such a company exists, galloping through the mizzling rain towards the Lincolnshire Wolds, it may mean nothing more than that Lord Stanley has decided to support his king and is coming out against the rebels. There's no reason to believe that Warwick has summoned him, still less to suppose Stanley would obey such a summons if he had. Green and tawny livery jacks, winking through the gloom, are as likely a sight as hen's teeth.

Clitheroe will be a welcome sight but empty without Katherine. The girl must be close to her time. He wonders whether James Haute is proving a kind husband or whether the thought of his wife being brought to bed of another man's bastard will reflect upon his care of her. She's a good girl, mild, modest, deserving of a caring spouse. When last they met, she'd kept her feelings close, thanking Richard for his choice, for the advancement it would ensure her. Marriage to a cousin of the queen, she'd told him, was an honour indeed.

He hadn't the heart to tell her the choice had not been his, that he was as grateful for it as she was. He will acknowledge the child, he'd told her, tilting her little round chin and planting a kiss on her still eager lips. 'And when he's grown, I will do what I can for him.'

'And if I bear a daughter?'

The fair, musical tone of her voice still had the power to rouse him. Grasping her by the shoulders, he'd buried his face in her hair. 'Then name her after yourself, my love, and I shall find her a good husband when the time comes.'

What happens in the birthing chamber is known to few men, save physicians and priests, and he can imagine little of what she will suffer, may be suffering even now, as he rides the bleak and sodden roads towards the land she once called home. She's young, healthy. She'll come through her travail as his mother did a dozen times. She'll care for the child, for her nature is warm and loving, and Haute, in his turn, will care for her.

Richard is not so foolish as to imagine she will pine away for loss of him. A pragmatist, Katherine has neither demanded nor expected anything, and for a lass like her, with little to recommend her but a pretty face and diluted gentility, she's attained heights lesser girls may only dream of. He does wonder, though, whether he's changed her life for good or ill, and what her fate would have been had their paths never crossed.

'Your Grace.' Pressing close, Thomas Parr points ahead. One of the scouts is returning, mount dipping and rising as it flashes through the gorse.

Yanking the reins, Richard holds up a hand. The cavalcade halts, eyes fixed on the bobbing figure. If Stanley is on the move, they must intercept him. Should there be a clash, it will be Richard's first, and he cannot pretend, even to himself, that it won't be daunting. His sojourn in Wales, though promising military encounters, provided little opportunity to bloody his blade. This situation, however, an outright attempt on Stanley's part to join the rebels, may prove more confrontational.

He seizes on Warwick's advice about hating the opponent and knows that this time, the task will be easy. Twenty years ago, his father returned from Ireland only to find that the king he'd tried to serve had branded him a traitor. Stanley retainers, in their tawny and green, had lain concealed amongst the Cheshire meres, keen to slay a man who bore them no ill, simply to ingratiate themselves with Marguerite. York had eluded them. Edward chooses to forgive. But Richard can't.

His outrider returns. 'Lord Thomas Stanley, Your Grace, moving north.'

Why would Stanley be heading north? If, as Edward suspects, Warwick has summoned him, does this signify further risings, this time in the Neville heartlands? A sudden chill slithers down Richard's spine.

'A large force? Accoutred for war?'

'They seemed suitably arrayed, Your Grace. But a small force, less than four score in number.' The scout is a local man, experienced and with a sure eye. Richard has no reason to doubt him.

'To ride with a company of armed men, equipped for war, and without the consent of the king, is contrary to the peace of the realm. We shall follow him.' Relinquishing thoughts of bed and board, he sends the carts to Clitheroe and presses on.

The route indicated by the scout takes them northwest. Stanley is ahead by the best part of a day's ride and knows the roads well. It might be possible, if they make good speed, to overtake him and head him off at the river.

The scout agrees. 'He will, like as not, halt to water the horses. But if our advance party can report his movements, it should be a simple matter to work out his intentions.'

Richard's cloak, worked with tallow, succeeds in keeping him dry, but the Lancashire retainers are drenched. Shivering, he casts an eye over them: men who've come to know him but recently, yet who are willing to accompany him on what could become either a bloody clash or a fool's errand.

'The king shall know of your good work,' he assures the scout, 'and I shall reward you whichever way I can.'

What in God's name that will be is far from certain, but he must do something when this business is over to encourage those who've agreed to serve him. In a country where King Stanley rules, it must have been a difficult choice.

A day into the journey, and Stanley has not diverted from his northerly route. He is, then, intent upon something. Richard's had plenty of time to consider his moves and believes that a matter of stealth on their part should allow Stanley to remain ignorant of their presence. Swift progress, a feint north-eastward, then westward once more, will bring them to the bridge over the Ribble, to which Stanley himself appears to be heading.

The route makes for hard riding, a powered, rhythmic gallop. Whatever Stanley's plans, Richard owns the right to challenge him. And his tightening gut looks forward to it.

Ribble Bridge: stone built with five arches. At its southern end, the advance party awaits them, shivering in their sodden livery. No sign yet, he's told, of the approach of Thomas Stanley. Has the bastard slowed his pace deliberately or turned back altogether? Ironic, Richard thinks, instead of outwitting Stanley, I may have been outwitted myself—a fine show of skill by the king's youngest brother.

At length, movement is spotted amongst the dun-coloured mounds. Stanley, with his company, is finally heading their way.

A human barricade. Arrayed three deep, the line blocks the approach to the bridge so effectively that Stanley will find it impossible to cross without forcibly breaking their ranks. Richard knows little of Stanley as a man but enough to suppose that such a blatantly aggressive manoeuvre will not be attempted.

He keeps his eye on the road ahead, tells himself that he's here to represent the king and that the lord of Lathom, for all his power in the region, represents none but himself. At length, Stanley emerges through the murk, banners of the Eagle and Child as limp and unimpressive as Richard's own White Boar, his men as bedraggled.

'My Lord Stanley.' Richard encourages Liard with a gentle nudge. 'I am here at the behest of the king and must enquire as to your intended course: where you are headed with a company of armed men at a time of uncertainty in the realm, if not to join him.'

Stanley urges his own mount—a black, admirable-looking beast for which Richard could almost envy him—and trots forward. With narrow shoulders, head like an inverted goose egg, which could be judged a little too large for his body, Stanley is well-dressed for a campaigning man. The blue perse doublet, visible beneath his cloak, is not a soldier's attire. Wherever he's going, it's clear the man doesn't intend to exercise any martial skills in person. But his retinue, armed with bows and poleaxes, is a different matter.

Eventually, Stanley nods; the goose egg dipping an elegant bow. 'May God save Your Grace. The journey upon which I am embarked is personal and concerns my castle of Hornby, which, at this present time, is inhabited illegally. I seek only to claim what was granted to me three years since, by his most noble grace, the king. I ride to uphold the law, not to breach it. And intend to do so without the shedding of blood.'

Richard flicks the reins, aligning Liard with Stanley's black charger. 'And yet you clearly intend to threaten. Surely, my lord, if you consider the Hornby estates to be your property and the castle to be unlawfully held, then the way to contend this would be to bring a case to Chancery. Any clash of arms, however slight, at a time of rebellion, can only be considered subversive and contrary to the king's peace.'

A raindrop drips from Stanley's hair and travels the length of his nose. With an aggravated swipe, he flicks it away. 'Begging Your

Grace's pardon, you may be unaware that this matter has already been arrayed before Chancery, the result of which afforded James Harrington a spell in the chancellor's prison. Refusing to quit Hornby when called to do so is in defiance of the legal judgement.'

'Had Chancery been possessed of the true facts, then its judgement may have been other than it was.'

Stanley blinks. 'And would these be the true facts, my lord of Gloucester, or the facts according to Sir James Harrington?'

Richard juts out his chin. 'I believe those to be one and the same.'

Stanley gives a weak smile as if humouring a simpleton. 'I've no argument with Your Grace on this matter. Chancery presented its verdict, of which I understand the king is content. Therefore, I request that you allow me to proceed in good faith.'

'No.'

For the first time during their exchange, the man appears discomforted. 'My lord duke—'

Richard glares at him. 'My Lord Stanley, retreat, or I will have no choice but to employ force. As I said, an armed party traversing the country at a time of rebellion can only be seen as seditious, a return to the anarchy of ancient time.'

Another intimidating silence. Stanley's men shuffle, unused to seeing their master repudiated, and Richard finds himself wishing Harrington were here to enjoy the affair. No matter, James will hear of it soon and from his own lips.

'I say again: withdraw, my lord Stanley.'

'Your Grace, this is not your quarrel.'

Richard remains motionless, watching with increased satisfaction as Stanley orders his men to withdraw. 'It is now.'

Chapter Twenty-Six

August 1470
York

*A*T THE abbey of Saint Mary, the king bestows on him the Captaincy of Carlisle.

'I've word of hostile assemblies in the area. If true, I need a man I can trust to put them down, and the earl's former office will, I know, be safe in your hands.'

The Wardenship of the West Marches is to follow; both offices stripped from their cousin like layers from an onion. Relieving the king of his goose quill, Richard leans across the indenture and appends his signet.

'My right arm,' Edward says, as the document is witnessed. 'You're my right arm, Richard.'

That evening, a summons reaches him with the dying chimes of the Compline bell. Hastings greets him at the door of the ante-chamber. The king, he says, will keep his brother no longer than it takes the royal bed to be censed and evening prayers recited.

While the chamberlain deals out duties for the morrow, Richard yawns and throws his weary body onto the settle.

'To ask for you at this hour, Richard,' Hastings says, dismissing one page and summoning another, 'it must be urgent.'

Richard heaves a sigh. 'Then you don't know why he's called me?'

'I don't know his mind in everything.

'Don't you?'

Hastings grunts. 'All I know is that he spent the hour after supper with his spymaster.'

News at the end of the day is never good, and Richard would have preferred some inkling of what's afoot. At least then, he could have prepared himself. If it's fresh news of the earl, and of their brother, he'll need to.

Neither had been active in subduing the Lincolnshire rebels, and in April, both Warwick and George had sailed once more for Calais: an action which could only be viewed as perfidious. Attempting to secure the *Trinity*, they'd been beaten off, in daring style, by Anthony Wydeville, the new Earl Rivers. Richard can only imagine how that particular defeat must have chafed against the grain. For his part, Edward had relished the news that Wenlock, Warwick's deputy, had closed the gates of Calais upon his old ally. Traitors, the king had pronounced, cannot expect their friends to help them. Traitors can expect nothing, not even mercy, if they choose to bite the hand that feeds them.

Spring had also confirmed Richard's fears: the earldom of Northumberland returned to Percy hands, and John Neville compensated with a marquessate. In part, he approves; a man's hereditary right should not be taken away and awarded to another, in the same way as James Harrington should not have been deprived of Hornby. Yet it's difficult not to consider the new Marquess Montagu's abiding service to York and how much the insult will sting. Does Edward really believe the prospect of marriage between his eldest daughter and John's only son will compensate their cousin for the loss?

Already, Neville pride is simmering. Fitzhugh has raised the men of Richmondshire against the king, and Warwick's stomping ground is now in revolt. Richard dares to wonder where it will end.

The chamber door creaks, breaking his line of thought. Thomas Rotherham, chancellor and chaplain, glides from the king's presence accompanied by two lesser priests with sprinkler and Psalter.

'My lord of Gloucester, His Grace would have you attend him.' Signing a hasty benediction, the churchman bids them good night.

Hastings raises his brows. 'In you go, Richard.'

Candle flames prick the darkness, a glaring torment for tired eyes. The abbot's bed, appropriated for the king's use, is heaped with pillows, its regal coverlet helping to create at least some semblance of majesty.

'Ah. Good lad. Sit you down.' The king himself is ready to retire and, at Richard's approach, dismisses the last of his servants. Shadows make a map of Edward's features: gullies, rivulets, low-rising mounds. 'I'll cut to the quick, Brother. Our cousin, much as you would like to believe otherwise, is finally lost to us.'

Richard groans. He's tired, and if Edward has nothing new to relate, he would prefer to repair to his bed.

The king sighs. 'Would it make things easier for you if I told you my intelligencers have brought further news? That our informants tell me how the earl is well housed by King Louis? That he has met with Marguerite and renounced the cause of York?'

'Marguerite! No. I won't believe it—'

'Sit down, Richard, for Pity's sake. It appears our cousin is prepared to destroy me and to return her half-witted husband to the throne. Don't look so incredulous, boy! I assure you it's true. The earl has even agreed a marriage between his younger daughter and the Lancastrian whelp, in order to seal things nicely.'

Richard dares not open his mouth; he's no idea what might come out. Warwick has forsworn the cause, allied himself with the She-Wolf. And George, likewise. George, of all people.

'You understand now?' Edward urges. 'You understand that I can in no wise forgive him? That he must be considered an enemy? Your enemy, as well as mine.'

Silence.

Brown eyes narrow. 'I said our cousin was lost to us. I didn't mention George.'

The chamber sways. 'George? You've heard from him?'

'I've written to him by way of a messenger.'

'When? Who?'

A weak smile plays around Edward's mouth. 'Would it surprise you to know that my agent is a woman?'

'Nothing would surprise me these days.'

'Elizabeth, wife of Roger Tocotes. He is familiar with George, and his wife has served in Isabel's entourage over recent times. Since Isabel has lost the child, it will seem nothing strange for the woman to be summoned. They are, I understand, close, and a woman needs the comfort of another at such times.'

Instinctively, Richard crosses himself. 'It's your intention to win George over?'

'What else? I've not given up on him entirely, Richard, and despite what you may think, I do recognise his loyalty to our father's name. Moreover, the proposed marriage between Anne Neville and Edward of Westminster has pushed our brother's nose out of joint. What future would there be for him in Warwick's new world, eh?'

Richard thinks, what kind of future would there be for any of us? Anne's marriage to Marguerite's son points to one intention only: the restoration and continuance of Lancaster. Surely, such an idea is as abhorrent to George as it is to him. Surely to Heaven.

He casts the king a weary glance. 'Tocotes' wife should not have so difficult a task on her hands, then.'

'God be merciful, no.'

'You say Isabel's child was stillborn?'

'Is what I hear, yes. What possessed Warwick and George to haul the poor girl with them, when she should have been confined, is beyond understanding.'

Within Edward's quiet outrage, there lies a sense of guilt. The queen's belly also hangs heavy, and Richard knows his brother's capacity for pity is not so narrow as to remain unaffected by the thought of Isabel's travail in the bleak confines of a heaving ship.

He swallows, unsure how much more of this he can take. 'Is there anything else, Your Grace?'

'No, Richard. That's all. Get you to bed.'

'Plymouth?' Hastings says. 'They are certain?'

At breakfast, the king massages his lids with quivering fingers. Further spies have broken the backs of their mounts, bringing the filth of the road in with them. 'Yes,' Edward says, grim. 'I'm to believe the earl has landed at Plymouth, others of his party at Dartmouth. That a proclamation has been issued declaring Henry, sixth of that name, as the rightful king. All of his "capital enemies" are to be pardoned, provided they ally themselves with the earl, the Duke of Clarence, and other lords of the "most noble princess, Marguerite, Queen of England."'

Hush permeates as each man flounders in a mixture of shock and disgust. Richard has nothing to say, still less the energy to say it. He feels empty. Numb. Tired.

'Jasper Tudor sailed with them,' the king continues, 'in allegiance to his regal half-brother, and I'm told their journey north afforded them the pleasure of Lord Stanley's company.'

'Neither of whom are renowned for their military prowess,' Rivers, at least, appears to be thinking ahead.

'No,' Edward is in agreement. 'But we must not forget, Anthony, that they have the Earl of Oxford in their retinue.'

Hastings snorts. 'No surprise there. De Vere must be smirking like a rutting pig. He's awaited this opportunity for years.'

Richard is sure he's going to be sick. Their cousin allied to Lancaster, George, too. It's not possible.

Edward rises. Unsteady, his bulk knocks the table edge and sets cups tumbling. 'Summon Harpisfeld, Will, and have a horse saddled. I need a rider to leave within the hour. The Marquess Montagu has promised me six thousand men.' His eyes seek Richard's, and a worrying glance passes between them. 'Pray God he will ready them and meet us on the road south.'

Chapter Twenty-Seven

November 1470
The Low Countries

*A*T MIDDELBERG, the abbey guesthouse is musty and mildewed. Richard shivers in its cavernous interior; his waxed cloak, having lately betrayed him, proves a sodden weight heaped across his shoulders.

Margaret eyes him with concern and urges the lay brothers to build up the fire. Only when they leave does she hasten towards him, breath vaporous and ethereal. 'Come, Richard, for the love of God, you'll catch an ague. Off with those wet things before you say another word.'

Fumbling for cloak hooks with stiff fingers, he makes little progress before his sister takes control, whipping the garment from him and arranging it before the swiftly growing flames. A pile of clean clothes - shirt, hose, gown - lie on a neighbouring chair, neatly folded. 'They may not fit you particularly well,' she says, 'but at least they're dry.'

Turning her back, she wanders to the shuttered window while he peels off the remainder of his clothes and wriggles with gratitude into their welcome replacements. Closing his eyes, he wallows in the delicious feeling of warmth. 'Ready.'

Margaret enfolds him in a belated embrace. Finding comfort in her sweet, familiar scent, he's too weary to utter anything of note other than to thank her for receiving him: a penniless exile, or as good as.

She ushers him to the hearth, towards the spattering faggots and the stink of drying wool. He begs her to take the solitary chair; it's not right that she should remain on her feet while he sits like some squalid waif rescued from the town ditch. Upright and stiff in her Burgundian brocade, Margaret shakes her head. 'So, Edward was surprised, was he, when Montagu abandoned him? Had it not crossed his mind that the restoration of the Percy earldom may lose him Cousin John's support?'

'What choice did he have but to restore it? Percy has assured Edward of his loyalty. And the earldom is his by right.'

Margaret is unmoved. 'Then Edward should have considered another way to reward John Neville for his services. He must have known the earldom of Northumberland, ancient and lineal as it is, cannot be tossed around like a pig's bladder. It's Percy's by right, I agree, but it's not in the character of a Neville to bear insult lightly. All Edward has done is to thrust Montagu into the arms of the earl.'

Richard nods and rubs his face.

'Come, then,' Margaret says, 'avail me of the rest.'

To speak of it is to experience it anew. The flight south, from Doncaster where they'd learnt of John Neville's defection, through Lincolnshire to the Norfolk coast; a living nightmare, punctured with constant reports from Edward's spies that Warwick and George were moving north-eastward, whilst Montagu was moving south. A pincer movement worthy of the Roman strategist, Vegetius.

Margaret lowers her head, arranges the folds of her gown.

'The rains were hellish,' he tells her, 'the roads a mire we often doubted our mounts could navigate. There was but one choice. We had to make for the coast. Rivers has influence in Norfolk; it was the safest route to take.'

Racing into oblivion under leaden skies, their status had meant nothing. The honours, the estates, the authority, Edward's anointing, his power, his kingship were reduced to the reins in their fists and the horseflesh between their legs. Richard had felt once more a frightened boy, running for his life.

'We reached Bishop's Lynn, the storms holding us ashore. No ship could be purveyed; no master prepared to set sail in such evil weather. Eventually, when the wind died a little, Edward managed to pay for passage. He took Will Hastings with him, Rivers, Duras—'

'What of you?' Dropping to her haunches, Margaret reaches for his hand.

'The king thought it best we didn't travel together. He would not have us both lost. Should his ship go down, the cause of York…'

'Go on,' she massages his fingers with her own.

'I sailed within the week. In the meantime, I used what influence I could to raise men, offering them promises of reward when—if—we return. By my Faith, I realise only too well how fortunate I was to barter a passage. And then, the voyage,' he falters, anxiety bubbling and rising, slapping his innards, 'it revived so many memories. The German Ocean. George and I, alone. Sister, you don't know how hard I prayed. I had no idea where we would land. I trusted everything to God's mercy.'

'You did wisely.' Margaret touches the small reliquary that hangs from her throat by a plain leather cord. 'Saint Barbara watches over us, over all of us. It was no matter of chance that you landed at Veere. Wolfert van Borselen is a reasonable man, and his letter made its way to me swiftly and privily. I take it Edward knows where you are?'

'Van Borselen put me in touch with him.'

'Good.' She pauses, then asks, 'You have money?'

'A little. The bailiff was forthcoming and lent me three pounds.'

'Be sparing, and I'll see what I can do.'

'How can I thank you?'

She strokes his cheek. 'I've done little yet to aid you. Remember, I took a great risk in coming here. Duke Charles knows nothing of this meeting. The earl's alliance with Louis means my husband must be careful.'

'Surely now, the duke must declare for York. He's always hated our cousin, and since his marriage to you, Edward is Charles' natural ally. The new alliance between Warwick and Louis can mean only one thing for Burgundy.'

Margaret pours two cups of wine from the waiting jug and pushes one into his hand. 'If it had pleased Edward to relinquish more of my dowry payments, then perhaps Charles may have leant a little closer towards England. If Warwick intends to re-establish King Henry – and yes, Richard, such news does find its way to me – then you know as well as I that, despite the Dowager Isabella's former kindness, Charles has always supported Lancaster and continues, officially, to do so. You know that, until recent days, he sheltered Somerset and Exeter in his entourage.'

'Then are we wasting our time if we appeal to him for help?' The abbot's wine is watered but refreshing, and Richard takes a long gulp.

'Not entirely. It's only a matter of a fortnight until my court leaves for Hesdin. Charles would have me fetch his daughter to him so we three may spend Christmas together. It's often remarked how Mary's presence softens him, and I believe I may make some progress in our brother's cause. Charles is not completely averse to Edward's presence on our shores. He did, after all, keep Edward informed of Warwick's movements and may be prepared to assist the king financially, if secretly. The fact that Edward is currently enjoying the hospitality of the Stadtholder is, of course, thanks to Charles. Gruuthuse has the duke's absolute trust, and I'm sure Edward also knows how fortunate he is.'

Richard detects a hint of wariness in his sister's voice, in addition to ill-disguised sarcasm. This is not simply a question of his own welfare, nor of Edward's; for Margaret, it's about what will happen to George.

Reaching for the drawstring bag which hangs from her girdle, she removes a sealed letter. 'As for me, I've not been idle these past weeks. I trust George was able to digest my missive without interference from the earl. This is a copy for Edward's perusal.'

Taking the letter, he slides it inside his shirt; the stiff parchment, pressed to his now warm breast, elicits the ghost of a shiver. 'He will be eternally grateful.'

'It's my understanding that Mother and our sister of Exeter have written to George, too.' Stroking the reliquary, Margaret proffers a wry smile. 'But I know that if George will listen to anyone, he'll listen to me.'

Dusk creeps over Des Graven Hage, presaged by darkening clouds. Approaching the walls with a meagre following, Richard sends his man ahead with letters of introduction from Van Borselen and hopes of receiving admittance before the storm begins. Reaching the Groenmarkt, his company waits at the city gate, shoulders hunched against the cold. Entry granted, directions offered, they clatter through the drenched and deserted streets towards the centre of the city. In the open squares and narrow *straaten*, signs of life are few; those lacking good reasons to be abroad having long since sought the comfort of their own hearths.

His note to Edward, hastily scribbled and sent in haste from Middelberg, has elicited a command to join the king as a guest of the Stadtholder, Louis de Gruuthuse. Their directions have brought them safely to the Binnenhof: a solid, impregnable bastion built on the banks of the Hofvijver lake.

A liveried man, bearing Gruuthuse's badge of the firing bombard, strides from the gatehouse. 'My lord of Kloster, you are most welcome.'

Richard entrusts him with his men, surprised as the Flemish he thought he'd forgotten tumbles out in hasty gratitude. Mounting a narrow stairwell, he's ushered into a vast chamber flickering with firelight and richly coloured hangings.

'Thank God, the giver of all good things.' The king, eyes glowing with pure joy, leaps to his feet and envelops Richard in a warm embrace. 'Oh, how I've missed you, Brother, and fretted for your safety.'

'And I, likewise. We've much to be grateful for.' Despite his exhaustion, Richard can hardly fail to admire the riches on display: the Turkey carpet spread atop the buffet, the display of golden dishes. 'The Stadtholder is indeed a wealthy man.'

'Indeed.' Edward gives a wicked grin. 'It shows how well a man can do for himself if he levies tax on every import of beer.'

Richard is glad to find his brother alone; a private reconciliation feels appropriate. Although news of their flight will be carried the length of Christendom, what has brought them here, to this place, to this state of existence, is a private - a family - matter.

'I've seen Margaret,' he says as Edward's chuckles die away.

'Have you?' Clearly, not even Edward could have credited him with so deft a move. 'How in God's name did you manage that?'

'It was unbeknown to the duke. She took a great risk in meeting me and entrusted me with this.' He draws the letter from its hiding place. 'She's written to George. This is a faithful copy. She wishes to prove how much she would have him return to us.'

'I don't doubt it.' Taking the parchment, Edward breaks the seal.

For Richard, the temptation to employ their cousin's methods of softening wax has been undeniable. But he's resisted. It wouldn't be right to read something intended for the king. 'What does she say?'

Edward's eyes, skittering back and forth, succeed in veiling his expression. Refolding the letter, he tucks it into the breast of his gown.

'Your Grace? What does she say?'

'Enough.'

'Might I be permitted to know?'

The king directs him towards the fire. 'Not until you stop shivering and have refreshed yourself. God's Blood, how it cheers me to see you, Richard.'

'And I you.' Weariness and relief are beginning to take their toll. 'You don't know how much.'

Advent is upon them, and Gruuthuse proves an obliging host. The luxuries offered at the Binnenhof belie the impoverished future they could have imagined for themselves two months past, and surely such honours would not be laid at their feet were Duke Charles not prepared to assist. When all's said and done, support for Edward must serve Charles better than any attempt to make peace with his hereditary overlord. Louis, now allied to Lancaster, is well placed to see Burgundy crushed, and if Charles has any sense, he'll come down in favour of York. But, as his father had, the duke chooses to play it safe, assisting covertly and from a distance. The best Edward can do is ply for favours, and ensure himself well-informed of events.

They sup, tonight, in Gruuthuse's parlour. Edward, sated, makes himself comfortable in the Stadtholder's chair, casting off his boots and wiggling his toes to the fire. Margaret's letter remains close, sealed between shirt and skin, and Richard still has no idea of its content.

'I hear you're proving an able ambassador to Van Borselen, Richard,' Hastings says, taking up an elaborate spoon and admiring its craftsmanship. 'Anything to report?

'Not much. Although, it's clear Louis' support of the earl still depends on Warwick conducting naval attacks on Burgundy.'

'Predictable,' Hastings snorts, 'but I imagine Warwick has enough work on his hands already without making a nuisance of himself here.'

'Either way, the citizens of Veere are taking precautions. They're in the process of building a gatehouse at Walcheren in order to withstand the earl's forces.'

Hastings shakes his head. 'No need. Warwick would be foolish to take on such a task.'

'The bailiff would disagree. The authorities genuinely fear an attack and are spending large sums on *"de Warwijkse Poort,"* as they're calling it.'

Hastings smirks. 'Your grasp of Flemish is to be envied, Richard. You must have acquired it courtesy of those pretty *deerns* you've been dallying with.'

Richard has soon come to realise that very little escapes the lascivious eye of Will Hastings. In the weeks since he made her acquaintance, Floortje has never crossed the threshold of Gruuthuse's mansion – the same goes for Mariette - yet Hastings seems to know of their existence. Is the chamberlain spying on him for his own aberrant pleasure, or is his interest purely political? Either way, Richard doesn't like it.

Edward barks with laughter. 'My brother's grasp of languages is enviable, although he's yet to better me in the use of the French tongue.'

A bawdy snigger from Hastings has both men hooting like wayward youths.

Rivers, coming to the rescue, chooses to ignore both the remark and Richard's rising embarrassment. 'It sounds to me, my lord of Gloucester, as if Warwick is allowing himself to be used. Still, desperation can make a fool of any man.'

Richard slides him a look of gratitude. He's finding George's opinion of Wydeville as a coward and a sycophant to be untrue. A scholar and a man of reason, the queen's brother cannot be summed up quite so glibly.

A snort from the fireside. 'I fear you're right, Anthony. It's well known that Duke Charles refers to Louis as 'the Universal Spider,' and if the same analogy is to be used, then Warwick is undoubtedly a fly, lured and entrapped in the Frenchman's sticky web.'

I have Louis eating out of the palm of my hand. Richard studies the tablecloth as Warwick's words creep back to him, along with so many other things about his cousin that have tormented him of late. Warwick's celebrated returns from France, Isabel admiring the gifts he brought her, Anne scrabbling for a place at his feet. Both girls gazing at their father in implicit approbation as he boasted how favourably Louis considered him, of how *Monseigneur de Warwicke* was, in the eyes of the French, the virtual ruler of the realm.

'Well, I still say he's enough trouble on his hands.' Hastings continues his admiration of the cutlery. 'Last time he tried to rule without Your Grace, nobody would listen to him.'

'And I doubt his ability to work alongside the likes of Somerset and Exeter,' Edward muses. 'Whatever he does, they'll always consider him their foe.'

'Neither of them is likely to venture upon English shores at present. They'll remain where they are, with Louis. And even if they do return to England,' Hastings waggles a hand in the vague direction of home, 'they'll only countenance Warwick for as long as it takes to re-establish Henry. You think Marguerite will care how much the Londoners love the earl once she has Somerset back? She'll tolerate Warwick while he helps her recover what she wants, then she'll force him to answer for his former behaviour. He'll be like Humphrey of Gloucester, quietly done away with. "Richard Neville?" people will say. "Oh, didn't he expire from a surfeit of something?" '

Angry, and tired of Hastings' derision, Richard trains his eye on the tapestry that frames him: Alexander, hair streaming, spear couched and level with the chamberlain's sandy head.

Leaning forward, Edward pats his footstool with a great paw. 'You did well in Veere, Brother. Come, warm yourself.'

Richard leaves the table, noting how chill and silent the chamber has become. While he sinks down, extending his palms to the flames, Edward turns to the others. 'Will, Anthony, do not feel the need to remain with us.'

Rivers bows ceremoniously, as if the place were swarming with Burgundians, then takes his leave. Hastings hesitates before inclining his head. 'As you wish, Ned.'

Once they're alone, Edward winks and indicates the gaming board propped against the settle. 'Merrills? Or do you have other plans for the evening?'

'Merrills, Highness, would be most pleasant.' Richard grabs the board and drags up a stool. Edward is silent as the game is set up, chest rising and falling in contented rhythm. When Richard is finished, he says, 'I'm in receipt of a letter from Mother.'

'Mother? Is all well?'

'Yes, she's hopeful of her attempts to influence George. And, of course, she assures us of her daily prayers.' Edward's splayed hands grasp his knees. 'But there's also news of the queen. Her Grace was delivered on All Souls' Day.' A slow smile lights up his face. 'Praise God, Richard, she has given me a son.'

Gruuthuse celebrates the Twelve Days in lavish style, his guests enjoying more seasonal comforts than Charles' five hundred ecus per month would have afforded them. Despite the revels, Richard muses. He thinks of his mother and her sombre vigils in Baynard's lonely chapel. Imagines the soft cheeks and tiny fists of the infant he has fathered but never met.

Most agonising of all, he allows himself to dwell upon Warwick, and upon George, wondering what his brother has done with the letters he received; whether he locked them in his clothes chest—or tossed them on the fire, bidding Isabel dispense with the services of Tocotes' wife. He wonders how George succeeds in bowing the knee to the woman he so joyfully named the She-Wolf. The mere suggestion of such an act, when as boys they had lain abed waging imaginary wars, would have been unthinkable. He would have dealt me a clout, Richard thinks, twisted my arm, or locked me in the jakes had I predicted any such fate for him in the fullness of ten years. And yet, here we are.

On the Feast of the Holy Innocents, when he finds Edward in the company of the Gascon, Lord Duras, Richard is hopeful. Loyal to the English and to Duke Charles, under whom he acts as chamberlain, Gaillard de Durfort has worked alongside Warwick in Calais and elsewhere. Perhaps his mediation could be useful.

'Read this.' Thrusting an opened letter into Richard's hand, Edward retreats to the window embrasure while Duras shivers and huddles into his furs.

Richard examines both halves of the broken signet: *Je Lays Emprins.* 'From Duke Charles himself?'

Burying his hands in the depth of his sleeves, Edward dips his head. Richard scans the parchment. 'Twenty thousand English pounds?'

'In payment of our expenses and in order to fund an army. It seems Charles has finally decided to act in his own best interests. He bids us meet him as soon as may be. It appears Gruuthuse has a castle at Oostcamp. From thence, we'll proceed to Aire, where the duke will receive us.'

Twenty thousand pounds: enough for a well-equipped, suitably arrayed army.

Tipping a signal to Duras, Edward waits until the Gascon

leaves before wandering back from the casement. 'You realise what this will mean?'

'Yes.' Richard hands back the letter as if its contents have scalded him. 'It means an invasion.'

'Indeed. I believe we may count upon Henry Percy for support. I'm entrusting Leventhorpe with letters to sound him out.'

Leventhorpe, a yeoman of the chamber, is a Yorkshireman and well-known to Percy. Providing support now, at such a crucial time, will seal Percy's position. A grateful Edward is a generous Edward, as a rule, and Northumberland will never have a more opportune moment to aid his king. And besides, the destruction of a Neville, particularly a Neville as powerful as Warwick, has ever been the dream of the House of Percy.

Edward's smile is slow and satisfied. 'We may have fled England as hunted men but could return as conquerors. I trust you've written letters to sound out your own supporters, Richard? You have made valuable alliances of late. Herbert, I'm sure we can depend on, what of Harrington?'

'James Harrington has responded most favourably. He assures me he can raise three hundred men, perhaps more.'

'Well done. What about William Parr? Is his young brother's devotion to you enough to sway Sir William from his Neville allegiance?'

'The Parrs are Neville supporters certainly, but I don't believe they would aid our cousins against you. They are committed to York.'

Edward wanders to the hearth, presents his palms to the flames. 'It's Warwick's alliances in the north we need to consider; those of the Midlands more so. Remember, George also has strong support in that region.'

'George? You told me Mother's letter spoke of a rapprochement?'

'I pray daily for such a conclusion. Knowing our brother, I can't see him sticking too closely to the earl now there's little remaining in the matter to benefit him. But when we set out our plans, we must make allowances for the fact that he could surprise us. He could continue in his loyalty to Warwick. And if he does, we shall face him across a battlefield.'

'One is our brother, Edward. The other is our cousin. Family.' Having uttered this statement so many times, its effect is lost even on Richard.

'I believe this whole affair will not progress to a clash of arms. The earl is a diplomat and a tactician; he's not a soldier. Not in the true sense of the word. If we procure a large enough force, he may throw himself on our mercy.'

'He'll not prostrate himself before you.' Richard sounds disrespectful, but of a sudden, etiquette fails to matter. 'For our cousin, pride is everything. I know that, Edward, even if you don't.'

'He must have prostrated himself before Marguerite, must he not? Her own savage pride would have demanded it.' Edward slides Duke Charles' letter into his purse. 'Besides, it's the opinion here in the Low Countries that the earl is a coward. That is my opinion also. The sight of a royal army swelled by the likes of Northumberland, and brother George—if he'll join us—could see Warwick bowing before my feet, too.'

It's not as simple as that. Edward knows it isn't, and yet, like George, like Warwick, he continues to play this spiteful, pitiful game. Only Margaret and I see where it will lead, Richard thinks, where it will truly lead: to death, and to destruction.

Thrusting protocol aside, he excuses himself.

At the Flemish castle of Aire, formality reigns supreme, and it appears that under Philip the Good's less-than-genial son, the ritualised behaviour of the ducal court has not diminished.

The Burgundians, spangling and bejewelled, have arranged themselves to the right of the hall, the English to the left. Arrayed like an archangel in the finest Venys gold, Edward clearly has an advantage over the rest of his party in their dull, unfashionable doublets. Nobody would think, to look at him, that two months ago he was on the road and in fear of his life, with an empty purse and nothing to his name but the clothes on his back. But why, Richard thinks, should we be surprised? If anyone can turn his luck around, it is Edward. As George once observed, with ill-concealed sarcasm, 'If he were cast overboard in a storm, he'd wash up in the Land of Cockaigne.'

Burgundy may not be that mythical land with extremes of abundance and loose living, but disregarding the latter, Charles' court makes for a fair emulation. The duke himself is like a man who has fallen headfirst into a casket of precious stones and emerged encrusted with gems. Even his black chapeau is peppered with pearls and sewn with rubies the size of plums. The visage beneath has changed little since Richard's childhood exile; the same solemn, sulky appearance of a man not easily impressed, not even by the vision of majesty displayed before him in the person of his brother-in-law. Perhaps Edward's golden gown, his hanging jewels, provided by the Stadtholder via a circuitous route from the duke's own purse, take the edge off the spectacle.

Charles descends from the dais, so the rulers can face one another upon the floor of the hall. *Le Téméraire* looks worthy of his epithet, and Richard has no difficulty in imagining how the duke's first meeting with Warwick dictated a subsequent relationship of mutual dislike. Edward, however, is no Richard Neville, and Charles' stiff, initial gestures are returned with a fluid grace few could emulate. Margaret hovers on the margins, Madonna-like in Virgin blue, exuding both quiet humility and stately determination.

'At least he's no longer harbouring Exeter and Somerset,' Hastings mutters in Richard's ear. 'But I imagine whilst here they'll have advised him to hold off in assisting us, pending events in London.'

'Duke Charles will have to make a choice: assist my brother in reclaiming his throne or throw in his lot with Lancaster. He cannot support both.'

'Supporting Lancaster will mean aligning himself with France,' Hastings says. 'And we all know how the duke detests his overlord. If he has any sense, he'll come to our aid. Ned is a generous man, he'll return the gesture when Louis snaps at Charles' heels.'

Below the dais, a conference has begun between the brothers-in-law. Richard strains to hear what he can amidst Hasting's incessant babble.

'Most generous…' Edward's fluent French is both charming and melodic, '… most thankful of Your Grace's largesse and promises.'

'Promises, le Roi Edouard? I made an offer, not a promise.'

'I assure Your Grace,' Edward's voice rises, 'that your letter led me to believe you were inclined to assist me. I have much support in England. The cause of York is strong.'

A condescending smile from the duke. 'Do not imagine that your predicament, and that of your country, is unfamiliar to me. My grandfather himself fell victim to such internal strife.' A shrug. 'It is the way of things.'

Edward takes a step forward. 'Whilst there are those who would deny my right, then yes, it is the way of things. Yet it is my intention, nay my determined aim, to reclaim that right.'

Hastings growls in indignation, and Richard silences him with a glance. From where they stand, it's clear that Charles' ample lips are clamped shut, his surly, solid presence a wall to be assailed, a drawbridge to be battered. Paying no heed to protocol, Edward falters as if he intends to throw himself at the ducal feet.

'For God's sake, Cousin, do not abandon me. We are brothers, bound by the laws of the church, as well as the laws of chivalry. The Garter binds you to me, and my acceptance of the Fleece assures my complete support should the need arise.' A flash of Venys gold and Edward's hands are joined in an act of supplication. 'In the name of the Blessed Saints, Charles.'

'For shame,' Hastings hisses. 'To see a man like Ned forced to beg.'

Margaret's steepled bonnet bobs as she glances from husband to brother and back again. She's gambled on Charles' co-operation, Richard thinks, she's as ignorant as we as to the outcome.

The duke arranges his gown. 'Certainly, Brother, I am fully aware of the great significance of your Order. Louis himself reminded me that, as his vassal, I should not have taken it upon myself to accept the Garter and, in order to exact punishment, promptly halted trade with Burgundy. He also declared me a traitor and looks to invade my lands.'

Edward's hands remain clasped. 'Under Yorkist rule, I can assure you that trade would be reopened and encouraged. Burgundy would fare better than it ever has.'

'Ah yes,' the response is not without a touch of sarcasm, 'for the traders, the merchants, they all love you, do they not?'

The duke's voice sinks so low that only his chosen audience is able to catch his words. Edward appears to respond, and they remain in conference for some moments.

'He's playing with him,' Hastings snarls. 'The man thinks himself an emperor.'

Richard's attention remains fixed on the desperate tableau. 'However he sees himself, we must pray he takes pity upon the plight of a fellow ruler. After all, Louis' alliance with England leaves Charles vulnerable. The duke may need assistance himself before too long.'

At length, Margaret is summoned by her husband and escorted across the floor. The voices of each remain muffled, but a gentle smile lifts the corners of her mouth.

Richard unclenches his fists, a series of crescents impressed on each palm.

'Thank God.' Hastings all but weeps in relief. 'That's it. We'll be on English soil before Easter.'

Gruuthuse's lofty casements bid welcome to the sunlight of early spring. Watery light, seeping through the leads, makes a chequered pattern on the floor, and Richard spends some distracted moments counting the squares, wondering how much he should reveal to Mijnheer de Vroede and whether he can trust him. The Fleming arrived at the Bruges mansion, supplied with paper and ink, linen and cord, as well as a pan of wax, which he sets to melting close to the fire.

De Vroede himself is short but sturdy, tightly curled hair cropped close to his scalp. Whether the scar running alongside his nose is an accident of his craft, or a more intimate experience of war, is impossible to tell. Methodical, he unrolls the parchment, weighting it at each corner, before unravelling his cord.

'You have harness in England, my lord Kloster? Yes?'

'Indeed, with which I am well satisfied.' Richard's tetchy, ill-mannered response is greeted with a protracted pause. Abashed, he looks the man in the eye. 'But it was fashioned for me during the latter part of my youth, so there's every reason to acquire a new one now.'

'Very well, my lord. You will please extend your arms.' Taking the cord, de Vroede measures his client's forearm from elbow to wrist bone before tying a knot. Using his measuring stick, he calculates then consigns the information to paper. Next, the cord is wrapped around the wrist. 'Hmm…very slender, my lord.'

Richard remains silent, deciding that when he does speak, his words will be brief and to the point. Thomas Parr looks on, eying him with feeling.

De Vroede shrugs in Flemish fashion. 'I understand you have no arming doublet to hand, my lord. A great pity. Used doublets retain the shape of their owner. It would have been of great use to me in sizing the vambrace, the rerebrace also. Arm movement is particularly important.' He tugs at Richard's doublet and glances up. 'Might I take one of your older garments with me?' He nods towards the hearth, 'If not, we could prepare a linen cast with the wax.'

Richard prays his anxiety is not obvious. 'One of my doublets is old and has been well worn. You may take that.'

The armourer circles him, tugging incessantly at his velvets. 'Did your tailors take measurements for this? I think not; it is a poor fit. Who made it? His Excellency Duke Charles would never be satisfied with such imprecision.'

Parr interjects. 'My fault, Mijnheer. Duke Richard's gown is new, made here in Bruges. I fear I sent my lord's measurements to the tailor in haste—'

'No,' Richard shrugs off de Vroede's probing fingers, 'the fault lies with me. I failed to visit the man in person.'

It's like Brocas' visit all over again, but he must try to oblige; the accuracy of full plate could mean the difference between life and death. Before Parr can attempt any further excuses, Richard unfastens his doublet. Casting it aside, he stands before the armourer in shirt and hose.

'Mijnheer, you must understand, I have a condition. You may have knowledge of such things, you may not. I am told it's not unheard of.'

De Vroede's brow creases with interest. 'Might I—?'

'I suggest you use your cord to measure my torso,' Richard fires the words like missiles. The faster they're out of his mouth, the easier it will feel. 'When you do, you will find an anomaly. I would like, if you please, for the breastplate and plackart to be fashioned to accommodate this.'

When he'd stood before Brocas on that cold afternoon, he had presented his body to a practising physician, a man used to the human form in all its variations. But an armourer is a different thing entirely, accustomed to the physique of the fighting man: men like Edward. Deciding to take control, Richard divests himself before he's asked, stoops before he's told. If this must be done, then let it be enacted with as little shame as possible.

De Vroede's hands are rough and decisive, palms hardened from the work of the forge. The fingers of Floortje, and those of Mariette, are soft and make no judgements, but there again, each believes they're caressing the body of a mere lordling, whose place amongst the entourage of *Koning Eduard* is inconsequential. This Fleming, with his court connections and his closeness to Duke Charles, will know at first-hand that the brother of the English king is flawed.

'A slight misalignment. This will be interesting work for me, Lord Kloster. However, it is the case that modifications are often required. No two men are the same.' De Vroede works carefully, measuring with the cord and pausing to note his findings. He concludes with a satisfied nod. 'If I may be so bold as to say, Lord Kloster, that not only is each man different, but no man is perfect.'

'My brother is.' Richard instantly regrets the retort. Why in

Heaven's name is he revealing such intimacies, such anxieties, to an armourer: a man he has never seen before in his life?

De Vroede laughs. 'Then, I would suggest that it is he who is unusual. The rest of us bear the imperfections with which God endowed us, in order that we might strive to honour Him by the strength of our efforts.'

Richard studies the man from beneath his brows. 'Did you ever consider training as a physician? It seems to me you have the manner for it.'

'Not I. I have witnessed enough spilt guts on the battlefield.'

Richard wriggles into his shirt. 'My purse, Tom. Please.'

Parr hands him his girdle with the purse attached. Rummaging inside, Richard proffers coin. 'I can trust to your discretion, Mijnheer?'

De Vroede holds up a hand. 'No need, my lord. The relationship of an armourer to his client is a close one. Between the lord and his enemies, between his life and his death, lies the skills of his armourer. If the lord trusts the armourer with his life, be assured he can also trust him with his secrets.'

Chapter Twenty-Eight

March 1471
Damme, Flanders

*N*ONE HAD expected such large crowds. Flemish burghers in bright wool with apple-cheeked wives and inquisitive children, farmers late from the fields, damsels fresh from their mothers' kitchens and curious gaping beggars. Each is intent upon viewing a spectacle they're not likely to see again: an English king, parading on foot from Bruges to the banks of the River Reie for no other reason than to reward the land which has sheltered him with a flagrant glimpse of his majesty. Gone is the pleading supplicant of Aire sur la Lys. Here, restored in glory, is the mighty Alexander, beautiful to the eye and bolstering to the heart, a glimmering Phoebus arrayed in all his splendour.

A gusting wind laden with the scent of verdure ensures blue skies, swift-moving clouds and radiant sunshine. It makes glittering pennants of Edward's sleeves, a spangled river of his trailing robes. It's as if the sun is his gift to the people, allowing those who have gathered beside meadows, ditches, and market squares to better admire him. Removing his bonnet, he waves it in triumph, takes the hands extended to him, kissing those proffered by women, and showering smiles like scented petals.

Richard watches, transfixed. Pride welling, expanding beneath his ribs, carries him on its fulsome waves back to Placentia, when a king had descended the steps of the dais to welcome two bewildered boys home from exile. Now, as then, he can conceive of no other who could draw such numbers to him by the strength of his beauty alone. Warwick can attract the crowds, yes, but it's his fame that attracts them, his liberality. Edward offers the people of Damme nothing but a glimpse of his own person, yet still they come, and the more they admire him, the more he gleams.

They turn into the marketplace, where the crowd is at its most dense, where the steps of the Stadhuis are crammed with town officials eager to show their respect. If one knew no better, one would assume it was their duke, Charles *Le Téméraire* , they had come to applaud, not a king from the far side of the German Ocean. Richard wishes Margaret were here to witness it; three years at the Burgundian court has done little to dull her pride in her family. He saw her last on the eve of Saint Valentine in Lille and remained with her at the Rihour Palace for three days, George's loyalty, or otherwise, providing the staple topic of conversation.

She'd held up a letter splattered with George's scrawl. 'I am certain of his commitment to the cause. He says the alliance with Marguerite was made against his advice. Although I doubt very much the earl would have cared for our brother's opinion one way or the other.'

Ignoring Richard's eager fingers, she'd tucked the letter into her purse. Whatever George had said was intended for her alone, and he knew enough about George to understand the missive would have been scribbled down, possibly in a flight of passion, and had decided not to encroach further. Regardless of any deception George may choose to practise upon the rest of the world, he would never lie to Margaret.

Richard scans the faces that line the market square, searching amongst the ready smiles. A hope, half-formed, has lingered since dawn: that he may catch a glimpse of his former guardian hidden amid the press. Wherever Jaagen is now, it's not inconceivable he might ride here today to view the spectacle. Richard wonders whether these ten years have been kind to his friend. He hopes so. True, kind, Christian souls are few, and the world a more treacherous and complex place than is suited to the nature of such a man.

324

'He could be Caesar, returned from Alesia,' Rivers interrupts his thoughts, smiling as a golden cup is presented to Edward and accepted with the king's usual aplomb.

Richard sniffs. 'He could be Caesar. He could be Hercules. He could be Arthur. But if battle is to be averted, we need him to become another Solomon.'

'You still wish for compromise?' Rivers is curious. 'After all our endeavours have borne fruit? When the authorities in Bruges, and the Hanse merchants, have agreed to aid us? When we've mercenaries from Holland, Zealand and Picardy? When financial assistance is coming in from Amsterdam and Leiden, and from the banker Portinari? You think His Grace will consider treating with the earl when he now has every chance of gaining victory in the field?'

You would think Rivers had all the papers to hand: the tallies, the account rolls, the list of monetary loans. Perhaps he carries the figures in his head, bobbing and buoyant: the means by which to destroy Richard Neville once and for all.

'Do I think the king will still consider treating with the earl?' Richard purses his lips. 'I do. And he will.'

Rivers' dismissive laugh suppresses a wisp of anxiety. 'My lord of Gloucester, I believe you are mistaken.'

'Do you?' The bells in the clock tower mark the hour as Richard takes his leave.

Thirty-six ships are anchored at Flushing. A small fleet for an armed invasion, yet the fact that it exists at all proves how reliant they have been upon the generosity of others. Such generosity has been wide-ranging, but they mustn't forget that their presence in the Low Countries has not pleased everyone. According to Hastings, the authorities of Middelburg had petitioned Gruuthuse: a tinkle of gold in the Stadholder's purse, if he could convince his English visitors not to bother them.

Gruuthuse had shrugged when he received the letter. 'Do not

condemn them, Highness.'

Edward had been dismissive. 'If they fear to support a man whose success is not guaranteed, then they must do as they will. Once we are returned to power, we'll not hold their circumspection against them.'

Gruuthuse's father-in-law, Henrik Van Borselen, has offered Edward the use of his ship, the *Antoine*, a great carvel with sundry crew; its master, a resident of Veere, its lodesman, a Yorkshireman from Hull, whose knowledge of the English coastline is like another gift from God. But the weather is against them; high winds in which only a fool would set sail. Despite this, Edward prepares to embark. Better to be aboard the vessels, he says, for when the tempests subside, we shall be ready. Waiting on the quay and huddling into his cloak, Richard wonders whether he'll ever be ready for what may lie ahead.

'You've made a good impression upon the Van Borselens,' Hastings yells above the pounding blast. 'Ned is pleased with you. Pleased, too, with the men you have been able to raise.'

Richard is tempted to explain that he's fully aware of Edward's pleasure in the matter, but such arrogance would be uncharitable. Besides, Hastings' habitual need to demonstrate his closeness to the king is something that brings the man a deal of pleasure and, Richard concedes, we must allow him to enjoy it.

The chamberlain observes the boarding of men and supplies: arrows acquired through Hanse connections, lead shot courtesy of Duke Charles, a contingent from Picardy, whose family legends speak to them of Agincourt and who have arrived provisioned with vengeful crossbows. Hastings monitors them all, eyes like abacus balls, keeping a mental tally. Richard recalls Rivers and his calculations at Damme. It's a pity, he thinks, the two are not better disposed towards one another; united, they'd comprise a formidable, mathematical force.

'How do you hazard our chances, Will? If it comes to it, I mean.'

'*If* it comes to it?' The abacus balls are still sliding. 'Peace can hardly be negotiated now the earl is fraternising with the enemy.

Warwick's made his choice, and Marguerite will hold him to it.'

Richard remains tight-lipped, unwilling to divert the conversation. He'd wished only for the chamberlain's opinion on their military capabilities and refuses to be drawn into talk of Warwick. Besides, what does Hastings know of him really? What does anyone know of him? If Warwick has revealed his soul to anyone, he thinks, it has been to George, and to me.

Sending his assistants further down the quay to assess the other vessels, Hastings honours Richard with his full attention. 'Returning to your question. Now that Duke Charles has finally thrown in his lot, I would say our chances are fair. Not certain by any means, but fair. Even better if we can take my lord of Clarence at his word.'

Two handgonners are arguing in Flemish, gruff, jangling oaths Richard recognises from the taverns of Des Graven Hage. The Gascon, Duras, intervenes, berating both in their native tongue.

'And you, Richard, how do you hazard our chances when it comes to your brother George?'

Another subject Richard would choose not to discuss. 'We must place our trust in God.'

Hastings gives a scornful wink. 'Better surety, I'd say, than my lord of Clarence.'

A gust seizes Richard's cloak. Snatching it back, he tugs it into place and goes in search of the king. His brother is not hard to find, soaring head and shoulders above every other man on the quay. 'Good,' Edward greets him with a nod, 'I was wondering where you were.'

Richard bows. 'I've been thinking of the last time I departed these shores. George and I were journeying into a more certain future then.'

'Things can't always be certain, Brother. In any situation, a man can only do his best, then leave the rest to Providence. And, of course, we each pray for success. Imagine the hours Mother must be spending on her knees. If that doesn't steer us towards a favourable conclusion, nothing will.'

'Don't make light of it, Edward.'

'You think I make jests in order to amuse myself? You'll discover that sometimes it's naught but a man's humour that eases his path. Even in camp, while soldiers arm themselves, preparing to look death in the face, they still swap irreverent jests as they seek to quell the demons in their bellies.'

Another gust batters the quay, slivers of desolation slicing through the blast. 'Will Hastings,' Richard says, 'doubts George's commitment.'

Edward drags his furs closer about him. 'It pays to be cautious where our brother is concerned. However, if George is committed, then he may prove useful in luring the earl back to the fold.'

'You still think—?'

'Ned!' Hastings bounds up, and Richard growls inwardly at the lost opportunity. 'All supplies and necessaries are now aboard the vessels. Do you wish to address the men before you embark?'

'My thanks, Will,' Edward says, 'I've spoken to many over the last few days and am content. This is not the time or place for a battle speech. Besides, how likely is it they'll hear me above these damned seabirds?'

The king extends a hand towards his brother. 'If the *Antoine* goes down, Richard, our followers must know of my trust in you.'

'But surely that is why we wait upon the weather.'

'But we must consider it. The German Ocean can prove treacherous, as you know from experience, and there's always the possibility that Louis—or the earl if he's so minded—may scatter some privateers in our path. If danger befalls me, you and Anthony must persevere. My son will need his uncles. The cause of York must continue to thrive, with or without me. Do I have your word?'

Such a future has been discussed already, but the thing Edward has declined to mention is their brother's place in the scheme of things. If George returns to the fold, but Edward is lost, then George—not Richard, or Rivers—will be the child's senior uncle. It's hard to determine how such an irrefutable fact would be received in the Wydeville camp.

Richard bows. 'Of course,' he concedes, 'you have my word. May God keep Your Grace.'

The king tilts his eyes to the heavens; thick, scudding clouds reflected in chestnut pools. 'Then we wait only on the weather. Pray to Saint Anne for a fair wind.'

Chapter Twenty-Nine

March 1471
Holderness Coast, Yorkshire

WET SAND clings to Richard's knees, an imprint of fervent thanksgiving. His legs feel like aspic as he dusts himself down and tries to steady his pulse. The sun is sinking over the leaden sea, whilst on the landward side, tussocky grass waves between random mounds of gilded stone.

There's little by way of feature to the ragged shoreline, and at this present time, he has no idea of their location. Equally, he's little idea who but his own party have survived the storm-tossed passage.

Their initial plan had seemed a good one. A landing on the Norfolk coast where its duke had shown himself true, and Wydeville estates are plentiful. But as they neared Cromer, a rowing boat, buffeted by the gathering squall, had drawn up beside Richard's own vessel. Nicholas Leventhorpe, Edward's messenger, had news.

'The scouts we sent ashore have returned with a warning from my lord of Canterbury. The Duke of Norfolk is in ward, and the Earl of Oxford's men are patrolling the coast. King Edward intends to put back to sea and head for Yorkshire - to my lord Percy's lands.'

The gusts that had blown Leventhorpe back to the *Antoine* had swelled into a ferocious tempest, battering the ships as they continued northward and eventually scattering the fleet.

Grateful for his life, Richard is pleased to be on dry land. But that is all. Licking parched lips, he squints into the distance. 'We need to find the king.'

Obvious.

Those gathered on the shore are watching, waiting for what comes next. But nothing comes next because he doesn't know what to tell them, what to suggest. He has no idea whether moving north or south from here would lead them into another trap, another Oxford-sprung snare. Moreover, they are no longer a mounted force: the ship that had carried the horses was seen to go down, and the *Antoine* itself was last sighted thrashing in the squall. It could have landed anywhere, if it has landed at all.

He sends for the Picard, Étienne Gaubert, and has him ready his men: a small contingent of archers clad with the cross of Saint Denis. 'Amongst your bowmen, Captain, you must have men of keen sight. Deliver me such a one to act as scout.'

Gaubert consults his captains, and the chosen man presents himself. Richard points due south, where the dun-coloured landscape expands towards the horizon and forms a rocky outcrop. A slow advance in that direction, a stealthy climb by the archer, belly to the soil, may reveal a little more of their situation.

He waits for the man's return, prayers circling with the white-winged gulls which swoop across the sands. What if the view from the promontory reveals nothing but a pile of wreckage? Well, the answer to that is clear. The king himself made it clear on the quay at Flushing. And if Edward has perished, then so too has his boon companion. Richard pictures them sinking together in a final, cordial embrace, Hastings hastily probing the seabed for a suitable place to lay the royal bones. That would leave Rivers. No sight nor sound of him in the salty wasteland, and no reason to suppose he has fared any better. If there is none but me, Richard thinks, in this wild and savage wilderness, what then?

The scout is sighted, returning at full pelt. Richard closes his eyes, mutters another brief prayer. Beside him, Gaubert crosses himself. 'Soon we shall know, Monseigneur.'

An anxious silence falls over the ranks. Richard grits his teeth. If the *Antoine* is little more than driftwood, then the only choice is to continue, to do as Edward asked. He thinks of James Harrington, of William Herbert, those whose support can be depended upon, but the obstacle is distance. And the ever-oscillating presence of Thomas Stanley.

Gaubert's man approaches, marram grass whipping his boots. The captain beckons. 'Très bon, Gaspard. Ici!'

The scout kneels, breast heaving. 'Monseigneur le Duc…'

Richard swallows. 'Oui. Dîtes moi.'

'I find men, Monseigneur. From your brother, le Roi Edouard. He has sent them out to look for you.' Gasping, the man turns and indicates the outcrop. 'They await you and will take you to him.'

'They are the king's men? You're sure?'

The scout's fist snaps open. In the centre of his palm, familiar and comforting, lies Edward's pearl and garnet ring.

The salt-washed village feels like the promised land. Having ensured his men are contented and Gaubert's company provided for, Richard makes for the shabby hostelry. Disengaging himself from Edward's embrace, he falls, exhausted, onto a wainscot bench in the tavern's solitary parlour and breathes in the tempting aroma of boiled onions.

Relief lights the king's face. 'Our captain lost sight of you once the storm hit. I prayed you hadn't been struck by the same wave which carried the horses down.'

Richard proffers a weary smile. 'I think we each prayed for the other. Any sign of Anthony?'

'Not yet. Please God, I don't have to tell Elizabeth that yet another of her brothers is dead.'

Signalling to their host, Hastings orders pottage and a cup of ale. 'We feared we'd lost you, Richard.'

The effort of conversation proves too much, and Richard is grateful when the food arrives. Grasping the dented spoon, he sets to, while Edward sinks onto a backless stool and tries, without success, to accommodate his legs under the narrow table.

Hastings retires to the shutterless window. 'To have washed up here, of all places, is surely a sign from Heaven.'

The ale, though murky and sour, is as nectar to Richard's parched throat, and he sees it off in one mouthful.

'Aye.' Edward watches with a satisfied grin. 'I don't suppose this soulless place means much to you, does it, Brother? It failed to impress me until I learned its name: Ravenspur.'

'Ravenspur?' Stirring the pottage, Richard discovers a solitary piece of stockfish lurking amongst the vegetables.

'Think harder, Richard.'

'Is it not said that the usurper Bolingbroke landed at Ravenspur when he returned to England?'

'Ha!' Edward smacks his mighty palms. 'If it were God's will we should return home safely, then where better to be washed up than here? Where Lancaster plotted to steal the crown, York prepares to snatch it back.'

Richard dips his head. A sign, certainly. 'And so, what next?'

'Henry Percy has great influence in these parts, and I've already sent men to Leconfield. If our luck holds, he'll have raised a company. In the meantime, we shall rest here for two more days in the hope that Anthony will join us. It should also give us time to consolidate our plans. If, during that time, there's no sign of him, we move out.'

But Rivers arrives the following day, breathless, dishevelled and stumbling into the hostelry, happy to be alive.

'We ran aground at Paull in the Humber. I had no knowledge of Your Grace's condition, who, if any of us, had survived.' He throws himself at Edward's feet. 'Thank God for His mercy.'

Offering a hand, Edward hauls him up. 'God has chosen to reunite us. He has plans for us, my lords. We must ensure we do not fail Him.'

Chapter Thirty

March 1471
York

RICHARD RIDES in silence, he and Hastings flanking the king like grim sentinels. Since leaving Ravenspur, they've attracted little support, and despite Edward's urgent letters, there's been no response from Henry Percy.

The gates of Hull have remained firmly barred, and the hope is that York may be more accommodating – with or without the earl of Northumberland.

'Percy could be at Tadcaster,' Edward is unwilling to consider a reversal of loyalty, 'or Topcliffe. He holds manors in each of those places.'

'He could be anywhere,' Hastings yells above the rising wind. 'He may be tucked in his bed, head beneath the coverlet, for all we know. His father died at Palmsunday Field fighting for Lancaster; we mustn't forget that. It could be that when it comes to the fight, Percy's allegiance remains divided.'

'You forget,' Edward says, 'he has pledged himself to me. Were it not for his communications to us in the Low Countries, we would not be as well informed as we are. We learnt much from Percy's intelligence. He's true, I feel sure.'

What is true, Richard thinks, is that even the king's winning ways have failed to furnish them with the numbers they require. Each of them, should they care to admit it, are fearful of what may lie ahead.

Edward twists in the saddle. 'When last we were in the city, Richard, you told me our cousin of Warwick had not managed to capture the hearts of the men here. How about Percy's family?'

'They have a long affiliation, Your Grace, yet the people of York seem neither Neville nor Percy in their allegiance.'

Edward bares his teeth in a lupine grin. 'No reason why they shouldn't support me, then. Unless a love for Lancaster has resurfaced since Warwick yanked Harry out of confinement and plopped him back on the throne.'

'I've had dealings with the aldermen,' Richard says, 'they are proud of their city—'

'Highness!' One of Edward's outriders has returned. Wheeling his mount, he attempts to control the feisty animal. 'A handful of men are approaching.'

'Don't tell me,' Hastings says glibly, 'Percy has decided to make an effort.'

Edward ignores him. 'Are they bearing arms?'

'There are city guards amongst them, but the man at their head is a civilian. They appear no threat, Your Grace.'

'Then we ride to meet them.'

At length, the party comes into view: a mounted man and six guards in city livery. Warwick had once explained to Richard the story of the red cross with its five passant lions. The lions, he said, represent five solitary men who defended the city against the Conqueror. William the Bastard, legend has it, admiring the courage of the small band, had consented to spare their lives.

The approaching contingent, however, looks in no way bellicose. On the contrary, its attitude indicates a desire to parley.

'Highness,' Rivers trots up. 'Give me leave to speak with them.'

'Very well,' Edward nods, 'but have a care, Anthony, until we know what they're about.'

'My lord of Gloucester should have been the one to converse,' Hastings objects as they slow their pace. 'He is known to them.'

The king's eyes narrow as he follows Wydeville's progress. 'Perhaps. And we may yet need him.'

Rivers is removing his bonnet, holding it aloft as a sign

of goodwill. The men from York draw rein, and their leader dismounts, long murrey gown and black chaperon revealing him as a man of note.

Hastings calms his whickering mount. 'Any idea who he is, Richard?'

'I believe he is the City Recorder.'

Rivers, bonnet replaced, is returning, his mouth downturned.

Hastings growls. 'Well, whoever he is, he doesn't seem inclined to welcome us. For Mercy's sake, don't say we have to skirt this blasted city as well.'

Edward remains calm. 'Well, Anthony?'

'Your Grace,' Rivers reins in. 'Thomas Conyers, City Recorder, bids us retreat. He says the city is acting upon instruction. When I asked whose, he said that of the king.'

The chamberlain glowers. 'This is their king.'

'And so I told them, my lord Hastings. Conyers says that if His Grace attempts to enter the city, he will be lost and undone.'

'Lost and undone? By God—'

'We advance.' Edward nudges his horse. Drawing level with Conyers, he passes the man without a glance, eyes fixed on the road ahead, while to either side, the city contingent falls like ninepins.

'My lords.' Bunching his skirts, Conyers attempts to run alongside. 'My lords, I pray you, the city is under instruction—'

'Hedging its bets.' Disgust puckers Hastings' brow.

Edward's smile is grim. 'Aren't we all?'

Walmgate looms wide and squat. Raising his eyes to the barbican, Richard spots movement between the crenels: more of the city guard in their proud, white tabards, more livery-clad descendants of the five.

As the great gates open a pinch and a further company slips out, Richard edges closer to the king. 'Let me try, Your Grace. There's some little chance these men may be prepared to negotiate.'

'Your offer is appreciated, Brother, but no, we shall continue together. I would hear in my own person what they have to say.'

Two men extricate themselves and kneel in the road. Gentlemen, by the look of them, their modest attitude at least promising. Edward draws rein, curious eyes flicking from one townsman to the other. He's waiting to see how they will address him, Richard thinks, a clever move.

Hastings coughs. 'Edward, King of England and France, Lord of Ireland, requests entry.'

Richard grimaces. Rivers, equally exasperated, catches his eye.

The citizens remain on their knees, bonnets clutched, pates exposed. 'Your Grace.'

The appellation pertains to many—king, duke, bishop—and in itself gives nothing away.

With a flick of his hand, Edward bids them approach. The more confident of the two is on his feet, brushing mud from the hem of his gown. Its quality indicates a man of business; the belt around his ample girth and fine leather purse speak of wealth, if not necessarily of standing. Etiquette awards a king the first word, but Edward's shrewd habit of calculated muteness inevitably has men cut to the quick, if only to break an uncomfortable silence.

'Your Grace,' the man clasps his hands, prayer-like. 'We apologise for the response of our recorder. There are those on the council who have received well your letters, who would be pleased to admit the Duke of York if he should choose to enter in peace.'

Richard shoots a glance at Hastings, sees that both he and Rivers are equally confused.

Edward's mouth twitches into a comely smile. 'My thanks, gentlemen. I, Edward Plantagenet, seek admittance merely to reclaim my dukedom, inherited by law from my lord father of blessed memory.'

An act of brilliance. The ruse by which the renegade, Henry Bolingbroke, filched the crown and founded a dynasty must now allow Edward of York the chance to regain what is rightfully his.

A sudden clank of weaponry, and Richard's hand flies to his sword hilt. Wheeling Liard in a swift arc, he finds it's only Conyers catching up, city guard in tow.

'Your Grace, I pray you, don't be deceived by aught these fellows have said. Robert Clifford and Richard Burgh know well enough that the city acts only as instructed, and for your own sake, you must gain entry elsewhere. York stands for the king.'

'If I may,' Richard speaks with more force than intended, but the sound settles all eyes on him, even the king's. 'Master Conyers, is it not so that my lord of Warwick is well known to each member of the council? The earl, as you will profess, holds great respect for the ancient blood and lineage of this land. He would not, I'm certain, have your city refuse entry to His Grace, whose father and forefathers have held the dukedom of York since the days of Edmund of Langley.'

Point made, Richard prides himself that, for once, Hastings has nothing to add. Conyers is clearly floundering, and the king's knees jab the flanks of his mount. With a flick of the reins, Edward makes for the gates. 'Á King Harry! Á King and Prince Edward!'

Conyers staggers from their path. Shouts echo from the barbican, and the great wooden doors are heaved apart. Edward, high in the saddle, clatters through the archway, yelling like a *huer* when the quarry is in sight.

Now, Richard sees how he did it. How, when he was taken and confined, he had eased his way out. How he'd trotted south, charming his way back to London. I may have presented the city with an undisputable fact, he thinks, but Edward is to present them with his own person. And none, it is certain, shall be able to resist him.

Chapter Thirty-One

March 1471
Sandal Castle, Yorkshire

*E*DWARD, PRAISING Saint Anne, declares their progress a miracle. Hastings attributes it to his monarch's skill, his presence, and the veracity of his cause. But, as they approach the town of Sandal, citadel grim and evocative against the setting sun, Richard believes they must also be grateful for the timely acquiescence of two significant men. Henry Percy, acknowledging Edward's letters, will allow them to pass through his lands unhindered - whilst John Neville, Marquess Montagu, lingering at Pontefract, is keeping himself to himself.

As expected, passing the night within the walls of Sandal is proving poignant. How could it be otherwise? In the cool, pink-tinged evening, Richard follows the king to the height of the ramparts and leans out over the parapet. They survey the fields beyond: the dark clumps of huddling trees, the acres over which their father rode, and where, in the grip of a northern winter, he died.

'Surely, he understood the possibility of an ambush.' Richard tucks windblown hair behind his ears and points into the distance. 'That copse, for example.'

'I've told you, Brother. The past is gone. It's the present which must concern us. But, yes, you're right, he should have considered it.'

Richard places his palm on the stone crenel, feels the day's warmth slowly dissolving.

'It's as if the world has shifted on its axis,' he says, 'as if we are reliving what occurred six months since.'

The king exhales. 'What, you mean the Marquess Montagu at our backs, holding our fate in his hands?'

'Yes.'

'But, if John Neville intended to attack, it's my belief he would have done so by now. He must know we would stop here. Sandal is ours; Harry of Lancaster holds no claim on it. Why then, certain of our destination, did Cousin John not leave Pontefract and march across country? If he'd wished to impede our progress, he could have done. He could have crept up on us.' Edward pauses, and wry laughter escapes him. 'After all, the populace is not exactly hurtling to join us. Montagu will never have a better opportunity. He could have chosen to advance, to destroy us here. What more fitting, ironic death could there be for the sons of York?'

'And so, tomorrow - assuming we last the night - we move on?'

Edward's mask slips to reveal a painful uncertainty. 'Yes,' he sighs at length, 'tomorrow, we move on.'

The roadside inn is shabby but sufficient, the village large enough to accommodate their meagre company overnight.

'I can levy three thousand,' Hastings says, swallowing his last spoonful of mutton pottage and belching softly. 'My messenger will leave at dawn. The company can meet us at Leicester.'

Richard is nursing a letter. With undisguised satisfaction, his wax-stained fingers drop it on the table amongst the tarnished pewter and scattered breadcrumbs. 'I have received a reply from Sir William Parr. Combined with the company of James Harrington, that makes for an additional six hundred. Both are to meet us at Nottingham.'

The heart of the city is brimming with the curious. As they

assemble at the stone cross in Nottingham's High Pavement, the locals gather despite the rain. It's not every day they see a former king wandering like a household steward to offer a personal welcome to the gathering troops. Shuffling, jostling, their new recruits cram into the square and spill over into the churchyard of Saint Mary. With growing pleasure, Richard picks out the blue livery of the Parrs, the black jerkins of the Harringtons, and James Harrington himself, bounding towards him over the rain-splattered earth.

'My lord of Gloucester.'

'James.' Richard waves the man's deference aside and embraces him, as the king would. 'Such a pleasure to receive you. His Grace is deeply grateful for your service, as he'll tell you himself.'

Harrington's eyes gleam. 'Thank God for your safe return, my lord. None knew how, or even if, you might set foot in England again.'

'As you say, James, God has his ways. Now, what news from Hornby? How has Stanley spent his time over the winter? Camping outside your gates? Laundering his shirts in the moat and hanging them on your bushes to dry?'

A harsh laugh bursts from Harrington. 'God forfend. Although he has made free with his threats. I imagine it's his hope that his brother-in-law, the earl, will whisper in King Harry's ear.'

Richard shakes his head. 'My cousin, Warwick, has never been enamoured of Lord Stanley.' The Warwick he knew, that is.

'I've heard,' Harrington says, 'that Stanley's brother, at least, intends to join us.'

'Yes. Edward is expecting William Stanley at Leicester with three hundred. Or so he has been led to believe. Come,' Richard takes Harrington's arm, 'let us find His Grace.'

They move through the crowd: a hodgepodge now of greyness and grimness, of dull, faded russet. Tricksters and whores have crept from the murky lanes and make for the churchyard seeking business, whilst others melt into the throng in search of charity. A footless cripple on a makeshift crutch hobbles across their path, filthy wrappings disguising his stump. Drawing a coin from his purse, Richard tosses it in the begging bowl. Something should be done for such people, he thinks. Something charitable.

Edward receives Harrington like a long-lost friend, an acquaintance he rarely sees but thinks about, nonetheless. Harrington, for his part, looks optimistic, and Richard resolves to keep the pot boiling. Another in Harrington's position could easily have turned away, rendered himself indiscriminate – like Thomas Stanley – or slid away to join the earl. When all is resolved, the question of Hornby will be resurrected, Richard will see to that.

'Benevolent of you,' Edward says later as they pick their way across the Leen Bridge onto the road south.

'Your Grace?'

'The halt beggar. I noticed your charity.'

Richard shrugs. 'The stump betrayed him for an old soldier. Must be difficult to earn a living once you've sacrificed a limb on your lord's behalf.'

'A fine gesture. However, whilst you were busy doling out alms, I received some news – my scouts have returned.'

The bridge narrows, and their spurs are in danger of snaring. 'George?'

'No. Exeter is back. He and Oxford are at Newark. Will has sent word to his troops in Leicester, commanding them to move north while we head for Newark. We can trap Exeter and Oxford between us in a pincer movement.' A laugh, sharp as a razor. 'Vegetius, I dare say, would be proud of us.'

Chapter Thirty-Two

April 1471
Warwick

THE KING has done with pretence. Any who believed he'd returned to claim his dukedom can now be under no illusion. He has indeed returned as his father's son, but their father, as must be remembered, had soared beyond his dukedom of York. As a monarch already crowned and anointed, Edward has nothing to reclaim, for supremacy is his already. But the rough voyage, the tense journey south, have taken their toll on them all. What is necessary, in the short term, is rest and comfort.

Bolstered by the countess' embroidered cushions, Edward weaves his fingers together and rests them in his lap, the epitome of contentment. Or so it would appear to those who don't know him.

Hastings makes free with the earl's wine cellar. Casks of Louis' Bordeaux, sent as covert gifts in more settled times, are opened and emptied. 'As Chamberlain of the King's Household, 'tis my duty to see that His Grace is well purveyed for. Even when the household he occupies is not his own.'

The company roars with laughter, and a sweep of Edward's sleeve offers a gesture of forced optimism. 'Please, my lords. Come, partake. All are welcome to whatever the earl has left behind.'

Offered a brimming cup, Richard takes it. Dipping his lips to the rim, he ignores the guffaws that continue to rise towards the cavernous ceiling. It gives him no pleasure to trespass here, in their cousin's fortress, where memories lie in wait around every corner, leaping with malice from every portal, lurking with recrimination upon every twisting stair. He almost expects to catch an echo of the rich, rolling staccato:

Is this how you choose to show your gratitude, Richard?

'Men will marvel at your generalship,' Hastings says, arranging himself at Edward's feet, as Richard had once arranged himself at Warwick's. 'The swift march to Newark was a brilliant move. Oxford will have heard that my own forces were heading up from Leicester, but the last thing he'd have imagined is that we would've borne down on him before they even joined us.' He waggles his cup. 'I heard from the mayor of Newark that the earth flew from beneath Oxford's hooves as he fled.'

The chamber resounds with mirth.

Edward gives a gentle smile. 'No general wishes to be caught in a pincer movement, and yet, had we hesitated, we ourselves may have faced the same prospect. I'm told the Marquess Montagu has eventually moved out and is riding south. If Oxford's intelligence was reliable, he should have heard the news and held his ground. Oxford and Montagu together would have made a formidable force.'

Richard caresses the stem of his cup. 'So, John Neville is coming upon us? That must be why our cousin has refused your offers of peace. He's awaiting reinforcements.'

Hastings laughs. 'He's awaiting your brother of Clarence. Or thinks he is.'

Why does he do this? Treating everything as a jest and, worse still, affecting an intimacy to which he's not entitled. He knows nothing of Warwick; none of them do.

Edward resettles himself, crossing his ankles and examining his boots. 'Well, we must all apply caution in that regard.'

On three successive days, they'd ridden to Coventry and tried to coax the earl from its protective walls, but to no avail. Edward had issued challenges, and when these were ignored, invitations to parley. He'd even promised a pardon, but with no response from Warwick, they'd moved out and headed here.

On the move, the king had seemed confident. 'Let's see what he does when he knows we have possession of the London road.'

'But if George decides to remain loyal to our cousin, then …'

'Yes, Richard?' Edward's sarcasm had been cutting. 'Don't tell me that you doubt our brother's promise. You, who've spent the last two years assuring me of his inveterate constancy to the cause of York?'

'The earl has chosen to remain in Coventry. He must be waging everything on George's arrival.'

'Or, to put it more simply, perhaps he's afraid to come out. Warwick's enemies have ever called him craven-hearted.'

Desperation had gripped Richard's guts. He must put this right. He must put it right: now, before it becomes irreparable. 'Send me to Warwick, Edward, I beg of you. I can speak with him.'

'Your task is already decided upon. Whenever, wherever, our brother makes an appearance, you'll ride out to converse with him. And then, we may consider sending him to the earl. Warwick's final chance. If he will not submit to me, then perhaps he'll submit to George.'

'Richard?' Back in the chamber, Hastings is leaning over him, proffering the wine jug.

Unable to dismiss his thoughts, Richard stares at him like a dullard. 'What? No…no, thank you.'

It occurs to him that he's not spoken with James Harrington since they arrived, and the company of an understanding friend is sorely needed. Rising, he makes a weary obeisance. 'May I beg your leave, Your Grace?'

Waking from his first sleep, Richard rubs his face and glances round his old chamber. Edward had offered him a choice from the earl's well-kept apartments, but he'd insisted on the familiar. It might ensure some safety, some guarantee, that the settled existence he had known here may return. 'Superstitious,' Edward would say, had he known his reasoning. 'The past is gone, and a night spent in your former room is not likely to change that.'

'Simon?' Flinging the covers aside, Richard swings his legs over the side of the bed. 'Simon?'

He waits, naked in the half-light, shivers prickling his spine. Eventually, the truckle bed creaks as Kyngston stumbles to his feet and fetches his master's bedgown.

'Forgive me, Your Grace. I was in the throes of a dream.'

Richard grasps the fur trim, drawing it close. 'A gentle dream? Or a nightmare?'

'Neither.' Kyngston stifles a yawn. 'A heap of nonsense, like every other dream. Bread, Your Grace? Wine?'

'Thank you.'

Richard drinks deeply, thoughts turning to the military volumes he read in Warwick's household. It was easy for Vegetius, he decides, for Tacticus. When they applied their pens to parchment, they had in mind the slaughtering of Barbarians, the advancement of empires. They'd never taken the field against those they loved. For them, the enemy was faceless: the fierce wielder of the spear and the club. None of their foes had ever shared their platters or their childhoods. Neither had they heard and kept their deepest secrets.

Kyngston bolsters the pillows. 'Anything else, Your Grace?'

'We must pray for my lord of Clarence. Pray he will renounce his recent actions and return to us.'

'Duke George has ever had a mind of his own.'

'Not so. He's open to persuasion. Always has been. Pray for him, Simon, before you return to your slumbers, that he may keep his recent promises. And when you've done that, I beg you, make like supplications for the earl.'

Following Mass, news arrives. A company has been spotted, approaching from the direction of Evesham and heading for Banbury. A company wearing the badge of the Gorget and displaying on its banners the Black Bull of Clarence.

Edward's jaw tightens. 'How large is this company?'

Leventhorpe is nervous. 'Forgive me, Your Grace, but 'company' does not perhaps best describe it. It's an army.'

Dismissing him, the king grasps his brother's hand. 'Well. This is your moment, Richard.'

At Edward's insistence, they ride out arrayed for war; the dogged squeak and jingle of harness a powerful reminder of what is owed to Duke Charles and the work of his master armourers. It will present George with a fearful sight, the king says. Let him know what he's up against, lest his loyalty be in danger of wavering. Again.

'You still don't trust him, do you?'

Edward shrugs. 'But I have his letters, Richard,' his head jerks to where Harpisfeld trots beside the baggage train, 'surely even George would find it difficult to deny he has promised himself to me.'

As they approach the river, Hastings rides up. 'Have a care, my lord of Gloucester, when you ride out to meet your brother.'

Richard steers Liard towards the ancient bridge. 'I have nothing to fear from George.'

'Nevertheless.'

'You forget. I trust him.'

The day is fair and bright, the road south unhampered and easy to navigate. Nearing Banbury, it's clear that word has spread; small groups huddle in the streets, gawping, whispering, clearly uncertain.

Hastings, leading the company, announces their presence. 'Á York! Á King Edward!'

While the townsfolk bend the knee, the king, bareheaded, keeps his eyes on the road. In time, they climb out of the valley and onto the road south, encased by far-ranging hills.

One of Leventhorpe's men approaches and speaks to the king. Edward thanks him.

'My lord of Gloucester. I'm advised that our brother is arrayed three miles distant. You know what is required.'

'Yes.'

Edward keeps his eyes lowered, lips moving in silent prayer. Falling back, Richard allows the king his privacy for the remainder of the journey, trusts Hastings has the tact to do the same.

Later, as they crest the rise, there's animation in the ranks. A glimmering aspect is visible in the noonday sun, an undulating wall of blinding steel. George and his company, straddling the road to London: the ideal position, whatever his intention.

Edward halts, commands the company to form a line, and beckons Richard with a mailed hand. 'When I command you, you will ride out. Take up position midway between the ranks. We must give our brother every reasonable opportunity to submit out of earshot. You know how he fears humiliation.'

A sharp breeze whips across the grass; from George's ranks, the occasional whicker of horses, the snap and thwack of banners. Richard knows he must make an end of this, must succeed in bringing his brothers together. If the family remains divided, they will each have failed: failed themselves, and worse still, failed their father.

He senses the king's fevered whispers, the swift, covert crossing of the breast. 'Go,' Edward says. 'Tell him I am prepared to forgive. But—'

'Yes, Your Grace?'

'Be careful.'

Richard knows all eyes are on him; his tension punctured by the creak of leather, the muffled thump of hooves on turf, the pumping of his own blood. He's passed beyond Edward's reach now, feels vulnerable and ill at ease. The distance between his brothers' companies is a short one, or would be, under circumstances other than this. He stares across the luscious green space; and from the centre of the opposing line, George stares back.

Richard eases Liard to a halt, unstraps his sallet and grips it stiffly in the crook of his arm. George advances until their mounts are aligned. Removing his own helm, he flicks the curls from his face.

'Dickon. Brother…'

The voice is unsteady, George is fretful, but Richard decides to make him wait. It's what Edward would do. Let him stew, he thinks, if only for a moment.

'My lord of Clarence,' he says at length, 'the king carries your letters with him. He is prepared to accept your submission.'

It's George's turn to hesitate. 'But what are his terms? I wish to place my army at his disposal. I seek his pardon, his forgiveness.'

Richard is immersed in a tidal wave of pity. 'George, thank Heaven.'

His brother looks cowed, round-shouldered, tears welling and threatening to flow. 'God in His Mercy, Dickon, the king must speak to our cousin. If I'm to be offered terms, then Edward must, by the same token, extend the same to the earl.'

Richard blinks. For distraction, he runs his eyes over George's company, watches the rising breeze taunting its banners in a flurry of blazing colour. 'He tried. We presented ourselves before the walls of Coventry upon several occasions over past days. Eventually, Edward called upon him to submit. Declared that if he would, he could leave with his life intact.'

They observe each other in silence, unprepared to consider the alternative.

'If Edward knew us at all,' George says, nodding vaguely towards the king's ranks, 'he should realise that you and I have one thing in common. We both care for our cousin.'

'I should hope we have more than one thing in common, Brother. But yes, it's true. We care for him.'

Indifferent to the attention of both armies, George is weeping. 'Edward was fortunate. He was granted the time to grow under a nurturing hand. Throughout his childhood, he had a father. Something we were denied.'

Richard clears his throat. 'The king wishes you to act as messenger, to be an intermediary, between himself and Warwick.' His mailed hand clashes against George's steel-clad shoulder. 'By all that is holy, I beg you, bring our cousin back to us.'

Just the three of them, closeted in their cousin's inner sanctum. Slumped in Warwick's favourite chair, George is quiet, edgy, eager to please.

'Why?' Edward, standing by the empty hearth, has yet to offer full conciliation. 'After everything we accomplished in the old days, why has he agreed to align himself with Marguerite?'

George studies the ring on his middle finger as if the answer can be found in its winking depths. 'He is proud.'

'So proud that he would consort with our bitterest enemy?' Edward yells. 'So proud he chooses to debase himself by bending the knee to a woman he despises?'

A sidelong glance from George, and Richard understands the irony of that statement is not lost on either of them. At length, George says, 'Our cousin feels you don't heed his advice, as once you did.'

'And he's made that perfectly plain,' Edward kicks the hearthstone with the toe of his boot, 'his manifesto was precise in that particular. But to come to terms with Lancaster, to deny everything he fought for, alongside me, alongside his own father. Does the cause of York mean nothing to him?'

It could be their cousin speaking. Perhaps, Richard thinks, Edward and Warwick are more alike than either would care to suppose.

'He still feels slighted,' George says. 'He feels you made a fool of him with the French.'

'Oh, so it's Louis' opinion that has brought us to this, is it?' Edward sounds incredulous. '*Monseigneur de Warwick* was found wanting in the eyes of the French king, and for that reason, he seeks to destroy his own blood?'

George rises from his chair. 'He…we… were foolish, Edward.'

'Foolish?' The king rolls the word on his tongue. Transforming it with mockery, he spits it out like a missile.

George plaits his hands, holding them aloft in supplication.

'The earl and I, both, are unworthy. That you have inclined to mercy in my regard, Brother, is more than I deserve. But please, I beg you, offer that same clemency to our cousin. He feels he has come too far and cannot now extricate himself from what he has done.'

'These are his thoughts?' Richard demands. 'He has confided in you?'

'Well, no…but it's true, I know—'

'Do not insult me, George.' Edward, at his quietest, is Edward at his most deadly.

George, increasingly tormented, throws himself to his knees. When Edward moves, he shuffles towards him like a Paschal pilgrim creeping to the cross. 'Please, Edward. I know him. If he believed he could return—'

The king observes the grovelling figure from the vantage of his great height. 'His honours intact? His position unchanged?'

Insensible to the tones of derision, George almost sobs with relief. 'Yes, exactly. Let me assure him. He'll swear himself to you entirely, stand beside you as loyally as he ever did.'

Edward rounds on him. 'You must be a bigger fool than I took you for if you believe such honours as our cousin once held could ever be divested upon him again. The earl had all of these things two years ago, yet they did not keep him from revolt. What he wants, what he's always wanted, is a mammet king whose every movement is directed by him.'

'But, Edward, consider—'

'Consider what, my lord of Clarence?'

Richard squirms. George's great ability for losing an argument has not diminished, and as always, Edward is outwitting him.

'Well…' George bleats, 'consider our cousin.'

'You speak of our cousin's pride?' Edward says. 'It seems to me that it was not simply an inability to submit which kept him confined behind the walls of Coventry. He was waiting for you. And if you'd remained steadfast, he would have sought to crush me.'

'I was trapped,' George is shamefaced. 'I'd given him my allegiance. We never sought to replace you. Not at first.'

'No? You sought to separate me from my family, and when that failed to work, you sought the throne for yourself.'

George's head jerks up, cheeks flushed as a milkmaid's. 'You must know, Highness, that was never my intent.'

'But you went along with it. You allowed him to convince people that an England under the rule of King George was a thing to be considered, even desired.'

'It just happened. To begin with, it was discussed, and then it became the intention, and then, well, it was out of my hands.'

'You were out of your depth, were you not? Led astray by foolish counsel? God's Blood, George, that excuse has been offered by duplicitous siblings since the foundation of the world. If this is how you argue your own cause, how do you hope to secure any clemency for the earl?'

Staggered by George's incompetency, Richard is on his feet. 'Your Grace, I must join with our brother in urging you to reconsider. It could be that the earl doesn't know how to approach you, that he recognises his perfidy, but is afraid for his life. If you would but send me, I would assure him of your forbearance.'

George, shuffling from one knee to the other, peers at him piteously from the tail of his eye.

Edward sighs. 'George, your efforts to commend the earl are poor in the extreme. However, Richard has always tried to convince me that it would be wrong to face Warwick in the field. Therefore, for the sake of the earl's loyalty to our father, I shall allow him one final opportunity to return.'

Deo Gratia. Richard drops to his knees beside George. Reaching for Edward's hand, he holds it to his lips. 'Thank you, Highness.'

George's shoulders fall, tension ebbing. Edward raises him to his feet, and soon they are locked together. When they disengage, the ring on George's hand catches the light. Richard recalls it now: a glittering emerald—a gift from their cousin.

'With regard to the earl,' Edward says. 'I shall send you, George, as intermediary. Tell him that despite his treachery, if he submits to me now, I will happily spare him.'

'Thank you, lord king.' George is like a figure on a faded Arras, rendered inconsequential by the rays of the sun. As if he is tired of the sight of him, Edward waves him from the chamber. When the door closes, Richard explodes in anger and desperation.

'You should have chosen me! You should have let me go. You can see how he is. He'll only make things worse. For Mercy's sake, Edward—'

One glare from the king shrivels him to silence.

Chapter Thirty-Three

April 1471
Daventry, Northamptonshire

*I*NTENT ON reaching the capital, they pause at Daventry only long enough to observe the rites of Palm Sunday. Richard and George process with the king to the priory church amid flapping fronds of willow and yew, their minds fixed on the earl.

'If only I could have convinced him,' George whispers as they pass beneath the ancient arch into cool and shady silence. 'I can't help believing I have failed.'

You have, Richard thinks, just as I knew you would. However, he must be charitable; it's not George's fault Edward sent him, not George's fault that he blights everything he sets his hands to. 'We have all failed, even Edward, with our army at his back. Our only option now, as our brother says, is an advance upon London.'

Unbuckling their sword belts at the church door, they remove their bonnets and dip their fingers in holy water. 'A man such as our cousin was never going to be persuaded by a show of force,' George says. 'But I did think he would respond to verbal entreaty. His own diplomatic skills have ever borne more fruit than his military tactics.'

'I know.' But if only Edward had sent me. If only.

The church is shrouded for Lent; altars veiled in hunger cloths, triptychs closed, the Saviour sealed within, waiting for rebirth. Images are ensconced behind wooden boards, hidden by purple silk. It's the time for reflection, and Richard knows that in addition to his meditations on the sanctity of the day, Edward will be pondering on Palm Sunday ten years past and his noted struggle to survive.

For himself, Richard thinks of the day at Paul's, twelve months since—the act of reconciliation, which Edward had recognised as naught but a sham. The fraternal, smiling George who'd sought to plot and deceive, to hold them in London while the rebels advanced, differs greatly from the George who stands beside him now: dipping and deferring and taking his lead from Edward. This is the brother Richard knew in childhood, who believed in the unity of the family of York.

Black-robed and hooded, the brethren shuffle into the choir, settling into their stalls as the laity congregates. The king pads reverently towards the rood screen, genuflects, while his retinue falls in behind him.

Richard's thoughts move in agonising circles. Why did Edward insist on sending George as intermediary? Was it deliberate? Did he want him to fail? Was it a ploy to avoid true reconciliation?

Hosanna filio David rises to the carved ceiling, to the angelic roof bosses with their gilded wings. Richard crosses himself. Edward must have known he would have been the better choice. Why did he not—?

A scraping sound echoes within the chancel. Cutting across the antiphon, it reduces the choir to silence. Heads jerk towards a niche in the vicinity of the rood. A wooden board, wedged against the stonework to cover the image within, has shifted precariously of its own accord. The sudden movement unbalances its neighbour. Soon, both boards clatter to the floor, shattering tiles. A gasp rises and settles over the assembly as worshippers cower in fear.

'O Blessed Mother of Mary…' The king clambers to his feet and strides to the front of the church. Throwing himself to the floor, he huddles, hands clasped, head bent. Hastening to his feet, Richard picks his way over broken terracotta. Kneeling beside the king, he peers towards the niche where a holy image is now revealed: Saint Anne, robed in scarlet and green, teaching the Virgin to read.

Edward wipes his face. 'A miracle, Brother. I prayed to her,

Blessed Saint Anne, on the homeward voyage. She saved us. She saved all of us. I've offered my thanks every day since then—'

'A miracle!' Hastings crunches over the scattered shards. 'A miracle. Everyone is witness.'

A woman bursts into tears, another staggers towards them, dragging, half-lifting, a crippled child. Fear and confusion take hold as a trickle of brethren creeps from the quire and array themselves before the image. One of their number races back through the screen, tripping on the soles of his sandals. 'Father Prior, a miracle…'

George moves in, astounded. 'What does it mean?'

Edward regards them all with a rare solemnity. 'It can mean only one thing. Saint Anne has answered my prayers, shown that the house of York retains divine favour. This, my lords, is little less than a promise of victory.'

They continue south, numbers increasing as the event at Daventry becomes widely known. Richard wonders about Saint Anne and of her plans for their cousin. Will she persuade him to yield? Will she lead him through their growing force to kneel at Edward's feet? Would Edward be merciful if she did? Something in the pit of his stomach tells him probably not.

Walter Devereux, loyal to the king and to their father before him, joins them on the road. Richard knows him, had the comfort and pleasure of his company during his time in Wales. It's reassuring to surround himself with friends like Devereux, Harrington and Parr, to find temporary relief from the constricting cords that bind him with every thought of the earl.

'The event in the church,' Devereux says as they ride flank to flank, 'was akin to the miraculous suns that appeared over Wigmore. If any Englishman doubted our king's right to rule, they can do so no longer.'

'Indeed.' Richard wonders if Warwick is aware of the intercession, of the mediation offered on Edward's behalf by the mother of the Mother of God.

'He will hear of it,' Edward says later. 'If he hasn't already.'

Whether he's heard or not makes little difference. Reportedly, two days' march away, their cousin is sweeping down on them, and possession of the capital is now their only hope. After days of unseasonable heat, the constriction of gambeson or brigandine is tortuous for the troops, the pace punishing for the horses. Conscious of losing men to exhaustion, the king has them rest the night at Dunstable and keeps George beside him at the only decent hostelry the town has to offer.

For his own company, Richard commandeers an inn, grubby and smelling of boiled fish. The hard mattress, prickly with protruding straw and adventurous ticks, is unsavoury but welcome enough as he submits himself to the ministrations of his squires.

'An improvement, Your Grace?' Kyngston wipes his hands after stoppering the oil jars.

Richard flexes his shoulders. 'Perhaps.'

'Are you sorely afflicted, my lord?' Parr, as always, looks sympathetic.

'Riding often loosens up the knots,' Richard shrugs back into his doublet, 'but this journey has necessitated long days, as well as uncomfortable nights. And we'll experience more of the same before this business is ended.'

Kyngston, quiet and reserved in recent days, folds Richard's linens while Parr combs his master's hair and jests about growing shadow and the necessity of a barber's blade.

'Lack of time, Tom. The king has summoned me to a council after supper. I believe he'll have more to concern him than my unkempt appearance.'

'If I may be so bold, Your Grace. The earl has ever been popular with the Londoners. What if the city were to hold for him, and for King Harry?'

Richard feigns optimism. 'Never fear. Saint Anne will

prepare the way.'

During supper, while tavern boys bustle in with eel pies and herring, the king dictates letters. Harpisfeld is at his elbow, writing slope balanced on the greasy board. Rivers, who has remained sleek and courteous since George's arrival, hovers, ready with advice.

Richard crosses to where George is perched on a wainscot bench beside the Burgundian, Duras, and eyeing Wydeville with ill-concealed spite.

'May I?'

'Sit you down, Dickon. We await Lord Hastings. One of his spies has returned. Apparently, he has news.'

They don't have to wait long before Hastings barges in, colliding with a serving boy. 'Word from the capital is that Archbishop Neville acts on instructions from the earl. Yesterday, Harry of Lancaster was paraded through the streets in the hope of raising support.'

'And how was he received?' Edward's jaw tightens.

'You need not fret yourself. My spy tells me George Neville held Harry by the hand as if he were an infant who's just outgrown his standing stool. Hardly a sight to inspire.'

A crack and shuffle of parchment: Harpisfeld collating his papers before the boys return with bread and cheese.

'Despatch those letters without delay,' Edward snaps, then looks to Hastings. 'What else have we learnt? Is the archbishop expected to remain loyal to Warwick?'

'It appears that way. He summoned support from the citizenry, asked them to join him at Paul's, harnessed and prepared to defend the capital.'

'What else?'

'It appears the earl himself, whilst yet in the City, wrote under the privy seal to those sympathetic to Your Grace's cause. Those answering the summons were placed in ward. A sly move, which explains the dearth of support on our way down here.'

'God in Heaven.' Edward's fist flies to his mouth. 'Who? Who is in ward?'

'Norfolk, we already know about. But also, your Bourchier

kin: Essex, Cromwell - Wiltshire, Mountjoy, even my lord of Canterbury.' Hastings counts each name on his fingers. 'Word is that Warwick released them shortly after, and they immediately claimed sanctuary.'

Another sharp move by the earl. The lords are no longer under official arrest, but they might as well be, for the use they'll be to York. Richard and George exchange glances: no matter what Warwick does, you can't help but admire him.

Edward stares at his plate as if the future can be divined amongst the burnt pastry crusts. 'With regard to the City, I've written to Mayor Stockton. He has always shown us his favour, and I believe he is dependable.'

Hastings takes a breath. 'Not as dependable as Your Grace might hope. Mayor Stockton has seen fit to take to his bed.' He stares pointedly at Rivers, 'Sir Thomas Cook deputised—'

'Lord help us.' George gives Richard a sharp nudge.

Few, with the understandable exception of Duras, can interpret this as good news. Richard had learnt of Cook's former situation one evening at L'Erber when Warwick's patience with the queen's family had reached boiling point, and news of Cook's arrest offered a perfect example of a case in point.

'Sickening.' The earl's ire had been palpable. 'A man is arrested and held in custody just long enough for Richard Wydeville to loot the man's house and carry off his goods.' But Old Earl Rivers had not been the only one to benefit from Cook's temporary imprisonment. His determined countess had seen to make free with a rich Arras she had long coveted. Hoisted from its hooks and rehung at Grafton Wydeville, it is said to have become a popular talking point at family feasts.

'Thomas Cook?' Edward says. 'You're certain, Will?'

'Yes, but again, we are fortunate. Word is that Cook took ship the day before yesterday and that Ralph Verney is now our man.'

George fidgets. 'Know anything about him, Dickon?'

Richard shakes his head. Somewhere in his mind, the name floats, flounders. A mercer? A vintner? If Verney is a merchant and known to Warwick, then there's a chance he will support him.

The king should never underestimate the effect of their cousin's popularity amongst the merchant class.

Edward stares pointedly at all present. 'We press on as planned. At first light, we make for Saint Albans. I would ask you to remember, my lords, that God is on our side and will guide us to victory.'

At Saint Albans, Abbot William has offered fair lodging, clean sheets and a welcome supper of salmon and pike. This morning shall see them in London, or at least within the shadow of its walls. Richard rises early. His back aches, but there's no time for self-pity.

Splashing his face, he gropes for a towel. 'Tom?'

Movement outside the door—clumping feet, harried voices. Kyngston answers the knock, then hurries back. 'Your Grace, the king is asking for you.'

Face dry, Richard thrusts the damp linen in Parr's direction and hastens to the abbot's lodging. Hastings is already there.

'It's Richard, Ned.'

'Good.' The king stands over a kneeling courier. 'Where's my lord of Clarence?'

Richard's heart thumps at sight of the man's crimson livery adorned with the archiepiscopal Cross Keys. Their cousin of York. Not another arrest. Not another trap Edward has led himself into. Through the open door, he catches sight of George pulling on his doublet and speeding down the passage as the bell clangs for Prime. As he races in, Edward brandishes a letter; its seal lozenge-shaped, clerical.

'The Archbishop of York desires to be admitted to my grace. He has renounced his brother, Warwick, to return to his former allegiance. This means, my lords, that with George Neville's defection, we now hold the person of Harry of Lancaster.' He beams. 'Who, in the capital, will choose to oppose us?'

Rivers arrives, bowing low. 'Your Grace?'

'I fear you're a little tardy, my lord earl,' Hastings says, eyeing

Rivers in triumph while George stifles a smirk. 'Notwithstanding, the king has received excellent news. London is ours.'

Richard pinches George's sleeve. 'Is this the end for our cousin?'

The smirk fades. 'Let us pray not.'

Chapter Thirty-Four

Maundy Thursday, 11 April 1471
London

*T*HEY PASS through Bishopsgate, engulfed by the stench from the ancient ditch and watched by a growing throng. The Burgundian contingent rides at their head: five hundred black and smoky gunners armed with weapons barely familiar to the gawping citizenry.

Thus far, Edward has met with no resistance, and in Harpisfeld's saddlebag sits a letter lately received. The City Fathers, it says, choose to be guided by the king's pleasure in all things. Alderman Ralph Verney, acting mayor, submits the City and its environs into Yorkist hands, while Thomas Urswick, recorder, sends the civic guards home to their dinners.

'We must remember,' Edward had announced as Richard and George had broken their fast with him in the frater at Saint Albans, 'that York has ofttimes found favour with the people of London. After Father's defeat, when Marguerite's troops swept south, the city aldermen agreed to her request for sustenance. But the citizens, protesting, waylaid the carts at Cripplegate.' He'd hesitated before grinning broadly. 'You see, the populace believed that our father still lived and was on his way to defend the capital. Despite all, the Londoners still had faith in his cause. This day, when we ride into their city, we'll demonstrate that the House of York does indeed still live and that, despite his turns of fortune, the Rose of Rouen still blooms.'

Even George could not have told a richer tale, and whether the fine words were true or not, Richard had been grateful for the telling. The latest word is that Marguerite and her son are preparing to return, ready to cross the channel, Somerset in tow.

Nudging Liard, he aligns with George. 'What manner of person is Edward of Westminster?'

'Much the same as other youths: brash and boastful.'

'I believe he's but a twelvemonth younger than I. Would you consider me "brash and boastful"?'

'Hardly,' George slides him an amused glance. 'Why do you ask?'

'Well, consider it. Harry may have appeared feeble to the masses, but if his son is expected to land within days, there are plenty who'll fight for him.'

'But he's no more Harry's son than I am,' George says. 'The whelp is of bastard stock; we've always known it. He's Old Somerset's by-blow.'

'And that may be enough for those who believe the Beaufort line still carries the blood of old King Edward and with it a claim to the throne.'

'Well, they'd be wrong, wouldn't they?' George says. 'For it is base blood and cannot run in the veins of kings.'

'I'm thinking what our enemies will say.'

'Well don't.'

Richard can see how insulting it must have been for George when Louis and their cousin had dreamed up the impossible: an alliance between the mighty Earl of Warwick and Marguerite d'Anjou. He imagines the humiliation when the focus of Warwick's ambition had transferred from George himself to the earl's youngest daughter, a girl of barely fourteen years, whose concerns in life extend to her pet squirrel and a dogged devotion to her father. After all he'd risked on their cousin's behalf, George had become superfluous.

At the far end of Bishopsgate Street, the crowds are increasing. Cries of 'Á York!' 'Á King Edward!' tumble from open mouths while Edward raises a palm in salute.

Stretching his back, Richard settles fluidly into the saddle. 'Edward of Westminster—'

'What of him?' George asks. 'Why do you care to hear of him?'

'Should his union with Cousin Anne eventually prove fruitful, then even if the son himself is defeated, a grandson may threaten York in future times. Will there never be an end to this?'

George sneers. 'Well, my presence at Amboise, when they were handfasted, furnished me with one useful titbit. Marguerite has advised her son against consummating the union. Cousin Warwick can't see that she is using him. If he secures the throne for Lancaster, he'll be disposed of, and the marriage easily annulled.'

The thought of a man like their cousin being duped is sickening. But perhaps he just can't see beyond the parapet of his own pride. 'Did you not advise him? Didn't you show him what a mammet he has become in their hands?'

George shakes his head. 'I tried. As God is my witness, I tried. But he never admits fault, you know that Dickon. He's too proud to consider that he can ever be wrong – in anything. And he continues to trust Louis. In spite of all, he continues to trust him.'

Richard espies a flash of crimson. A goodwife, leaning from an upper window, is snatching at a painted cloth which lolls from the casement.

He knows his brother has seen it, too. A hanging cloth sewn with an image of the Ragged Staff ripped from its tenterhooks and tossed aside like refuse.

Shrinking within himself, George diverts his eyes. Richard expects him to comment, but he doesn't. Perhaps he doesn't need to.

Cornhill, Poultry, Cheapside: Ralph Verney is as good as his word. As the streets draw them into the heart of the city, Richard watches the crowds grow, springing up on either side like wayside blooms. The king sits high in the saddle, absorbing the adulation and showering his people with smiles.

The goldsmiths, the silversmiths, the mercers—it's true he

owes them money, yet despite his debts, they love him. For Edward, like his cousin before him, knows how to charm, how to woo. He is Zeus with his thunderbolt, bending the weather to his will. He is Midas with his golden touch. By the time they reach Paul's Churchyard, his seduction is complete.

The spectacle of the Ragged Staff, ripped from its hooks by the goody's fists, has quieted George. He'd remained pensive for the remainder of the journey, and as they kneel within the sanctity of Paul's, Richard can hear his brother's mouth working, whispering, pleading in the weighty silence. He's not alone, Richard thinks, in wondering how events could have fallen out the way they have.

As they leave the abbey, they offer mass pennies at the Crux Borealis. Destined for the Bishop's Palace, they could slip neatly through the prelate's own private entry, but Edward wishes to be seen. They have not, he says, come this far only to take possession of old Harry by privy stealth. Crowds move in, calling out, as they cross the west churchyard. After the dispiriting sight of the former king, the vision of the comely, amiable giant must seem like a gift from on high. Edward, dazzling, acknowledges every cheer, every wave, and as upon his wanderings along the highways of Damme, holds each of his admirers in the palm of his hand.

At the palace, men of the Crossed Keys fuss and flatter. George Neville falls to his knees with Bishop Kempe beside him.

'My lord of York,' Edward rolls the words around his mouth, savouring. 'God give you good day.'

The archbishop tilts his face. But for the cropped fair hair, he could be a younger, more compliant version of his brother. 'My lord king, you are most welcome.'

'Clearly.' Edward gestures towards the palace walls, beyond which the cheering continues, then pauses, allowing his sarcasm to settle. 'I am in receipt of your letter, Cousin, in which you submit to my authority both your own person and that of your prisoner.'

George Neville folds his hands, linking his fingers with care, as if there were some form of protocol involved in the action upon which his whole person could be judged. 'Yes, Highness. Please accept my homage and all due allegiance as my sovereign, without blemish and without equal.'

Edward is silent but accepting. 'Lead me to your charge.'

Bishop Kempe has vacated his chamber in order to house his former king. High-ceilinged and inhabited by a distinct chill, the room smells of must and ancient vellum.

A hunched figure sits atop the bed, encircled by sunlight and dust motes. George Neville hastens across the matting, skirts bundled as a prelude to obeisance. Checking the habit just in time, he approaches the former king with the simple deference he would show to anyone of noble birth.

The prisoner raises his head. To a casual observer, his mild expression, plain black bonnet and gown would mark him as little more than an ordinary clerk.

The weak mouth smiles. 'My lord archbishop, where is Lord Sudeley? One of the books I brought with me is missing, I would have him search for it.'

By the door, hovering like an afterthought, Ralph Boteler looks discomforted. 'I am here, your lordship - and shall seek the volume anon. Once the king has left us.'

Harry of Lancaster seems quietly satisfied, if vaguely bemused.

George Neville coughs. 'If you please, my lord, may I present your cousin, His Grace, King Edward.'

Richard remembers a winter's day, dusk creeping in, when George first sat him down to tell him about Henry and his hated queen. 'Father would make a fine king,' he'd said, 'a better king than Harry the Mad.' Richard recalls his own childish perplexity, his inability to fully understand. 'All you need to know,' George had pointed out glibly, 'is that Harry is an imbecile. Like his grandfather, Charles the Glass King.'

But Richard can detect no trace of madness in this mild-mannered, bewildered man, simply confusion - as if lately woken and finding himself otherwise than he would have supposed.

Henry takes in Edward's height, his girth, his radiance. He looks expectant, but not fretfully so, as if nothing more is amiss than a delayed dinner, a morning's ride postponed due to foul weather. At length, Edward extends his hand. Folding back his clerkly sleeve, Henry takes it. 'My cousin of York, you are very welcome. I believe that in your hands, my life will not be in danger.'

He makes to rise, and George Neville, upon instinct, hurries to assist.

'Do not fuss, my lord archbishop,' Henry says. 'I am quite well.'

Edward leans in. Grasping Henry's hand, he allows himself a moment to survey the man before him. Richard can hazard no guess as to his brother's thoughts; can barely keep pace with his own. When he and George were children, Henry's was the name that had rattled around the nursery, in ballad and in rhyme. Later, it had crept into the stairwell, loitering in the shadows, pulsing with danger. Later still, it had burst upon their lives, distorting them beyond recall. Never, in all that time, had Richard laid eyes upon the man himself.

Yet here he is: the king their father had tried to serve and who, ultimately, he had tried to replace. The man who had allowed others to colour his views, who'd seen their father exiled, marginalised, hunted down in the bloodied snow. Yet Richard finds he cannot hate him. With his wax-splattered gown and shuffling gait, Henry seems but a feeble man, distanced from his surroundings, craving only his supper, his prayers, and his misplaced book.

Any hatred must lie, as it always has, at the feet of his wife and her malicious, vengeful favourites.

York holds the reins once more, and Edward's charger is kicking its heels. At Westminster, the crown is placed momentarily upon his head, the sceptre in his fist. He stands in the sanctuary, upon the pavement of the cosmos, a sun amongst the spheres and stars, while

Harry of Lancaster and his elusive library return to his apartments in the Tower.

As they leave the abbey, George falls into step with Richard. 'The archbishop says he has never supported Lancaster; simply that he was forced to do as his brother—as Warwick—wished.'

'And wasn't that your excuse also?' Richard's voice is terse, accusatory. He can no longer defend Warwick, neither of them can, and the impotence makes him angry. It's also more painful than he cares to admit.

George lets it go, jerks his head to where Edward can be seen hastening towards the palace, in order to greet his queen. 'How long do you think he'll be? I'm eager to see Mother.'

'We're all eager to see Mother,' Richard says. 'Who could have imagined she would ever offer to house the Queen's Grace under her roof?'

'Not I, for one. I was hoping she would be able to plead for our cousin, but that's unlikely now, I suppose, in Elizabeth's presence.'

Richard's gaze sweeps the length of Dean's Yard. 'There may be an opportunity. If not, we must arrange it, but whether Her Grace's company will incline our brother to listen is another matter.'

Chapter Thirty-Five

Maundy Thursday, 11 April 1471
Baynard's Castle

A FORMAL meal, their mother has insisted. Despite their Lenten fare, all custom and protocol is adhered to. Never let it be said that the Duchess of York was too proud to fête her daughter-in-law with the respect due to a queen consort. Or that a Neville fails to honour a future king, even though he sleeps, swaddled and mewling in his cradle.

In her turn, Elizabeth is appreciative; she compliments the duchess on her velvets, her jewels, the efficiency of her servants. She commends the excellent freshwater fish, the purslane and primrose salad. But says little, if anything, to George.

What must it be like, Richard wonders, to dine with a man who has executed your kin? Certain he himself could not, he oscillates between disgust and admiration. The conversation turns to the new prince and the duchess' intention of visiting her grandson upon the morrow.

'I should be honoured, my lady of York.' The queen's heavily lidded eyes shine like chestnuts. 'I shall inform Nurse Welles to prepare him immediately after Mass.'

When she retires, and Edward with her, the duchess invites Richard and George to her solar. As it's Holy Week, the marchpane dish is empty.

'You must speak to him about Warwick,' George is the first to leap in. 'You will, won't you, Mother? Edward must understand.

We're ready to engage with the enemy, but surely we can never make war upon our own cousin.'

The duchess remains unmoved. 'Are you not simply grateful for his forgiveness, George?'

George's brows meet. 'Edward was always going to forgive me....was he not?'

Richard sighs. Sometimes, it's as if his brother views life through a lens, one which distorts the world beyond recognition.

Their mother folds her hands in her lap. 'Life is not a game.'

George laughs, a snuffling snigger tinged with shame and not a little fear. 'My lady, I beg you—'

Closing her eyes, the duchess massages her lids with weary fingers. 'No, George. *I* beg. I beg you to understand that it's too late. Two of my nephews have turned their backs on York. Their brother, the archbishop, is a weathercock and cannot be relied upon. They have betrayed your father's cause, and that has been their choice. Our own allegiance is to the king, and so it must remain.'

George flashes Richard a glance: *She has given up on him.*

Richard wipes an anxious palm the length of his thigh. 'There's still time, Mother, despite all. The earl could revert to his former loyalties at the last moment. Others have done so in the past—'

'Andrew Trollope,' George snarls. 'God rot him!'

'Yes. Trollope. I agree the name is painful to our ears, but the point is that in betraying our father at Ludford Bridge, Trollope also betrayed Warwick. Therefore, our cousin knows only too well that desertion is an option. Perhaps that's what he plans to do.'

'Enough!' Their mother's swift movement sends tremors through her women. Jane Lessy, flushed and concerned, flaps across the floor only to be confronted by a warning hand. 'Stop. You know I cannot abide fuss.'

Cowed, Mistress Lessy retreats to the embrasure. Her young, comely companion, budging closer to the light, keeps her eyes on her stitching. The soft crescent of the girl's cheek reminds Richard of Katherine, and he wonders how his daughter is faring. The child must be almost a year now, tottering perhaps on small, unsteady legs in the household of her stepfather.

Sensible of the prevailing silence, he says, 'Forgive me, Mother. It was not my intention to upset you. I suppose I was just thinking aloud.'

The duchess purses her lips. 'You were scouring the wildest reaches of your imagination, Richard. George seeks to do the same. You both must know that I can do naught to influence your cousin. Even if I wished to.'

George shuffles to the edge of his chair. 'You mean you *don't* wish to?'

'Why should I?' The retort is like a lash of the birch.

'Well,' shame creeps back into George's voice, 'you supported him before. The uprisings, my marriage—'

'Whilst he championed York, yes. Whilst he tried to separate your brother from his mistakes. But that is no longer the case. Warwick has his own cause now. Isabel will not become queen, so he hopes to raise Anne. His espousal to Lancaster, it seems, is a small price to pay for such honour.' Their mother glowers, white knuckles fringing furred cuffs. 'If you would have me beg him to return, then you're more deluded than I thought.'

Good Friday. Following Mass in their mother's chapel, Edward summons a council of war. Those newly emerged from sanctuary join them in the hall at Baynard's, four trestles forming a square, men pressing together, shoulder to shoulder, eager to hear his plans: John, Lord Howard and Thomas, his son; Mountjoy; Cromwell; the Bourchiers. And Ralph Hastings; face, like his brother's, red and peeling in the unseasonable heat.

Casements wide to a peerless blue sky, there's little breeze. Perspiration clings and the acerbic stench of armpits has men reaching for pomanders. The king calls for small beer, and they fall upon it gladly, draining cups and smacking lips, eager for more. Richard glances around the company. Is it loyalty to York that brings them here? Or an aversion to Warwick, a chance to settle scores? Allegiance to the cause would be the preferable answer, of course.

But with a man as divisive as the earl, one can never truly know.

'We thank you, my lords—my friends—for coming to us in such haste,' Edward is down to his shirt sleeves, and they billow like sails as he signs to his audience. 'We are overjoyed that so many of you have come to us, defensibly arrayed. It's our hope that the adventures which are likely to come will settle us once more in our rightful place. And that all opposition to our kingship may finally be crushed.'

Appreciative roars echo to the hammerbeams. Hastings pummels the board while Thomas Howard shuffles on his bench with ill-concealed excitement.

'We've heard rumours,' the king says, 'much to our full marvel, that our brother-in-law Duke Charles has signed a three months' truce with the French king.'

There's muttering and a growing wave of consternation. An alliance between the two would see them united against England. To Richard's left, Duras writhes in discomfort. To his right, George leans in, tipping his head in the king's direction.

'Why does he do this? Keeping such things to himself, only to make a sudden announcement in the hearing of all? Surely, he should share such things with us first. We're his brothers. We should be briefed.'

Richard shrugs. 'For whatever reason, that is his way.'

Or, he thinks, Edward may simply choose to keep things from George for as long as possible, lest lines of communication with their cousin are still open.

They're joined by John More, Edward's keen, lanky intelligencer, who converses quietly with the king. Following nods and affirmations, Edward says, 'My spies are attempting to discover the truth of the reports, but I wonder, my Lord Duras, whether you are in any way aware of your master's intentions?'

Duras, floundering under scrutiny, holds up his hands. 'This comes as much of a surprise to me as to Your Grace.'

Richard seeks George's ear. 'He's telling the truth. I'm sure of it.'

A judicious nod reveals the king to be in no way suspicious of the Gascon. 'You've served us well, Gaillard. Please, do not concern yourself. Once we know the truth or otherwise of this rumour, we shall require you to write to your master to ascertain his intentions.'

George's mouth puckers as his mind races. 'Warwick is playing a dangerous game; it seems he may soon be caught between two fires. We have to try harder, Dickon. If Mother isn't prepared to intercede, then we'll press Edward further. He must offer our cousin another chance to submit.'

He must. But will he?

Edward pushes hair from his brow, swiping sweat. 'The Earl of Warwick is advancing upon London, which means he intends to attack despite the holiness of the season. As we know from the piteous experience of our own father, whom God assoil, the enemy is not averse to practising deception during times of observance.'

'He'll not strike now,' Richard murmurs, eyes fixed on the brilliant blue beyond the casement, 'not during Passiontide. Our cousin is not an impious man.'

Thrusting back his chair, Edward is on his feet. 'We leave upon the morrow, my lords, and head north. I'm told the enemy is approaching Saint Albans, and with God's help, we shall confront them. Until then, preparations will continue.'

The hall resounds to the scraping of benches, the clumping of feet, as men file out into the pounding heat of the day.

With the greatest of effort, Richard assumes a settled countenance. To the death, then.

Chapter Thirty-Six

*J*HE RIVER, green and opaque, laps the barge as they approach the Water Gate. Richard and George share their mother's own vessel, and taking her lead, Richard keeps his own counsel. He's never considered, until now, how it must be to watch the residue of your male offspring prepare themselves for war.

The royal barge has already moored and Edward steps onto the wharf; helps the queen alight with his own hand before lifting his daughters, Elizabeth, Cecily and Mary, and depositing them beside their mother. The youngest wobble on their fat little legs, while the eldest fusses over her infant brother.

Margaret had been right about siblings, Richard thinks, they feel responsible for one another. He observes George hugging his knees and averting his gaze from the filial proceedings. But for his hasty escape across the Narrow Seas, such fatherly concerns might now be his.

Engulfed by shame and pity, Richard touches his brother's hand. 'Begging your forgiveness, I've never asked—'

'All is well, Dickon. All is mended.'

'But I've not made enquiry after Isabel. Please, forgive me.'

A tight smile. 'She's safely housed in the West Country. No need for concern.'

The vessel bumps against the landing, and the bargemen relinquish their oars. The duchess shifts, tight-lipped, and the bench creaks beneath her.

'You will be safe here, my lady,' George says. 'Whatever happens.'

London is tense and perplexed. Two kings in the capital and the world, again, turned upside down. Cannon is hauled from the Tower, Harry is hauled from his books. Better, Edward says, that they take the old king with them than leave him in the hands of those who may seek to raise him up once more as soon as Yorkist hoofbeats disappear along the Great North Road.

'If time has taught me anything,' he adds, 'it's that trust cannot be freely given. Archbishop Neville may well be confined, but if he were able to assist his brother, he'd find a way to slither out of his cell and do it.'

Cynicism has become a habit for Edward, and Richard isn't sure he cares for it. 'Our cousin of York has declaimed his loyalty to us. He has given his oath upon the Gospels, Brother.'

Edward is unmoved. 'Indeed. But this is George Neville we speak of.'

They ascend the steps of Saint Thomas' Tower, boots skimming smooth stone. There is one final task to fulfil before they march out, and it's something they must perform together. Edward, leading, takes the steps two at a time and dips his head to navigate the doorway. George follows, and Richard takes up the rear. Stepping from the heavy glare of late afternoon, they emerge into a dim interior, hazy with greenish shadow.

The place bustles with their mother's servants—Mistress Lessy, shaking creases from velvet, pages scattering rosemary sprigs and crushing them underfoot. In the far corner, the door to the oratory stands agape. Their mother is alone and on her knees. Alerted by their footfall, she rises, wipes her face, then presents a countenance both ordered and sedate.

'My sons.'

It's easier for us, Richard thinks; we three have each other, at least for the moment. We shall leave together, ride together, and, God willing, we'll return together. During that time, she will have none to share her anguish but Elizabeth, a woman she despises. This evening, she will pray with her chaplain, be consoled by her women, but know nothing of how we fare until word finds its way to her: for good or ill.

'Lady Mother,' the king makes obeisance, 'we've come to take our leave.'

Before she can respond, he jerks his head towards the doorway, bridging the gap between duty and fear with forced banality. 'I'm pleased to see you have sufficient comforts here. Enough, at least, for your needs.'

Richard nods in vigorous, unnecessary approval. Jane Lessy has hung the gowns, the comely girl has arrived, and between them, they're making the bed, wafting the coverlet and allowing it to fall on the overstuffed mattress.

'Yes,' the duchess says, 'I am well provided for.'

She lifts the crucifix from the altar and presents it to her sons to kiss before studying them intently. She's consigning our faces to memory, Richard thinks, the way she must have done with Father, with Edmund.

Embracing each in turn, she crosses herself. 'May the Trinity keep you.'

Chapter Thirty-Seven

Saturday 13 April 1471 – Afternoon
The Road to Barnet

THEY LEAVE the city by the old Roman road, foreriders sent ahead to discern the position of the enemy. Richard's courage is playing him false, threatening to betray him with every hoofbeat that leads them towards the inevitable. Somewhere, on the route to Saint Albans, their cousin is waiting in the midst of a Lancastrian army. How Richard will feel when he's forced to confront him, he cannot begin to imagine.

Five miles on, the foreriders return, desperate, bloodied, whipping up a sweat. Reining in before Edward, the leader dismounts, falling to the earth like a consignment of baggage.

'Your Grace…the earl's scouts. We encountered them nigh on Chipping Barnet. We clashed but saw them off, chased them north beyond the village.'

'Did we lose many men?' The king's voice is steady.

'Injuries were sustained, Highness, on both sides, but flesh wounds only. We set them fleeing, and those who could, gave chase.' The man pauses to catch his breath. 'We glimpsed the earl's division. His men are drawn up on a ridge, straddling the road north—'

'How far from here?'

The scout pants, and Hastings yells for a wineskin. Sustained, the man makes a vague gesture. 'At Gladmore Heath, a half mile or so beyond Barnet village, no further.'

'And as to number? What would be a fair estimate?'

'We think - that is, we assumed - around fifteen thousand.'

There's movement amongst the company as horses sense the mood of their riders. Richard soothes Liard with the flat of his hand. 'Your Grace, we are outnumbered.'

'Consider our uncle of Salisbury in times past,' Edward says. 'Faced twice his number yet won a resounding victory.'

Richard chews his lip. Such stories should hearten him: their uncle's ranks having been swelled that day by Harringtons and Parrs. Instead, old tales of Blore Heath seem unfitting. The world has changed since then, and the family of York with it.

The king makes camp, calls his captains to him while he thinks aloud. Richard stays close, and when he listens to Edward's tactical plans, he does so with as much detachment as he can muster. He can't falter, can't allow himself to think beyond the current moment. This is war, or soon will be. It's what he's been trained for.

'We wait here,' Edward says, 'let your men sleep if they will. Having clashed with our outriders, the enemy knows we're in the vicinity but will not come in search of us. They have the advantage of higher ground and won't wish to lose it. We'll set out at dusk and approach them quietly as darkness falls. According to our scouts, the armies are drawn up in battles: Montagu has the centre, Exeter their left, while Oxford commands the van. The earl himself commands the reserve.' He turns to Hastings. 'Will, I want you on the left, facing Oxford. He appears to be taking advantage of the hedgerows, and I fear your task will not be an easy one. My lord of Clarence will remain with me in the centre, where we shall keep Harry of Lancaster in ward. Earl Rivers will bring up the reserve. My lord of Gloucester, you will form the vanguard.'

'The van?' Richard pauses, wineskin halfway to his mouth. 'Me?'

The vanguard leads an army. It is the first to deploy.

'Yes, Richard, you. Oxford is experienced, and therefore,

it is sensible that he faces Lord Hastings.' Edward's wry grin is designed to tease. 'What is it? Do you not believe yourself capable of facing Exeter?'

Henry Holland, their brother by marriage, whose devotion to Harry's queen had placed him at the walls of Sandal one freezing day in late December. Henry Holland, whose loyalty to Lancaster had served to render them fatherless. *Hate your opponent, boy. It's the only way.*

A steady thump rises in Richard's chest. 'Brother, you mistake me. Given my lord Exeter's former career, I believe you will find me more than fitted for the task.'

The night before a confrontation is always the same. He's been advised of this many times since leaving London, not least by the king himself. What Edward also said is true: the night before battle, men do make light of their lives, of their situation, even of their destinies. As they rest, men share flasks of small beer, they piss in the surrounding ditches, recall old comrades-in-arms. They speak of youthful scuffles in side streets and narrow lanes, they compare scars. They talk fondly of their women. They pray to God and the saints. They confess, if not to one of the chaplains, then at least to each other. A fortunate few sleep.

Voicing encouragement to his own troops, Richard speaks to them of tenacity and courage, of duty and pride, before retiring to rest his aching back and shrink before the looming spectre of his own hypocrisy. What can he possibly tell these men that they don't know already? What morsel of advice has he for those whose experience of war far outranks his own?

Pressing his spine against the gnarled oak, he spies James Harrington weaving his way through the seated mass. Rising to greet him, Richard clasps the man's hand with both of his own, Harrington's sapphire and death's head rings grazing his palm. They talk, but Richard finds he has little appetite for conversation.

'Courage is in your veins, Your Grace,' Harrington assures him as he takes his leave. 'As it was in your father's.'

Such praise, proffered by another, would smack of sycophancy. From a man such as this, it is a compliment. 'Thank you, Sir James. May God keep you.'

Harrington returns to his fellowship, releasing the scents of evening as he stumps through the grass. Hungry for solitude, Richard calls for his travelling Psalter, but when it arrives, it remains in his lap unopened. Fingers creeping towards his scabbard, he fights the compulsion to draw out the blade. Compulsion wins, and he tilts the flat of the blade towards the dying sun until the incised letters wink back at him: *Optimo*. The best.

Closing his eyes, he waits for the agony to pass. How could he have known, in the keen, rapturous days of the practice yard, how his daily labours would ultimately find expression? How his cousin's ardent tutelage would witness its fruition in this: the necessity of their facing each other across a rough and unremarkable heath, marking the road to London.

A swish of footsteps and he's on his feet in a moment, sword gripped, heart pounding, 'For Pity's sake, Brother!'

George's chest heaves as fiercely as his own. Richard returns the blade to its scabbard and reclaims his place beneath the tree. 'Has none bothered to tell you that the only person you should ever creep up on is your enemy?'

With a shaky laugh, George flops down beside him. 'Thought I was done for.'

'Well, you might be if you do anything like that again. Thank Saint Loy, you didn't try that with Edward. Instinct would have him run you through before he bothered to look at your face.'

'Or Hastings would get there first. Anyway, I'm hardly likely to creep up on our brother, now am I?'

Richard is in no mood for levity. Eyes turned to the horizon, he watches the glowing ball sink below the trees, fingers returning to his scabbard to caress the Spanish leather.

George's eyes follow. '*He* gave it to you, didn't he?'

Richard rounds on him. 'How do you know that?'

'He told me himself. And before you growl at me, I can

assure you he had nothing of a similar kind made for me, nor for anyone else.'

The sun has almost gone; nothing now but a weak and fading blush pursued by the advancing dusk. 'I don't mind telling you,' George continues, 'that when he described it, I was in sore envy of so singular a gift. "But your brother wants for encouragement," he said, "and has a great longing within him."'

Richard clutches a handful of grass; the blades cool in his hand, popping and snapping as he rives them from the earth. 'Not strictly true. The king himself has always encouraged me.'

'Cease feigning, Dickon. Be honest—at least with me. We love our cousin, and the morrow is going to be hard for both of us.'

'But what I cannot understand is his betrayal. What possessed him to make his peace with her—with Marguerite? He hates Elizabeth and her kin, that's clear to every man, but surely to God, his hatred cannot have overtaken his abhorrence of Lancaster—of those who killed his own father, and ours.' Richard's breaths quicken, and he knows he's on the verge of despair. 'It…' he makes useless gestures with his hands '…it makes no sense to me.'

George is quiet. Grasping the discarded blades of grass, he sifts them through his fingers. 'I know what you're thinking, Dickon, that I went along with it myself, to a degree. Yes, I wanted to change things. I wanted to tear Edward away from those who would influence him. And yes, I admit, if the king would not submit to us, there was some talk of exile, of imprisonment. Of my—'

'Shut up, George! For Heaven's sake.'

George lowers his voice. 'You must know—both you and Edward must know—that I was never part of Louis' plan. It was all of Louis' own devising. I could never have reconciled myself with the enemy. Even Warwick, to an extent, opposed rapprochement with Marguerite but saw no other way—no other way to receive the help he needed from the French. I don't doubt he has his own plans, of becoming as indispensable to Harry as he was to Edward. But the truth is, Dickon, the only person he's fooling is himself. If he's doing even that.'

Richard looks him in the eye. 'I still pray for a defection at the last moment.'

'As do I. But we both know his pride and how far he will go to preserve it. We know him, Brother. Better, probably, than he knows his own self.'

As dusk descends, Edward has them arm and prepare themselves. 'My lord of Gloucester's contingent shall be the first to ride out.'

Pride, disappointment and resentment vie for prominence in Richard's gut. It's like the pottage they ate as children; many ingredients stirred into the mix, but it's the least appealing which always rises to the top. His first engagement, and he's riding to face the one man on earth he loves above all others. This isn't how it should be, nor would be, had Edward allowed him to mediate. In another world, the family of York would be united, their Neville cousins swelling their ranks. Warwick and Montagu are not the enemy: he can't consider it, even now.

His squires prepare the Burgundian harness: Mijnheer de Vroede's masterpiece in steel. Wiggling his arm so the vambrace squeals, he attempts a weak smile, an even weaker jest: 'The king requires stealth, but it will be no easy matter to steal upon the enemy in full harness. This clatter would haul a man from the deepest sleep.'

They laugh for the sake of courtesy before an awkward silence descends. Feigning bravado, Richard breaks it, 'According to our scouts, the terrain below the ridge offers ample cover. It will enable us to position ourselves closer to the enemy than will be expected. The king intends to join battle at dawn, allow Lancaster no opportunity to play us false.'

Parr smiles. 'None can deny the king's skill, nor his fearsome reputation in the field. I should rather be with His Grace, facing the enemy, than in their ranks, facing us.'

The optimism is welcome, and Richard claps him on the back. 'Well said, Tom.'

Chapter Thirty-Eight

Saturday 13 April 1471 – Evening
Barnet Heath

REACHING THE heath as night falls, they array themselves according to the king's command. Their enemies may believe they have the advantage, deployed as they are upon the ridge, but the swelling ground between the armies works in favour of York. Edward has his men move silently in the gloaming, slithering into position as close to the rise as they can without giving themselves away.

Richard settles his own men, mindful of Edward's instructions. No undue noise. No campfires. Darkness to be used as a shield with which to deceive the enemy. While they warm themselves by their own fires, Lancaster will be blinded to what is happening in the hollow beyond.

He'd been determined not to sleep, but his eyes are heavy, and soon, a soft nudge finds him cursing himself. 'Your Grace,' Parr is hunching over him, 'a messenger is here. You are to attend the king.'

Hauling himself upright, Richard follows the retreating tabard over uneven ground, the vague impression of a Sun with Streams leading him through the gloom. He finds the king seated on the ground like the rest of his army, his voice little more than a whisper. 'Can you hear anything from your position, Richard?'

Not daring to own that his senses had been momentarily dimmed, Richard shakes his head.

'I've spent the last hour listening,' Edward says, 'seeking to decipher their mutterings.'

A lithesome clink, and George slips towards them through the purpling shadows. 'I've heard a little. There's been some talk of a bombard, and that noise just now…there, do you hear it? They're rolling their cannon into place.' He hesitates. 'Our cousin. He wouldn't fire at us now, would he? When we are in repose?'

'Well, if he does,' Edward says, 'he's not likely to hit us. They've no idea how close we are.' He signals to the waiting messenger. 'Send to Lord Hastings, to Earl Rivers. Remind them, no sound, especially now. Go.'

The man leaves in haste, and they each gaze after him until his Sun with Streams is finally eclipsed. Up on the ridge, the trundling of cannon continues: squeaking wheels, thumping carriage.

Edward exhales. 'I've not called you here to discuss tactics, Richard. We've done that already. As I told you then, we are united as a force, but each of our three battles must fight independently. Once a commander is in the thick of the fight, he's conscious only of the movements of his own battle; remember that. Though he may not be aware of the movements of his fellows, he must continue, to the death if necessary. But I've yet to lose a field—'

'Please, Your Grace, no.' Richard's voice is rasping. 'There's such a thing as tempting the Fates.'

He senses, rather than sees, Edward's grin. 'But God, as we know, is on our side. Has Saint Anne not shown us that? Besides, Lancaster may have the advantage of the ridge, but dawn will reveal to them a very different sight from the one they imagine lies before them.'

George peers in the direction of the enemy.

Edward studies him. 'What are you wishing for, Brother? Do you still imagine the earl will sue for peace? Even if he wanted to, which I doubt, there's no likelihood of him being able to extricate himself now. If he showed any inclination to defect, he'd be struck down. Oxford and Exeter have hated him long enough, it would be no great effort for them. They might even enjoy it—'

A blast of cannon from the ridge. They, and all around them, flatten themselves against the earth.

'He's firing on us!' George is incredulous.

'Well observed,' Edward jeers. 'Although even I did not suppose he would attempt to bombard us whilst we slept.'

'But…' George creeps close, the whites of his eyes flickering, 'for all he knows…'

The truth hits Richard, too, with as much force as the iron balls whistling over their heads. For all Warwick knows, any one of his cousins could be dead, crushed into the dried mud, limbs wrenched and scattered. He licks parched lips. 'It was probably Oxford.'

George gives a vigorous nod. 'Yes, Oxford. It has to be.'

The king has another message for his captains: no retaliation, despite the bombardment. At this vital moment, they must not reveal their position.

'You too, Richard,' Edward urges. 'Go. Tell your gunners, no retaliation.'

Gauntlet crushes gauntlet. 'Remember all I've told you and accept my blessing. God be with you, Brother.'

'And with you, Your Grace.'

'The Trinity bless you, Dickon,' George murmurs. 'Remember, we must pray for… for each other.'

A swift embrace. 'Just so,' Richard says. 'And be assured—I shall be praying for us all.'

Chapter Thirty-Nine

Easter Day, 14 April 1471 – Dawn
Barnet Heath

*T*HEY WAKE—THOSE who have dared sleep—to a grey and muffled world. Overnight, heavy mist has fallen, and the air of early dawn is like a breath of winter. Beneath his coif, Richard's hair sticks to his skull like goose grease, and his cheeks feel sore and clammy. Worse is the effect of the sodden grass, wet and slimy under his arming shoes, as he drags himself to his feet. Not only does York give battle in the holiest seasons, he reflects, but we're cursed each time with the most malevolent of weather.

Chaplains pick their way through the waking men, balancing the Host on patens. After a brief confession, each man receives the Eucharist and bows his head in receipt of a blessing. To Richard, the king sends one of his royal chaplains, Richard Martin, chasuble creased and grubby from travel. Kneeling on the damp earth, Richard's heart begins to pound.

Confiteor Deo omnipotenti…

This may be his last confession, his final chance to clear himself of fault, in thought and word and deed. His mind scrambles, searching for things that may have harmed, may have hurt, may have troubled those whose paths he's crossed. He thinks of Katherine and of their child, of the lusts of Des Graven Hage. But these sins, long confessed, are as nothing to the festering desire for vengeance that has lodged in him since childhood and for which he can never truly feel contrite. It has always felt that to forgive would be to forget, to disregard the pain inflicted upon his family, to reduce the atrocities of Ludlow, the tragedy of Sandal to things banal and mundane, as if they had travelled beyond those scarred landscapes to pleasanter realms without a backward glance. But none of them have, and none of them shall, until the enemy is crushed.

Martin elevates the Host, voice flat, hurried and detached.

Ecce Agnus Dei, qui tollis peccata mundi…

The wafer cleaving to Richard's palate gradually dissolves. Crossing himself, he wipes the moisture from his cheeks and rises in a cacophony of clanking steel.

Martin signals a final blessing, then vanishes, piecemeal, into the growing mist. Richard feels alone, disjointed, severed from the world. In his sudden desolation, he's beset by a need to draw his people close. These boys, these men, are his friends. And not merely his friends; they're those with whom he may be sharing his ultimate morning on earth. He recalls the priest with a sudden yell.

'Father, minister to my squires also. And shrive them.'

'If it please Your Grace, the king bade me minister to you expressly. Your men must seek the services of the camp chaplains.'

'Minister to my squires. And shrive them.' Voice firm, toneless in the murk, he calls them forward: Tom Parr, Thomas Huddleston, between them conjuring memories of the north; Christopher Worsley, John Harper, whose friendship he forged on the Welsh Marches; John Milewater the Younger, whose father served his own. Loyal men each, whose redemption should not be dependent upon the time constraints of wandering clerics. Before Martin can object, Richard bids the squires kneel at his feet.

One is missing. He spots Kyngston crouched on the ground, face in his hands.

'Simon! Come, receive the Host like your fellows.'

Kyngston refuses to move. 'I'm unworthy, Your Grace. These others risk their lives for you while I'm to be sent to cower by the baggage train. I'm not a soldier, and it would be presumption, my lord. I do not deserve it.'

With a swift motion, Richard drags him to his feet. 'We're all equal when we take the Sacrament. Now go, kneel with the others.'

His master's hand on the small of his back, Kyngston staggers forward. When all are shriven and blessed, Richard propels Martin back into the mist.

'Simon, say your farewells and retire to the horse park.'

The youths embrace, ruffle Kyngston's hair, throw playful punches. When they break apart, Richard enfolds the boy, thanks him for his services – just in case. 'Get you to the wagons. And, if it goes amiss for York, seek out my lord of Warwick. He'll do right by you.'

Watching the boy slip through the fog, he flexes his arms as Huddleston checks his harness for movement and prepares to fit his gauntlets. 'Harper, send a message to my captains. I would speak with the men. Hurry, we don't have long.'

There's not much to say, but he wants to say something. He wants to bestow a blessing - from lord to squire, from master to servant, from one friend to another - before the bloodletting begins.

The mist has tightened its grip; the surface of Richard's harness beaded with moisture, his banners little but sodden rags. Harrington's contingent to his left, William Parr's to his right, he's chosen to deploy a number of Gaubert's archers upon each flank. Their captain has promised to pray to Saint Denis that the fog may be lifted and that his keen-eyed *garçons* catch at least a glimpse of the enemy.

The king's trumpets, flat and barely audible, sound from the centre of the Yorkist ranks. Richard relays the command, and an order is hurled down the line to Gaubert. While the Gascon's roar rebounds like an avenging spirit from Crispin's Day, his bowmen can see nothing, still less take aim. Richard squints as shafts hurtle into the mist, then snaps his visor shut, awaiting the exchange. But nothing appears from the direction of the enemy. Vague blasts of cannon fire prove that somewhere, beyond them, men have engaged. And yet, there's no repost from Exeter. Does the bastard intend to lure them on, then bombard them at close range?

Another arrow storm is loosed, but smoke from the king's artillery thickens the wall of cloud and Richard curses. It's like waging war in the netherworld.

When, once again, nothing is returned, he calls for Gaubert. 'Why do they not respond, Étienne?'

'It cannot be certain we have made any impact, Monseigneur le Duc. We cannot truly know their position. Our aim may well have fallen short.'

Richard growls. His own lack of experience is infuriating. 'Ever fought in such conditions before?'

'Non, Monseigneur. Never. But had our volleys reached the enemy, be sure we would have received a swift *réplique.*'

A decision must be made – and quickly. 'We have no choice. We must advance.'

Richard's squires surround him. Worsley ahead, bearing his standard, Harper and Huddleston fore and aft, Milewater and Parr closely flanking. Whispered prayers gush within the confines of his sallet, that those who protect him may be themselves protected.

Their arming shoes struggle to grip the slimy earth, and he realises they are descending into boggy ground. The king's scouts had spoken of a hollow in the landscape, which Exeter appears to be using to protect his left flank.

'Halt!' Richard raises a hand, his squires move in, and around him, the screech of movement subsides. At length, muted sounds of conflict slice through the fog from the far left of the company.

'My God.' Realisation assaults him like a battering ram. Their armies are misaligned.

A burst of voices, and he spins to find Huddleston exchanging words with a black-liveried messenger. 'Your Grace, Sir James Harrington comes—'

Before he can react, Harrington himself, Boreas-like, strides through the growing fog. 'My lord of Gloucester. The battle rages beyond us. Sounds of engagement to the left of my contingent, dulled by the mist, yet clear enough. Our lines are set awry.'

Richard springs open his visor. 'And for our part, we're advancing downhill. James, if each of our battles is equally misplaced, Exeter must now be engaging with the king. If we swing our forces to the left, we can advance from this depression and attack Holland from the rear. The last thing he'll expect, given the terrain, is a flank attack.'

His heart pounds as his brain races. In his mind, he's already scaling the incline, launching a reckless charge through the mist. 'It might just be possible, but in God's name, James, once we ascend to even ground, we must hold firm. If we allow the enemy to force us back into the hollow, we're dead men.'

'May God save Your Grace.' Harrington, certain of his orders, hastens back to his company as word is sent to William Parr and Gaubet. The move will prove daring and difficult, but they have little choice.

The leftward swing helps propel them, and soon, they're clambering up the bank towards the edge of the hollow, drenched grass and uneven terrain increasing the ordeal as they struggle to gain a foothold. Richard prays harder than he's ever prayed. If he can do this, if he can creep up on Holland like a cutpurse…

Approaching the plateau, a wave of his arm signals the call to advance banners.

'Á York. Á Gloucester!'

They burst like cannon fire onto level ground, yells resounding as primal instincts rise. Patchy colours are visible through the fog— banners of red and white: the golden wheat ears, the fiery beacons of Henry Holland.

Summoning his strength, Richard surges into the leaden murk.

His first confrontation: the man is down as another falls from view. Those lacking a visor are easy pickings, and after the first eruptions of blood and brains, horror becomes commonplace. The enemy is naught but hunting quarry. They're the dashing, flickering prey of the forest. They're the flayed hinds and the cornered harts, they're the limp and bloody stags.

His war hammer crashes on steel, crushing all beneath. *Hate your opponent, boy.* And he does. Each blow delivered is for his father, each thrust for what was lost. It's for Cousin Warwick, for his care, for his love, for his pride in him, and for the ruin of those who have enticed the earl away. It's for what he wants. For what he needs. For the chance to become what his father intended. For another chance at life.

Gasping for breath, he wheels in every direction, dodging blows and slithering on the gore-splattered earth. Righting himself, he gags. The glistening mass was a man's guts: a man's guts, still digesting his barley bread. This isn't real, he tells himself. If it were, I would spew. But he doesn't spew, and it *is* real. This is the horror Edward pronounced: the antithesis of the shimmering knight on the painted page. It gives the lie to the glittering harness, the rippling, silken banners. It is vengeance, still yet, survival, and he continues to attack, to hit out, to smash breastplate and sallet, to believe that somehow, despite the horror he's forced to inflict, that Christ will forgive him.

Exeter's crimson livery, its golden wheat ear, flashes across his sight. A man-at-arms, poleaxe gripped, spear thrusting. Richard is swift, Milewater swifter, and the man is skewered, swimming in his own blood. Gasping, heart pumping, he owes his life to his squire, but there's no time for gratitude, and Richard recovers himself just in time to counter another thrust.

Strength he barely knew he possessed builds and releases; builds and releases, a relentless, maniacal rhythm, as if his body has finally found its purpose. He longs to lift his visor, to see beyond the circumference of his own position. He has no idea how long they've been engaged, nor how long they can continue. All he knows is that they must.

Huddleston and Harper close in tight as Worsley points in desperation towards a flurry of banners now mingling with the duke's. 'Your Grace, Exeter is reinforced. The earl has sent in his reserve!'

Insignias of his cousin, Warwick—Neville saltires, Ragged Staves—are beating towards them like demons from Hell. My God, Richard thinks, he intends to destroy us, to force us to the brink of the hollow, to thrust us back the way we came. *Jhesu Mercy.*

'Á York! Á Gloucester!' Worsley screams encouragement above the moans and shrieks of the wounded, the nerve-ripping screech of harness. Sweat trickles down Richard's brow, he blinks it away, dealing out death with every blow of his war hammer.

He feels their position slipping, a slow but certain sense of being pushed back. The effort of retaining ground, of gathering strength, of hurling himself against the thrust of the renewed onslaught is agonising. They mustn't weaken before the assault. They weaken, they die.

Urged on by the sound of his own cries, his belly is a leaden vessel of fear, of pain, of desperation. Prayers burst from him: pleas to both his Heavenly and earthly fathers. He cannot die here, cannot allow his men to die. *Blessed Mother of God…*

His foot meets resistance, and he all but stumbles. Metallic, yet pliant, the obstacle can be but one thing. His urge is to kick the body aside, to move on. Yet he can't dismiss the need to pause, to glance swiftly down. A scream erupts from his lungs: the obstruction is Thomas Parr, writhing in the mud, clutching his innards as they gush between his mailed fingers. Parr: loyal, dutiful—sallet ripped away, nose a bloody mass of gore. A soldier in Exeter's livery, having despatched the squire , now turns his attention to the master. Chest heaving, Richard launches himself forward. Forcing his hammer into the man's skull, he wallows in grim but brief satisfaction, then turns to find John Milewater sprawled on the earth, eyes cast heavenward.

A sob escapes him. Curses and obscenities follow. *I didn't thank him. He saved my life, and I couldn't thank him. Lord Jhesu…*

'My lord of Gloucester!' A mailed fist grips his arm. Disorientated, he spins. Glimpsing the livery of the sunburst, he recognises a familiar voice.

'Your Grace.' It's Thomas Huddleston. 'Stand down. A message from the king.'

Shielded by Huddleston and Worsley, Richard retreats through the heaving mass to a safe distance. Springing his visor with a trembling hand, he gulps the air, but the stench is fouler than his stinking sallet. It's like the slaughterhouse. Without warning, he retches.

The king's man is breathless. 'My lord of Gloucester, His Grace wishes to know if you can hold.'

Wiping his mouth, Richard stares at him inanely. 'Hold? That is my purpose. Of course I—'

'My lord duke, there is confusion in the ranks. Word has reached the king of disarray amongst the enemy. He wishes to apply his full reserve in the centre, where it can make most headway.'

Richard takes the wineskin that is handed to him and gulps deeply. The centre. His cousin Montagu's command. Undoubtedly bolstered by whatever company remains to his brother, Warwick.

He takes a deep breath. 'Assure His Grace. Gloucester can hold.'

The respite has eased the strain but broken his rhythm. Flanked by Huddleston and Worsley, he launches back into the fray. Motion resumes, pace returning to his driving limbs, vicious as before. Time loses its meaning: existence nothing but the rapid motion of thrust and jab. He cannot tell how long they've fought; can barely see the impact they've made. Life has shrunk, brief moments lived between one blow and another, one breath and the next.

Soon, the wall of crimson livery crumbles before them, fragmenting, falling away in a sprawling mass. He's like a man bewitched, pushing forward, regaining ground with every potent step. God will not allow them to fail. They've come too far.

'My lord of Gloucester!' Worsley flashes into his line of sight. Beside him a royal messenger: his Sun with Streams glinting through the fading haze. Chest heaving, Richard raises his visor as Edward's man bends the knee.

'Your Grace. The king sends word…the field is won.'

Chapter Forty

Easter Day, 14 April 1471 – Forenoon
Barnet Heath

SURGEON, WILLIAM Hobbes, stands by Richard's cot, appraising the underside of his gauntlet.

'You were fortunate, Your Grace. Had the leather ripped any further, the dagger could have opened an artery.' Thrusting the mailed glove aside, he peers at the wound, which gapes like a bloodied mouth at the base of Richard's thumb. 'A flesh wound only, but it will need treatment; we would not wish for infection to take hold.'

'As you will.' Richard, assailed by a bout of violent shuddering, finds he cannot keep still.

'Shock,' Hobbes explains. 'It grips all men in the aftermath of battle. You do what has to be done, but when it is over…' he gives an elegant little shrug. 'In the field, a man's eye is trained upon his enemies, his thoughts upon their destruction. Only when combat is over does his body, and it has to be said his mind, react to the horrors he has witnessed.'

Taking an ointment jar from his assistant, the surgeon waggles it in triumph. 'Rose honey. Used by the eminent John Bradmore to cleanse Prince Hal's wound at Shrewsbury Field.'

Richard's exhaustion allows but a brief acknowledgement. The tent flap opens, and Kyngston ducks in, bearing a wineskin. Eyes red, face mottled, it's clear he has been weeping for his friend. Richard thanks God that at least Huddleston, Worsley and Harper remain with them and that Kyngston has not been left entirely alone. When the youth presents the wineskin, Richard bids him keep it and go to seek them out.

'But Your Grace—'

'Go. There's nothing I require.'

With a thwack of heavy linen, Kyngston disappears through the flap and the stench of the field seeps in. The rose honey, smoothed over Richard's wound, provides a pleasant antidote.

'How long will this take to heal? Our business, as you know, doctor, is yet to be concluded.'

'Healing varies with the individual, Your Grace, but you should notice some difference in a sennight, if care is observed.'

Men-at-arms stumble in, bearing a bloodied sheet between them. Rivers, peering from its folds, essays a half smile and bites his lip as he's bumped onto a waiting cot.

'My lord of Gloucester, I am most happy to see you.' Wydeville's squires arrive to divest him of his harness, and Rivers lowers his hand to his groin. 'A slight yet bloody wound, I'm told. I trust Your Grace's injury is equally superficial.'

Richard raises his bandaged limb.

'Ah,' Rivers nods, 'not your sword hand, at least.'

'No, as Hobbes says, I was fortunate.' Richard diverts his gaze, willing Rivers to silence. He doesn't wish to know what Wydeville knows, if indeed he knows anything. If Edward is aware of their cousin's fate, he would prefer to hear of it from him.

A commotion beyond the tent, and George bursts in, harness smeared with congealing blood.

'Dickon. Thank God.' Espying Rivers on the opposite side of the tent, he thrusts out his chin, then retreats through the flap. 'I'll wait outside.'

With Hobbes' leave, Richard rises and follows him out. Finding his brother pacing the earth, he reaches for his hand. 'You cannot know how glad I am to see you.'

Close to weeping, George takes a moment to compose himself. 'We heard you were beset by great numbers. I was afraid. Was so thankful when I heard…'

Richard swallows. 'Where's the king?'

George glances towards the horizon, where the church tower of Monken Hadley rises above the trees. 'Giving instructions to his heralds. Wants them to count the dead. Harpisfeld is with him; Edward wants to write to Mother and to the City, announcing our victory.'

Richard nods, mute. He daren't ask what happened in the centre. He daren't, yet he must.

George stares straight ahead. 'Edward ordered that…that if he were to be found—our cousin—then he should be taken alive.'

'Then he will pardon? Thank God—'

George tilts his head. 'Rather, it's my opinion that the king was planning a trial. A trial for high treason. Well,' he kicks the earth, 'he won't get the chance now, will he?'

Panic sets in. 'The earl, where is he?'

George turns a wretched face towards him. 'Where is he? Piled onto a cart with Cousin John. Respect and formality, it seems, are rarely offered to the slain. Not even those of Neville blood.'

As they pick their way towards the royal camp, Richard needs to retch again. Determined to fight it, he takes short, quivering breaths, unsure which need is most pressing: to vomit or to weep. He doesn't have the strength for either.

'They both knew, didn't they? Edward. Our cousin. They knew how it would end.'

'And so did we, if we're truthful.' George, blinking repeatedly, surveys the hideous spectacle around them.

The scene is like a Doom painting. Yet, unlike the painted scenes over chancel arches, the fates of the dead are not visible to them. All they have is a mound of empty carcasses, and cannot see whence the souls have flown. Richard seeks out Yorkist livery. But it's impossible to gauge the loyalties of the fallen, so many have been stripped and despoiled.

'Sweet Jhesu,' he snarls. 'Can't Edward do something

about this?'

'If you've lost anyone of note,' George says, 'make sure they're found quickly, before those bastards pick them clean. Some whoresons are even prepared to rob from their own.'

'I've already seen to it,' Richard tells him. 'Two of my squires, Parr and Milewater.'

George crosses himself. 'May God assoil them. I've lost men, too. Hurts, doesn't it?'

Richard thinks of their mother, of Margaret, and the horrors they must have faced over these last days. He imagines the consolation Edward's letters will bring, the alleviation of distress, the soothing of pain, and for that, he's glad. But his own pain, that which he'd thought long soothed, has risen up once more, bringing with it the presence of a skinny, whimpering boy who would rather conceal himself in his pony's stall than show his face to the world.

'My lord of Gloucester.'

Wrenched from his thoughts, he spots the striding figure of James Harrington and inclines his head in greeting. 'James, my dear friend, well met. Accept my deepest gratitude for your loyalty and service.'

Sweat drops from Harrington's brow. 'I thank the Trinity for preserving Your Graces. And for our victory.'

Richard clasps him by the shoulder. 'Indeed. I'm on my way to find the king and will, you can be assured, render high acclaim of you and yours.'

Harrington's gaze is earnest. 'And, if it please you, offer him my personal greeting.'

'I will, my friend. God keep you.'

'Is he a good man?' George says as they press on.

'Yes. He's a good man.' Richard tries to keep the sun banner in his sights, but the obstacles which litter the field make all diversions impossible. Edward's heralds, vivid against the filth, wander with their portable desks, recording each ripped and bloodied corpse while men-at-arms clear away the innards: the bowels, guts and brains, the offal of those who have died for the cause.

'Oh, George…' It's coming: the sob he knows must burst from

him or choke him in the attempt. It's coming, and there's nothing on God's earth he can do about it.

Grasping him by the elbow, George pulls him aside. 'We must talk. We must talk before…while we can.'

'What happened to him? If you know, you must tell me.' He's trembling again, limbs trapped in violent spasms.

'Word is, Montagu convinced him to leave the mounts in the horse park. It was the only way that Oxford's men would truly trust them. No escape, you see, if it went against them.'

'And you know this, in truth?'

'Aye, one of John Neville's captains has been taken. A northern man, I believe, Elyot, or some such. Do you know the name?'

Richard shakes his head.

'Well, Edward has this from him, so it's probably as close as we'll get to the truth. Oxford's men had routed Hastings—'

'Will? He is fallen?'

'No, he survives, but made no great display of himself. After the assault, he tried to rally his men, but Oxford's force pursued them and cut them down. Although some managed to reach London.'

Richard closes his eyes. 'Can you imagine what news they would have spread?'

'No need to imagine. Edward despatched a messenger to proclaim our victory, only to have him return, saying none had believed him. All in the City had supposed we were lost.'

'Then thank God Edward has thought to write to Mother.'

'According to Neville's captain, when Oxford's army returned to the field, Montagu's men saw the approach of the Streaming Star and launched an attack. They thought it was Edward's Sun with Streams. The fog, you see.'

Richard nods. The reorientation of the battle. The blurred and wretched time when he had marched into the hollow, then risen out of it, when he'd fought to the death to assault Exeter's flank. In forcing Holland to reposition, he had repositioned the whole field.

George continues, 'Oxford's men cried treason as they fled. I imagine Oxford himself blamed our cousin. He never really trusted Warwick, despite being his brother by marriage.' A breeze whips up, lifting the king's distant banners: a garden of golden, winking *soleils*. 'Edward took advantage of the confusion. Beset by the king, Montagu and most of his army fell. It seems the earl saw no other way open to him than to flee the field.'

Richard drops his head. The mighty *Monseigneur de Warwick* fleeing the field like a hunted beast. 'Don't stop there, Brother. If I must know, which I must, then tell me all. Remember, I hate equivocation.'

'Like I said. Edward ordered he should be taken alive, and he was, by all accounts.' George swallows. 'But some whoreson recognised him and skewered him in the throat with a bollock dagger.' He begins to tremble. 'A lowly bollock dagger. A man like our cousin…'

Richard feels light-headed. Part of him is still anchored in the fray, Ragged Staves bearing down on him. 'George? It was required of him, wasn't it? When he sent in his reserve, he simply pitted them against his enemy. Could afford no thoughts as to whom—'

'His argument was never with us. We both know that. He loved us, Dickon, as much as we loved him.'

George grasps Richard's shoulders, burrows his face into his neck like a sobbing child. A pain rears up in Richard's chest. Howling in silent despair, it calls out to its twin across the space of ten years and joins with its lamentation.

When all is spent, he lolls in his brother's arms.

'Come,' George says, swiping a hand across his own face, 'Edward is waiting.'

Hastings, lingering by the tent flap, is the first to greet them.

'My lord of Gloucester. Thank God in Heaven.' Throwing his arms around Richard, he pummels him like a haunch of meat.

'Faith preserve you, Will.' From Lord knows where, Richard summons up a weak smile. Hastings takes him by the elbow, as if they were Archbishop Neville and old King Harry, and ushers him into Edward's presence.

The king, divested of his harness, rises from his camp chair. The embrace is silent yet overwhelming, each shudder of Edward's body rippling with the movement of muscle and sinew. 'Both of my brothers safe and well. In the name of all that is holy, I could wish for nothing more.'

Richard could, but cannot tell him so.

'I commend you, my lord of Gloucester, and I thank you. If you had not held out against Exeter, then…well, the action in the centre was fierce, I had few men to spare.'

Richard continues to shake, teeth striking each other, the impact echoing around his skull. 'I did my duty.'

Edward snorts, incredulous. 'Never one for praise, are you, lad? I'm proud of you, Brother. God alone knows.'

Accepting the compliments, Richard digests them, but the pleasure is shallow and transient. It's not how he would have wished to receive such accolades. None of this is as he would have wished.

Edward, frowning, points to his bandaged hand. 'A flesh wound,' Richard explains, 'Hobbes says a fortnight will see it right.'

A brief smile lifts the king's lips. 'Good. I'll need you.'

Rivers is announced and limps in. However he came by his injury, Richard thinks, the wound must be paltry if he's managed to follow us across the field. But he can't deny the queen's brother looks pallid, the shadows under his eyes like great bruises.

Hastings mutters something about needing to be elsewhere. Slapping Richard's shoulder on the way out, he makes a graceful bow. 'Accept the admiration of us all, my lord of Gloucester.'

Conscious of Rivers, Richard keeps his voice low. 'Edward. Where is he?'

'With those of our own men we have managed to recover. He died the death of a craven, Richard, in retreat and fleeing from the field. But we will do our utmost for him and the Marquess, despite all. Now, you must rest.'

A camp stool is fetched, and Richard sinks down. His back is raw. He needs Kyngston and Parr—he swallows. He needs Kyngston. And he needs the ointments.

Edward has thrown a solicitous arm around Rivers. 'Anthony.

You must take your rest, also. With such a wound, I dare say a pallet will bring you more comfort than a stool. Here, man.'

The king directs Rivers towards his own palliasse. It's as well Hastings has absented himself, Richard thinks, the outrage of Rivers utilising the royal couch may have proved too much. With the queen's brother settled, Edward signals for wine.

'Saving your wound, Anthony, I should have sent you to London. It seems my messenger has already returned, claiming news of our triumph is not believed in the City.'

'The fault of Hastings' men,' George says, peevish, 'fleeing the field and spreading false reports.'

Edward ignores the barb. 'Whatever the cause, I've been compelled to send one of my gauntlets to the queen to put her fears to rest. Once word is received at the Tower, our victory will be declared.'

A pensive silence descends, each of them lost in their own thoughts. Richard must speak with William Parr, tell him he wishes to take charge of Tom himself and bury him with honour. He'll do the same for John Milewater. Both squires gave their lives for him. It's the least he can do.

Chapter Forty-One

15 April 1471
London

*T*HEIR ARRIVAL is announced by military trumpeters. Donning his bloodied harness and gore-encrusted coat of arms, Edward processes to the sound of growing adulation. Behind him, amid a column of archers, Harry of Lancaster sits astride a docile gelding, bound for the shelter of the Tower and the companionship of his books.

No Neville saltires to be seen this time, no Ragged Staves snatched by anxious fists from open casements. Instead, blossom petals, pink and bountiful, are cast in Edward's path. Some attach themselves to his hair, powdering the bronze with signs of spring, others adhere to tarnished steel, covering the spoils of death with symbols of life.

Since leaving London, they've come full circle. And coming full circle means returning to one's former position. York has regained power, as well as the person of the old king. Yet, as before, they still have the baleful presence of Marguerite, lingering with her son on the French coast. The latest word is that they still have Oxford, too, or at least the Scots do. Rumours of de Vere's flight across the border appear to be correct, and it's certain he'll seek sanctuary there, as his erstwhile queen did in former time. Exeter has also survived, hauled from the field, and kneaded back to life. Moreover, it has escaped nobody's mind that there remains the malignant presence of Edmund Beaufort, Duke of Somerset so-called, sticking rigidly to his queen's side and planning to restore the old regime by means of his battle axe.

As far as Richard can see, the only tangible change is that the House of Neville has lost two of its scions, and that he has lost his cousin.

At Baynard's Castle, he begs a favour: leave to provide what he can for Parr and Milewater. To his eternal gratitude, Edward agrees to provide funds for the purpose. The Warden of the Greyfriars proves obliging, and Parr and Milewater are dutifully laid in the Chapel of Saint Francis.

'An inscription, my lord duke? Upon the ledger stone?'

'Be sure to record their courage,' Richard says, 'and that they died together on the sacred day of Easter.'

The journey to Paul's is a short one. Edward strides ahead, kingly in murrey silks. Richard and George follow, dragging their heels, to where twin catafalques have been erected on the steps of the quire.

Richard cannot bring himself to look, knowing that when he does, what he sees will break his heart.

The king approaches first, kneeling at the foot of the steps and duly dipping his head. Whatever he's praying for, Richard cannot tell. Nor does he wish to. Edward's dealings with the earl were not his, and he wouldn't care to ponder on them. Rising, the king crosses himself, and, with a swift turn, marches the length of the nave. Passing through the west door, he emerges, triumphant, into the arms of the crowd.

Richard and George approach the quire in unison. Sunlight, filtering through glass, peppers their cousins' newly washed skin with spangles of colour, ornamenting wounds and dignifying scars. Levelled by death, the Nevilles could be warriors; they could be costermongers; they could be kings.

'He held everything in the palm of his hand,' George's voice trembles like birdsong, 'once.'

Richard kneels on the pavement, laces his fingers - and remembers. Eyes clamped shut, he could be anywhere: cathedral church or pony's stall. He could be anyone: soldier, duke or frightened child.

'I think you should know he was proud of you.' George's sigh is deafening in the chill vacuity. 'I was his ally, became his son by marriage. But you became a true son. The son he would have wanted.'

Opening his eyes, Richard sees his brother's hand, palm open in invitation. Taking it, he composes his features, compresses his grief.

'Come, Dickon,' George says. 'Blades to the whetstone. We've work to do.'

END

List of Sources

ASHDOWN-HILL, J. (2014) *The Third Plantagenet,*
The History Press

ASHDOWN-HILL, J. (2019) *Elizabeth Widville, Lady Grey:*
Edward IV's Chief Mistress and the 'Pink Queen', Pen & Sword

ASHDOWN-HILL, J. (2020) *Cecily Neville: Mother of Richard III,*
Pen & Sword

BARNFIELD, M. (Due for publication 2024) *The Itinerary of Richard*
Plantagenet, Duke of Gloucester, 1452-1483, Richard III Society

BURLEY, P., ELLIOTT, M., WATSON, H. (2007) *The Battle of Saint*
Albans, Pen & Sword

DEAN, K. (2015) *The World of Richard III,* Amberley Publishing

FABYAN, R. (d. 1513) *The Great Chronicle of London*

HAMMOND, P. W (1990). *The Battles of Barnet and Tewkesbury,*
Alan Sutton Publishing

HICKS, M. (2008) *Warwick the Kingmaker,* Blackwell Publishing

HISTORY GEEKS, THE
https://www.facebook.com/1039059642858367/

LEWIS, M. (2018) *Richard III: Loyalty Binds Me,* Amberley Publishing

KENDALL, P. M. (1955) *Richard III,* Unwin Hyman Limited

KENDALL, P. M. (1957) *Warwick the Kingmaker,* Phoenix Press

MOUNT, T. (2015) *Dragon's Blood and Willow Bark,*
Amberley Publishing

ROSS, C. (1981) *Richard III,* Methuen London Limited

ROSS, C. (1974) *Edward IV,* Eyre Methuen Limited

SANTIUSTE, D. (2010) *Edward IV and the Wars of the Roses,*
Pen & Sword

TAYLOR, A. S. (2001) *Isabel of Burgundy,* Tempus Publishing

VISSER-FUCHS, L. *Edward IV's 'Memoir on Paper' To Charles,*
Duke of Burgundy, Nottingham Medieval Studies, Vol 36 (1992),
pp. 167-227

WILKINSON, J. (2009) *Richard III: The Young King To Be,*
Amberley Publishing

WEIGHTMAN, C. *(1989) Margaret of Burgundy,*
Alan Sutton Publishing

Author's Note

I suspect that for many authors, the experience of writing a debut novel resembles a roller-coaster journey of highs and lows. The process is certainly a labour of love, and yet at the same time, a gruelling test of endurance. For me, *The Traitor's Son* has proved to be just that. Taking over a decade to complete, the novel has played a huge part in my life, and I'm still getting used to the fact that it has finally flown the nest.

My passion for all things medieval goes back a long way. A serious and enduring interest in Richard III was triggered at the age of eight by a visit to Middleham Castle in Yorkshire. But I'm far from being alone in that regard. Despite living over five hundred years ago, King Richard continues to fascinate and divide opinion worldwide. Almost everyone has heard of Richard III, but it is my belief that an individual's view of the king may well depend upon *how* they heard of him. If their initial encounter is with the Shakespearean Richard, for example, or the opinions of traditional historians, their views will differ considerably from those who have met the king through more modern and enlightened means.

The historian Dr Michael K. Jones has observed that Richard is all too often considered in isolation, rather than as part of a family.[1] And this is certainly true. Return Richard to his kin—consider him as son, brother, cousin, father—and you will find a devout and honourable man possessed of strong personal loyalties, as well as a deep consideration for those who gave their lives in the cause of York.

In this fictional re-telling of his early years, my aim has been to keep the action close. Focussing on Richard's most intimate circle,

---

1 M.K. Jones, *Bosworth 1485: Psychology of a Battle* (2002), pp. 35-38.

it concentrates on the family and events which shaped him, and presents, I hope, a credible picture of his life and times. Whether or not I have achieved this, I will leave to the judgement of my readers.

Whenever Richard's whereabouts are known, I have adhered to the facts, trying hard not to place him in one location when he is recorded to have been elsewhere. Naturally, there are gaps in our knowledge, particularly when it comes to Richard's childhood, but it is certain that he lived with his mother for the first eight years of his life, prior to exile in the Low Countries. Following his brother Edward's accession to the crown, Richard was housed with his siblings, George and Margaret, before leaving for the north country. It is not known specifically when Richard joined the household of his cousin, the Earl of Warwick, but a record exists of him making an offering at St Mary's Church, Warwick in September 1465. The fact that he was accompanied at this time by William Hastings and Henry Fitzhugh suggests all were moving northward to attend the enthronement of Archbishop George Neville, which took place in York later that month. Richard's first official duty on behalf of his king appears to have been in January 1469, so it is not unreasonable to suppose that by this time he had left the earl's household and joined his brother, Edward IV. Throughout the writing process, I have relied upon a detailed itinerary produced by the Richard III Society, which is due to be published this year, and Kristie Dean's wonderful account of his travels in her book *The World of Richard III* (Amberley Publishing, 2015).

Richard's father, the Duke of York, is said to have lost his life close to his castle of Sandal, during what is known as the Battle of Wakefield. However, as George informs Richard that their father died at Sandal Castle, I have used that particular placename throughout when discussing the conflict, in order to avoid confusion. An interesting point to note is that the Battle of Wakefield monument is in fact located in Manygates Lane, Sandal. Its plaque informs us that 'Richard Plantagenet fell here' and, although erected in the nineteenth century, the monument is said to have replaced a medieval memorial constructed by Edward IV. This would suggest that the precise spot upon which his father perished was known to the first Yorkist king, and that it took place close to Sandal Castle.

The extravagance of Archbishop George Neville's enthronement feast is well known. It is generally assumed to have been held at Cawood Castle, yet although the extensive menu has been preserved, I have not been able to find any contemporary testimony which confirms this location. On that basis, I have chosen to set the banquet scene at the Archbishop of York's Palace, in what is now known as Dean's Park, on the assumption that its close proximity to York Minster would have presented an easier alternative to a ten-mile horse ride, or river journey, to Cawood.

When discussing Richard and Edward's sojourn in the Low Countries, I have used the medieval name for The Hague — Des Graven Hage. The allusion in Chapter Four to the 'colours of York' refers to the blue and white livery colours formerly used by Richard duke of York. Why York adopted these colours – associated for the most part with the House of Lancaster – is unknown. Upon his accession to the throne in 1461, Edward IV adopted the colours more often associated with the House of York: murrey and blue. For the sake of authenticity, I have chosen to use the medieval terms 'henxman' and 'henxmen' when referring to Richard's fellow trainees at Middleham. Although their modern equivalents, 'henchman' and 'henchmen', are more familiar, these often carry unsavoury connotations which would not have applied in the Middle Ages.

The interpretation of Richard's relationships with his siblings, and particularly with his cousin, the Earl of Warwick, is purely my own. Yet, I do believe that during Richard's troubled childhood, he must have forged a deeper attachment to his middle brother, George, than to Edward, who was more than ten years his senior and largely engaged in fighting for the family cause. The fact that Richard is known to have remained fiercely loyal to the memory of his father, the Duke of York, has led me to believe that a mutual bond could conceivably have existed between himself and his cousin, Warwick: the former having lost a father, the latter seemingly unable to father a son of his own. The mothers of Richard's illegitimate children are unknown to history, but it has been speculated that Katherine

Plantagenet may be the result of an association with one, Katherine Haute, a relative of the Wydevilles, to whom Richard is known to have granted an annuity. Many novelists have followed this intimation and it seemed reasonable for me to do the same.

I have made every effort to depict events chronologically and in only one instance have chosen to place an event out of its lineal order. Following the Battle of Hexham in May 1464, a number of Lancastrians are known to have been executed. However, for the purposes of dramatic effect, I have depicted further executions at Middleham the following year, when young Richard joins his cousin's household.

King Edward's furious outburst at his discovery of Warwick's plans to marry the Neville girls to the king's two brothers was set on record by the French chronicler, Jean de Wavrin. The anti-Wydeville antics of Edward IV's jester, Woodhouse, are also a matter of historical fact and recorded in *The Great Chronicle of London*. With regard to the surname of the queen's family, I have chosen to use the medieval spelling of *Wydeville* for the purposes of authenticity. Thomas Parr and John Milewater were indeed buried in the Church of the Greyfriars, London. Richard always remembered the loyalty of his former squires, and in 1477, whilst endowing Queen's College, Cambridge, requested eternal prayers to be said for the souls of Thomas Parr, John Milewater, Christopher Worsley, Thomas Huddleston and John Harper. The fact that Parr and Milewater were buried together, and reference made on their ledger stone to them having perished at Barnet, has led me to wonder whether Richard himself arranged their obsequies, and also to deduce that Worsley, Huddleston and Harper probably died in the following confrontation, the Battle of Tewkesbury.

The Traitor's Son is the first in a proposed Ricardian trilogy. Whether you are familiar with the details of Richard's life, or a newcomer to his story, I hope you enjoy the novel and feel that I have respectfully interpreted his life upon the page.

Wendy

Wendy has a lifelong passion for medieval history, its people, and for bringing their incredible stories to life. Her specific areas of interest are the fifteenth century, the Wars of the Roses, and Richard III in particular. She enjoys narratives which immerse the reader in the past, and tries faithfully to recreate the later Middle Ages within in her own writing. She has contributed to a number of historical anthologies and was a runner up in the Woman and Home Short Story Competition 2008.

A member of the Richard III Society since 1986, Wendy is also a founder member of Philippa Langley's *Looking for Richard Project*, which located the king's lost grave in 2012. She co-authored *Finding Richard III: the Official Account of Research by the Retrieval and Reburial Project* in 2014, and in 2019 received the Richard III Society's Robert Hamblin Award.

THE TRAITOR'S SON, volume one in a Richard III trilogy, is Wendy's debut novel and she is currently working on the sequel.

Book Club Questions

1. *The Traitor's Son* re-imagines the early life of the future Richard III. What did you know about Richard III before, and has this book altered your view of the man he might have been?

2. Young Richard and his elder brother, George, are sometimes at odds. How would you describe their relationship, and are you more inclined to sympathise with Richard, or George?

3. Richard's mother, Cecily, has been thrown into crisis by the death of her husband, the duke of York, and her teenage son, Edmund. With her youngest children in mortal danger, how do you feel she handles the crisis, and what does that tell you about her character?

4. How would you describe Richard and George's life in the Low Countries? Do you feel their exile brings them closer?

5. King Edward's clandestine marriage to the Lancastrian widow, Lady Grey (Elizabeth Wydeville) fatally damages his relationship with his cousin, the earl of Warwick. What are your thoughts on the marriage? Was Edward right to follow his heart, or should he have followed his cousin's advice and entered into a dynastic marriage?

6. Both Richard and George are extremely close to their elder sister, Margaret. What do you feel is Margaret's natural role within the family, and how does her personality influence her brothers?

7. Richard Neville, earl of Warwick, emerges as a powerful and forceful figure. How do you view his relationship with Richard, and to what extent do you think he influences the young boy?

8. What are your impressions of Warwick's wife, Anne Beau-

champ, and their daughters, Isabel and Anne? How do you think Warwick's daughters view him?

9. The triangular relationship between Richard, George and Warwick is a complex one. How do you feel Warwick affects relations between the two brothers?

10. Whilst in his cousin's household, Richard develops a spinal condition – scoliosis. How do you feel he copes with this diagnosis? Discuss.

11. When Warwick and George rebel, Richard is forced to make a life defining choice: whether to join them, or to support his brother, Edward. Despite his deep bond with the earl, Richard eventually sides with Edward. Why do you think that was?

12. Richard, George and Edward are reconciled prior to the battle of Barnet. Were you surprised by this coming together, or did you expect George to abandon Warwick and return to his family? Who, ultimately, do you feel was responsible for the breakdown of relations between the king and the earl: Edward, or Warwick?

13. 'May the Trinity keep you.' Cecily, duchess of York, bids farewell to her three remaining sons, Edward, George and Richard, as they ride out to face the Lancastrians. What emotions do you imagine she would have experienced, given the fact that she had already lost her husband and son, Edmund, to the conflict ten years earlier? How much do you feel her religious faith would have sustained her at this time?

14. As with all medieval engagements, Barnet was a bloody affair. How do you think the brutal experience of his first battle affects Richard? And how do you feel he shoulders the responsibility of leading the vanguard?

15. *The Traitor's Son* takes Richard from an eight-year-old boy to a courageous warrior of eighteen. Do you feel Richard has changed over the course of the book, and what characteristics have remained constant?

Historical Fiction from MadeGlobal Publishing

I Am Henry - **Jan Hendrik Verstraten & Massimo Barbato**
The Sebastian Foxley Series - **Toni Mount**
The Savernake Forest Series - **Susanna M. Newstead**
The Death Collector - **Toni Mount**
The Falcon's Rise & The Falcon's Flight - **Natalia Richards**
The Reversible Mask - **Loretta Goldberg**

History Colouring Books

The Mary, Queen of Scots Colouring Book - **Roland Hui**
The Life of Anne Boleyn Colouring Book - **Claire Ridgway**
The Wars of the Roses Colouring Book - **Debra Bayani**
The Tudor Colouring Book - **Ainhoa Modenes**

PLEASE LEAVE A REVIEW

If you enjoyed this book, *please* leave a review at the book seller where you purchased it. There is no better way to thank the author and it really does make a huge difference!
Thank you in advance.

Printed in Great Britain
by Amazon